DETACHMENTS

DETACHMENTS

R.C. Charles

MEADOWBROOK CREATIONS, LLC

Meadowbrook Creations, LLC
@RealMeadowbrook

ISBN: 979-8-9928760-1-7
Library of Congress Control Number: 2025904931

"███████████ non-concurs with [R.C. Charles] using '███████' and/or '███████████'....and especially the connections he makes on ██████████ as this will most certainly drive ██████████ interest that we prefer to avoid."

(A senior official's comments from the publication review process)

For the most important people in the
world:
My family.

CHAPTER 1

A sudden scream pierced the night air. John's heart jumped from his chest, dragging him from his slumber. The old cabin's rickety floorboards strained under the vintage chair's wooden rockers. Silence once again chased away the haunting sound. *Was it a dream?* John wondered. He tried to convince himself for a moment, almost pleading against hope for that to be true.

The night was otherwise calm and still. The chirping of crickets filled the quiet air in the shallow canyon. A soft breeze stirred the dust and dried brush on the desert floor as it swept against the rocky slopes. Stretching its reach, a rogue gust joined the property's lone ragged tree. It swayed and waved on nature's dance floor.

Thick, fluffy clouds hid the moon from sight. The silvery light struggled to carve its way through but remained trapped above like a haunting glow among the stars. The nights were always the same: dull and routine. But this night was different. It was unforgettable.

The scream returned, louder and with greater urgency. John sprang to his feet, tipping the old rocker over backward. It crashed to the floor, but Mary's screams drowned the noise out. John ran to Mary's bedside to find her writhing in pain. Her hands strained for a tighter grip on the bedspread as she pulled herself upright. Beads of sweat rolled off her forehead. She clutched her swollen belly as she called out, "John!"

John kneeled at her bedside and wrapped his left arm around her back. "Mary? Mary? What's wrong? What's wrong with—"

John paused as the moisture that soaked Mary's nightgown pressed against his arm.

"The baby! I think it's coming!" Mary shrieked.

"No! You're not due for another month!"

"Something's wrong, I don't…" Mary's words gave way to another scream as she winced in agony.

"Okay, okay, everything's gonna be fine," John said as he rubbed Mary's back. His eyes shifted to the scarlet tinge staining her white gown and bedsheets. His heart pounded against the wall of his chest. Several thoughts clattered around in his confused mind. He gave himself an instant to consider the well-being of his unborn child before returning all his attention to Mary.

Mary panted as if she had just finished a marathon. A mask of pain shrouded her beautiful face. John could barely recognize her as another wave of pain slammed into her.

John had reached his limit. He wrapped Mary in their bedspread and swept her up in his arms. Dread gripped his mind, giving him a notion of the heartache his father must have endured when John's mother and younger brother died during childbirth. John's eyes glanced around the cabin, a ghostly inheritance where his father lost his battle with grief.

John carried Mary through the sitting room. As fear washed over him, he opened the heavy wooden door that led outside. His hair stood on end as goosebumps dotted his skin. He shuddered as he glanced at the clock on the wall—it was nearly midnight.

He rushed Mary to the barn at the rear of the house. The doors were already open, exposing the grille of his old Ford. For once, he did not regret forgetting to close them. The Ford logo on the old truck had faded and was barely visible. The original paint had suffered from years of abuse in the scorching desert sun. Rust and dents scarred the body. The truck was an eyesore, save for a few shiny hood vents on the driver's side. It had served for over fifteen years, making it possible for John's father and now John to help on ranches across the county.

John opened the truck door in a flash and carefully laid Mary across the seat. She was no longer panting; she just took slow, weak breaths.

"Please, Mary," John said as he rested his hand on her abdomen to feel his unborn child still moving within. "Please hold on, Mary. We'll be there soon… just hold on."

John and Mary lived in a desolate, sparsely populated area. A handful of homesteads and ranches dotted a landscape that stretched for hundreds of square miles. Their modest home sat ninety miles as the crow flies from the closest thing that could be called a real town. The nearest hospital was a three-hour drive across unimproved desert roads.

John closed the passenger door and rushed to the driver's seat. The truck's keys were waiting where he always left them—in the ignition. He pumped the throttle a few times and twisted the key to crank the old pickup. The truck sputtered to life briefly and stalled.

"No, no, no! Not today! Not today, please!"

John tried again. His hands trembled as he turned the key. The engine coughed to life with a bang from the exhaust pipe before settling into a low rattle. Crickets scurried from the barn.

John stabbed the accelerator. The Ford jerked forward abruptly before catching traction on the dirt floor of the building. The worn tires stopped spinning and thrust the old truck forward with haste. John sped onto the dirt roadway, leaving a cloud of dust behind in his wake.

The road was long and winding. It carved its way through the hills and down to the desert floor. Once a month, John would take Mary to town to get supplies, so he knew the road well, but he had never driven it so late at night and never in such dire circumstances.

A hollow groan escaped Mary's lips as the rigid vehicle bounced over the pitted and potholed dirt road. Her head thrashed from side to side; her eyes were glazed and filled with tears. Mary's fists tightened as she fought through the pain.

"Mary, please hold on. We'll be there soon. Everything will be okay," John said, his voice cracking. He glanced at Mary, and his heart sank. *No!* he thought. He could not possibly survive another death.

He floored the accelerator to beat the unforgiving passage of time. The needle on the speedometer approached the 85 mph mark, pushing the rickety truck to its limit. The truck clattered along the road, bottoming out over the rough surface. He floored the pedal for several minutes before focusing on the passenger seat.

"Mary? Mary?" John's voice strained.

There was no response. He realized that the screams and grunts had stopped minutes ago. Fear grabbed hold of John's soul. He slowed down and reached to check for a pulse. His worst fear subsided as he confirmed she was alive—unconscious, but alive.

He sped up again, pushing the old pickup as fast as it could handle the curves. After about twenty minutes of restless solitude, the worn-down Ford sputtered. As the engine stumbled, the hair on John's neck stood up, and a chill ran through his body. The truck slowly came to a stop, releasing a long hiss from its engine.

"No! No! No! No!" John shouted in frustration as he slammed the steering wheel.

He swallowed hard as he looked around. It was still quiet, and Mary remained unconscious. He almost cried at that point. That familiar sense of hopelessness crowded his thoughts, tormenting his soul. John sat there motionless, his hands gripping the steering wheel, paralyzed by the haunting realization that he was all alone and ill-equipped to manage the crisis. Sweat soaked through his shirt into the worn seats of his father's old truck.

John broke free of his cognitive prison, hoping to repair whatever had caused the Ford to fail. He hopped out of the truck and rushed to the hood. Steam rushed into his face as he popped it open. He wiped the concoction of sweat, coolant, and condensation from his brow as he searched for any damage. Steam continued to rise from the front of the engine

4

compartment as coolant dripped down from the inside of the propped hood and soaked the dirt road below.

John tried in vain to find the source of the draining fluid. He knew enough that it could be as simple as a hose or as devastating as a failure in the engine itself. Regardless, without coolant to refill the system, there was no point in trying to repair the truck. Recognizing the pickup was a lost cause, John returned to check on Mary. She had grown more pale. Her breathing was shallow, and he could barely find a pulse. He was sure he was losing her.

"Mary!" John screamed in horror.

John's yell reverberated through the desert as he desperately tried to revive Mary by tapping her cheek and lifting her eyelids.

"Come on, Mary. Don't you leave me!"

He sprinted down the road toward his home, making it a half-dozen feet before he ran back in the other direction. There was no one for miles in either direction and no hope of finding help on foot. He accepted his fate and dropped to his knees.

John screamed in anguish as his vision blurred with tears. He looked to the sky, pleading with God for anything, anyone, that could help. Then, a faint white light burst into his periphery as it crested the hill on the horizon. As the light grew brighter and larger, John believed it was approaching and that God had answered his prayers. John stood up and began waving for help. An unusual sensation rose through his body, and he collapsed to the ground as the world faded to black.

John struggled to open his eyes. His eyelids felt like damp leather pressed heavily on them, slowing every movement. He fought through the resistance. He peeled one eye open, then the next, and took in the bright white light that flooded the room. His body was in agony, worse than after a full week of tough ranch labor. John scanned his surroundings. The ceiling was unlike anything he had ever seen. It looked like steel, but the bright light created the

5

effect of looking through a domed window directly toward the sun; however, the light was soft in his eyes, and he felt no warmth on his face. The walls curved up to the peak, creating the appearance of the ceiling and walls being one.

John felt the soft bedding beneath him. It was something familiar. He looked and saw a medical gurney. *Oh, thank God! A passerby must have brought us to the hospital,* he thought. He could not see Mary, but he knew they were in a place much better than the desert.

John struggled to get up and search for Mary, but he could only move his eyes. Someone must have restrained his head, his arms, his whole body. He could not see any restraints on him, though. It was as if an invisible hand was clamping his body to the gurney. As his hopeful thoughts faded, a knot of worry tightened in his stomach.

He was unsure of Mary's whereabouts but believed she was there. He screamed for help, only to learn another shocking reality: John could not speak. No sound escaped his mouth. The feeling of being buried alive overwhelmed him. He struggled in a frenzy of fear, but his limbs would not obey, leaving him helpless.

John's pulse quickened. Panic surged through him; his breaths became short and rapid. His chest heaved with each passing moment, the rise and fall growing more rapid and forceful.

John strained his eyes in every direction and could make out several other gurneys around him. He tried to calm himself enough to bring the entire picture into clarity. Judging by the size of the room, he figured it must accommodate at least a couple of dozen gurneys, and to his amazement, he could tell there were people on at least all of those he could see positioned near him. They all appeared to be sleeping. He wondered what they were all doing there. *Are they like me? Can they not move? Can they see?*

As John regained his composure, he noticed a shadow passing, first near him, then toward him. Eventually, the shadow cast directly over him. His body shuddered, and his eyes shut.

John woke up again. This time, he was certain someone was in the room with him. He cracked open his eyes as he realized he had developed the ability to move his head. Ever so carefully, he scanned his surroundings. The gurneys were now empty, devoid of the people he had seen earlier. He had a clear view across the gurneys, all the way to the walls. *Were all the beds occupied? Where did they all go? Am I alone?* John wondered.

The lighting had dimmed, creating a soft shimmering metallic appearance on the ceiling. The effect created something closer to a moon-like glow than the sun-like appearance he recalled from his last awakening.

John wrestled to turn his head in the other direction to push beyond his limits. Convinced he could increase his range of motion, he tried to force his voice to comply and scream for Mary, but no sound came forth.

As John brought his head back to the center, he felt what was becoming a familiar sensation and blacked out.

John awoke a third time. The muscles in his face painted a canvas of frustration. He struggled to get up, but his limbs continued their betrayal. He tried in vain to break free from whatever held him back, but his efforts produced no benefit. His body remained motionless.

"Stop!" a voice said. It sounded calm and confident, striking a perfect balance between authority and concern.

John strained to see who it was but could not make it out.

"Don't worry," the voice reassured. "Everything will be okay."

John responded by thrashing his head around on the gurney within the limits his body would allow. He felt an urge to shout, *Where is Mary? Who are you? What have you done to us?*

"Please calm down. You're only going to hurt yourself," the voice said.

John continued his futile attempts to set himself free. He tried to speak again.

"Safety protocols have been engaged. You should be resting. Please don't worry. You'll return to normal in no time." The voice was matter-of-fact, without a sense of urgency or noticeable emotion.

"Relax now. You need to rest."

John saw something that resembled a hand, but it was not human. It traveled over his face, quite close to his eyes. John felt an unusual sensation and the urge to sleep. He fought to stay awake until the hand pressed softly against his temple, and his eyes closed.

CHAPTER 2

John rolled onto his back and woke up. His arm landed on the emptiness beside him. A gasp escaped his mouth as he snapped out of his groggy state to scan the room. The sight of familiar walls sent sparks of hope through his body.

"Mary!" he called. His surroundings came into focus.

As hope dwindled, his eyes wandered from the bed to the wall, then around the room. He was alone. John buried his head in his hands as tears welled in his eyes. He fought to suppress the dark thoughts crowding his mind.

"No! No! No!" he repeated, wiping his tears and banging the heels of his hands against his forehead, fixated on thoughts of Mary. *This can't be real. She can't be gone!*

John forced himself out of bed and walked across the hard floor. Sunlight filled the room, but it provided no warmth. It was soft in his eyes, not like he had expected.

John looked down at the drab gray clothing he was wearing. He walked across the room to the metal door. After contemplating, he grabbed the door handle and stepped into the sandals by the wall. He pulled on the door, expecting it to be locked, as though he were confined in a prison cell. To his surprise, the door popped open, and John entered a long corridor.

His eyes moved along the well-lit hallway. Numbered doors identical to his own lined it on each side. He took his first steps toward what he believed was the exit. His door shut with a loud thud that caused him to freeze. As the echoes subsided, John continued down the empty hall.

Where am I? The question danced in his head. He ran his hand across the wall as he walked. He had never felt one like it—slick like oiled steel but soft and dry. Angular shapes below the surface reflected light at different angles despite the lack of windows or obvious light sources. The effect reminded John of an old dystopian movie he had seen at a special screening with Mary after his father passed.

As John walked down the hallway, he heard something. *Are my ears deceiving me?* John moved closer. It was chattering. *People! Finally, I'll get some answers!* John rushed toward the exit, where he found a staircase. He descended the stairs and stepped out into a courtyard, feeling the warmth of genuine sunlight. His eyes took in the scene—dozens of people: men and women of different ages, races, and sizes. Some were standing, while others were sitting and talking together.

The people all wore different clothes and shoes, although some were dressed in the same gray clothes as John. The courtyard was large, with several metal benches. Some were under trees, others against the apartment buildings, some in the shade, and others in the sunlight. As people took notice, the chatter turned to silence. One by one, they all turned to face him. John felt uncomfortable with so many eyes on him. He struggled to find his voice to break the awkward silence.

"Hey! The new guy's awake!" a skinny man declared as he stood up from a metal bench. He pointed at John as if he had been the topic of discussion all along.

Murmurings and whispers filled the courtyard as people welcomed John, some with warm smiles, others with just a nod to acknowledge his presence.

John had found his first reason for hope. Someone here could at least make sense of things and tell him where he might find Mary. He walked into the crowd, heading nowhere in particular. As he drifted among the group, he heard different questions thrown at him—questions like:

"Where do you come from?"

"What's your name?"

Others bombarded him with jibes. "Some sleep that was, huh?"

"You ever shave?" one person joked.

None of the voices inspired the confidence John was seeking as he measured potential allies. Exasperated by the noise and lack of information, he reached his boiling point and yelled, "Where am I? What the hell is happening?"

It was loud enough and sufficiently robust to hush the crowd. They all remembered being in John's shoes and overcoming their circumstances, but no one answered. As he was about to demand further answers, a short, middle-aged man wearing a smug grin pushed through the crowd.

"You've been abducted, my man! Abducted by Big Brains!" he said with a cackle.

"What did you say?" John asked. "Abducted? By who? Where's Mary? What the hell is this place?"

He looked around for cues that others thought the man was crazy, but they all looked at him with acceptance and a hint of despair, a truth they did not dare acknowledge.

"You're not gonna believe it, but that's the case. You're not in Kansas anymore, Dorothy," the man smirked. "Worse, you're not gonna be able to click your heels to get back home," he teased.

John's heart sank. He shook his head slowly, hoping that none of it was true.

"What the hell do you mean, I can't go home?" John's eyes wandered. "Where am I? How do I get out of here?"

"Shit, son," another voice announced. "I don't know who Mary is, but I know she's not here."

An older man walked closer to John. He was in his mid-fifties. His eyes were beady and lay behind thick glasses. "I don't know how to tell you this, kid. Not only can you not go home, but you're not even on the right planet." The man noticed John's bewilderment and pointed at the sky. "Look!"

John looked in the direction the man pointed and stared for a while. The sky was ashy and pale. It wasn't blue, as he had expected. More shocking, there were two moons in the sky, both about the size of the moon back home. It was something John could not quite comprehend. He reached his limit. Mary was gone. Hope had vanished. He could take no more and shuffled his way to the apartment building walls, where he collapsed onto the ground and into a level of despair he had never felt before. Tears glistened in his eyes. He tried holding them back to present a brave face, but the tears won the battle and forced their way down his cheeks.

The older man came to him. He put a hand on John's shoulder.

"Hey, kid. There's nothing to be upset about. They treat us real good here."

John tried to rub his eyes and conceal his emotions.

"Hell... it's not like you had anything to go home to. None of us do. I figure that's why they took us," the man said reassuringly.

John lashed out, "Nothing? Nothing to go home to? Is that right?" He shoved the man's hand off his shoulder and stormed away, seeking refuge. He headed toward the stairwell as the people in the courtyard looked at each other and began talking. He heard someone in the crowd yell, "You'll get used to it!" John disappeared into the apartment building, escaping to his room.

Another man from the crowd approached the man in glasses. He was large and physically intimidating. His voice was soft, with a British accent that conveyed a sense of calmness and concern for others.

"What d'you reckon, Doc? Think he'll make it? Mate looks proper shaken, he does."

"I don't know, Gus," Doc said, adjusting his glasses. "Let's give him some space for now."

Rex joined in. He was the shorter man who first greeted John. Rex always moved with a sense of purpose. "I've never seen anyone react like that," he said.

"Yeah," Gus said as he looked toward the apartment building. "I thought the Big Brains only went after people who didn't have nothing."

Doc stood there, pondering the situation. *Something was not right*, he thought.

A loud, warbling tone echoed throughout the courtyard for a few seconds, and the people filtered out.

"Come on, guys," Doc urged. "It's time for lunch. I'm sure the Big Brains wouldn't have brought him here if he had attachments back home."

The large lunchroom was buzzing with excitement and gossip. It was obvious John was the subject of every discussion. Everyone spoke in hushed yet animated tones. The place wasn't officially the 'lunchroom.' It said 'Dining Facility' on the wall, but the residents called it the lunchroom, even though they had breakfast and dinner there.

Doc and his friends stood in a long line, each with a metal tray in hand. In front of them stood an extended structure that looked like a table. On it were several food containers distributed by some others, mostly female captives. The servers worked mechanically and rhythmically. They only spoke when they asked what kind of food a person wanted.

"Which one?" an Asian server asked. Her lips cracked the slightest of smiles.

"Just starch," Doc said as he collected the pale-looking meal and moved to a table where his clique sat. He sat down and surveyed the room. He wondered how John's reaction amplified the enthusiasm.

The mealtimes were long, so many captives would wait for the initial rush before arriving for their meals. Some would stay in their rooms or lounge in the courtyard, but today was different. Doc was sure everyone would gather early to see the "F.N.G." and confirm the rumors. Rex popularized the acronym for "Fuckin' New Guy" several years ago, but the camp had not seen an F.N.G. in at least five years.

The lunchroom had circular tables everywhere, and each could accommodate five people. Some tables were still empty, though.

The room had strange music playing. No one had ever heard anything like it before arriving from Earth, and many guessed it was some Big Brain technique to trick people into liking the food. It was just a joke, but for food composed of various synthetic substances, it was oddly satisfying and flavorful.

A honeycomb pattern that slowly changed colors covered the ceiling. The lighting created a calming effect that only exacerbated the conspiracy theories about the music. Doc believed the ceiling was trying to mimic the northern lights on Earth. The walls had the same pattern but were just a static gray color with thin strips of light in the seam between the top of the wall and the ceiling.

"So, this new bloke's all everyone's talking about round town, isn't it?" Gus began.

"Yeah, what do you expect from the way that guy reacted? No one's ever acted like that before," Rex responded in between bites of the synthetic food.

"Except that one guy," Chris added with his thick Swahili accent and trademark smile.

"That one guy? What are you talking about, Chris?" Rex asked in disbelief.

Chris arrived at the camp about a decade earlier. Adapting to life in the camp had been difficult for Chris, but Doc took him under his wing, and the two became close friends.

"Do you not remember?" Chris said, stealing occasional glances at Doc with a hint of concern. "The man who kept trying to break out. He was holding on to something, too, yes?"

"Oh… I remember now. The stupid fool would only make it as far as the first Big Brain." Rex shook his head, disappointed in his failed memory. "How many times did he try, Doc?"

Doc ignored the comment. He focused on his meal and tried to disregard the conversation.

"I heard it was dozens, maybe more, right?" Rex asked, prodding Doc for more insight.

"Yes, it was the same thing every time," Chris recalled. "He would get within a few yards of a Big Brain and, boom! Right to the ground… knocked out cold."

"Hey, whatever happened to that guy, anyway?" Rex asked, forcing Doc to engage.

Doc responded by banging his fists on the table. The clatter in the lunchroom stopped as people turned their attention to Doc. He stood up slowly, with a steely expression on his face. He looked at the men individually, as if they had uttered a forbidden word.

"Dead! Mark's dead!" Doc said in a tone of finality. "He couldn't take it anymore and jumped off Apartment 15. Okay?" Doc stood up, causing the group to go silent. He turned and walked toward the exit.

"Oi, Doc, we're real sorry, yeah? Don't think anyone meant to wind you up. Come on back, mate." Gus, always the peacemaker, pleaded for Doc's understanding.

"Oh goodness, we are dumb. I am so sorry, my friend," Chris declared. He slapped his palm to his face. "I completely forgot."

Doc paused for a moment, contemplating his next move. His friends touched upon a still-frayed nerve, forgetting the person who was once Doc's best friend. Doc never fully understood Mark's reason for needing to escape—something about being unable to accept being held captive despite having everything they needed. He never imagined that the futility of the repeated attempts would end up being too much for his friend. It took Doc years to come to grips with the loss, but he still blamed himself.

Rex stood up with his empty tray to approach Doc, and the other men followed his lead. Gus patted Doc on the back, helping him escape the thoughts in his head. "You okay, brother?"

"Yeah, yeah, I'm, uh, I'm fine." Doc snapped out of his thoughts. "Let's, uh, get out of here, guys."

The men took their dirty food trays to a lady near the exit. As they were just outside the lunchroom, a shout came from an area near the courtyard. Voices clashed, and pandemonium reigned.

"What's that?" Rex asked. He was a little startled.

"I am betting the gangs are going at it again. We should get a closer look," Chris said.

They rushed to the scene of the fight, where two opposing gangsters were throwing punches. The crowd jumped with excitement when one of them landed a heavy punch. His opponent retaliated with a swift kick, causing drops of blood to dot the ground.

"Blimey, this ain't good. Betcha we'll have one of them Big Brains turnin' up any minute now!" Gus said.

"Yep, you're right. Look!" Rex pointed to a unique barrier that disappeared like a portal—a human-like being glided through; it was a Big Brain guard. Its arms were longer than a human's, and its legs were long and thin. Its skin was gray and seemed thin, like paper. The Big Brain had large, dark eyes that glowed with a bluish hue around them. Rather than walking, the Big Brains floated through the air like balloons.

The Big Brain moved toward the scene of the fight. As it arrived, everyone in the area crumpled to the ground—those who were not so close dispersed and hurried back to their rooms.

The men continued to gaze at the scene. Rex was most excited, as if he were watching a movie.

The Big Brain guard settled over the two fighters. It stretched out its hand, causing them to float off the ground. It then drifted toward the barrier with the two men floating behind. They all disappeared through the portal in a matter of seconds.

"Whew! How long do you think they'll be gone?" Rex asked.

"That fight was not too serious," Chris said, scratching his beard. "I do not think they will get a full Tom. He was gone for about a year. Either way, the gangs will want replacements. Those men are done."

CHAPTER 3

John sat on his bed, hugging his knees to his chest as though his life depended on it.

He rocked back and forth, mumbling words that not even he understood. All he could think of was Mary and the unimaginable distance between them. He did not know where he was or how to get back to her. All he knew was the paralyzing fear of the possibility that he would never see her again.

He remained lost in his thoughts until the lights in his room came up automatically, like the sun rising over the horizon. John did not move. He sat in the clothes he had been wearing since the previous day. The dust and sand from the courtyard discolored his gray pants, leaving their mark on his bed.

Several hours passed when someone knocked at his door. The knock was light yet urgent—enough to cause John to stop his back-and-forth movement but insufficient to prompt a reply. Moments later, the knock returned. This time, it was louder and rattled the door with loud thuds.

"Kid? Hey, kid?! You awake?" Doc's voice filtered through the door. "Kid! Are you alright in there? Come on, open the door!"

John stopped rocking but said nothing.

Doc feared the worst. *What if the kid had hurt himself or something?*

"Come on, kid! Let me know if you're all right in there. It's been twenty-four hours. You gotta come out of there and get something to eat. Come on, kid! Look, if you don't come open this door, I'm gonna open it!"

John kept his voice in check and resumed his rocking movement.

Doc took a few steps back and delivered a straight kick to the door latch. The door gave way, and he rushed into the room.

"What's the matter with you, kid? I've been..." Doc paused. The words fell back into his gut. His frustration disappeared when he saw John's face and reddened eyes.

"Oh, man..." Doc approached the bed slowly. "Hey... you alright? Come on, we gotta get you up." He reached out to touch John's shoulder, but he pulled away with such force that Doc's arm shot up, causing him to step back in defense.

"Get away from me!" John yelled. "Just leave me alone! Can't you see? It's over! It's all over!" He screamed and hit his head with his hands. He did that for a few seconds before turning to the wall. Doc lunged forward and wrestled John off the bed to the floor before he could hurt himself.

"Leave me alone! Let me go! Let me go!" John screamed under the weight. Doc struggled to control the larger man.

"Hey! Hey! Hey! Everything is going to be all right. Now, calm down. It's all going to be okay—"

"How can it be okay?" John kept trying to break away from Doc. "Mary is gone, my child is gone, my whole world is gone, and I can't do a damn thing about it. I can't—"

Doc loosened his grip. "Wait... hang on. Hang on. What did you say? You had a family?" He made it sound like having a family was an impossible thing.

"Yes!" John said emphatically. Doc's confusion surprised John, creating a moment of calmness and opportunity. Doc seized the chance to gain John's cooperation.

"Wait, what happened?" Doc asked as he released his grip on John and gave him some space. "Tell me the whole story, kid. We've never heard of anything like this happening before."

"What's the point? Is it going to get me back to them?"

"No, no, sadly it won't. I'm afraid there's no way out of this camp, but I'm willing to listen. Tell me what happened, and maybe talking about it will help. Maybe a little?"

John sat up on the floor and leaned his back against the bed. Doc propped himself up against the nightstand so he could remain close to John.

"She was in labor… We were headed to the hospital when my truck broke down. I was… I was trying—"

Doc could see the difficulty John was having recounting the story.

"You were trying to fix the truck?" Doc finished John's thought.

"Yeah, but when I couldn't fix it, I went for help. Then I saw some light coming over a hill, and the next thing I knew, I was in a room with a bunch of other people on gurneys. I figured I passed out and woke up in the hospital." Doc's eyebrows perked up at the mention of John waking up.

"I couldn't move while I was there. There was this voice. It kept telling me that everything was going to be fine. That happened twice, and then I woke up here."

Doc closed his eyes. "I'm so sorry, kid, but this is quite unusual. I've never heard of the Big Brains taking people with families. They should have known about your wife. What's her name?"

John looked Doc in the eyes. "Mary… She wasn't my wife, though. We were going to get married in a few months."

"Oh…" Doc sighed. He realized the Big Brains had made an error. *It had to be. They couldn't just capture the kid like that*, he thought. He looked at John in understanding and said, "I'm so sorry, kid… Look, we can't possibly know what happened. Maybe someone came along and saved your girl."

"Yeah, right," John said under his breath. He looked away in disbelief.

"Have some faith. We can hope that everything will work out. No matter how hard you weep, it's not gonna help anyone. Your child is there, and you're here. Now come on, sitting here wasting away isn't gonna help you, and it sure ain't gonna help Mary."

The words breached John's armor. He wiped his tears and stood up.

"Kid?"

"Yeah?"

"What's your name?"

"John."

"All right, John. Take a shower and clean up. I want to show you a little about this place."

Doc stood outside the apartment building, waiting for John to arrive. He stood below the large sign on the wall that read, "Apartment 3."

John eventually exited the building. He looked better, having showered and changed clothes. All the dirt was gone from his hair, and his eyes looked less distressed. It was amazing what a good shower could do for someone. He walked up to Doc, who wore a huge grin.

"Feel a little better now, kid?" he asked. He still called him 'kid.' For Doc, it fit better than John's name.

"Better? No, but I needed that shower, so thanks for coming to get me."

"I know this has to be tough, kid. I can't imagine what you're going through, and I wish there was something I could do to help. But we're all stuck here. Stuck like prisoners."

"I just… I don't know what I'm gonna do without her. How could this happen?" John asked.

"I wish I knew, kid. I wish I knew."

"I don't think I can—" Tears filled John's eyes.

"Hey, kid, come on now, let's get your mind off things. There's lots of stuff here to see."

John wiped his eyes. "Oh, uh, yeah... no, I'm fine, I'm fine... So, it's not all just apartments here?"

"No, of course not," Doc said as he walked toward a path through the courtyard. Rows of buildings lined the courtyard, each with numbers painted on the walls.

"So, there's twenty apartment buildings. Each of them has about a hundred and twenty rooms. That's Apartment 7," Doc said. He pointed to the rundown structure. It had an ominous aura that was well punctuated by the glare of one of the residents standing with a group of menacing-looking men.

"How do you know? There's no number," John said as he shifted his gaze away.

"Yeah. Everyone knows Apartment 7. That's where most of the Drongs live."

"The Drongs?"

"Yeah, it's a gang. We've got a couple here in the camp. As long as you steer clear of them, they're nothing to worry about."

"Wow," John said. "What's that?" He pointed to a large, tall building with a dome-shaped roof and rhythmically blinking red and blue lights around its edges. The building had a big sign that read "Hub" right above the entrance. "What is this place?"

"You're about to find out, kid. Come on."

They strolled toward the doors, which opened automatically, catching John by surprise.

"Welcome to the Hub," a robotic voice droned.

John looked around in wonder. He marveled at the colorful lights, the beautiful architecture, and the overall atmosphere of the place. For a brief instant, his amazement overpowered his grief.

The interior was captivating. It was like a large hall with different levels and sections, each with its own color code. A shimmering green hue illuminated the first floor, the second floor glowed red, and the third floor shone blue. They toured the green zone first. It had a bowling alley, several casino games, and pool tables. A few men shouted over bottles of beer and bowling balls—light music filtered through the building. A small bar sat nestled in a corner. Several beer bottles decorated the metal shelf behind the chubby bartender.

"This... is our relaxation spot. Fun, games, drinks. All you need to unwind is right here."

"This is incredible—" John looked on in awe.

"Pretty amazing, right?" Doc asked rhetorically as he waved to the men at the bar. The bartender smiled back.

"Wait till you see level 2, kid."

Doc wasn't kidding. Level 2 was more impressive. It was a movie theater that had been upgraded and remodeled. The room had seating laid out in typical cinema style. A big screen displaying some war film clung to the wall up front.

Like the lunchroom ceiling, the walls had a unique honeycomb pattern. The sound from the speakers was crisp and clear, far better than any movie theater John had ever been to back home. It was almost as if he were in the movie's action. Once again, his jaw dropped in awe.

"Don't be too surprised, kid. Level 3 awaits."

John followed Doc to a small elevator. They stepped inside the futuristic lift. It had geometric patterns on the walls and ceiling, with lighting that seemed to come from nowhere, like his apartment.

"How do we control this thing? There's no buttons?"

"You'll see," Doc assured. The elevator doors closed with a beep.

"Level 3," Doc announced.

The ceiling took on a bluish glow. The journey upward was so smooth that John could not tell they had moved.

As the elevator doors opened, the men stepped out.

They reached the blue level at the top of the building. The ceiling was dome-shaped and almost seemed transparent. He found himself so fascinated by the lighting technique that he developed a mild stiffness in his neck from looking up at it for too long.

A tall, curved wall separated the floor into two equal parts. The first part contained about a dozen batting cages. Gently sloping away from home plate, each floor directed the balls toward the pitching machine. The user would then reload them into the hopper that fed the metal pitching arm.

"As you get better, you can adjust the pitch speed to nearly big-league levels. It's a fun way to challenge yourself," Doc explained.

"Hmm. Are there any competitions or tournaments here?"

"Not that I've ever seen, but I guess anything is possible."

Outside the cages were several batting helmets and bats from which to choose, all neat and in good repair.

"What's on the other side?" John asked.

"Yeah. That's the tennis court. It's better to avoid them and use the outdoor courts."

"Why? What's wrong with using the indoor courts?"

"Lemme show ya."

Doc led John to the tennis courts, where the fencing stretched to the ceiling. Papers, old clothes, and broken rackets littered the courts. There was a nauseating smell that John suspected came from the dirty clothes. Right next to the court was a small machine that dispensed rackets. Dust covered the machine. John ran his fingertips across it, leaving four stripes through the caked-on dust.

"Wow. No one comes here, huh?" John's voice echoed a bit.

"I told ya, kid. This place is just gang turf at this point. That's about it for the Hub. You can come back anytime and spend as long as you want, but let me take you to the market so you can see that."

The market was a few minutes away from the Hub. It was a dusty, dry area enclosed in a circular clearing with rocks as barricades. People had bunched the stones together and piled them slightly higher than the average human. An opening in the barricade served as an entrance.

As soon as they went through that entrance, John could feel the energy and excitement of the place. The stalls and shops displayed their wares, forming an abstract painting of mismatched colors and textures. A cacophony of laughter, shouts, and haggling came from every direction. The shops had everything from food and drinks to shoes and clothes, board games, and books, and much more.

"Wow, it looks like everyone is here."

Doc laughed. "It's not everyone, John. I guess a lot of people prefer the market over the Hub or the apartment buildings because it's livelier and has more freedom." Doc shrugged.

"Freedom?" John asked. "How can there be freedom when we're prisoners here?"

"It's true, we are in a kind of prison, but the Big Brains pretty much leave us alone. Hell, the only time we see a Big Brain is when there's a fight, and they have to break it up."

"All these people? They live their lives here like this?"

"That's right, kid. In fact, the sense I get is that most people seem to feel like life here is better than it was on Earth."

"Better? Most of them?" John asked. "How many people are we talking about... here in the camp, I mean?"

"I don't know. I guess about two thousand. Could be more—"

"Wait... what about money? What are all these people shopping with?" John asked.

"Oh, there isn't any money. Well, not really. Everything here is based on the barter system."

"Seriously?" John asked, surprised by the implication.

"Yeah. Just bring what you have and get what you want." Doc snapped his fingers. "Just like that! Look! Look at that guy over there."

Doc pointed to a tough-looking man draped in a leather jacket and faded jeans, carrying a bunch of rackets and eyeing a pair of shoes on display.

"He's gonna try to trade those for the shoes."

"Yeah, I see, but... the shoes look more expensive," John said.

"They do, sure, but that doesn't matter. What matters is need. If both parties have what the other needs, they make an exchange."

John nodded in understanding.

"Look over there; you see that guy? He's trading poker chips from the Hub. Since they're in limited supply, they can be valuable, but only to people who want to play in the casino. See what I mean?" Doc asked.

"That makes sense, Doc."

"So, where does all this stuff come from, anyway?"

"People can just submit a request to the Big Brains for anything they might want. Sometimes they give it to us; sometimes they don't. We don't always know because the gangs get their hands on the supplies first. So, unless it's the synthetic food in the lunchroom, you'll find it here."

John nodded along, taking in the information Doc provided.

"Okay, kid, let's get out of here. It's about time to get some chow."

CHAPTER 4

Doc led John away from the market. They strolled along a dusty, winding path created by years of people using it as a shortcut. John paused for a moment and reflected on everything he had seen at the Hub and the market.

"I've been thinking... why do you figure they brought us here? The, uh—" John struggled to recall what he had heard Doc call their captors.

"The Big Brains?" Doc clarified.

"Yeah, the Big Brains. Why bring us here to lock us up like this? It just doesn't make sense to me."

Doc nodded. "I know. It seems pretty odd. You know what I think? I don't think it has anything to do with us. I think it's something to do with them."

"What do you mean?"

"These Big Brains... I think they only put us here to study and observe us. I'm betting they visit Earth all the time. They observe our atmospheric conditions, the suitability for their survival, and, most importantly, the potential for colonization."

"You think they want to take over our world?"

"Basically. Yeah. I think that's their plan." Doc nodded. "I'm betting they want to see how we behave in captivity. Like they're trying to decide if they should just kill all of us on Earth or if they can keep us all locked up in camps like this."

"You mean like internment camps?"

"Sort of, yeah. But they leave us alone to run things the way we want to. Maybe it's more like an Indian reservation, but one we can't leave. Ya know?"

"And no one ever gets out of here?" John asked.

"No. That's why we figured the Big Brains only took people no one would miss... always figured they didn't want anyone who would put up a fight."

"But they took me. Why would they take me?"

"I dunno, kid. I wonder if you're at the start of some new test phase. You are the first person to arrive in... well... I guess it has to be about five years."

"But why only grab me then? What did they do with all the other people I saw?"

"Wait. What?"

"Yeah. When I first woke up, I was in a room full of people on gurneys like me."

He stopped. His eyes stretched wide open as he turned to face John. "Hold up, kid. What room are you talking about?"

"Before I got here," John said, "we were all on gurneys packed in a room. There had to be a couple dozen of us. When I woke up later, though, they were all gone."

Doc became more interested. Enthusiasm filled his voice. "You mean you were actually awake on their ship? You could look around?"

"I... I, uh... ship? I... I don't know... it, it, uh, didn't feel like we were moving or anything. All I know is every time I woke up and tried to move, I felt this strange sensation. Then, I would pass out again."

"Oh, that..." Doc responded with a slower nod. He behaved as if what John was describing was normal. "That's how the Big Brains control us."

Doc continued the tour noticeably slower to focus on the conversation. John followed, still getting a feel for his surroundings.

"It happens anytime they get near us, or we get close to the borders, like that one over there." Doc pointed to the defensive barrier that shimmered and glowed. John took in the information with visible wonder in his eyes. "That's where they come from. They glide right through, but our muscles lock up, and we pass out anytime they get close."

"The Big Brain told me it was a safety feature. I couldn't even open my mouth to talk."

"Yeah, sounds like the same thing as the security line. Hell, I'm shocked you could wake up at all, let alone talk. I've never heard of that happening before."

A loud tone sounded throughout the camp.

"What does that mean?"

"Dinner. Come on, I want to introduce you to a few friends of mine."

They walked for a few minutes before Doc spoke up again. "You actually woke up, huh?"

"Yep. It had to be two or three times. The last time, the voice told me to relax. Everything would be okay. Then, this thing that looked like a hand touched my head. The next time I woke up, I was here."

"So, you haven't seen them yet?"

"Nope. Just that weird hand."

"Well, I'm sure you'll get your chance soon enough," Doc said. "We see them come in here occasionally to break up fights."

"Oddly enough, I can't wait."

John walked into the lunchroom, which was near capacity. The sounds were almost overwhelming as plates clanged and spoons clashed against forks. Whispers about the F.N.G. moved from one person to the next.

"Oi, Doc!" Gus called from a table at the far end. John let out a barely audible groan as he recognized all the eyes upon him.

Doc waved at Gus and made his way to the table.

"Come on, kid, that's our table."

"F.N.G.!" Rex said as the two reached their seats. "You finally left your room… well, alright."

John responded with a nervous grin. He tried to assess everyone seated at the table.

"F.N.G.?" John asked as he looked to see how people reacted to his query.

"It means fucking new guy!" Chris hollered in his thick accent, causing the table to laugh in unison.

"You must be starving, mate, yeah?" Gus asked. "Here, take a load off." Gus shimmied his chair to the side to make enough room for the two men to join.

As the men sat, Doc said, "This is John. John, meet the only friends I have in this place."

"Hello, my friend. I am Chris." He extended a hand, and John shook it.

"I'm Rex."

The group looked to Gus to provide his introduction. "Oh, er, I'm Gus. Pleasure to meet ya, John," Gus said as he put his fork down to focus more on the conversation.

"Have a seat there, and I'll go get us some food," Doc said as he moved away from the table. John settled into his seat.

After a few minutes, Chris finally broke the awkward silence. "Where are you from, John?"

"Oh, uh, I live in the desert hills in the Southwest," John announced.

"Oh. That sounds boring as shit," Rex said with a smirk.

John hesitated before responding. "Yeah," he said with a hint of sadness.

A wave of silence threatened to return before Rex asked, "What did you do out there?"

The conversation felt more like an interview.

John swallowed. "I, uh, I worked some ranches out there. Not my own, just ones in the area when they needed an extra hand. I—"

"Are y'all done grilling the kid yet?" Doc asked as he returned to the table with two trays of food. John sighed with relief. "Here you go, kid. Eat up. You'll need the energy. You look like you could pass out any minute."

John took the tray and set it on the table. He eyed the synthetic food with suspicion and doubt. It did not look like anything he had ever seen before.

"Your parents. How'd they die?" Rex asked out of nowhere. The question startled John.

"How did you know?" John said.

"Oh, man. It's a thing here. The Big Brains only capture people who don't have any real family left. Doc hasn't told you?" Rex asked.

John contemplated how to answer. Before he could, Chris doubled down on the question.

"Yes, how did they pass on?"

"Oh, uh, well, I lost my mother first. I was young when she died giving birth to my brother."

Before silence became uncomfortable, Gus asked with sadness in his voice, "And what about the little 'un?"

"He died too," John said in a hushed tone. "My dad was never really the same after that. He ended up taking his own life while I was waiting to ship out after boot camp a couple of years ago. I guess being all alone was just too much for him."

"Oh, that's just awful. Really sorry for your loss, mate," Gus said as he patted John on the back.

"Thanks, Gus. Thanks for that." With Gus's supportive tone, John nearly mentioned how Mary had been his rock since his father passed. As soon as the thought entered his mind, he could feel the despair growing within. He fought against the raw nerve, not wanting to break down in front of the men he had just met. "Uh… what about you guys? What, uh, what's your stories?"

Gus began first. "Well, I'm from just outside London. Used to be a cabbie, driving people all over the gaff. But then I had this proper nasty accident—nearly did me in, it did. Spent months stuck in hospital, and when they finally let me out, things just weren't the same," Gus said. His speech slowed. "The pain, mate, blimey, it was more than anyone could handle. Ended up turning to the bottle, I did—only thing that took the edge off. And food? Well, that was the only bit of comfort I had left. But then, these Big Brains, yeah, they did something to me. Don't ask me what, but it worked. Took the pain right away, and now? I feel more like myself again, like I did before the accident. Never thought I'd see the day, but here we are."

"What about your parents?" John asked.

"Never met 'em. Heard they passed a few months after I was born. Grew up in an orphanage till I was old enough to leg it and make my own way."

Moved by how Gus had become such a caring man despite all he had been through, John attempted to express his sympathy, but before he could utter a word, Gus asked, "Who's next?" John assumed Gus was still trying to cope with his difficult youth.

Chris adjusted his seat and sat up. "I… I am from Kenya."

"Where's that?" John asked.

"It's in Africa. Like Gus, I grew up with no parents. I worked with a group of missionaries who helped me learn English, but I was pretty much alone in the world. I guess that's what the Big Brains wanted."

"Same here," Doc said. "I pretty much lost everything when the pandemic took my wife. We didn't have any kids yet, and I had no one. Back then, I was still a practicing doctor. I didn't see much point in that after losing Rose."

Rex looked at them, poker-faced. Everyone at the table stared at him expectantly.

"Me? Well, there's nothing much to say. I had a job in Germany. Had a life, or at least I thought I did. I was going to start my own trucking business, but then the Big Brains showed up. And yeah, it's weird that all our parents and relatives are dead. No one's there to remember us. Is there anything sadder than that?" He took a swig of his drink.

"There's not a lot we can do about it," Doc said. "Do you know what's weirder, though? This guy here," pointing to John, "he woke up while the Big Brains were bringing him here."

"Woke up? That's impossible! Nobody wakes up!" Rex said as he turned to John. "Are you sure?"

"Yeah. I woke up a few times."

"How was that? What did you see?" Chris asked in wonder.

John narrated the entire experience—the gurneys, the people, the unusual hand. His description of his abduction that night captured everyone's attention.

"Who's Mary?" Gus asked.

"She's my girl. I was driving her to the hospital." John fought to keep his emotions in check.

"Hospital? What happened to her, then?"

"She was in labor. Our truck died, and that's when the Big Brains got me. I still—I just, I can't believe I'll never see her again." John broke down.

"Oh, man… that's terrible. I'm so sorry, man. Don't give up, though. You never know. You might still see her again. Anything is possible," Rex said with an undertone that conveyed reassurance and disbelief simultaneously. The others around the table nodded in agreement.

"Yeah. Sure, the Big Brains will just release us and bring us back to Earth, right?" John mocked the suggestion as he regained his composure.

"Hey, you never know," Rex said, trying to convince himself that such things are possible. "I guess you could always try escaping."

Chris and Gus's eyes widened as they recalled the conversation from the day before. Doc looked like he would explode at any second from Rex's needling.

Rex's words fueled John's imagination. For the first time on the planet, he developed something that offered at least a glimmer of hope.

"You wouldn't be the first to try, isn't that right, Doc?" Rex looked over at Doc to see the reaction he had provoked.

At first, Doc wanted to ignore the question, but his face revealed his frustration with Rex.

"What, too soon, Doc?" Rex laughed and diffused the situation.

"God, you're such a dick," Doc chuckled, trying not to give Rex any further satisfaction. "No, Rex. John wouldn't be the first."

"Hey, John, Doc here helped the last guy who tried. Maybe he can help you, too?"

John turned to Doc excitedly, locking onto anything that could feed the hope growing within.

"Is that right, Doc? You can help?"

"Seriously, Rex, don't you have any limits?" Gus said.

Rex continued to force the conversation. "I mean… what could go wrong, Doc?"

Doc scrunched up his face in anger and once again banged his fist on the table, drawing the attention of most people in the room. He turned to John. "Get this straight, kid! There's no escaping this place. We're stuck here. Stop listening to this fool and get used to your new life." Doc stood up from his chair and stormed out, leaving his tray of unfinished food behind.

The sudden outburst surprised John. He wondered if he had said something wrong.

"Do not worry about that, my friend," Chris began. "Rex was just giving Doc a hard time."

"I don't get it. What happened?" John asked.

Rex took it upon himself to explain. "Listen, Doc's a great dude, but a long time ago, he helped a buddy of his try to escape. Doc thought there was some kind of weakness in the Big Brains' security system or something. But after repeated failures, the guy threw himself off Apartment 15."

John's eyes widened.

Rex said, "Doc blames himself. I figure, though, if I give him shit about it, he might finally realize it's not his fault. That guy pushed Doc to help him. Doc doesn't own any of the blame. Anyway, I think you remind Doc a lot of that guy. I can tell by the way he's already taken to ya. I don't know, maybe I went a bit too far, but if there's a possibility to get out, it's going to take someone who needs to get out of here, like you, and someone like Doc to help. So there ya have it. Do with that information as you like."

John nodded along as the men got up, returned Doc's and their trays, and left the lunchroom.

CHAPTER 5

John spent the night thinking of ways to escape his prison. He tried to encourage himself the way Mary would, but nothing eased his mind. Sleep all but abandoned him as he tossed and turned. He woke the next morning from what little sleep he found with red, swollen eyes. His neck and back ached, causing him to groan as he stretched. Pain coursed through his body.

As he washed up in the bathroom, John concluded that despite Doc's feelings, he was the only person who could help. He got dressed and headed downstairs, determined to make Doc his ally. He made it to the courtyard before he realized he had no plan for where to go. He headed to the lunchroom, where he joined Gus, who was already seated at a table.

"Hey, Gus. Good morning."

"Alright, mate. How's it going?"

"I'm hanging in. Have you seen Doc?"

"Nah, haven't seen him all morning."

"Where do you think I might find him?"

"If he's not in his room, I'd bet he's down at the Hub."

"Oh. Hey, what's Doc's room number?"

"He's pretty much just upstairs from you, mate—room 305."

"Thanks, Gus."

DETACHMENTS

John hurried out of the lunchroom and headed to Apartment 3. He stopped at the Hub on the way, believing Doc might be there. The place was as congested as it had been the previous day. He wondered why the people had gathered there so early in the morning. It eventually dawned on him when he realized he was still thinking like people on Earth. Here, people had no families, no jobs, no responsibilities at all. John realized some people might see the camp as the ultimate freedom, even though they were being held captive. To John, though, it was complete oppression.

John scanned the area intently, taking in the sights and sounds of all the clinking bottles and profanity that filled the atmosphere. The Hub was remarkable, but John preferred to hang out alone in his room. If not for Mary, staying alone at his father's homestead would have been John's entire life.

He spotted Doc near one of the billiard tables in the bowling section of the Hub. Doc was watching someone roll a ball. At least it looked like Doc was watching. He was physically there, but John could tell Doc was somewhere far away in his mind. He stroked his jaw with his fingers while his other hand tapped his thigh several times a second, but without a distinct pattern or rhythm. John rushed toward him.

"Doc! Can we talk?"

"Nope. I'm not gonna do it; don't even bother."

"I haven't even asked anything!"

"You don't need to, kid. I already know exactly what you're thinking." Doc sighed, recognizing the excitement and hope in John's eyes.

"Ah, fuck. Jesus Christ. Fine, let's get out of here. We can talk up on level 3."

Doc led the way to the elevator at what seemed like a snail's pace to John. They arrived at the empty batting cages and were finally alone.

"Go ahead, spit it out, kid," Doc said.

"Doc, I gotta get home. I gotta get back to Mary."

Doc took a deep breath and then released it. "I know, kid. I know what you're feeling, but it's not possible! You don't want to hear this, but you need to let go. We've tried everything. It's impossible."

"There has to be a way. You're the only one who can help. You tried it with your friend, so you can show me what you learned. I need you to help me out with this, Doc," John pleaded in desperation. "Doc, I need you—"

"Look, kid. I'm not doing this again. I don't think you understand. Mark didn't just decide to throw himself off that building. That was me; that was my fault. I might as well have pushed him off that building."

John stepped back. "Doc, you can't blame yourself for that."

"I can't? I watched him try and fail over and over. Whenever I came up with a new idea, I gave him another glimmer of hope to try again. I should have known and seen what it was doing to him. Who am I kidding here?"

"It sounds like you were just trying to help."

"No, it wasn't just that. I didn't want to see him quit. That was me! I wanted him to keep trying. I wanted—" Doc's voice broke as he choked back his emotions. He was on the brink of tears before he collected himself. "Honestly, I don't know what I wanted. Hell, I'm not always sure if I'm more upset about losing a friend or that I couldn't keep trying. I mean, would he have even tried to escape if it wasn't for me filling his head with the possibility?" Doc shook his head, disgusted with himself.

"Listen, Doc. I get it was hard on you, and you blame yourself, but it wasn't your fault. Mark made his decisions, and I've made mine. I'm doing this with or without you. If there's a way to get back to Mary, I will find it!"

"Listen, it's just not possible, and I'm not gonna help you. If you're doing this, you're doing it alone."

"Fine." John stormed out, more determined than he had been when he arrived. He was going to find a way. He had to.

DETACHMENTS

The following day arrived, and with it, a new focus for John. He woke excited to explore his options for escape, a new obsession that distracted him from the dread that otherwise preoccupied his thoughts. He knew trying to escape would be a considerable risk, but it was a risk he had to take.

During the previous night, John began his research on the barrier. He knew the key to escape lay behind that tall, shimmering barrier.

John went to the courtyard as the sun peeked over the horizon. He hurried through the vast, dusty area, trying to avoid the attention of the other residents. As he neared the perimeter, he slowed down and became more deliberate. John crept toward it, half expecting to fall to the ground, paralyzed. He paced the area for a minute, unsure of what to do or how to begin his experiments. A few people took notice and gawked in wonder. For some, this would be the most exciting thing to happen in a long time. They sat on the benches and watched as if they were attending a movie at the Hub. John focused on his work and barely noticed the people watching. Normally, he would, but at this moment, John thought only of getting back to Mary.

Doc and his friends eventually made their way into the courtyard. They noticed the stillness and what had captured the attention of the others in the area.

"What in the world is going on?" Doc asked.

"Damn, it's your F.N.G.," Rex said. He pointed toward the perimeter. "He's about to learn a lesson the hard way."

"Shit!" Doc said. "What the hell is he doing?"

"Looks to me like he wants a sleep aid," Rex said.

They watched John pace back and forth. He would move to a certain distance and mark it off with his foot. Then he would step back and repeat, inching closer and closer to the defensive wall.

"Oh… the kid's trying to figure out how deep the perimeter is. I bet he's going to try to jump through it," Doc said as he rubbed his forehead in disbelief.

John edged closer to the perimeter—a half step, then another. He put his hands before him to see if he could better detect the threat. As John edged closer, he felt a familiar sensation grip his body. He quickly stepped back, satisfied he had found the closest he could get to the perimeter, and made a mark with his foot.

"Well, can he?" Chris inquired.

"Hell no! We tried and tried, but we couldn't get anywhere near close enough to get through to the other side."

As Doc spoke, John loosened up by shaking his arms and legs. He walked up to the line he made with his foot and slowly leaned toward the fence line—first an inch, then another. He leaned over the line another inch, intensifying the sensation. The move garnered gasps and murmurs from the onlookers. The barrier flashed a bright red light, sending him straight to the ground. He tried to stand up but could not. John could not talk, but he remained awake, trapped in the barrier's grasp.

Doc saw this and initially groaned, but then accepted that they needed to act. "Christ! Come on, let's go get him before a Big Brain does."

They all hurried to the spot where John lay motionless.

"Don't get too close. Get his feet!" Doc said.

Gus and Chris dragged John back from the security system's grasp. John sat up as he regained muscle control.

"Thanks, guys. Thanks so—"

"What were you thinking?" Doc barked. "What would have happened to you if we weren't here? What if we couldn't reach your feet? You ever think about that? Next time, tie yourself to a tree before you do something stupid. You can get a rope at the market. Until then, stop your dumb shit!" Doc's eyes bulged as he chastised John like a disappointed father.

"What the hell did you expect?" John snapped back as he sprang to his feet. "You won't help me! You won't tell me what won't work! What the hell am I supposed to do?"

"I already did, kid. I told you everything you need to know—nothing works! There is no way out. We never made it more than halfway into that perimeter, and every time, boom, knocked out cold. Just give it up. There is no way—"

"Knocked out? No, I didn't get knocked out. I was awake. I could see. I just couldn't move or call out."

"You were awake?" Chris asked.

"Yeah, the whole time. I could feel y'all pull me out and everything."

"Doc, did you hear that? He was awake in there," Chris said.

"It doesn't change a damn thing. There's no way through that barrier unless you're taken through it by a Big Brain," Doc insisted.

"Hey, wait, maybe we could—"

"Forget it, kid! The only way through that perimeter is by Big Brains. And when they take you, they do something to your brain. They'll wipe your entire mind. Then where would you be? Face it, you're fucked." Doc looked at John and realized he was talking to a brick wall. He grumbled something under his breath and walked off.

"I am so sorry, John. It's quite special that you stayed awake. I am afraid Doc is right, though. You should probably listen to him," Chris said as he and Rex left.

Only Gus remained there with John. "If you're gonna keep at it, mate, I'll give you a hand."

"You'd be willing to help? Thank you… but… why? What makes you want to help?" John asked.

"You have a family to get back to. That's why. And, well, it just feels like the right thing to do."

John and Gus wasted no time. The following day, they headed to the perimeter again, armed with some rope and two small rolled-up mattresses like those used with a cot. They used the straps on the mattresses to tie them end to end, then pushed them into the perimeter, positioning them to shield John's fall.

"Gus, where did you say you got these mattresses again?" John asked as he assessed the mattresses to see how well they would break his fall.

"The market."

"And what did you trade for 'em?"

"A basket."

"Damn, I guess that's a good trade. Did you need to get ones that smelled so bad?"

Gus laughed. "Beggars can't be choosers, can they?"

"I hope that wasn't a very nice basket."

"Well, it definitely smelled better."

The men laughed momentarily before they prepared for the first attempt. John secured the rope around his waist, dug his feet into the loose ground to get a firm push-off, and then sprinted for the mattresses. As he reached the edge of the first mattress, he jumped into the air. He hoped his feet would land near the joining of the two mattresses so he might fall forward enough to avoid the perimeter's effects on the far side. He barely made it off the ground before the perimeter knocked John out cold, and he collapsed on the first mattress in an awkward clump. Gus pulled John back from the perimeter's effects, and after a minute, John woke to unfamiliar aches and pains.

"Holy shit, that hurt! What happened?"

"Mate, you barely got off the ground, and the way you went down in a heap—looked like you didn't have any bones at all!"

"I definitely got knocked out that time. How far did I make it?"

"You didn't even make it to the second mattress. Don't think you even got a proper jump in before it took you out."

"Damn it. Do I gotta jump sooner, ya think?"

Before Gus could opine, Rex made his presence in the courtyard known. "Hey! Gus! John! That looked painful as hell," he said with a laugh. "Go on, give it another shot. You can do it!" Rex goaded.

Doc entered the courtyard just in time to hear Rex ridiculing John.

"Oh man, you should have seen his last try," Rex said.

Doc and Rex watched as John tried to loosen up his muscles and joints from his first failed attempt.

"He crashed hard, Doc. Hysterical."

Doc sighed, shaking his head in disbelief.

"What? I thought it was funny," Rex explained.

"This kid doesn't want to give up."

Rex nodded in agreement.

They watched as the two continued with a string of failed attempts. John aimed for a jump angle that would give him enough distance for the second mattress, but the optimal angle for distance was too far ahead of the first mattress, making it impossible to gain any useful ground toward the second.

John's efforts continued through the breakfast hours and into the late morning. His repeated attempts took their toll, both physically and emotionally, but he continued to try every viable approach.

"John, mate. Listen, I reckon it's time to stop," the big man said as he pulled up the slack in the rope connecting him to John.

"No, not yet. I can do this!"

"You're all banged up. You're nowhere near as quick as when we started, and you haven't even had a bite to eat. It's time to pack it in, mate."

Frustration drenched John's face in dirt, sweat, and hate. Despite Gus's sage advice, he readied himself for another attempt.

"No. We're trying again. Come on, give me some slack," John demanded as he tugged on the rope.

"Nah, don't think I will, John." The big man looked down at John calmly but firmly as he strengthened his grip on the rolled-up rope.

John pulled harder. "Gimme the fuckin' rope. Just leave, and I'll do it myself."

John was a powerful man from years of back-breaking work on ranches around his father's home in Torrance County, but he was no match for Gus, who was easily six feet four inches tall and must have weighed close to two hundred and fifty pounds. It may not have been all muscle, but he was a formidable man who knew how to use his strength when he wanted. It was clear Gus had suffered with his own challenges in life. Despite his imposing physicality, Gus was a kind man who put others' needs before his own.

"I ain't leaving this rope here, John. It's time to take a break, and that's the end of it."

Before John could utter a response, the lunch alarm sounded, and Gus continued.

"Come on. It's lunchtime. We'll have another go after." John relented and, with a sigh, untied the rope, dusted himself off, and followed Gus to the lunchroom. They went up to their usual table. Doc and Rex were already there. Chris ate his lunch at the Hub.

"Alright, lads," Gus greeted with his normal cheeriness.

"Hey," John said, practically under his breath.

"So, first off, you suck at this," Doc scolded John. He was trying to be as calm as possible. "Second, what does it take to get through your thick skull? What you're trying to do is impossible."

"Look, maybe this whole thing fails, but if there's even a chance, I've got to try."

Doc sighed as he recognized there was no way he could convince John to stop.

"Yeah, he's not gonna give up, Doc. So, how's that been working out for ya, John?" Rex inserted his unique brand of support.

"To be honest, it's a lot harder than I thought," John admitted. He wiped off the beads of sweat remaining on his brow. "I... I mean, we... could really use your help," John said as he glanced over to Gus in his first demonstration of appreciation for Gus's efforts.

"Why? What do you need us for?" Rex asked. He sat up and focused all his attention on John.

"I... um. I think I've got another idea. It's gonna sound nuts, but I—"

"You mean, more nuts than what you're already doing?" Rex said.

With a sigh, John said, "I need you guys to throw me over the perimeter. I think that just might work."

Doc and Rex looked at each other. They had that *he's gone bonkers* look on their faces.

"What?! No way! That's insane!" Doc blasted.

"Let me worry about the dangers, Doc. I'll be fine."

"Yeah, Doc, let John worry about the danger. Hell, I'm in." Rex laughed, excited at the opportunity to hurl John into the barrier.

Doc sighed and shrugged. He could not bother himself with John's nonsense any longer. If John wanted to kill himself, there was nothing he could do about it.

After lunch, John's accomplices returned to the perimeter to try their plan of tossing John toward the unrelenting barrier. Rex and Gus positioned themselves, with Rex grabbing John's hands and Gus holding John's ankles. While not as strong as either Gus or John, Rex spent much of his life proving he could outdo bigger men. For his size, he was formidable, able to hold his own in most situations, and was all too willing to prove it.

"Okay, just make sure my head lands on the mattresses."

"Mate, this is gonna hurt. You sure you wanna give it a go?" Gus asked.

"Yeah, I'm sure; let's do it."

The men lifted John from the dirt below. Realizing what they were about to see, laughter and jeering rose from the crowd that had gathered to watch the spectacle. If the size disparity between Rex and Gus wasn't sufficient to garner such a reaction, the expected result certainly was.

"Okay, I'm ready, guys."

Rex counted down as he and Gus swung John back and forth to create as much momentum as possible. They released on three, and John sailed through the air with a slight spin caused by Gus overpowering Rex. John landed parallel to the mattresses, with his head and torso on the first mattress and his legs and feet on the second. John was still nowhere near as far as he would need to be to endure the barrier's effects. The men dragged John back from the perimeter with the rope.

John awoke to greater laughter and mockery from the growing crowd that had collected to see the shenanigans.

Gus gave John a look that made it clear he disapproved of trying again. John recognized Gus's displeasure and said, "I think we're done for the day, Gus. We can try again tomorrow."

"Ahh, come on, this is fun. Let's try again," Rex said in his patented sarcastic way. Neither John nor Gus even smirked. "Okay, that one was too soon, wasn't it? In all seriousness, man, I genuinely hoped it would work. Hopefully, we will have more luck tomorrow."

The men tried various tactics to get John across the barrier over the next several days, with modest improvement as they refined their methods. One day, after another round of futile attempts, a fight broke out in the courtyard.

"Why are they fighting?" John asked.

"Power, territory, controlling the better jobs in the camp for supplies—all that sort of thing," Gus said. "People join the gang mostly 'cause they get all the best stuff, don't they? I reckon the Big Brains drop supplies here, but the gangs run the show. Most of the lot working in the lunchroom, the market—pretty much anywhere but the infirmary—they're all working for Drongs or the Serpentis. Those gangs are always at it, fighting."

John listened intently as Gus said, "See that bloke over there, the one in the red shirt? He's one of the Serpentis. And the poor sod on the ground he's kicking? He's a Drong—"

"Hey, won't the Big Brains—" John paused as Gus pointed again to the perimeter. A Big Brain was coming through. John watched in awe as the creature floated toward the fight. All the gang members slumped to the ground, unconscious. The Big Brain lifted them and floated them across the perimeter. It all happened so fast. John wished he could watch the moment over again. He felt a surge of adrenaline rush through his veins. He knew he had to see Doc. "Hey, Gus, I think we can stop for the day. I'll catch up with you later," John said as he walked off before Gus could respond.

CHAPTER 6

John entered the apartment building after passing through a group of about ten residents who remained in the courtyard. He barely noticed their mockery and snide comments, focusing instead on his destination. John swallowed as he reached Doc's room. He filled his lungs with air to prepare for the conflict he expected. He summoned all the courage he could muster and knocked on the door. His hand had hardly landed before Doc opened it, as though he had been waiting for him to arrive.

"Hey, John."

"Doc. I need to talk to you. Can I come in?"

"Yeah, of course." Doc stepped aside as John walked in. He surveyed the corridor briefly before stepping back into his room and shutting the door.

John scanned the room. It was pretty much identical to his. Doc had a pile of books sitting on a small table in a corner. The room had a slight aroma of old laundry and was in a general state of disarray. John wasn't a clean freak, but Doc's room was chaotic. Books, clothes, various trinkets from the market, and poker chips from the Hub were all haphazardly set about the room. There was laundry stacked up in the corner, and his trash can was nearly full of beer bottles.

John stood while Doc sat on his bed, leaning against the headboard with his legs outstretched. He gestured toward a chair. "Have a seat, kid."

John moved a pair of pants and some books from the chair. He dragged the chair closer to the bed and sat down. John sat there silently for a moment, trying to choose his words carefully. The silence did not bother Doc, but for John, the moment felt like it stretched well beyond awkward.

"So… what brings you here?" Doc asked, knowing precisely what John hoped to discuss.

John shifted in his chair. "Look, Doc," he began with a shaky voice. "I know you don't want to help, and I realize I'm never getting through that perimeter the way I've been trying. But what if there were another way?"

Doc's left eyebrow perked up.

"What are you getting at, kid?"

John edged closer to Doc and spoke in a lower tone. "What if there was a way to get through with a Big Brain?"

Doc shook his head in disappointment. "Kid, what did I tell you about that? Sure, they might take you out of here, but then what? It's too risky; it's just too risky."

"But, Doc, I could—"

"Kid. I can't stress this enough. We don't know what's out there. People don't come back the same. You could lose your memories of Mary and everything that makes you who you are."

"There's gotta be a way, Doc. If we can't get through that barrier, we'll find a way."

"John, I wish that were true. I do. If I thought you had a chance, I'd be right there with you. But the Big Brains are just too powerful. No one has ever resisted their power—no one except… uh, well… no one, never mind."

John's eyes perked up. "What did you say? What do you mean, except?"

Doc groaned. He had said too much. "Shit! Damn it! Look. Don't go thinkin' this is going to help. Hell, I'm not even sure it's true. I heard it happened over at Apartment 19—"

48

"What? What happened at 19?"

"Shirley. Shirley happened."

"Shirley? Who's Shirley?"

With that, Doc became the uncomfortable one in the conversation. He did not want to give John hope where there was none, but he could feel John's suffering. Before he knew it, Doc had helped John more than he ever intended. He released a deep sigh and said, "Shirley's the first and only person to be born here in the camp. The Big Brains, it seems, took Shirley's mother shortly after she became pregnant."

"I guess I've been too preoccupied to notice, but now that you mention it," John said aloud as he realized he had seen no children or pregnant women in the camp.

"Yeah, I'm not sure why it is, but no women here get pregnant. I don't know. Maybe it's something about the planet or something to do with population control."

John nodded slowly as he realized why the women there seemed so carefree, especially the ones affiliated with members of the gangs.

Doc continued. "The story goes that her mother couldn't take all of this anymore, so she threw herself off the roof of Apartment 19. The Big Brains were there, keeping everyone away. When Shirley heard about it, she ran to her mother. Many expected the Big Brains to subdue her, but she just ran through them. As the story goes, she even knocked one of them right to the ground. She stayed there, crying over her mother's body. I guess it took a long time before she let go, and the Big Brains could clear the area."

"Hmm. If that's true, she might know how to do it again. Maybe I can learn it." John stroked his beardless chin with his fingertips. The key to his escape was becoming clearer and more accessible. His hope and energy from the first day of his trial and error came back in full force. John was grinning from ear to ear.

Doc smirked. "You're grasping at straws, kid. Even if she can block the Big Brains' powers, you weren't born here, so you won't be able to. I'm sure of it."

"We don't know that, Doc," John said. His voice brimmed with enthusiasm. "You're the one who said no one had ever woken up before coming to the camp, and I did! Three times! And that was the first time with the perimeter, too! There's gotta be something to that, Doc. There has to be!"

Doc groaned. "All right, kid, fine. I'll help you find Shirley, but you've gotta promise that once we find her and she can't help us, you'll give this whole thing up and set about living your life here. Deal?" Doc stretched out his hand for a shake.

John took it with a huge smile. "Deal. Tomorrow morning?"

"Yeah. Okay, kid. Tomorrow morning."

The next morning, John appeared at Doc's door before the lights came up in the building. He had spent the entire night tossing and turning in his bed as thoughts of Shirley, Mary, and freedom filled his mind.

He knocked on Doc's door. No response. He knocked again a few moments later with a bit more conviction. Time seemed to stand still as John readied for a third knock when Doc opened the door with a grunt.

"I've been knocking, Doc. Are you ready?"

"No. Wait. Uh… Ready for what?" he said, with reddened eyes and messy gray hair that surrounded the balding crown of his head.

"Oh, come on, Doc. Don't tell me you forgot." John lowered his voice. "We have to go see Shirley!"

"Oh shit… yeah, okay. Gimme a minute."

Doc grunted again and shut the door. He emerged a few minutes later. John wondered how Doc could shave, shower, and choose clothes that fast, but Doc appeared well-prepared for the day.

"How come you're up so early?" Doc asked as he closed his door, and they walked down the corridor.

"I'm an early riser."

"That's a lie." Doc laughed. "Your first day here, you slept so long that some of us started calling you Sleeping Beauty."

John's face flushed red, and he laughed to conceal his embarrassment.

They arrived at a twisted path through a wooded park that led to the other buildings. The wind whipped at their faces as they walked along. In two minutes, the path curved toward the building that was Apartment 19. They stood at the entrance, confused at first as they watched the residents file out almost mechanically.

John leaned over and whispered in Doc's ear, "Where are they all going?"

"At this hour? Probably the market. Come on, let's head in."

For whatever reason, the residents of Apartment 19 kept to themselves. John assumed that stemmed from the tragic story of Shirley's mother. They walked up to a petite woman who sat on a bench like the one in the courtyard.

"Hello," Doc greeted.

"Hola," she said, with a thick Spanish accent.

"We're looking for Shirley. Do you know where she is?"

The smile disappeared from the woman's face. She suddenly looked nervous, or perhaps scared.

"Shirley? No Shirley. No habla inglés."

"Shirley. We're looking for Shirley," John repeated, slowing his speech and speaking more loudly.

"No Shirley. Yo soy Isabella."

John was about to clarify when Doc intervened. "Okay, de nada." Doc held up his hand to wave and thank the woman as they moved on. "Let's find someone else, John. She either doesn't speak English or won't speak English because she doesn't want to tell us."

They continued their search for Shirley, gaining the attention of several residents. After more than an hour wandering about the building and surrounding area, Doc noticed someone following them.

"John," Doc said in a whisper. "I think we might have a problem."

"What? What is it?"

"That guy over there. I think he's following us."

John looked over and saw the man looking in their direction. Not one to be intimidated, he said to Doc, "Hey, let's go find out."

"Hey, hey, is there a problem?"

"I dunno. Maybe there is. Why don't you tell me why you're looking for Shirley? I'll let you know if we have a problem. How's that sound?" The man was not concerned by John's willingness to call him out. John wondered if the man expected or perhaps intended for them to do exactly that.

"I... uh... need her for something very important," John said. He moved closer to the man and explained his situation, careful enough to add Mary and his unborn child to generate as much sympathy as possible.

"Oh. Interesting. Thanks," the man replied as he disappeared into a hallway as mysteriously as he had arrived.

Doc wiped his palm across his face. Both men stood there, confused by the interaction for a moment.

"Huh, that was, uh, well... odd."

"Yeah, it was. Okay, come on, kid. We're wasting our time here."

John could feel his face warming with frustration. "No, I'm not—"

"You said you were looking for Shirley?" a woman asked from behind them.

They spun around to see a woman draped in a shawl covering her shoulders. Her dress was otherwise mundane, but the bright colors of the shawl highlighted her dark eyes and hair, creating an almost regal presence.

"Yes! Yes, please," John said.

"I know where to find her. Please, come with me." The woman turned to lead them. After a few moments, she said, "I couldn't help but overhear the story about... it was Mary, right? And your unborn child. I'm very sorry for what you've been through."

John and Doc exchanged glances, then looked back at the woman suspiciously.

"Thank you, uh, Miss?" John tried to find out the woman's name, to no avail.

"From which building are you, gentlemen?"

"Uh, we're from Apartment 3."

Doc remained quiet throughout. He was still suspicious of the woman. After the unusual interaction with the man moments before, he worried she might be a gang member.

"How long have you been here?" the woman asked.

"I don't know. It's been a couple of weeks now, I guess?"

"You're the new guy I've been hearing about?"

"Yeah," John admitted.

"And you?" She turned and pointed at Doc.

"Twenty years, give or take," Doc said.

John's mind nearly exploded. He had never asked or realized how long Doc had been in the camp. His mind briefly wandered. *How could this man have survived in this place for twenty years without going mad?* For the first time, John understood why Doc was sure escape was impossible.

The woman turned back around. "Well, now, that's quite a long time," she said as she led them into a quiet area outside the back of the building. The woman stopped and turned to face the men again. "This will do. This will do just fine."

Doc felt uneasy about the location. He knew the gangs had found places around the camp where it would take longer for the Big Brains to respond to violence. The men found themselves at a dead end, leaving them just one way out—back through the building.

CHAPTER 7

John could sense Doc's unease and wondered if they had been led into a trap. The moment grew tense until he could stand it no longer.

"So, where's Shirley? Why'd you bring us out here? You said you were taking us to see her."

The woman cracked a smile, realizing the apprehension she had caused before letting the men off the hook. "And that's exactly what I've done. I'm Shirley. I'm glad to meet you both."

John stared back in relief. "Oh, thank God, we've been looking for you all morning."

Shirley's smile widened as she extended her hand to shake John's.

"Oh, Shirley. It's nice to meet you, ma'am," John responded with heightened respect.

"Why should we believe you?" Doc asked, still apprehensive about their current situation. He kept his arms folded and close to his chest.

"I understand your reluctance, Doc. But I am Shirley, the daughter of Margaret, the woman who died here sixteen years ago. You're welcome to continue looking for her if you don't believe me." She nodded toward Apartment 19.

John and Doc eyed each other and, in unison, nodded in agreement that they had found Shirley. "Well, thank you for taking the time to talk with us. I really appreciate it," John said.

"It's okay. Sorry, it's been difficult to find me. The people of Apartment 19 have taken care of me since my mother passed when I was thirteen, so they're very protective."

"Do you mind if we ask what happened that day? Not about your mom, but the rumors that you knocked a Big Brain down. Did that happen? Were you able to resist them?" Doc asked, revealing his curiosity about the event.

"Oh, it's true, all right. It was a horrible night, but it's all true."

"How?" Doc asked. "How did you do that?" Doc shook his head, amazed by Shirley's confirmation.

"I'm not exactly sure. I didn't have time to think, so I was just focused on my mother and what happened that I didn't even pay attention to the Big Brains when I ran to her."

"My deepest condolences," John said as he fought to keep the memories of Mary from breaking through the dam of emotions he was feeling.

"Thank you, John. I know this must all be very difficult for you as well."

"It is, yes. That's exactly why we came looking for you. We thought you could help me do what you did. Once you knew you could stop the Big Brains, why didn't you escape?"

"Escape to what? There's nothing for me on Earth. Life here isn't so bad if you can stay clear of the gangs. That's what you want, isn't it? You want to escape."

"Of course. I have to find a way back to Earth. If there's any chance Mary and my baby are alive, I have to. Will you teach me how you did it?"

"Teach you? I'm not sure I can still do it. I only did it that one time and haven't been near a Big Brain since then to even try. Besides, you weren't born here, so how could I teach you?"

"I don't know. Maybe I'm crazy. I just… I think it might be possible. I mean, I did wake up before getting to the camp—"

"You did what?" Shirley asked in surprise.

"I woke up before they brought me to the camp. Three times, and once when I got too close to the barrier. That's gotta mean something, right?"

Shirley paused. She was deep in thought. "I think it just might, John. It just might."

Doc could not believe what he was hearing. Not only was Shirley's story true, but she thought John could develop the ability she had that day. "Wait, do you really think John can do this?"

"I'm not sure, but maybe we've been thinking about this all wrong," Shirley wondered aloud. "Maybe my ability that day had nothing to do with being born here. Maybe it was just because of how much I loved my mother."

John's eyes nearly jumped out of his head. The dots of information in his mind connected the similarities between his and Shirley's experiences. "When I woke up before camp, I had just lost Mary. Do you think that could be it?"

"It could be, John. I think it could be. But you'll have to get up close and personal with the Big Brains to find out."

John and Doc agreed with a nod of their heads.

Shirley said, "You're going to need to keep an eye out for fights between the gangs. That always brings the Big Brains. When they come, you'll need to get as close as possible without getting mixed up in the fight. If you can get near them while they're using their power, maybe you can train your mind."

"Train my mind?"

"Yeah, if this theory is correct, we were both able to resist their abilities by being so focused on our loved ones taken from us. Focus on that loss, the feeling. Maybe that detachment is the key," Shirley suggested. "Once we know it works, it will just take some practice."

"That makes sense to me," John said. "Doc, what do ya think?"

For the first time, Doc was no longer certain John's goals were impossible. Doc caught himself getting excited by the possibility. Perhaps all his efforts with Mark had been worthwhile. Maybe helping John would ensure Mark did not die in vain after all.

"I think I've got some ideas to help make sure we get you near some fights too, kid," Doc said, surprising John with his support.

"Okay. That's good for the practice, but how do I get through the barrier?"

"I guess if you could stay awake once and you get good enough, you can probably just walk through the barrier," Shirley said.

"That might work. Right, Doc?"

"Nope, not gonna work. Forget it."

"What do you mean, Doc? You can't still be refusing to help."

"No, no, I'm in. I'm gonna help. In fact, I'm helping right now. Remember when you saw the Big Brains coming through? They deactivated the barrier before floating across, right? Why do you think that is? The barrier has an alarm, kid. You cross that line without taking it down first, and you'll have more Big Brains than you can deal with."

"So, we've gotta figure out a way to get out at basically the same time the Big Brains are going through the barrier."

"Gentlemen, I think the answer is simple. You need to stage a fight with each other for the Big Brains to come after you. When they do, drop and let them take you through the perimeter. Once you're in their city, John can overpower the Big Brains, and you can sneak onto their ship and back to Earth."

"Yeah, that's simple enough," John joked, eliciting a laugh, even from Shirley.

"Yeah, you gentlemen have a tough road ahead, but if there is a way, it will be something along those lines."

John and Doc sighed almost simultaneously.

"Do you know what we'll find if we get out of here?" Doc asked.

"You mean the Big Brain city? I just know that's where they take all the offenders. I heard that they have some special cells or facilities where they keep the people till they've been able to alter their minds and send them back here. You should talk to Tom. He might have some insights to share."

"Tom?" John looked at Doc and then at Shirley.

"He's... well, he was a gang leader here. He was one of the worst. The Big Brains thought he was becoming too violent, so they took him away and changed all that," Doc said.

"What happened when he came back?"

"He was completely different," Shirley said. "Now, he may be the nicest person in the camp. He spends most of his time helping people and improving the place."

"Where can we find him?"

"He lives in Apartment 8 but frequents the courtyard, especially in the morning."

"Thank you, Shirley. You've been so helpful," John said.

She nodded and walked away, leaving the men to consider their next steps.

"That was smooth," Doc snickered. "So, what do we do now?"

"We go looking for Tom, of course."

After a short walk, the men reached Apartment 8. It had to be one of the tidiest buildings in the entire camp. The occupants of the building had erected a small fence made of branches and pieces of metal that they got from some spare materials from the Hub and the market.

"Wow... this is incredible. Do you think Tom did all of this?" John asked, noticing beautiful frames and designs that clung to the walls. There was lively chatter among the residents outside the building. That atmosphere gave John a sense of peace and belonging.

DETACHMENTS

As John and Doc entered the building, they spotted a man sitting by his room door, listening to some music.

"Good morning," they both cheerfully greeted.

"Yeah," the man said with a smile. "Y'all looking for someone?"

"Yes… Do you know who Tom is?" Doc asked nervously. Still in disbelief, the Big Brains fully reformed the notorious gangster.

The man paused for a moment. He still had a smile on his face. "Tom?"

"Yeah, Tom."

"Sure, I know Tom. Who doesn't? You'll probably find him in the yard." The man gestured toward a metal door that was a few meters away. "Go through there… You'll find him on the other side."

"Thank you," John said.

"The yard?" Doc asked as he and John approached the door. John shrugged and turned the handle. The door creaked open. A narrow, dimly lit corridor lay ahead.

"What is this place?" Doc adjusted his glasses as he spoke.

In a few moments, they arrived at another door.

CHAPTER 8

John opened the door to reveal a small patch of land about a quarter of the size of the courtyard. The place was lush, almost tropical. It was unlike any other area Doc had seen in the camp before. It was like walking into a hidden paradise.

"Hello?" John called out.

A tall, broad man stood up from behind some bushes. His face was strong and angular. A heavy scar ran from his left ear to his eyebrow, partiality hidden by his short, dark hair, disheveled from his gardening. His massive arms and chest bulged through his faded shirt.

"Hello," Tom said with no discernible accent. "I'm Tom. What can I do for ya?"

After introducing themselves, Doc said, "We were hoping we could talk to you about something. It's very important."

"How could something I know be so important?" Tom approached the men and exchanged a handshake.

"It's about the Big Brains and the perimeter," Doc said. "We understand you've been to the Big Brains' city. We're hoping you can tell us about that."

"Tell me, what is it you'd like to know?" Tom's lips curved in a smile. His voice landed with a soothing tone that gave no hint of the danger his appearance communicated.

"Uh, the Big Brains. We're, uh, we're trying to understand what happens... I mean, what happened to you when they took you," Doc said.

"Oh..." Tom sighed. "Come on, gentlemen, let's sit and relax a little." Tom led the way to some nearby rocks they could sit on. "Listen, I understand I was a pretty awful person before my rehabilitation. I hope I never harmed either of you during those days."

"No, uh, never directly, no. The gangs have definitely made life harder here than it needs to be, so I guess if, uh... you—" Doc stammered as he realized what he almost said.

"It's okay, you can say it. It's fine."

"Oh, uh, well, I was just going to say, if you had never created the Drongs and controlled things so much, maybe life here would have been more enjoyable, and maybe Mark... well, never mind, we're not here for that." Doc pulled himself back from getting too personal.

Tom leaned over to Doc and gently placed his hand on Doc's shoulder. "I can see I have hurt you, Doc. I'm very sorry for my previous actions. I know I don't deserve forgiveness, but I hope there's some way I can make amends for the pain I've caused you and the people you care about."

Doc lifted his head to look up at Tom. He reached over and patted his hand resting on his shoulder. "I appreciate you saying that, Tom. It means a lot to me." Doc returned his hand to his side as Tom settled on his rock.

John sat silently as the entire scene played out before him. For a moment, Doc became the most important person in John's life. It was clear Doc needed Tom's full attention. Whatever the gangs forced Mark to endure was significant enough to push him toward escape and, ultimately, his death.

"And how 'bout you, John? How have I hurt you in the past?"

"Oh, uh, me? You haven't. I, uh, I'm new here."

"Wait. Are you the F.N.G.? I try not to leave the building here too often. With all the pain I've caused, I don't want to cause more by showing my face when it's not needed. I spend most of my time here in the yard."

"It's beautiful here. How have I never heard of this place?" Doc asked as his eyes wandered about the area, taking in the sights and scents of the blossoming flowers that outlined their sitting area.

"Those of us who know about it keep it a secret. With how secluded it is, we're worried the Big Brains can't access this place, and the gangs would want to take it over, like the tennis courts."

"Do you take care of this whole place?" John asked.

"Not alone, no. Many of the residents here come and help, but it's pretty much what I do every day. It keeps me occupied, and I find it fulfilling."

"Did you always have an interest in this kind of thing, or is that something the Big Brains did while you were with them?" Doc asked.

"No, I think I've always had an interest. At least I have vivid memories of helping my mother in her garden when I was a child."

"You still have memories of your childhood? I heard they wiped your mind," Doc said.

"I have tremendous gaps in my memories, that's for sure. There isn't much I remember from my childhood or even from here in the camp. Yeah, mind wipe is a fair description, I guess."

"Do you remember what happened when you were in the Big Brains' city? How did they do that to you?" John asked.

"I wouldn't say I remember anything specifically, no, but I feel like I remember being there. It's hard to explain."

"Anything you can tell us will be helpful. Please, anything you know."

"From the things I can remember, I only recall waking up back here in the camp with three shaved spots on my head."

"Were there sutures on your scalp from any incisions they made?" Doc asked.

"No, just shaved patches—two back here and one up front in this area," Tom said, pointing to the areas on his scalp. "The oddest part of it was that I wasn't surprised by any of it."

"What do you mean by that?" John asked.

"The whole thing seemed normal, like… I fully expected to see the shaved spots on my head. I expected to wake up here, and it felt like I'd been gone for close to a year."

"If that's the case, you couldn't have been under the whole time, then," Doc surmised.

"That's the sense I have, yes."

"John, if he wasn't under the whole time, it's reasonable to believe there might be some opportunities there." John nodded in agreement.

"Opportunity for what?" Tom asked.

After a pause, John sought Doc's counsel. Doc tilted his head in concurrence. With that, John told Tom the story of his arrival and his intent to get back to Mary.

"I understand your predicament, John. I wish there were more I could do to help."

"Are you sure you can't recall any other details that might help? Like where they kept you? How they treated you? Anything?" John tried to get some more details.

"All I have are some feelings that remain. I can't see anything in my head, but I feel like they treated me well while I was there. As you were telling me the story of what happened to you, I couldn't help but think they didn't mean to do any of that."

"Doc, do you think if they could wipe his memories, that they could make him feel those things as well?"

"I dunno, kid. Messing with memories, implanting feelings—this is all way beyond anything I ever learned about what's medically possible. I guess I'm open to almost any possibility."

"You're saying there's a potential they just made me feel pleasant things about them? Could they make it feel real, like I legitimately experienced it?"

"I'm so sorry, Tom. I hope none of what we're telling you is going to disturb the harmony you've found here. We don't want to cause any problems."

"No, John, it's okay. I still don't feel any ill will toward the Big Brains, but I do hope you're able to achieve your goals. Do you think you'll even be able to get past the perimeter?"

Doc explained their plans and intentions of using the fights to train John's mind.

"Seems like you've got a good plan there, but how are you going to make sure you're around the fights when they happen?"

"That's a good point, Doc. I hadn't thought of that."

"I've got some ideas, but if I'm being honest, I was hoping Tom here could fill in some details for that."

"You're wanting to incite gang violence, aren't you?" Tom asked.

"That's my basic idea, yeah," Doc said. "But with your memories wiped, I don't know how much help you could be."

"Sadly, much like my memories of the Big Brain city, I just have general feelings about the gangs. Maybe if you tell me what you know about them, I'll be able to help spark some ideas for your plan. What do both gangs want? If you can find something, some kind of wedge you can drive between them, that could give you the conflict you'll need."

"That's the thing," Doc said. "They've been on a truce since not long after the Big Brains took you. The Serpentis control the Hub and all the supplies that come to the camp, except for the individual requests made by residents. The Drongs control those and the market. They both seem pretty content with their level of control in the camp."

"Well, that won't work then, and any move to upset that balance will cause a war that won't do you any good at all. You're going to need to do something at a more personal level."

"What do you mean, Tom?" John asked.

"My gut tells me the gang members, especially the leadership, are very possessive of their women. They treat them like property."

"I wouldn't want to get any of the women hurt if they—"

"That's gonna be a risk, John, for sure, but you're not thinking like they do. If a gang leader's woman is stepping out on him, she'll be in for a beating, no doubt. But if someone from another gang is just trying to take her, that's about as disrespectful as it gets. Imagine what would happen if the Serpentis tried to steal a delivery of alcohol from the Drongs. Now multiply that by ten, and you'll get a sense of how they would react to someone trying to take one of their women."

"Hey, that could work!" Doc agreed. "We could probably make it seem like Sal from the Serpentis is interested in Mick's girl. This is gonna have to be done just right. He's not the Drong's leader for nothing, ya know? He's no idiot."

"If you can make it believable, that would get some tensions going. Mick would probably put his pawns on notice to keep a closer eye on things. That could work. You'll have to be careful that people don't realize what you're doing," Tom said.

"Considering how much the Big Brains have taken from your memory, you've been a real help, Tom. Thanks so much."

"Yes, thank you," Doc agreed.

"No problem at all. Just do me a favor and keep this place to yourself, okay? Neither of us wants our secrets revealed to the gangs, so I trust that won't be a concern, right?"

Both John and Doc nodded in agreement and left the yard to finish their planning, enlist some help, and start making John's escape plan a reality.

Doc and John revealed their plan to their friends during lunch the next day.

"Wait... Doc, are you really getting in on this? Have you lost your mind?" Rex said in a harsh whisper. Their talk about Shirley, Tom, and the gangs made Rex drop his spoon in shock, unable to respond with a more typical smart-ass retort.

"I know it's crazy and dangerous, but I think we've got a good plan, and more importantly, I believe in John."

Chris sat up in his chair. "What happened? How do you believe so strongly now when just two days ago you washed your hands of this?"

"I know, Chris. I know. But that was before we talked to Shirley. Now, I think this kid might pull off something miraculous."

Rex's eyes stretched wide, and his mouth dropped. "Shirley! You guys talked to Shirley?"

"We did, and we think John might just be able to do what she did."

"You mean you think he can escape the Big Brains' power?" Gus asked.

"I think he—"

"I can, I know I can!" John insisted.

"Well, we'll figure that out, but we need some help," Doc said.

"I'll help, mate. Just let me know what you need."

"I knew you would, Gus. I very much appreciate everything you've been doing to help already," John said. "Chris? Rex? What about you?"

"I want to help you, my friend. I need to know more before I can agree, though," Chris said.

"Yeah, I don't want to end up getting my mind wiped on some shitty plan. No offense," Rex said with a laugh.

Doc and John laid out their plan.

"Hold on... you want us to hang around with gang members and spread rumors about them? Have you lost your fucking mind?"

"Rex, I know it's a risk, but if we're all coordinating closely on this, everything should work out fine. We need to be careful, but if we do this right, none of this will ever come back on us. That's why we can't do this alone," Doc explained.

66

DETACHMENTS

Chris sat quietly, leaning his head into his hands. Doc had never seen Chris so seriously contemplate anything.

"I know…" John started, then paused as Chris's eyes opened above his hands. "I know you guys barely know me, and I've not done anything yet to earn your trust or your favor, but I'm going to ask you to put yourselves in my shoes. Would you not do everything in your power to get back to your loved ones?"

Chris nodded in agreement. John had successfully won him over. His eyes shifted back to Rex, hoping his appeal had a similar effect. The moment stretched on, and all eyes turned to Rex. His gaze shifted from one friend to the next. John's fate hung in the balance. He knew that without Rex, their plan had no hope. They would not have enough people to help hide the origin of the gossip and protect his co-conspirators.

CHAPTER 9

The lunchroom grew quiet as the awkward silence loomed over Rex's decision. Despite the soothing music playing in the background, John's heart pounded. He teetered between euphoria and desperation. Rex's continued silence burned like salt in an open wound. John was about to lose his patience when he noticed Rex develop a faint smile.

"Fine! Fuck! I'll help," Rex announced as he stood to shake John's hand. "But don't go thinkin' I'm doing this for you. I'm just doing it to get rid of your dumb ass."

John stood and shook his head in disbelief at how Rex played with his emotions. He stretched out his hand and shook Rex's.

"What is it with you, man? You just can't stop yourself, can you?" John asked.

"What? Did I say something wrong?" Rex laughed.

"Hey, look at it this way, kid. He must like you. He only messes with the people he likes," Doc said.

"But wait," Chris chimed in. "Rex never messes with me. You do not like me, Rex?"

"Ha… just the opposite, Chris. You're the only one here I do like. The old man is nuts."

"Alright. Alright. We got work to do. Sit down. Let's figure this out."

Doc took control of the group. They all sat back down and developed their plans. They were the last ones to leave the lunchroom as the meal ended. After they departed, John and his friends immediately got to work sharing fragments of information among disparate groups of people. They knew their salacious gossip would eventually reach the right ears. It was a necessarily subtle campaign to avoid detection.

The first altercation happened some days later as John rested in the courtyard, trying to maintain his patience. On that day, the Serpentis entered the area first. Sal had an entourage of about six men. John took notice and sat up. Doc rushed to John's side. His feet slid in the loose dirt as he took a seat.

Through heavy breaths, Doc said, "The Drongs are right around the corner, kid. They're headed this way. You ready for this?"

"I couldn't be more ready." John sat up and leaned forward. He did not want to miss a moment.

John and Doc watched as Mick led a handful of Drongs into the courtyard. As Mick laid eyes on his rival, his face revealed the fury he kept in check. They approached the Serpentis like pawns on a chessboard. Each of the gangs' foot soldiers positioned themselves in front of their leaders—a well-established show of force any time violence might become necessary. It was a standard tactic to keep their leaders out of the fight and safe from any Big Brain intervention. Maintaining their grip on the camp's critical facilities outweighed any beef between the gangs. Only the leaders and their deputies knew all the ins and outs of how they controlled the supplies, how they ran their respective grafts, and how they managed the workers.

"You got some fuckin' nerve showing your face!" Mick said. The Drongs in front of him puffed their chests out and readied themselves for a fight.

"I don't see your name on the courtyard," Sal said. "I'll show my face anywhere I want. Rumor has it a lot of people like my face. You know anyone special that likes my face, Mick?"

"You stay the fuck away from Ava, you piece of shit!" Mick tried to lunge through his goons, driving them into Sal's men, causing a momentary scrum. The gangs' foot soldiers pushed and shoved one another as Mick's deputy held him back.

"Ooh, kid. It's about to happen," Doc said.

"Aww, you worried I'm gonna take your girl, Mick? What makes you think I'd want that scrag after you've had her, anyway?"

"That's it, you're fuckin' dead!" Mick's face burned red as he drove into his men, trying to reach Sal's neck. "Lemme fuckin' through." His momentum pushed several Drongs into expendable Serpentis, reigniting the fracas. One of the Serpentis landed a clean shot on a Drong. The two men exchanged blows as those around them worked to keep their bosses out of the fight.

John watched the perimeter anxiously as he moved closer to the scene. The two men continued exchanging haymakers. The rest of the gang members stepped back, knowing the Big Brains would not be far behind.

John barely arrived near the fight when the perimeter lights changed. A moment later, a Big Brain drifted through. John's heart quickened. He looked back at Doc for a last dose of encouragement.

Doc's grin and nod were all John needed. He readied himself for the Big Brain's influence. John got his first up-close look at the being. Its skin was gray and wrinkled. The creature's head looked too large for its small, slender body. Its arms and legs were skinny, with no muscle mass—they were little more than twigs.

The Big Brain approached from the Serpentis side of the scrum. Sal was the first to fall to the ground in slumber, his men a heartbeat later. Before John knew it, he could feel the effects envelop him. He focused his thoughts on Mary and his unborn child as hard as he could. John channeled all his love and frustration over being taken from them. He focused it all into one thought, as Shirley recommended. The Big Brain moved closer. The two men fighting were out cold, and those next to him fell to the ground. John's drowsiness intensified, but he refused to give in. He fought back with more memories of Mary. As he battled with his mind, he felt his knees getting weaker. Then it hit him. He realized he was the only person still standing. John dropped to the ground to avoid detection.

Doc worried John had succumbed to the Big Brain guard. He watched the guard lift and float the two fighters beyond the perimeter. As Doc approached, John gasped as he lifted his head from the dirt. Doc leaned down and helped John to his feet.

"Man, I thought it got you. Let's get you to your room before these guys wake up."

Doc steadied John as they walked back to his room and helped him onto his bed.

"Tell me what happened. Tell me everything."

"It was rough, Doc. I felt really tired. It was as if a voice was in my head telling me the best thing to do was to lie down and sleep."

"How exactly did you fight it, kid? What did you have to do? Was it like Shirley said?"

"I just thought of Mary and the baby. I focused on memories of her, how I left them, and how much they needed me."

"Damn, I can't believe it. This might work."

"It will, Doc. I need more practice, but I know this will work," John said as he sat up and looked at Doc.

"No doubt, kid. For now, though, you need some rest. This isn't over for Mick and Sal. Don't worry, you're gonna get another chance, for sure."

"Thanks, Doc. Thanks for everything."

Doc patted John's shoulder and walked out.

John lay on the bed, thoughts of Mary and home swirling in his mind. He was going home. He knew it. He could feel it in his bones.

Over the next few weeks, John's friends helped him instigate several more fights. John practiced at every opportunity the gangs gave him. His ability to resist the Big Brains grew stronger with each encounter, the last of which he could stand his ground without feeling drowsy.

John sat on his bed, more confident than ever—he was ready. It was time to leave this planet, and he would not wait another minute, so he charged out the door to find Doc.

"I'm ready, Doc! It's time. We need to plan our next move," John said as Doc's door barely closed behind him.

"Good evening to you as well, kid," Doc said with a smirk as he sat down on his bed.

"Sorry, I just—"

"I know, kid. I'm excited for you, too."

"You agree, then? It's time?"

"I don't think it's a bad idea," Doc said. "Things are getting pretty tense with the gangs. They're gonna start to wonder why you're always around when they fight, if they aren't already."

"You don't think—"

"No, I, uh, I wouldn't worry, John." Doc's eyes looked down and away from John as he pressed his left hand against his forehead.

"What, Doc? Have you heard something?"

"No, no, kid, it's, uh, everything's fine," Doc said as he lifted his eyes back to John's.

Doc could see the desperation in John's eyes, the same desperation he saw when John first learned there might be a way off this planet. Doc tapped his fingers on his thigh with uncertainty.

"Hey, kid. There's nothing we can do tonight. So, morning?" Doc proposed.

"Yeah. Okay, morning. I want to do it in a place with a lot of people. That should get the attention of the Big Brains faster."

"I think outside the lunchroom would be the perfect place," Doc said. "Should be a pleasant change of pace for everyone tired of seeing the gangs fight. But hey, try not to hit me too hard," forcing a half-hearted smile to his lips. "I'm getting too old for this shit, kid."

"Don't worry, old man," John jested while making quotation marks in the air around 'old man.' "I'll go easy on ya, but make it look good, would ya?"

They shook hands and patted each other on the back in a brotherly embrace. All their preparations had led to this. The next morning, the Big Brains would take John and Doc through the border. John knew, somehow, he would be near Mary again soon.

"I owe you an enormous debt of gratitude for all you've done, Doc."

"Thank me when you're on that ship headed home, kid. There's a whole lot that's still gotta go our way before that happens."

"I know, Doc. I know. Okay, let's get some sleep. I'll see you in the morning."

"Sounds good, Doc. Have a good night."

John opened the door, and before his mind could register the imposing figure before him, a deep Italian accent crashed against his ears.

"Where the fuck you think you're goin'?"

CHAPTER 10

John's eyes adjusted to the sight before him. He stepped back instinctively to create distance from the threat. Doc knocked the pile of books beside him to the floor as he struggled to maintain his composure.

The shadow of Sal and five of his men cast deep into Doc's room, blanketing the atmosphere with gloom. Sal's face looked hardened by weeks of anger. His eyes were wild and unblinking. Sal's rage was clear.

"What, uh, what do, uh, you want, Sal?" Doc said.

Sal and his men pushed their way into the small room. One man stayed at the entrance, keeping the door open a crack. Sal stood quietly, surveying the room, wringing his hands near his chest. After a moment, he tilted his head up ever so slightly, prompting his goons to force Doc and John down on the edge of the bed. They sat helplessly. They had no means of escape.

"Good, I've got your attention. Now, listen closely. We're gonna do this real quiet. Not a fuckin' noise from either of you. You got me? I swear to Christ, you do anything to bring in the Big Brains, and I guarantee at least one of you will be dead before they get me, clear?" Sal growled, his voice deep and penetrating.

Sweat beaded on John's forehead. He nodded in agreement. Doc nodded along as he picked up John's acknowledgment out of the corner of his eye.

"Good! Get 'em up," Sal demanded.

Sal's men yanked John and Doc off the bed and pushed them toward the door.

"Fuckin' move!" one of the Serpentis ordered as he shoved Doc from behind.

The Serpentis led John and Doc to the Hub. The journey was quick. Too quick. Before they knew it, John and Doc had emerged from the elevator on the third floor. Their demise felt close at hand. Away from bystanders, Sal's men shoved them toward the deserted tennis courts beyond the batting cages.

"Put 'em on their fuckin' knees!" Sal ordered as he leaned against a dusty racket dispenser.

Sal's troops forced John and Doc to their knees. They hovered over them, ready to deliver punishment. A pungent smell wafted through the air after one of the Serpentis kicked some old bloody clothes aside.

"You fucks thought you could start some shit about me and Mick's girl and get away with it?"

John let out a sigh that betrayed any hope of convincing Sal he was mistaken. His face turned a ghostly white. Doc's head dropped in acceptance of their fate. They had played their hand, their only hand, and Sal was about to play his.

"Doc had nothing to do with it. It was all me."

"No, kid—"

"Ha," Sal huffed. "You expect me to believe that shit? You've been here, what, a month?"

"It… it was me. I did it! It was all my idea! I masterminded everything! Please let my friend go," John pleaded. "He did nothing. It's all my fault."

His voice became weak, riddled with anxiety and fear of the unknown.

"Don't give me that bullshit!" Sal said.

John's left cheek burned with fire as he slammed down on the hard court floor. He caught himself with his hands mere inches before his head bounced off the surface. He shook his head to fight off the haze from the blow. *What the hell happened?* John wondered. Sal's slap had been so fast, John's eyes could not perceive the motion.

"Leave the kid alone! We did—"

"Am I fuckin' talkin' to you, Doc? Shut your fuckin' mouth, or I'll beat this piece of shit harder and make you watch. You got me?"

John pulled himself up to his knees, still reeling from the impact. "I got it, Doc, this is on me," John said in little more than a whisper as he struggled to catch his breath.

"You got a lot of balls spreading that shit about me. You put me and every member of my clan in danger. Do you have any idea how many people I lost to the Big Brains over this bullshit?"

John caught the motion of Sal's hand in time to stiffen his neck and ready his body for another blow. The smack landed harder than the first, but John took the full force and maintained his composure. Not to be denied, Sal clenched his fist and delivered a hard right cross to John's jaw. The punch landed on its target, knocking John back to the court floor, balled up on his side and dazed from the shot. Sal stepped in and kicked John's forehead, causing his head to snap back and spatter blood on the nearby wall.

John struggled to orient himself on the floor as muddled echoes of cheering Serpentis seeped past the fog in his brain. The cheers became clearer as he regained his composure. Doc instinctively reached for his friend but learned Sal's men had no patience for that and snatched him back to the only spot Sal would allow.

John raised and vigorously shook his head. He stammered out some unintelligible words. Half expecting another shot from Sal, John's voice gained some clarity as he balanced on his hands and knees, "I'm sorry, sir. I had no choice… I'm so—"

He could not finish his sentence before Sal delivered another kick, this time to John's abdomen. The shot forced a gasp from John and sent him sliding across the floor.

"You had no choice? What the fuck is that supposed to mean?"

John struggled to catch his breath and find the right words to escape another blow from Sal.

"Again, sir, I'm very sorry. I had to, though. It was the only way to get off this planet."

Sal noticeably rocked back in his stance. The words landed with unexpected force. It was as though John had reared back and smacked Sal in retaliation. John recognized the opening. It was a slim one, but it was an opening.

John worked his way to his knees. He stretched his right hand in meager defense while cradling his abdomen with his left. "My girl—" John struggled to catch his breath. "My girl's pregnant back home. We… we were on the way to the hospital. She was in labor. Then these fucking Big Brains took me. They weren't supposed to take me!" John cried out in frustration as he coughed and spat blood through his words.

"Wait, what? Okay, you've got my attention. This I've gotta hear. Go ahead. I'm listening," Sal said as he resumed his lean against the racket dispenser.

John's voice trembled as he described the night the Big Brains grabbed him, the desperation he felt that night, and the fear he felt at the thought of losing Mary and his child.

Sal listened on, waiting to hear where this tale would lead and how it would justify John's actions.

"After I got here, I told Doc I had woken up three times before I got to the camp—"

"Bullshit!! No fuckin' way," one of Sal's lieutenants said. "No one wakes up till they're in the camp. Boss, you aren't buying any of this BS, are you?"

Doc could not stop himself. "No, it's true, it's all true."

Not revealing his intentions, Sal nodded for John to continue.

"I don't know what became of Mary or my child. I fear for the worst. Doc and I have a plan, though. The Big Brains can't stop me. I can stay awake. I can beat them!" John insisted.

Sal rolled his eyes in disbelief as he stood back up from his resting position against the tennis racket dispenser.

"No, I swear. That's why I did it. The rumors, the fights, all of it. I needed to be around the Big Brains when people were fighting so I could train. It was the only way."

"That's it!" Sal said. "You needed us to fight so that you could practice? That's the bullshit you want to sell me?"

"No, really, it's true; the Big Brains can't knock him out. I've seen it. He can prove it, I'm telling you," Doc said.

Sal's followers mocked Doc's assertions to support their boss's disbelief.

"Hold on, guys, hold on! Shut the fuck up!" Sal hushed his gang and looked back at John.

"The Big Brains can't stop you? That's what you're telling me?" Sal tilted his head back while rubbing his chin.

"Yes," John said with confidence.

Sal leaned back against the racket dispenser as the truth took hold in his mind.

"I think I like Doc's idea… how 'bout we make him prove it?"

"Boss? We're gonna fight and risk losing more guys? Boss, you can't be—"

Sal sprang back upright. "Did I say that? Did I fuckin' say anything like that? How 'bout you shut the fuck up and let me decide what we're gonna do? Is that okay with you?" Sal's voice returned to a more conversational tone. "See, I've got a better idea. This piece of shit can prove it by restoring Tom's mind. He's gonna help us end the Drongs forever."

As the words floated across the room to the rest of the Serpentis, Doc could practically see a collective light bulb form above their heads. They nodded in approval with a barely audible hint of sinister affirmation.

Sal revealed his plan. "If this bullshit you're spinning is true, here's what you're going to do to prove it. There's a small vault at the back of the infirmary where they keep a special serum called 'Rev Rehab.' It's in a shiny blue vial. My men and I have been trying to get into that vault ever since Tom's been back. We don't have a lot of details, but we know it's closely guarded by Big Brains. If this story you're telling is true, you should have no trouble getting me that serum. You get that, and I'll consider your debt paid in full."

John was silent. His mind raced. He did not know where the infirmary was, let alone the vault behind it. He knew if he disagreed, though, his mission to leave this planet would end right then and there.

CHAPTER 11

With little time to think, John looked at Doc with hopelessness in his eyes. Doc flashed a nearly imperceptible smile that gave John the confidence he needed to respond.

"Okay. Okay. I'll do it."

Sal's taut expression spread into a broad, ominous grin.

"Haha... I like this deal," Sal announced.

The Serpentis all smiled and cheered along, acknowledging the brilliant win-win situation their boss created.

"You have till dinner ends tomorrow to bring me the Rev Rehab. If you don't deliver it or you play any games with me, I'll shock the Big Brains with what I do to you and your three other friends," Sal warned. "Yeah, I know about them too... Now, go get my fucking serum!"

Doc helped John to his feet and into the elevator. He left the encounter battered and bruised, but alive. As they walked from the Hub to the infirmary, John broke the uneasy silence.

"What the hell is Rev Rehab, Doc?" John asked.

Doc sighed heavily. "It's not good, kid. It's not good."

"What do you mean?"

"Rev Rehab is short for Reverse Rehabilitation. Supposedly, it's a serum created by the Big Brain scientists to undo the mind-wipes they do to people. I assumed it was a legend at this point. The first I ever heard of it was shortly after Shirley's mom passed. I guess the Serpentis believe it's true."

John scratched his head and wiped blood from his eye that had flowed from the cut on his forehead caused by Sal's kick.

"It makes sense that Sal would want to restore the minds of his gang, but what did he want with Tom? Wasn't he a Drong?"

"He was," Doc advised. "He was the leader of the Drongs when they controlled the whole camp. I'll bet Sal wants to know the Drongs' secrets."

"So, they want Tom's info to take over the Drongs' territory?"

"It has to be. If they use the serum, they can torture him till they get everything they need. They'll take over the entire camp."

"No, you're right. No one would be safe, and no one could stop them," John said as he hobbled with Doc. "And I'm gonna make that all possible?"

"I dunno what choice we have, John. I just don't know." Doc patted John's shoulder like a father trying to soothe his son.

"So, what do we do?" John asked. "How do we get the serum?"

"I dunno. We're gonna have to figure something out." Doc's words trailed off as he completed his thoughts.

"You okay, Doc?"

"Yeah, yeah, I'm okay, kid. I just—Dammit! We were close. I thought you were gonna make it. I—" Doc's voice cracked as the emotions of the moment closed his windpipe.

"You what?"

"Never mind, it doesn't matter," Doc wiped at the corner of his eyes. "We got a job to do, John. Let's just get it done."

"You sure, Doc?"

"Yeah, I'm good. Let's get you patched up so we can focus on the task at hand."

As they walked toward the entrance, Doc pointed to the infirmary door and helped keep John on his feet. John stood fast momentarily, holding Doc back from his next step.

"Hey, Doc, wait a minute. Maybe we shouldn't go to the infirmary now. Maybe—"

"What? No, you need to get that looked at. They're gonna need to close that wound on your head, and we should make sure you don't have any broken ribs."

"No, hear me out. My injuries… they'll get me in the door. I can use them to find the vault. If we go now, I'm not gonna be able to go back tomorrow."

"You make a good point, kid. If you've got broken ribs, though, you shouldn't wait. How's your pain level? You feel any sharp pains when you breathe?"

"No, not sharp. No, it's fine."

"Cough for me."

John coughed a few times. His face winced ever so slightly.

"How'd that feel?"

"Fine, Doc, I'm fine."

"Yeah, okay, sure," Doc said, shaking his head. "All right, kid. We'll do it your way. Let's get you home and cleaned up. We'll figure things out."

John and Doc arrived back at John's room. John cleaned up the dried blood on his forehead, eye, and mouth while standing at his sink. A light trickle of blood oozed from his forehead, and he could still taste blood in his mouth from his swollen and split lip. He looked quite the sight in his mirror.

"I don't get it," John called out to Doc. "If this serum would undo the mind-wipes, why would the Big Brains trust it being in the camp?"

"Only thing I can figure, kid… the Big Brains must trust the infirmary staff. You know, like trustees at a prison. There must be some medical need for them to have it here. That's the best I can figure."

John stepped out of his bathroom, sucking on his lower lip. He held rolled-up toilet tissue to his forehead to clot the blood from the wound.

"Got a nice little knot on your head there, kid. At least the laceration itself isn't too bad."

"Yeah, I've seen better days. That much is for sure."

"No doubt, you're a sight. Ya know, if you get in that vault, the Big Brains are gonna come for you. Maybe a bunch of 'em. You may have to get violent to get out of there. Do you think you can handle several of 'em?"

"Not sure I've got much choice there," John said, still clutching his left side.

Doc could see the concern in John's eyes.

"I wish I could be there to help ya."

"Yeah, I know, Doc. They'd knock you out, and I'd be struggling to get both of us out of there."

Doc nodded with a hint of a frown.

"You gonna head over first thing in the morning? I know I can't go into the vault with you, but maybe I can keep watch or something?"

"Yeah, I plan on getting up with the morning lights and heading on over. No need for you to tag along. I want you as far away from the Big Brains as possible."

"All right, John. The lights are gonna come up soon. You should try to get some rest." Doc stood up and gave John a firm handshake. "Good luck, kid."

"Thanks, Doc."

Doc turned and left John's room. The door shut softly behind him. John settled into his bed and drifted off to thoughts of the challenge ahead.

Dawn arrived sooner than John was prepared to accept. He shifted his body to hide from the light, his ribs protesting the move with agony. The pain caused John to recoil, reminding him of how Mary would place her cold feet on his side in the winter months back home. The memory drove John to his feet. He had work to do.

John readied himself for the day and headed out to the infirmary. His mind wandered into contemplation—the camp, his life, and his uncertain journey home.

Like the apartment buildings in the camp, the infirmary was large and formed part of the northern border. It stretched more than the width of the park that separated the two rows of apartment buildings on the east and west sides of the camp. The residents used east and west based on the sun, as if they were still on Earth, but no one knew for sure which direction the sun crossed the sky.

Thick forestry flanked both sides of the infirmary. John could not make out whether the barrier was active beyond the woods but wondered if it provided an opportunity. He presumed Doc must have tried that with Mark, or he would have suggested it. Regardless, the woods made it impractical to try accessing the rear of the building to get to the vault.

John approached the entrance of the infirmary. The shiny glass door slid open, surprising him.

"Welcome," an automated voice spoke. "Please step onto the Dia-Glass to your right," the voice instructed.

John stepped inside. To his right was a flat pane of thick glass on the floor. It was glowing green with wavelike lines darting about on a screen.

"Dia-Glass?" John muttered aloud. He had heard the infirmary automated most systems but never imagined talking glass would make a diagnosis.

He moved in closer and stood on the glass floor. The Dia-Glass released a low hum for a few seconds. The greenish glow turned red.

"Acute conditions include a mild laceration, facial contusions, and costochondritis. Chronic conditions include anxiety and prehypertension. Please follow the guide to Ward 8," the voice said.

As John stepped off the Dia-Glass and headed into the empty infirmary hallway, he heard another voice. "Please follow me." A light from within the wall to his right flashed with each syllable. It glided down the corridor, creating a vapor-like trail behind it. It led John past different wards and jumped across hallways to adjacent walls, showing John where to turn to find the proper treatment area.

DETACHMENTS

Without passing another person, John entered Ward 8. The light continued to lead him through a labyrinth of rooms for various examinations, tests, procedures, and a few that appeared to be for inpatient use. John had never seen a hospital laid out like this one. He could not determine if Ward 8 had a specific medical focus, as he would have expected, or if Ward 8 had some other purpose. Regardless, John had no intention of remaining long.

The light arrived at its destination, turned green, and announced, "Please wait in this exam room, and a nurse will be with you shortly." The light then disappeared as quickly as it had arrived. John opened the door to a small exam room. It wasn't much larger than the bed it contained. He stepped inside and heaved a heavy sigh as he shut the door and readied himself for his next move.

Outside of the vague instructions he received from Sal, John did not know where to find the vault. He opened the door a crack to assess his options. The hall was empty. He exited his room and entered the ward to begin his mission.

John tried to recall the route the light took through the ward to his exam room to form some semblance of a mental map. He was cautious not to draw the attention of guards or staff as he crept along the empty hallways. Only the occasional clatter of medical equipment disturbed the otherwise stillness in the air. John made what he believed would be the last turn, where he expected to find the vault. Instead, he found only a dead end. *It should be here. Where did I go wrong?* John wondered as he second-guessed his sense of direction.

As John turned to retrace his steps, his eyes caught something unusual on the floor at the end of the hall. He could see marks from the soles of shoes as though someone had walked beyond the wall. John scrutinized the area more closely. He noticed fingerprints on the smooth, steely surface. He placed his hand near the prints, causing the wall to react with tiny red lights that outlined his hand and rippled outward. John pulled his hand away and stepped back.

He looked around to check his surroundings. After a few moments, he confirmed he had the hallway to himself and placed his hand back on the wall. The red lights radiated away from his hand, then became a solid red outline that blinked. A voice announced, "Staff access only. Please step away."

This must be it, John concluded.

Before John could contemplate his next move, he heard footsteps rapidly approaching.

CHAPTER 12

John burst through the door of Ward 7, surprising a nurse. Before she could make a sound, he rushed her. He cupped his hand over her mouth and squeezed her head back against his chest, pinning her. He could see the look of fear in her eyes as she whimpered. His hand dwarfed her face.

"I'm not gonna hurt you. I'm so sorry to do this, but you need to stay quiet," John whispered as he pushed the nurse through the open door of a nearby exam room.

John closed the door with his hip, which caused an audible thud that only added to his worries. He caught his breath with the nurse still trapped in his grip.

"Sorry, sorry, I'm so sorry. If I release my hands, do you promise to stay quiet?" John asked in a whisper.

With tears forming in the corners of her eyes, she nodded in agreement.

John slowly released his hold but remained ready to reimpose his grasp. To his relief, the nurse obeyed. She stepped back from her captor as the terror slowly drained from her face.

"Don't be scared, okay? I promise I won't hurt you." John cut to the chase. He now knew how to get the best reaction from people. "I know you have no reason to trust me, but the Big Brains screwed up. They took me from my home and my family. I'm not supposed to be here."

The nurse's face turned from fear to something between disbelief and shock. She quickly composed herself and said, "Wait, come again? You said the Big Brains pulled you away from your family?"

John nodded as desperation filled his eyes. He once again explained the story of how he had been rushing Mary to the hospital shortly before the Big Brains captured him; how he had woken before reaching the camp, hatched his escape plan, and practiced defeating the Big Brains.

The conversation lasted only a few moments before the nurse said, "So, what do you need from me? You've got only minor injuries. Anyone here would have been able to treat you."

"No, no, it's not my injuries," John said, clutching his ribs. "It's how I got them and what's going to happen to my friends and me if I fail."

"Fail? Fail at what?"

John elaborated on his dilemma with the Serpentis and the Rev Rehab. The nurse grasped the severity of John's situation, as any disbelief she had about his predicament appeared to fall away from concern.

Seeing this look on her face, John asked, "Will you help me?"

The nurse struggled to form the words. "Help you? To get the Rev Rehab? I'm sorry, I really am, but there's no way. Even if I wanted to help, I can't. Accessing the Rev Rehab without a specific order is impossible."

"I've got to try. If I don't bring it back to the Serpentis—"

"I understand, but even if I let you in—"

"You can get me into the vault?"

The nurse sighed. "Yes, I can get you into the pharmacy. But it won't do any good. If you take the serum without authorization, it will trigger an alarm, and the Big Brain guards will—"

"I told you, I can handle the Big Brains."

The nurse realized she could not dissuade John from his pursuit. "God, I can't believe I'm doing this!"

John's eyes lit up. "You will? You're going to help? Thank you so much!"

"Don't get too excited. You're likely not going to enjoy how this ends. The Big Brains are very serious about the serum."

John ignored the warning. He heard the one thing he cared about: she would take him to the vault.

"Thank you again. I really appreciate it. My name's John."

"I'm Helen. Something tells me we're not going to see each other again after today, and if we do, I'm willing to bet you won't remember this, but I hope I'm wrong… for your sake."

"It's good to meet you. Sorry it's under these conditions. Don't worry about the Big Brains, though," John said. "Just get me to the serum, and everything will work out."

The nurse shrugged her shoulders in doubt, but she knew John had set his course. He would not turn back.

"Okay. Check to make sure no one is in the hallway looking for me."

"Looking for you? Why would anyone be looking for you?" Nurse Helen asked.

"Because I tried to get into the vault door, a voice told me to step away, and I heard security coming down the hall."

"Security? There's no security here. Everything is automated. The door does that with any bad palm scan. You must have just heard staff in the hallway."

"Oh, my God. I'm so sorry. That was the whole reason I grabbed you the way I did."

"Don't worry about it. It is a staff-only area, though. I'm not supposed to escort anyone through there, so we'll need to be careful."

John nodded. "Okay, I understand. You ready?"

Helen agreed as she led John from the exam room, out of Ward 7, and approached the staff area entrance.

Nurse Helen placed her hand against the door. A green outline of her hand flashed once, and what had appeared to be a solid wall split open like a double door sliding to each side. She looked down the corridor toward the pharmacy and motioned to John.

She led John down the hall without saying a word. John could sense she was worried about being caught.

"Is that the vault?" John asked, pointing to the smudge marks on the wall at the end of the hallway.

"We don't call it the vault, but yes, that's where you'll find the Rev Rehab and all the other controlled medicines. It's our controlled pharmacy," Helen said.

"And you can get in there?"

"I can, but the automated security will respond if we remove any unauthorized medication… especially the Rev Rehab."

They arrived at the pharmacy door. Helen looked at John before opening it, silently questioning the wisdom of their next move. John nodded, urging her to open the door. She placed her hand against the wall, and the door slid open.

John stepped into the pharmacy. It was a large rectangular room that was at least as long as the hallway. The nurse stood at the threshold for a moment before entering. Metallic cabinetry that nearly matched the walls lined the expansive room. None of them had labels, causing John to wonder how anyone could find anything. There was another door on the far side of the room.

"Each cabinet is like the door. They're all controlled by identity," Helen explained. "Here, watch. I've got an approved order in for some codeine."

John looked on in confusion.

"Pharmacy, codeine," Helen announced as she watched John's reaction, bringing a faint smile to her lips.

A small cabinet glowed with a green outline. She walked over and pressed her hand to its side. It opened, revealing an assortment of medicine bottles. She retrieved the proper dosage and quantity, then shut the cabinet. She returned to the open doorway, where John stood, amazed.

"So, that's how it works," Helen said. "But when we ask for the Rev Rehab, whichever cabinet it's in will glow red, but it won't open. You'll have to force it open to get to the serum."

John looked around the room, searching for anything he could use to pry open the cabinet.

"It's not too late. We can stop now. No one has to know any of this ever happened."

"Pharmacy, Rev Rehab," John called out.

A cabinet on the left side of the room near the far door glowed red.

"Okay, there it is. I don't know how you'll get it out of there, but now you know where it is."

"What's on the other side of that door over there?"

"We don't know. None of us have access to that one. We assume it leads to the Big Brain city, and that's how they keep the pharmacy stocked."

"Okay, stay here in the doorway. If this works, I'm gonna have to move fast."

Helen positioned herself to give John as much room as possible to clear the doorway while keeping it clear for his exit. He made his way toward the Rev Rehab storage door, took a deep breath, and grabbed the upper corner of the cabinet. John pulled hard to force it open. It barely budged. John repeatedly tugged down and out on the corner, to no effect.

John tried again and again to find new ways to apply leverage. Each time, his hands slipped from the corner. The gap between the door and the cabinet itself was too narrow to get a strong enough grip. John's frustration grew. He reached back up to the corner, pulling and grunting as he tried with all his might to get in.

"Fuck!" John screamed at the cabinet standing between him and the Rev Rehab... between him and the only way he would avoid the Serpentis' wrath... between him and any chance of seeing Mary again.

"John, you need to keep quiet! People may hear us."

John did not care. He knew everything depended on freeing the serum from the locked cabinet. He went back to it. His grunting grew louder.

His futile tearing at the cabinet grew ever more violent and unhinged until he fell to the floor in dejected anger. He stood back up in a rage and pounded his fist against the taunting cabinet. The explosion of noise cracked across the room and echoed down the hallway, causing Helen to recoil in fear.

As the dust settled from John's outburst, his common sense returned. He looked at Helen and saw renewed terror on her face. John was unsure if his rage caused her fear or if it was the noise from his outburst. He sat, defeated, regret clear on his face—a reflection he could see in Helen's eyes before she looked away to assess the damage. As she fixated on the locker, her mouth dropped in shock. John snapped his head around to discover his tantrum had proven fruitful. His fist had deformed the cabinet, causing the center to buckle and expose a gap in the upper corner.

"Helen!" a voice echoed from far down the hallway. "What the hell was that noise?"

"Oh, uh, Dr. Thompson. I was, uh, getting a script, and I fell back against the cabinets. Why do those upper cabinets have to be so high?" she said with a forced smile.

"Are you okay? Any injuries?"

"No, no injuries, Doctor. Well, maybe my pride," she said with an artificial laugh.

"Okay, are you getting breakfast this morning? I'm grabbing something before they close. Would you like to join me?"

"No, I'm fine. I've already eaten."

"Okay, well, try to be careful, Nurse."

"Will do, Doctor."

Dr. Thompson turned and walked away as the staff entrance closed behind him.

"Phew. That was close, huh?" John said.

Helen tilted her head down to look at John like a child who had misbehaved. "Can you try to be a little quieter now?"

John nodded in agreement as he reached up and sank his fingers deep behind the exposed corner of the cabinet door. He readied himself for one hard pull by placing his left foot against the lower cabinets. After a few tests to prepare himself, John lifted his right foot and propelled himself backward, ripping the door open. John slammed back against the lockers. An alarm wailed throughout the pharmacy and the staff area. John sprang to his feet, reached into the cabinet, and grabbed one vial with its thick blue serum.

The door to the Big Brains opened. In an instant, five Big Brains descended on him. He closed his eyes and summoned visions of Mary and his child—the dream of a family to which he so desperately wanted to return. His feet remained solid on the ground. He was neither frightened nor did he feel the urge to lie on the floor.

The Big Brains drifted lower to increase their effect on him. John opened his eyes and punched at a frail-bodied Big Brain blocking his exit. It felt like hitting a wad of bread dough. He knocked the Big Brain to the floor. It lay motionless.

Helen stood in amazement. The look on her face told John she thought he might succeed.

As John stepped toward the hallway, a slew of Big Brains joined the fight. There had to be fifteen of them, maybe more. The pharmacy was full of them. The effect grew far stronger than John had ever faced. He shut his eyes to gather as much strength as he could. John steadied his breath and focused his thoughts. He was still standing, his mind still fighting. The Big Brains continued their assault. They moved closer to strengthen their effect.

CHAPTER 13

John's knees buckled. He heard a voice urging him not to resist. His thoughts of Mary faded as the furrowed skin between his brows relaxed. His whole body grew weak, and he longed for rest. The Big Brains moved in, closer still. Their effect increased over John's mind as he slumped to the ground. His eyes closed.

John felt a tingle in his fingers. He moved his head from left to right. He struggled a bit but finally opened his eyes to a blurry existence. John burst up from his back like a startled rabbit, nearly falling off the gurney he lay upon. He took in his surroundings and brought his environment into focus.

This was not the pharmacy. He was not in his room, but he knew he had been in this place before. The curved roof, the gurneys—this was where he had woken up for the first time after the Big Brains captured him.

"Take me home," he grunted in a low whisper. He tried again to be sure he had not lost his voice, then immediately focused on more immediate concerns. John knew he would have to find some means of escape before the Big Brains could wipe his mind. Getting caught would make his situation worse.

John stepped down on his left foot, then the right. He shifted his weight and rose to his feet, realizing the pain in his ribs and the wound on his forehead were gone. John used his hand to steady himself as he regained his balance from the Big Brains' powers and listened for signs anyone had detected his movements. He readied himself to lie on a gurney and feign unconsciousness if needed. He noticed a door on one side of the mostly spherical room. He glanced around one more time and then made his way toward it.

A light whoosh reached his ears from a direction he could not discern. He rushed back to his gurney and shut his eyes. After a minute, he reopened them to confirm no Big Brains had arrived. Once John concluded his paranoia had gotten the better of him, he stepped back down from the bed. He sneaked his way back toward the door. But, like the ones in the pharmacy, there was no handle.

He placed his hand on the door. He surmised that only authorized people could open it. He expected to see the red outline of his hand, but the door did not react at all. He tried several areas, all to no effect.

John moved to the center of the room and looked around in search of an idea… anything that might give him some possibility of escape. He thought about forcing the door open, even using a gurney. *Would that be strong enough? Could it force the door open? Would the noise alert security?*

He further scanned the room before returning to the door. He ran his hands across it, looking for a soft spot, still considering ramming a gurney into it. He quickly realized the door was rigid, well beyond anything a gurney could overcome. He could not find a weakness.

Unable to conceive an immediate solution, John returned to his gurney to contemplate his options. He concluded he must be in a holding room where they keep captives before sending them to the camp. *Is this where they'll wipe my mind? Is this room in the Big Brains' city? How can I take advantage of this situation?* He had so many questions.

John and Doc had been trying to escape the camp for so long, but what lay beyond was entirely unknown to them. John hoped to answer those unknowns and find the information to complete their escape plan, a plan that now required him to reunite with Doc without the Big Brains wiping his mind. There were too many unknowns.

The ship to take him back to Earth was at the top of the list of unknowns. He also needed to learn when it would make that journey and, of course, how to stow away on it without detection. John knew that if he could answer these questions, he and Doc would be much better prepared to bring their plan to fruition.

A loud whoosh filled the room. John noticed a five-to six-foot wall section next to the door open to each side like a set of double doors. A Big Brain glided into the room. John froze. He shut his eyes to prevent the Big Brain from realizing he could overpower the room's safety features. John could feel the paralyzing effect of the Big Brain trying to take control. He had dealt with fifteen Big Brains, though—one was no match.

John could sense the Big Brain hovering over him. He remained motionless until the effect waned and then disappeared. John opened his eyes a slit. He knew someone had switched off the safety feature. Three additional Big Brains entered the room through the opening. As they approached his gurney, his view crystallized.

These were not Big Brains. These were humans, a man and two women. The women wore plain white dresses resembling a nurse's uniform. The man wore black trousers, a white-collared shirt, and a dark tie. John struggled to contain his bewilderment. He thought only Big Brains inhabited the city. *Perhaps these humans would help him.* To John's chagrin, though, the looks on their faces gave him little reason for such hope.

The doctor and the nurses stood over him next to his bed.

"Please wake him up," the man directed.

One nurse tapped lightly on John's shoulder. He continued to act as though he was asleep. The nurse tapped him again, then a third time.

John shuffled about on the bed as though he were waking up from a deep sleep. He then slowly opened his eyes. He could feel their gaze upon him as though they were ready to react to poor behavior.

"You can try to talk. The safety features have been disabled," the man said. "We will re-enable them if you get violent. Is that understood?"

John rubbed his eyes, swallowed hard, and said, "Uh... yeah, I, uh, I do."

He brought himself up to a sitting position.

"What is this place? How did I get here? And how are you here?" John asked.

"This is a medical facility. It was built to handle cases like yours. I mean... psychological problems and modifications. I'm Dr. Harry. These are my nurses: Clara and Jean. We're your medical team. As for how you got here, you were brought in for theft and for striking Big Brain security staff. It's our job to evaluate you and determine the treatment before we can return you to the camp. May I ask your name?"

"Yeah, it's, uh, John Callaway."

As he told them his name, one nurse took notes.

"I don't understand. You're human. How can you be helping the Big Brains?" John asked. "Why would you help them keep us here? We belong back on Earth with our kind."

"I understand how you feel, John," the doctor said. "But there's nothing we can do about that. We're only here to do our job. I'd appreciate it if you calmed down and answered my questions, please."

John saw the look in his eyes and knew trying to enlist Dr. Harry's support was a fool's errand. John gave up and nodded affirmatively.

"Thank you. We understand you were caught trying to break into the pharmacy at the infirmary in the camp. Is that right?" the doctor probed.

"Um... yes," John said.

He knew they already had the truth and assumed lying would only extend his evaluation time. He needed to get the information he could from this city and return to the camp as soon as possible.

"Okay," the doctor said. "Do you mind telling me what prompted you to do that?"

"You mean, why did I go to the pharmacy?"

"Yes, exactly. We'd like to understand why you tried to break into the medicines. Why did you try to do that?"

"I… I wanted to steal a serum," he answered.

The doctor was silent for a while. John thought he was trying to read the truth about what he had just revealed. The Big Brains may not know the exact reason he tried to break into the pharmacy, but they knew it was to steal the serum.

"What is the name of this serum?" the doctor asked.

"It's called, uh, Rev Rehab," John said.

"Okay. Thank you for being honest and not getting violent with us, John. We will return tomorrow to discuss this with you further. Please lie back in bed. We're sorry, but we're required to re-engage the safety feature until we begin your treatment," the doctor spoke in slow, measured tones.

The nurses on both sides were writing the entire time, barely looking up from their clipboards. When the doctor finished talking, they turned for the door. John lay back on the bed, but his eyes remained open a sliver to see how the doctor would open the wall. He could feel the safety features re-engage as the opening closed tightly behind them. He pondered the wisdom of telling the medical team about the Rev Rehab but figured that lying about the name of the serum would only protect the Serpentis—something he had no interest in doing.

As they departed, John took in every detail and listened for the faintest sounds. The doctor pressed what appeared to be a button on the wall. John could not be sure, though; a nurse had partially obstructed his view. He knew there was a button, though; it made a subtle clink sound when the doctor pushed it.

John waited several minutes to ensure there were no further visitors. The silence in the room had become too much for him to bear. He rose from the gurney and began his search. *The doctor was to the right of the opening when I heard the button. It must be on that side.* He skimmed his hands across the area and pressed all around. He felt a slight variance on the wall. *This has to be it.*

John pressed his ear to the wall, paused, and pushed the button. His face went aglow with a broad grin as it opened. He hugged the jam to avoid being seen, closed his eyes, and prayed for the hallway to be clear.

DETACHMENTS

He worked up the courage, opened his eyes, and peeked around the corner. John discovered a fifteen-foot-long, dimly lit corridor with a set of doors at the end. The passageway presented its own challenges. John worried whether he could figure out how to open the other set of doors when he reached them. Of more significant concern, he wondered if he could return at all. He had no way of knowing if either doorway used security like the pharmacy.

John had few options. He would have to breach the far set of doors if he wanted better intelligence. He contemplated wedging both sets of doors open but thought that might increase his risk. He had no way to ensure he could return and would have to commit to escaping that night.

He stepped into the passageway. It had no windows. The doors shut behind him with a light thud that rippled through John's bones. He braced himself against the wall and felt its unusual construction. It was unlike any texture he had experienced before—rough yet somewhat pliable, like thick burlap.

John continued toward the doors, focusing his attention in search of a button. He scanned in frustration, noticing that the way the passage connected near the door made it impossible for a button to be where he expected.

As John reached the doors, they suddenly opened. He jumped back against the wall. His weight caused it to bend and flex like a net stretched tight. He regained his balance and looked through the doors for guards. The panic subsided as he realized the hallway appeared to be empty. He stayed a few feet from the door as he circled from the right side of the doorway to the left. The doors began closing at one point, causing John to move toward them instinctively. The doors reopened.

Bright lights illuminated the hallway. The air felt cool and sterile. John contemplated his next move as he studied his surroundings. There were doors down the hallway in both directions, but none on the near side. *If I hear anything or can't get back here, I'll have to jump into one of those rooms.*

John looked back at the first set of doors, then ahead to the open hallway. He knew that being captured would extend his time away from the camp and make his rehabilitation more severe. He also knew he would never have a chance like this again. John threw caution to the wind and took his first steps into the hallway.

He turned left and headed down the chilly corridor, passing several rooms to his right, but nothing that appeared to be any form of exit. As he neared the end of the passageway, he could see stairs that spiraled upward to the left and downward to his right. He hoped that this could provide his way out.

As he arrived at the spiral staircase, John concluded the exit would be on the ground floor. He made his way into the stairwell and headed down. The stairs were not as brightly lit as the hallway, illuminated only by a red glow. He crept down the flight of stairs as the red glow grew brighter until he reached the landing, revealing a white door surrounded on every edge by red lighting. Symbols appeared on a sizable window-like screen on the door that quickly disappeared, replaced by the word "SECURED."

Committed to escaping, John moved closer to the door. Unlike the doors he had seen thus far, this one had what appeared to be a bar he could push to open. He pushed the bar, but it was in vain. He pushed harder, but again, the door did not budge. John continued to push, throwing his body into it while pressing the bar. Aside from a light creaking noise, the door did not give at all.

John stepped away for a moment to catch his breath. He prepared himself for another attempt. The instant John prepared to hurl himself against the door, a familiar feeling came over him. He turned to see a large group of Big Brains floating down the stairs. It was too late to fight. John's legs quivered as the Big Brains moved in. His knees could no longer support his weight. He dropped to the ground, obeying the eerie voice. His eyes shut, and he drifted off.

It was four hours after breakfast. Doc had yet to see John. He expected him to be in the lunchroom so they could talk over their meals about how everything went. But the seat he reserved for John remained empty.

"What about John? Is he not joining us?" Gus asked.

"I don't know. I think maybe he's in his room. Maybe he's not hungry. You know, he's probably too excited about going home," Doc added as he rapidly tapped his foot. Doc barely believed himself. He worried his friends would dig deeper. Doc tried to deflect their inquiry by discussing the fight between the gangs. He thought it better to shield his companions from the Serpentis' demands, hoping John would arrive soon.

Not long after, Doc excused himself and left the lunchroom to search for his friend. Doc checked John's room first, then headed to the infirmary to find any sign of him. Like a worried parent, Doc struggled to find any reason for hope. He saw no sign of John, nor anything that would give him a better sense of things. He waited and waited but accepted reality: John had been subdued by Big Brains and taken beyond the perimeter.

Doc returned to his room, defeated. He found his way to the edge of his bed, where he sat hunched over. He supported the weight of his head by burying his face in his hands. His elbows rested on his legs. He tried to find some solution or an alternative course of action. *What do I do now?*

Despair crept into Doc's mind. He failed again. He failed another kid trying to escape. It was on him, and he knew it. John would have to face having his mind wiped. *It is his first offense, though, so maybe he'd be back in just a few days. Maybe they'll hear his story and take some pity on him.* Doc struggled to find hope. He knew the truth, though. John's mind was gone. John was gone. The high cost of Doc's folly. Two lives destroyed by his weakness.

To pull himself out of the dread, Doc forced his mind to shift its focus to the Serpentis. *It would have all gone well,* Doc thought. *He'd probably be on Earth now if not for the fuckin' Serpentis.* Doc knew the Serpentis would come the next day to collect. He had no concerns. In fact, he concluded there was no point in waiting for the inevitable. He might as well pay them a visit tonight.

He stood up and stormed out the door. If he engaged the Serpentis in a fight, the Big Brains would float in and take him to their city behind the barrier. *That might work. I might get to see John. We might finish our plan after all.* Doc could not resist the Big Brains, though. He was unsure if he would ever find John, but he could try to take down some of the Serpentis, maybe even their leader, Sal.

CHAPTER 14

Doc went to the Hub, hoping to find Sal and members of his gang. His boiling blood cooled with each step, giving way to a more thoughtful plan... one to take the gangs down for good. To do that, though, he would need help. Doc walked past the Hub and continued to the lunchroom, where he knew he would find his friends. He arrived at the lunchroom to find Rex, Gus, and Chris on their way to a table with their food trays. Doc skipped the line and went straight to his seat to sit with the men.

"Geez, Doc, what the hell's the matter with—"

"Shut up, Rex. Listen, we... we fucked up," Doc whispered, which caused the men to crowd the table and lean over their trays.

"What do ya mean... what happened? What's going on?" Gus asked.

"Serpentis grabbed John and me last night. Fuck, I thought they were gonna kill us."

"What? What happened?"

"They figured out we spread the rumors."

"Shit, are they coming for—"

"No, no, uh, don't worry... listen, we have little time. They beat John real bad. He might even have some broken ribs. We only got out of there because we agreed to get this Rev Rehab serum they wanted from the vault in the infirmary."

"What the hell is Rev Rehab?" Chris asked.

"It's bullshit. It's some made-up garbage people think can undo the Big Brain's mind-wipes," Rex said.

"The Serpentis must believe it because they tried to steal it before. John went to steal it first thing this morning. I'm really worried, though. He should have been back by now," Doc said. "They gave us till the end of the dinner meal tonight to bring them the serum."

"And you don't think John's gonna make it back, do you?" Gus asked.

"No, I think by now he'd either be back with the serum, or the Big Brains have taken him."

"You think the Serpentis are gonna come for us, then? Is that what you're saying?"

"That's exactly what I'm saying, but that's not why I wanna talk. We're fucked; there's no way around that. But if I'm gonna take a beating, I'm gonna take as many gang members out of this camp as possible... hopefully, enough to keep you guys safe."

"You wanna do what?" Rex asked, as his voice strained to find a higher octave.

"Yes, Doc. That is crazy. You can't fight all the gangs. Even if we helped, we would never get more than a handful of gang members to fight with us," Chris said.

"I know, but..." Doc motioned for the men to crowd closer. His whisper grew quieter and lower. "... I think, considering how on edge we've got the gangs already, we might be able to start a full-scale war between them."

"What more can we do? If they already know it's all bullshit, why would—" Rex said.

"They won't... I've got another idea, though. We're gonna have to be even bolder with this one. I figure we've got about eight hours for this to reach the right ears before they come looking for us. You guys in?"

The men agreed, and Doc laid out his plan to lead the two gangs to war and hopefully significantly reduce their control over the camp. The men all left the lunchroom to carry out their tasks. Hours felt like seconds. Before Doc knew it, the dinner alarm sounded, and Doc returned to his room to await his fate.

John lay in the bed of a single-occupancy room. The nurses had already brought his breakfast, but it had little appeal. His mind focused on a means to escape—a means to return to Earth. The Big Brain's effect thinned out, but unlike the larger room with the gurneys, his current room did not appear to have the same safety feature. He was surprised to find he wasn't being restrained or drugged. Having just tried to escape, he expected to wake up to greater security. Instead, he was in an individual room and had breakfast delivered before being visited by his medical team.

"John, how are you finding the facilities? Are you comfortable?" Dr. Harry asked.

"Um… yes, I think it's fine here."

"No issues? You've not been injured or needed something we haven't provided?"

"No, nothing. Nothing specific anyway."

"John, can you tell me why you tried to leave last night?"

"Leave? Oh… uh, no, I wasn't, uh, trying to leave."

Dr. Harry's eyebrows raised in skepticism as he peered over the top of his glasses. "It was pretty late last night when security found you trying to leave through a secured door. You weren't trying to get away?"

"No, no, I wasn't trying to leave. I assumed I was free to roam around like in the camp. That's until I saw the Big Brains and realized I must have stumbled into a restricted area. That's why I didn't resist at all."

"Resist? Do you believe you could have fought them off?"

"No. Of course not," John said.

"Is that so?" Dr. Harry asked. His expression revealed to John that his assertions were unconvincing.

"Well, I, uh—"

"That's fine, John. When we last spoke, you said you were trying to steal the Rev Rehab from the pharmacy before the guard caught you. Is that right?"

"Yes."

"Today, I'd like to know why you tried to do that. You're a fairly new resident in the camp," Dr. Harry said. "How did you become so interested in that serum in such a short time?"

"It's a long story, but basically, I had no choice."

"What do you mean, you didn't have a choice?"

"We have these gangs in the camp. Are you familiar with them?"

"Sadly, John, yes. We're all too familiar with the gangs. We've treated several of them recently."

"Well, the leader of the Serpentis was forcing me to get the serum. He said if I didn't try, he'd kill me and my friend."

"The Serpentis. Okay. So why did the Serpentis force you to steal the serum for them? You understand why I'm asking, right, John?"

"I guess you just want to make sure I'm not lying to you?"

"In a way, yes. But more so about whether or not you're trying to hide being one of the Serpentis. If they forced you, your treatment would be entirely different from what we would do if you were one of them."

"No, I am not. I'm definitely not! I could never be one of them. They made me do it to punish me because of the rumors I was spreading about them."

"You were spreading rumors? About the Serpentis? Why would you do something like that?"

John went silent for a while, contemplating his response. He had to ensure he revealed nothing that would give away his plans to return to Earth. He knew he could not trust anyone cooperating with the Big Brains.

"It wasn't about the Serpentis, so to speak."

"No? The other gang? That's the Drongs, right?"

Dr. Harry looked over to his nurses to ensure they were writing the information John was sharing.

"Yes, uh... I mean, no. I mean, the other gang is called the Drongs, but no, I wasn't spreading rumors about them either," John said.

"Look, John, I know you're nervous, but there's nothing to worry about. We're not here to harm you. This is a medical facility. We just want to help you adjust to living here. There are no wrong answers, but we can't prescribe the best treatment for you if we don't understand the situation. Do you understand?"

"Yes, I understand."

"Tell me then. Why did you spread these rumors and take such risks?"

John sighed and said, "It was just out of hatred. I hated them so much. They're so disruptive to life in the camp. All the fighting, the threats, the way they try to control everything. So, my friends and I thought we could get away with tricking them into fighting each other. We figured if they were too busy hurting each other, the rest of us might be safer. But when they figured everything out, they came after us."

"I see. Yeah, that makes sense, John, sure." John knew he failed to convince the doctor, but Dr. Harry continued rather than question John's veracity further.

"John, Rev Rehab is quite important and particularly dangerous. We only use rehabilitation for those who have serious behavioral challenges— behavioral challenges that endanger other people. Imagine if such people realized and could access a way to undo all the work we had done to protect the humans in the camp. How could we ensure safety for most of the people there?"

John nearly gasped as he heard this human doctor use the term "we." *How could a human relate himself to these Big Brains?* John wondered. He collected himself and hoped the jarring nature of the comment did not reflect in his body language.

"I want to make sure you're telling me everything here, John. There's no other reason the Serpentis need it. Is that right?"

John regained his focus. "Oh… uh, yeah, I guess. They claim they lost a lot of men because you wiped all their brains. They seem concerned about their dwindling numbers and are worried about the Drongs. My sense is they wanted the serum so they could get their members back and stay stronger than the Drongs."

"Okay. One more question, John. How did the Serpentis discover the Rev Rehab's location?"

"I honestly do not know," John said.

The doctor was silent again, gazing at him as if he could read the truth in his eyes.

"Okay then. Thanks very much for your cooperation, John. We're going to let you get some rest while we determine the best treatment plan for you. I know this all seems very confusing right now, but we only want what's best for you and the other people here. We'll be back with you soon."

"Okay, Doctor."

"One more thing. You're our guest here. Please, if you need anything, just let one of the nurses know. Please don't go wandering around or get close to that secured door again, okay?"

"Okay, Doctor," John said. It was a necessary deception. He planned further exploration.

The medical team left the room. John thought he had done well enough to shield his bona fide motives. He knew he would have to act soon before their treatment plan robbed him of his mind.

The day dragged on, and there was little to keep John's mind occupied. He wondered if the absence of any form of distraction was part of whatever rehabilitation they planned for him. Dinner had arrived, no more appealing than lunchroom food, but a good indicator that he would not have another session with the medical team that day.

With that, John concluded it was time. If he was ever getting back to Earth, he needed better information, but he would have to be more careful.

DETACHMENTS

He got off the bed once again and went to the door. He listened through the door for any sound, then pushed the button. The door slid open.

CHAPTER 15

John looked down the corridor and stepped out of the room. He stood by the door with his eyes closed momentarily, trying to detect if Big Brains were nearby. He felt nothing.

The hallway was bright, cool, and silent, like the previous night. John did not understand why he had no footwear, but while his bare feet amplified the floor's chilling effect, they also allowed him to move more silently. John's confidence that he could avoid discovery grew with every step. He walked along the corridor, his senses at full alert as he applied the lessons he had learned at boot camp. He had been through so much in the two years since he left San Diego. His thoughts drifted to the moment he met Mary before shipping out.

He reached the end of the hall, and the likelihood of nearby danger forced his attention back to the matter at hand. He knew the threats that lay ahead. There was a long staircase, the handrails reflecting the colors of the lighted signage on the "SECURED" door just beyond. John knew not to try that route again. He only hoped the stairs would prove a workable option and took his first bold step toward them.

He got to the foot of the stairs and looked up. If there was a horde of Big Brains up there, he hoped to find out before they could detect him. John took the stairs one at a time. He sharpened his senses, feeling for Big

Brains in his mind and listening for every sound he made. Each step gripped at his cold, bare feet as he lifted them from the floor.

Halfway up the stairs, he heard voices. They did not sound quite like those of humans. They overlapped with one another and were unclear. John listened carefully to make some sense of the chatter. He was sure the voices were coming from Big Brains. They were talking about some technology involving gravity. John focused on the conversation long enough to figure out it would not help his escape and continued his search.

He approached a landing with a perpendicular passageway leading to his left. John stretched his body across the stairs. He peered down the hall with his eyes barely above the corridor's floor. It was empty.

Glass lined the upper half of the corridor walls, allowing the lights from outside to shine in. A red glow filled the far side of the bottleneck. *That must be another stairwell,* he thought. John crawled into the hallway. He remained below the windows to avoid being seen as he moved to the second building's stairwell, which spiraled up to his right and down to his left. He took the first step down. Then the second. By the third step, John felt confident he was alone and made quick work of the remaining steps.

John reached the corridor at the bottom of the stairs. It was as long as the one in the other building. The brightly illuminated corridor echoed every sound. His every breath reverberated off the walls. He could see several doors on each side of the hall. The one to his immediate right appeared similar to the emergency door he had found the night before. The unusual characters on the screen scrambled and then displayed 'EXIT.'

John took a deep breath and pushed the door's opener. The latch actuated, shooting sparks of excitement through him. He opened the door a crack and let the cool evening air embrace his face. This was it. This was his way out.

John pressed his right ear to the door to look through the opening. Easing the door open further, he slipped his head past the jam and scanned the area. Palm trees decorated a large park area outside the door and across a narrow road-like surface. To John's far left, he saw three Big Brains facing each other. *They're not searching for anything. Are they talking to each other?* John wondered.

John could see no clear path that ensured he would remain undetected. He considered creating a diversion for a moment, but he had to act fast before someone noticed that the door was open.

The Big Brains' field of view covered every route. John searched for options until his eyes caught something familiar on the ground in the park—a manhole. In an instant, John had his plan. It was risky, but it was an opportunity, one John refused to waste.

John took another look at the Big Brains, surveyed the area one last time, and was off. He darted across the narrow roadway and into the park, where he hid behind a bush. He pushed the branches apart to see the Big Brains. *They didn't see me.*

John turned his attention to the manhole. He pulled on it, expecting it to be heavy like those on Earth. John stumbled backward, falling to his back with the cover still in his grasp atop his chest. He remained still and listened for any sign the Big Brains had taken notice. John summoned the courage to resume his plan. He placed the cover on the ground to his side, crouched near the tunnel's entrance, and took one last look toward the Big Brains. John grabbed the cover, slinked into the utility shaft, and closed himself inside.

With each click, the minute hand on Doc's clock boomed off the walls, pounding louder in Doc's mind. The dinner meal would end in three minutes. Click. Two minutes. Click. One minute. Click. The final click gave way to thunder at Doc's door. He leaped to his feet. His mind conjured images of the angel of death standing in the hallway.

"Open this fuckin' door!"

To Doc's chagrin, it was not the Grim Reaper. It was far worse. It was Sal.

"I know you're in there hiding, you—"

Doc turned the handle on the door, and Sal pushed Doc back inside and stormed in. Several other Serpentis streamed in behind him.

Doc stumbled backward until he reached the bed and sat down, gazing up at his tormentors.

"Where's my shit?" Sal exploded, overpowering the sound of the door slamming shut behind him.

"I... I don't know. I think the Big Brains got him when he was trying to get the serum," Doc said.

"You think? What the fuck do you mean, you think? You didn't go with him?" Sal questioned.

"No, no. I, uh, I tried, but he said I'd just slow him down if the Big Brains showed up and knocked me out."

Sal banged his hand on the pile of books next to Doc's bed. The loud blast rocked Doc back in fear as the books tumbled to the floor.

"Are you two fucking stupid? Did I have to plan the whole thing out for you? You think I let you both go just 'cause I liked you?" Sal stormed.

"What good would I be? The Big Brains would knock me out the second they saw me," Doc said in a measured tone.

He did not want to provoke Sal into violence too soon. He knew the Big Brains could detect violence in the apartments and wanted to make the most of this opportunity to take down as many gang members as possible.

"What good would you be? Are you serious? I thought doctors were supposed to be smart. Lemme ask you this... if John were to break into the vault and steal the serum, where would the Big Brains be?"

Doc was silent. He only stared at the door as if waiting for someone to come through.

"I'm fucking waiting!"

"Oh, uh, I guess the vault, right?"

"Duh, exactly, the fuckin' vault."

Doc narrowed his right eye as he tilted his head in confusion.

"I can't fuckin' believe this. You're gonna make me spell it out for ya? Jesus Christ… Doc, you didn't need to be in the vault. John could have grabbed the serum and, before the Big Brains arrived, tossed it to you on the outside of the vault."

"I don't… No, I think… There's no way that would… I guess. No, surely they would still have come after me."

"By the time the Big Brains—"

Antonio leaned in and whispered something in Sal's ear. Doc had not met Antonio before, but he displayed a good deal of respect for Sal. The way he handled himself suggested he was probably Sal's second in command.

"Oh yeah, bro. That's exactly what we're going to do," Sal said.

"Yo, get this fuckin' piece of shit on his feet," Antonio commanded the three henchmen standing behind Sal as a knock sounded at the door.

"Listen to me, Doc," Sal said in a harsh, whispered tone. "Ask who it is like normal. You give any sign we're in here, and you'll be dead before the door opens. You got me?"

Doc nodded, "Who, uh, yeah, who is it?"

"Boss, you in there?"

"Is that—"

"Yeah, Capo. It's Nick," Antonio said with a roll of his eyes.

"Fuck. All right, let him in. This better be good," Sal said.

"Can I talk to you, boss, alone?" Nick said with a look of timidity as he glanced at Antonio.

Sal stood glued to his spot with his eyes still fixed on Doc. He slowly turned his attention to Nick with a glare of disgust at the interruption.

"This better be good," Sal growled.

Sal pivoted his full attention to Nick, shoving him toward the door. He pulled the door open and shoved Nick out, allowing the door to slam behind him.

Doc could hear voices on the other side in muffled tones. A word here or a "how the fuck" there is all Doc could piece together. The men weren't gone more than a minute when Sal pushed the door back open. The door swung with such force that it slammed into the doorstop, loosening it from its mount.

"What's the deal, Boss?" Antonio asked.

Sal glared at Antonio, his face twisted with rage.

Antonio stepped back and raised his hands in a stopping motion, making it clear he realized it would be ill-advised to ask again.

"Listen, you piece of shit," Sal said, banging his pointer finger repeatedly into Doc's chest, knocking him back onto the bed, "this ain't fuckin' over!"

Doc did not move or say a word. Sal turned around to his men. "We gotta get the fuck outta here. Get back to the club." Nick pulled the door open, and the Serpentis filed out.

"Did I fuckin' say you could move?" Sal blasted Antonio. "No! I don't think I did... just stand there and shut your fuckin' trap."

"Wait, Boss, what the—"

"What the fuck did I just say?"

"But—"

"One more fuckin' word, and the next time you see me will be the last time you see anyone!"

Antonio's eyes sank in confusion. Doc almost felt bad for the beast of a man. Sal and the other Serpentis left the room, slamming the door behind them as they thundered out. Antonio and Doc remained motionless for a few moments. Antonio regained some semblance of composure as he looked down at Doc, still sitting on the bed. He looked away to avoid eye contact, but not fast enough to avoid Antonio's glare.

"What the fuck are you lookin' at?" Antonio turned his attention to Doc. He grabbed him by the shirt on his chest. "I don't know what the fuck's going on, but I'm gonna find—"

At that moment, Doc's door flung open, sending the damaged doorstop spiraling across the floor.

CHAPTER 16

The enemy of Doc's enemy finally arrived. Too late for the damage he hoped to cause. But they had arrived.

"Where the fuck is Sal?" the Drongs leader asked.

"Go fuck yourself," Antonio snapped.

"He's gone," Doc said. "Couldn't have been more than five minutes ago."

"Who the fuck are you?" the leader of the small group of Drongs asked Antonio.

"None of your damn business."

"That's Antonio," Doc announced.

"Motherfucker, how 'bout you shut your fuckin' mouth before I close it for good," Antonio warned as he peered down at Doc.

"You're Antonio?" the lead Drong asked.

"Yeah, what of it?"

"No, uh, nothing. We don't got no beef with you. Paddy said he appreciated the tip, though."

"What? What are you fuckin' talking about?"

"I don't know. I just know we were supposed to come here to get some blue vial. They don't tell me a lot. Don't matter. It's all above my pay grade. So, where's the vial?"

DETACHMENTS

Antonio kept his mouth shut.

"We never got the vial," Doc announced.

The lead Drong nodded his head and instructed the other men to leave. Antonio remained stunned by the events of the last ten minutes. He had not pieced everything together, but he knew Sal was mad enough at him to leave him alone to deal with five Drongs. Antonio paced around the room, looking down at the floor for a while before he turned his full attention to Doc.

John stood inside the large tunnel. It easily accommodated a twenty-three-year-old man of average height, like himself. Rather than a sewage odor, the tunnel gave off a chemical smell that made it difficult for John to breathe. He worried it was toxic and might kill him. As he crawled along the corridor, straddling the muck below, the tunnel grew darker. The vapor grew more intense with each step. Doubt crept into John's mind. *Does this tunnel have an end or not?* The chemical smell intensified the further he got from the entrance. John coughed repeatedly as he walked. He had traveled nearly a hundred yards. Short of breath, he quickened his pace, desperate for an exit. He held his breath to avoid taking in more of the harmful fumes.

He made it another fifty yards before releasing his breath into a coughing spasm, becoming lightheaded. He knew he would never make it back before passing out. His only choice was to move forward. He cleared the gag-induced tears from his eyes enough to see a patch of light another fifty yards away. John composed himself as best he could, still gasping to force his lungs to filter each molecule of fresh air they could. John staggered his way to the light as the air improved. The tunnel continued, but John did not dare follow it further. He looked up and began his climb up the three rungs. John slid the cover ajar to let in more fresh air and catch his breath.

After clearing his lungs, John lifted the cover and moved it to the side. He peeked out to briefly scan for Big Brains. In the distance, he noticed a handful of them in what could be called a street. They did not appear to be of immediate concern. The moment he was about to climb out, what he could only describe as a car passed immediately over his barely exposed head.

John's spine locked in fear. His nerves fired throughout his body like a shock. His grip loosened, and he slipped down the ladder. He caught himself mere inches before he fell into the waste at the bottom of the tunnel. His chest pulsed in near panic. He climbed back up the ladder and peered out again. John realized the car that had caused such fright had no wheels or tires. It made no contact with the roadway below at all. He let out a deep groan and climbed out. He looked from one end of the street to another and put the lid back in place.

John walked along the road amidst the wonders of the Big Brain city. He continued until his eyes caught an orange glow illuminating several ships and unusual-looking craft. *That must be the shipyard,* John thought. He wanted to move closer but realized he had been gone quite a while. He knew that if he did not return soon, the Big Brains would discover his absence. Worse, they could lock the door to the medical facility, trapping him in the Big Brain city overnight.

John turned and traced his way back to his underground route. He took several deep breaths to prepare for the caustic journey and crawled back inside. He emerged in the park outside the building. After catching his breath, he scanned the area.

The Big Brains were no longer on guard outside the building. John retraced his steps through the door, up the stairs, back across the sky bridge, and down to his room. His feet were sore; the rough texture of the tunnel walls cracked and chapped the soles of his feet. The journey had been well worth it, though; he had found the shipyard. Next, he would need to find the ship that would take him home.

DETACHMENTS

Doc struggled to break free, his wrists bound and stretched between two trees. Ropes bound his ankles and feet tightly together. The total weight of his body dangled from the remaining strength in the ligaments of his shoulders. His head slumped down onto his chest. His chin bore the burden of the load, causing his head to rock with each breath. A slurry concoction of blood, mucus, and dirt drained from Doc's face like molasses from a cruet. Doc summoned enough strength to lift his head as Antonio delivered another hard right cross to his cheek. The strike sent blood raining down on John's and Mark's lifeless bodies lying on the ground below.

"I told you! I told you that you'd fuckin' pay!" Antonio roared as he delivered another bone-crushing shot directly into Doc's rib cage.

In the distance, Doc heard a soft thumping sound: "thud, thud, thud."

Antonio drove Doc's head back, delivering another blow straight to his nose. The pace of the blood streaming from each of Doc's nostrils quickened.

The thumping sound returned, but louder, faster, and clearer: "bang, bang, bang."

"Doc, you there?"

The voice was unrecognizable, too muffled to identify. Antonio readied his final blow. He pressed his blade against Doc's throat.

"Almost a pity not to keep you around long enough to make you watch what I'm gonna do to your friends."

The cold steel dug into Doc's neck. He could feel the knife tear through the outer layers of his skin, slashing into his nerves and muscles. Blood spurted from his carotid artery as the crowd of Serpentis cheered Antonio on.

"Doc, come on, mate… you're gonna miss breakfast!" Gus banged hard on Doc's door, ripping him from his nightmare.

He sprang up from his pillow and caught his breath with a sigh of relief. Sweat dripped from his forehead into his salt-crusted eyes as he rubbed them clear.

"Hold on… I'll… I'll be right there."

Doc stood and lumbered across the room to open the door.

"Oi, Doc, you coming to breakfast or what?"

"Hey Gus, yeah, lemme just freshen up real quick. Come on in, have a seat. I'll be right out."

Doc headed into his bathroom. Like the other apartments, Doc's bathroom was a small, simple room with a sink, commode, and a small shower, barely sufficient for his toiletries. As Doc went through a minimalist version of his morning routine, Gus called out, "Reckon we've stirred up some proper trouble with the gangs, Doc."

"Oh?" Doc said with a mouthful of toothpaste.

"Everyone's chatting about the Rev Rehab now. The Drongs clearly wanna shut down the Serpentis."

"That was kind of the plan," Doc said as he dried his face and returned to the main room. "I'm not sure if we caused more problems for the gangs or us, though."

"Us? What d'you mean? Why would it cause more problems for us?"

"Well, since the fight didn't happen, Sal's gonna have time to figure things out."

"Yeah, that's true, isn't it?" Gus said.

"Damn it! I really hoped they'd gotten into it last night."

"You're proper worried about this, aren't you?" Gus could see the concern in Doc's eyes.

"Yeah, I—I just worry we're gonna have more problems. Like, what's going on between Sal and Antonio?"

"Antonio?" Gus asked.

"Yeah, I think he's, or he was, the number two in the Serpentis. He was here last night, then Sal and the other Serpentis abandoned him to deal with the Drongs."

"Did they give him a proper beating?"

"No," Doc said. "Actually, they acted like he was the one that tipped them off. I don't get it, Gus. When the Drongs left, it was just me and

Antonio here. He was pacing around. I thought he was gonna lose it on me. But then he just walked out without saying a word. I dunno. I guess we'll figure it out. Let's get some chow."

"Chow can wait, Doc. You alright?" Gus asked. "You've been through a lot. Anything I can do?"

"No, Gus, I'm fine. It just… it feels like I keep making things worse."

"Worse? How can you think that, mate? All you've ever done is try to help people."

"I try. Sure, I try. But look what happens when I do. Does it ever truly help? Did I help Mark? Look at the help I gave John… where's he at now? And now I've gone and pulled you, Rex, and Chris deeper into this mess. I'm—"

"You can't blame yourself, Doc. Same as Mark and John, we all made our own choices here. You didn't force anyone to do anything. Do you really think Mark would've been any better off if you hadn't helped? And John? You reckon he'd have even had a chance without you there to guide him?"

"I dunno. I just don't know," Doc said.

"Well, I do! I know both Mark and John needed you. What happened to Mark is proper tragic, yeah, but you gave him a chance—a real chance. Sadly, there was nothing you or anyone else could've done for him. But John? You can't give up hope. I know he'll be back. Things will work out, you'll see."

"I just don't think I can handle it if something happens to you guys. None of you needed to be involved in this, and I—"

"Doc… come on, mate. What d'you think friends are for? Let's grab some breakfast, yeah? Then we'll sort it so the gangs pay, not us. Deal?"

"Yeah, okay. Thanks, Gus."

Doc and Gus headed out to the lunchroom. They arrived in time to get some food. The place had emptied, leaving Rex and Chris at their table. They had finished eating and were waiting for Doc and Gus to arrive to discuss what happened.

The men grabbed their food and joined their friends.

"Hello, my friends," Chris welcomed the men to the table.

"Shit, that didn't go as planned, did it?" Rex pointed out with his traditional wit. "You kinda suck at this, huh?"

Doc shook his head with a subtle hint of laughter. Rex always had a way of lightening the mood with pointed sarcasm.

"Yeah, I guess not, but hey, we're all still alive. That's something, right?"

"That's a pretty low bar, but yeah, that's something, alright," Rex goaded. "So, what happened last night?"

Doc took a few moments to describe what happened the night before in his room and how the fight he had hoped for never materialized.

"I do not understand. How did the Serpentis know to get out of there?" Chris asked.

"I don't know, but whatever Nick told Sal was enough to make him lose his shit with Antonio."

"Antonio? The big muscular one?" Chris asked.

"Yeah, that's him. I think he's their second in command, or at least he was. I dunno," Doc said.

"You reckon Nick's got an informant in the Drongs, maybe?" Gus asked.

"I guess they must," Doc said.

"That's exactly what it is," Rex said, "and I'll bet you a million bucks the Drongs suspected they had a rat in their gang all along."

"What? What makes you think that, Rex?" Gus asked.

"Think about it. Look how things worked out. We wanted a fight between the Drongs and Serpentis, right?"

"Yeah, what does that have to do with it?" Doc asked.

"Look at what ended up happening. The Drongs sent five newbies to go after the top leaders of the Serpentis."

"Yeah, so what?"

"You think they would have done that if they really believed the serum was there? They had to at least suspect we were setting them up. So, they played it safe."

"I can see playing it safe, but how does that help them? They still don't have the serum?" Doc wondered aloud.

"Damn, are y'all just not thinking today or what?" Rex said. "Again, look at how things worked out. The Drongs know about the Rev Rehab, right? And we told them how the Serpentis wanted to use Tom to take full control of the camp, right?"

The group all nodded, still trying to figure out where Rex was going with his conclusions.

Rex said, still shaking his head in disbelief, "Well, now Sal thinks his deputy might be a traitor, and the Serpentis are in disarray. You think that's all coincidence? Whoever they think Nick is getting info from must have made that person believe Antonio told them about the Rev Rehab instead of us."

"Ya know, I can't fault your logic there," Doc assessed. "Do you think the Drongs will come after us since we never had the serum?"

"I guess technically we never told them you or John had it. We just told them the Serpentis were going to get it from you," Chris pointed out.

"Still, you reckon they'll suss out our plans?" Gus asked.

"Will they? No, I think they already did... well, maybe not that we were trying to get them rehabbed by the Big Brains, but they knew we were putting them at risk. They just figured out a way to reduce that risk," Rex concluded.

"So, what's the plan now, then?" Gus asked.

"Yeah, Rex, you seem to have the gangs all figured out. What's the plan?" Doc laughed, relishing the opportunity to prod Rex for a change.

"Honestly, I don't think we do anything. Seems to me the Drongs already have a plan. We should just let them handle it."

"We just do nothing?" Chris asked. "What do you think will happen?"

"If I'm right, the Drongs are pitting the top two Serpentis against each other to take them both out. They do that, and they'll run the whole camp whether they get the Rev Rehab or not."

"Oh, hey, I bet that would make a good fight. Who do you think would win?" Chris asked.

"I'd put my money on Antonio. That guy is huge," Doc said.

"No way!" Chris said. "Antonio may be stronger, but Sal knows how to fight. I've heard some stories. That man is scary."

"I'm betting on Sal as well," Gus said.

"Who the fuck cares who wins... as long as they're both gone. This will all be worth it," Rex said. "Hopefully, they'll be gone as long as Tom was, and they come back equally wiped."

"I just hope John doesn't come back like that, and he gets back here real soon," Doc said.

"I know I'm not as close to John as you are, and I'm kind of a dick sometimes—" Rex began.

"Sometimes?" Doc laughed.

"Yeah, sometimes... what? Anyway, I hope he gets back soon, too."

John's medical team visited after lunch to conduct a few tests and get clarifying information about John's understanding of the gangs in the camp. Fortunately, John's outing from the previous night never came up. That left John hopeful that his efforts had gone entirely undetected.

John had a newfound enthusiasm for his escape plans. Finding the shipyard was a stroke of luck. He took it as a clear sign he would eventually be successful. His confidence had grown to new heights. He was no longer convincing himself he could escape this planet; he believed he would.

Looking back over the conversations from earlier in the day with his medical team, John wondered if they had noticed any change in his disposition. He knew Dr. Harry was a keen observer of behavior. John concluded he might have gotten away with it once, but he would have to do a better job in their next session to ensure he did not further elevate the team's suspicions about his true motives.

During their visit, the nurses gave him standard patient clothes: black pants and a white shirt. After the medical team left, John entered the bathroom, where he had already cleaned up from the previous evening's adventure through the Big Brain's sewer system. As John pulled his worn clothes from his body, he caught a faint whiff of the chemical-like odor of the tunnels he had traversed. Fortunately, there were no other signs of the distress he had been through. The pain in his feet and hands from trying to stay above the waterline in the sewers had been worthwhile, despite the wear and tear on his skin. He donned his new patient garb and disposed of the old clothes in the laundry bin on the wall.

John sat on his bed, waiting for the nurse or an orderly to take his dinner tray so he could set out for the shipyard to learn more. He knew his route.

The door opened, and an orderly walked in.

"Are you all done with this?"

"Oh, uh, yes, thank you." The orderly disappeared as quickly as he had arrived.

The time was near. John counted the moments until he knew the hallways would be clear. He took a few deep breaths and glanced down at his feet. They were still sore from the night before, but he made his way to the door, activated the switch on the wall, and set out.

John followed the same route as the previous evening, trying to remain undetected. He again heard the voices of the Big Brains as he ascended the stairs to the connector between the two buildings, but he was no longer worried. He figured if the Big Brains used harsh punishments, they would have already done so. Rather than punishment, John felt they preferred to persuade people to see things their way. He thought that revealed some legitimate goodwill, but he mostly saw it as an advantage to achieve his goals.

He crossed the overpass to the other building and exited. John saw more Big Brains than he had the night before, but that would not stop him from tracing his way to the manhole. He quietly slid it open, prepared himself for the caustic atmosphere with several deep breaths, and then slipped inside.

John rushed through the tunnel and reached his exit, dizzy from the fumes. A hacking cough wracked his body, stealing what little strength he had left, and he struggled to grip the ladder. His arms trembled with exhaustion. He could feel himself losing consciousness.

CHAPTER 17

John closed his eyes and tried to catch his breath, praying for fresh air to reach his lungs. The dizziness took hold and caused him to doubt whether his feet could keep their grip on the tunnel walls and remain suspended above the mess below. His vision faded as a voice entered his ears. Mary called his name, a spirit in the fresh air drifting down to him like a feather descending from heaven. He breathed in the fresh air as deeply as he could. He grasped the bars once again and pulled himself up. He pushed the lid aside and filled his lungs.

Once he regained his senses, he left to find the shipyard. It reminded him of the ports in San Diego, but it was a beautiful spectacle. Futuristic ships floated in the water outside a great dome-like structure. It stretched at least thirty stories above the ground. The dome was semi-transparent. Orange-hued lights made the dome appear like a giant campfire, and movement from within the structure created a flame-like effect in the night sky.

John made his way closer. There were several ships moored outside the dome. They were unlike anything he had seen. It was too dark to make out much detail, but their silhouettes were wide and sat low against the night sky. He could not see the water but assumed it was a lake since he could not hear waves lapping against the ships' hulls.

John made his way to some machinery near the dome's exterior. He hid there to form his plan. Through the dome wall, he could see Big Brains working with humans. They were moving various ship parts. He assumed they were building a new one.

John searched for a way inside. Inching closer, he skulked behind bushes, trees, and equipment outside the dome. He figured out the only way in was from the waterside of the building, where he assumed the Big Brains launched their ships. John planned his route. In a few moments, he was twenty yards from the entrance, behind the last concealment he could find.

A man entered the dome and looked in his direction. He ducked down and prayed. He had no hope of hearing the man approach over the whirring of machinery inside. John waited, first a minute, then two. If someone had detected him, he would have known it by now. He leaned from his hiding spot and could see the man through the walls, now inside the dome. He was too close to the entrance to risk moving any closer.

John could make out various objects and activities in the building from his vantage point. He saw a Big Brain and a human working together to move a large panel. He also saw what looked like two ships hanging from the ceiling, but John could not determine how. Toward the back of the dome, he saw a couple of Big Brains that appeared to be talking with a human. *Maybe I can get close enough to hear them through the wall?*

John low-crawled from safety to the base of the dome, as close as he could get to the conversation. He pressed his ear against the wall, hoping for more clarity, but what he assumed was glass was something he had never felt before. It felt closer to metal and coarser than expected. He found a vent in the wall and listened through it, but the noise from the work inside made it difficult to hear. Only a few words filtered into his ears. The conversation seemed tense.

"Listen… you understand… we're… rehabilitation… as we speak." The words landed in fragments on John's ears, grasping for every sound he could parse. He wondered if they were talking about his rehabilitation. *They must be.* His heart sank. *They're going to wipe my mind.* His time was running out. He needed to get off this planet while he still had his memories intact.

"Looks like... need... to help... but... ship... launch."

John listened, but upon hearing the word launch, his attention became more focused.

The voice changed to another speaker: "But... easier... told me... ready..."

The noise from the construction site had grown louder, but John could piece together the human's last sentence, "But it would be much easier if you told me when you will be ready to—"

"You must sleep now."

The words echoed in John's ears. *Why would one of them say that?*

The voice distracted John enough to feel the presence of Big Brains inducing him to sleep.

"No!" he screamed as he spun around to find five Big Brains closing in on him. He pressed his back against the wall to stabilize himself as he struggled to focus his mind to fight them off. *It's only five; I can recover.* His thoughts turned to Mary as her voice again called to him. He could feel his focus returning as he pulled himself back to his feet and off the wall.

John clenched his fists as the Big Brains moved closer, revealing his intent. The Big Brains hovered just outside John's reach, recognizing they were ineffective in subduing him.

"Come down here and see what happens. Come on!"

"You can fight us if you must, but we will just bring more guards. Why make this harder? No one wants to harm you, John."

John could not believe he was effectively conversing with this Big Brain. He tried to keep his focus but could not ignore the wisdom of the Big Brain's point. *What would I do if I got away? How long would I make it before they caught me again? How much worse would things get if I keep resisting?*

Distracted by his thoughts, John found himself on the ground, helpless and barely conscious. He succumbed to a deep sleep as a Big Brain swooped in closer.

By the time the dinner meal in the camp finished that night, virtually everyone knew Antonio was effectively out of the Serpentis. The Drongs would have pulled off a remarkable ploy if Rex's theory was correct. Word traveled that the Serpentis planned to punish Antonio for his apparent treason. It was the only thing people talked about. The Serpentis could not allow Antonio to walk freely for too long, or they would look weak. With every hour, the tension grew stronger in anticipation of the battle to come.

Typically, after dinner, most people would go their separate ways. Tonight, the crowd followed Antonio, hoping for a show. He went to the Hub after the dinner meal. Doc, Gus, Chris, and Rex were no different. If the fight was going to happen, they wanted to see it for themselves.

Antonio was in the casino part of the Hub, playing hold 'em with some random men. That was Antonio's favorite game, and he played it like he played the game of life, with no fear. His aggressive risk-taking earned him the nickname "River Rat" for his penchant for catching a winning hand on the river card. He used to gather members of the gang, including Sal, and thrash them silly, one hand after another. Sal teased him that it was the only thing he was good at, and Antonio relished proving him correct.

Sal and some of his confederates were loitering about, drinking, triangulating, almost certainly preparing the battlefield for the coming war. Amidst the music blasting from the speakers, Sal was ready to explode. Doc saw Sal signal something to one of his men. The men fanned out in a choreographed display. Sal's eyes stayed fixed on Antonio, his fists tightly wound, veins bulging.

Sal's men positioned themselves at each of the three exits and the elevator. If Antonio tried to flee, he would find no safe harbor. If the Big Brains arrived, they would have difficulty getting into the Hub with the doors held shut. Satisfied, he set his trap; Sal moved in like a lion stalking his prey. He approached Antonio's table, bumping into him to make his presence known. "My men and I want to play, so all of you can get the fuck away from my table, capiche?"

Antonio ignored the insult. He could tell Sal was trying to rattle him. The other players at the table collected their chips to back away. Antonio sneered and threatened under his breath, "Touch those fuckin' chips or leave this table, and you'll be waking up in the infirmary." Antonio's words had the desired effect, and the other men froze, realizing the dilemma they had stumbled into.

"We're not going anywhere!" Antonio said. "You and your crew can sit there and shut the fuck up till we're done playing." He finished his retort with a sarcastic, "Capiche?" and returned his attention to the game, as though Sal was inconsequential.

Antonio's reaction surprised Doc. Initially, he thought Antonio was unaware Sal was in the building, but he had missed nothing.

"Oh… you're here. I didn't notice," Sal mocked as he glared down. "Look, guys, Antonio is here." One-on-one, Sal was no match for Antonio, but a fate worse than a beating would be the loss of credibility with the other Serpentis if he did not act.

Antonio secured his chips and readied himself for the fight.

"You knew this was coming, you piece of shit. You know what's going to happen. Why don't you make it easy on these nice people and get your ass up to the tennis courts? Don't make me spill your guts right here on this table," Sal said.

"You? You? I doubt that. Maybe you should rethink your plan… you sure you brought the right men with you?" Antonio taunted.

"You think I'm fucking around? You think you're something special? Just 'cause we go way back, you think I'm gonna let your treason slide?"

"Treason? Man, fuck you." Antonio sprang to his feet, enraged by the accusation. He shoved Sal back against the adjacent table. "I didn't betray shit. You're fucking nuts. Whatever Nick told you is total bullshit," Antonio said, pointing at Sal while regaining his balance.

That was more than Sal could tolerate. He lunged back at Antonio, delivering a bone-crushing punch right to Antonio's jaw. The blow echoed like a thunderclap across the room. Onlookers reacted with similar intensity to the men in the brawl. The fight everyone expected was on. The crowd roared with excitement. Everyone would remember this battle for years to come.

The impact of Sal's right cross pushed Antonio back against some chairs. Before he could regain his balance, Sal pounced on him and lashed out with everything he had. This was not a disciplined assault. It was a mad thrashing of uncorked rage. The crowd yelled his name. "Sal! Sal! Sal!" That fueled Sal's fury as he landed a torrent of punches.

He grabbed a bottle and broke it against Antonio's head. Then he drove his knee into Antonio's ribs. Antonio was bleeding from his head and mouth. The first punch had broken open his nose and his lower lip. Several of Antonio's supporters had arrived at the Hub but did not dare to intervene or hint at anything their capo might perceive as disloyalty. But the downcast looks on their faces revealed their disappointment at seeing the Serpentis' leadership at war with each other.

Of course, most in the crowd hoped for a lasting finality in the result, be it from the Big Brains wiping the minds or from the combatants' respective deaths. Doc and his friends were among those in the crowd cheering them on and banging on the tables. The Serpentis oppression needed to end.

The Drongs also loved what they were seeing. Their voices were the loudest in the crowd. Their jubilation confirmed Rex's suspicions that the Drongs had outsmarted the Serpentis.

Sal's punches slowed. Sweat dripped from his brow. His breathing neared that of hyperventilation. *Did Sal punch himself out?* Doc wondered. *Did Antonio weather the storm?*

CHAPTER 18

Antonio maintained a proper guard for most of the assault, but Sal landed several heavy blows. Blood spilled from Antonio's nose and a deep gash above his left eye. His right eye had a pronounced lump directly below it. Sal delivered a beating from which almost no one in camp could have recovered—no one except Antonio.

He had played possum long enough. With Sal's energy drained, Antonio delivered an elbow strike from his guard that changed the tide. It thrust both men toward the center of the casino floor, scattering chairs and tables about. Broken bottles littered the floor. An iron-like stench of blood filled the air. Antonio's attack was so powerful that Sal stumbled backward and struggled to reach his feet. Unable to defend himself from the incoming blows, Antonio grabbed him by the throat and threw him back onto a table. The table collapsed under the force.

Sal reeled in pain. He got to his feet before Antonio could begin a ground-and-pound series of strikes. Sal, still rocked by Antonio's assault, could not fend him off. Antonio snatched a fistful of Sal's hair and smashed his head against the edge of the casino table. Sal's forehead split open, pouring blood like a waterfall from a deep gash. Everyone thought this would be the end. Sal slumped to the floor after his head hit the table. Barely conscious, Antonio turned away, perhaps hoping to avoid the Big Brains' inevitability.

"Get back here, you piece of shit. This ain't fuckin' done. This don't end till one of us is dead!" Sal howled, spitting through the blood draining across his mouth.

Antonio, too, was getting exhausted, blood still dripping from his face. If death was the only end in sight, then so be it. He took one of the few unbroken bottles and smashed it down on Sal's head. Sal collapsed, but Antonio grabbed him by the collar with his left hand and pulled him up from the floor, closer to his face.

"You said you were going to kill me, right? Well, who's gonna die now? Huh? Tell me. Who's gonna fucking die now?"

Sal could barely stand. He was gasping for air, choking on the blood and spit that kept flowing back into his mouth. The crowd knew what Antonio wanted to do, and the Drongs among the crowd cheered him on.

"Kill, kill, kill—" they chanted.

Antonio was holding a piece of the bottle he had broken on Sal's head. He held it there, contemplating his next actions. Sensing that Antonio was about to kill their capo, Sal's men rushed from the exit door to stop the lethal blow. Before they arrived, Sal, with the last strength he could summon, grabbed Antonio's arm and yelled at his men, "Get back to those fuckin' doors!"

His command was too late. A swarm of Big Brains glided in and knocked out each of the Serpentis near the doors and most of the crowd. They carried off Sal and Antonio, hopefully never to return. The whole melee took only a few minutes to unfold, but it was an eternity for those involved.

Severely handicapped without Sal and Antonio, the Drongs had the Serpentis on their deathbed. Doc may have started the ball rolling, but the Drongs had made the most of the situation—one that almost certainly included a desire to get the Rev Rehab for themselves.

DETACHMENTS

The Big Brains' effects wore off. John woke from what felt like a deep and peaceful sleep. As he swept the cobwebs from his head, he reached to clear his eyes, only to find his wrists bound. He thrashed hard against the restraints before realizing that doing so might bring several Big Brains to his room to knock him out again.

John scanned his surroundings as best he could. The room appeared unchanged from the previous night. Despite the familiarity, his current situation had become far worse. Escape had become virtually impossible. John's frustration gave way to anger—anger at the events that led him to this predicament, anger at himself for getting caught, and anger at the world. Perhaps more than anything, anger at the unknown.

Question after question strafed John's mind. *Who were the figures at the dome? Was one of them Dr. Harry? And who was he talking to? Why would they need the ship for my treatment? When is the launch happening? How do I find out?* John left too many questions unanswered. The only voice he heard now was that of self-doubt, a grim reminder of his father's war within. John struggled to find the will to go on.

A light beep sounded from the door—a noise John had not previously heard that pulled him from the shadows in his mind. The door to his room slid open, and Dr. Harry walked in with his nurses. John could see the solemn expression on Dr. Harry's face, no doubt aware of John's covert activities. He approached like a father entering his child's room, ready to deliver well-deserved punishment.

The door closed behind the medical team. Dr. Harry looked around the room and tilted his head to the ceiling. He inhaled deeply and gathered the strength to restrain his frustration. "Good morning, John. It seems our initial assessment was inaccurate. I suspect you knew that already, considering the restraints. John, are you listening to me?"

John shifted his gaze more directly to his doctor to acknowledge that he was listening.

"Do you understand why we have you in restraints now?"

135

John lay quietly, still brooding over his circumstances, hearing every word but refusing to respect the doctor's query.

"You left the room again. Not only did you leave the room, but the building. Then you found your way to the Empyrean? None of this helps your—"

John said, "The what? What did you say?"

"The Empyrean. That's the name we hear the Big Brains call it. It's the dome you visited last night. Think of it as an air and seaport. You—"

John cut the doctor off again. "Am I a prisoner here or not?"

"John, none of that matters now. You need to relax and stop worrying about such things. We can't help you if your mind is too conflicted. All we want to do is help you enjoy your life here, but the more you resist and the more dishonest you are with us, the longer the process will take. Now, can you explain what you were doing last night?"

John kept his cards close to his chest. "I just—I... I just wanted to go for a walk. Can you blame me? I was bored out of my mind. Look at this place; there's nothing here. You just stick me here with not even a book to read. You didn't think I'd get curious? So, I went for a walk. That's all it was."

"I know it's frustrating, and I wish there were more for you to do, but we need to clear your mind before we can begin your rehabilitation. Everything we're doing, John—everything from the food you've been eating to the design of these walls to the reduced noise we expose you to—it's all part of building a common baseline for your treatment. That's why we had the door locks turned off until now. We wanted to avoid the beeping of the door every time we enter."

"If you've locked the doors, why do I need to be in restraints?" John yanked hard with his right arm to show his frustration.

"Well, John, the truth is we don't trust you. You've shown us you can withstand being incapacitated by the Big Brains. So, we're worried we wouldn't be able to restrain you before you could hurt someone."

John's face twisted with disapproval, but he could not argue with the doctor's point. The look of concern on the nurses' faces made the truth clear. They saw him as a threat.

"I am sorry that we have to do this," Dr. Harry said. "But we simply don't have a choice."

"You don't have a choice? Of course you do! I can't leave. Just take off the restraints! I'm not going to hurt anyone! I didn't hurt that nurse in the vault, so why would I hurt—"

"But you hurt the Big Brain. You almost killed that guard."

"Why should I care about the Big Brain guard? They're nothing—"

The nurses each let out a gasp of disbelief. Their reaction stopped John in his tracks.

"I'm sorry, I shouldn't have said that, I guess... I guess I've just been so caught up in my own problems that I haven't really stopped to think about anyone else, let alone our Big Brain captors. But they are... they are our captors." The frustration of being the only one resisting the Big Brains got the better of John. "I guess I don't feel the same way about hurting them as I would if I hurt another one of us, ya know?"

The nurses behind Dr. Harry stole glances at each other and swallowed hard, clutching tightly to the pens in their hands.

"Look, we understand why you feel the way you do. But that's exactly how the rehabilitation will help you. We want to allow our patients as much freedom as possible within the baseline that works with our protocols. Sneaking around at night can never work, though," Dr. Harry said. "You will get another chance to see the city. It's all part of the rehab process—taking a walk around the city with us—"

"With you?" John said. "You mean I can't walk around like you?"

"Eventually, perhaps by the time we've finished the rehab process, you'll be able to walk around as much as you like. We find many people want to return to the simpler life of the camp, but many of us choose to stay here in the city. But those are bridges we can cross when we come to them. For now, though, we need to get your protocol set up, which I'm afraid you've significantly delayed."

John sighed but refused to speak. He felt caught somewhere between rage and hopelessness. The reality of his situation set in. He could fight them and further delay his return to the camp, or worse. Alternatively, he could be honest and allow the medical team's efforts to ease his mind, despite the risk of having his mind wiped. There had to be a path forward. What that path was, John could not yet discern.

"John? Are you listening? We really are trying to help you, John."

John had again closed his mind to his medical team, done entertaining their treatment.

"Okay, we'll give you the rest of the day to process everything. Hopefully, when we return tomorrow, we'll get a fresh start on your rehabilitation." As Dr. Harry completed his goodbyes, Nurse Jean approached the door, causing the security system to beep. She pushed the control button on the door, and it slid open.

As John's medical team left, he lifted his head as if he wanted them to stay. The door closed quietly as John fought back the urge to scream for them to return. He thrust his head back down onto his pillow in frustration. He knew he had caused another unnecessary delay—a full day wasted.

The familiar beep of the door's security chimed, and the door swished open. Nurse Jean entered alone with John's breakfast. John had suffered mightily throughout the night trying to sleep in his restraints, a fact he shared with the nurse before she could ask how his night was.

"I barely slept, so how is this supposed to be helpful for my treatment if I'm not sleeping? Can you tell me that?"

"It's not at all helpful. This is all going horribly, John. I'm so sorry we had to do this, but you gave us no options. This isn't enjoyable for me either. Do you think I want to spend my morning feeding you?"

Jean reached toward the bed and raised John into a seated position.

"Now, if you can behave, I'll release your arm restraints so you can feed yourself. Can you do that?"

John nodded and shifted his eyes downward in shame—shame for the fear he had inadvertently had caused the other humans.

"I swear on my... uh... uh... my life," John caught himself almost revealing to the nurse his true reason for being so intent on escaping his captors. He was sincere, and Jean believed him. She reached over him and removed the restraints from his wrists, then slid the tray stand with food over to him.

"You go ahead and eat, John, and if you're ready to work with us, we'll see about getting you out of those leg restraints so you can care for yourself, and maybe we can take you out for a tour. I think you'd like that."

John's eyes lit up as the carrot Jean dangled captured his genuine interest. He had not considered the possibility that his medical team legitimately cared about his well-being. The idea of including a tour of the city in the treatment reminded him of his visit to downtown San Diego when he was waiting to ship out to the Pacific—the day he met Mary.

"I'll be back in a bit, John," Nurse Jean said.

John finished his meal and slid the tray out of the way. He stretched his shoulders, still sore from the night in restraints. A few moments later, the door's security beeped, and Nurse Jean walked in. She was pleased to find John had not attempted to free himself from the leg restraints, as if he had passed a test.

"How do you feel now that you've got some food in you?"

"Not too bad, I guess. I'd like to use the bathroom and get a—"

Jean interrupted, "I'm not supposed to undo your leg restraints without security. Your bed is equipped to handle your waste needs. The buttons are there on the rail. I feel like I can trust you, though. I can, right, John?"

"You can indeed, Nurse. I promise you that."

139

Jean, with almost complete confidence, continued to remove the restraints from John's ankles.

"You may have a hard time standing at first. You've been lying still for quite a while now."

Jean helped John sit up, pivot to the side of his bed, and then get to his feet. He stretched his back as Jean relaxed her support. John then lifted each foot, flexing his legs and working his knees to remove the stiffness.

"Thank you so much, Nurse. I appreciate you trusting me enough to let me out of those restraints."

"No thanks necessary. We just want you well. I'm going to leave and let you get yourself cleaned up. There's a new set of clothes in the bathroom for you. Please dispose of the old ones in the bin. I'll check on you again around lunchtime."

Jean turned to exit as John's pulse quickened. He could easily overpower the diminutive nurse. This could be his last chance to escape.

CHAPTER 19

The now-familiar beep of the door sounded as Jean approached. He took a step toward her, then stopped. *What am I thinking?* John was certain that even if he got past Jean and broke out of the medical facility again, the Big Brains would eventually catch him. More importantly, though, John made a promise, and he intended to keep his word.

A few hours later, Jean returned. John noted a tinge of excitement in her voice as she greeted him.

"I've got great news, John."

"I assured the Big Brains and the medical staff you could be trusted and convinced them to give me special permission to take you for a short city tour. Does that sound like something you might like to do?"

"Of course," John said. "I'll be on my best behavior."

"Oh, I know, John, and I do trust you... but just in case I'm wrong about you, I got this." Jean displayed a device John had not seen before. "If I activate this, the Big Brains will be with us in a flash. I know I won't need this. Right, John?"

"No, you definitely won't."

Jean nodded in approval of John's response and handed him shoes that slipped on like socks but formed to his feet, providing support and protection like a quality shoe. A moment later, Jean led John out on their adventure.

Jean guided John down the hall toward the stairs.

"We're in the medical building now, John. The sky bridge you crossed will take us to the crew support building before we can venture out. What did you think of the city's skyline from the view of the sky bridge?"

"I... well... I was too nervous to stand in front of the windows, so... I haven't seen it yet."

"Oh, my goodness." Jean laughed. "You crawled? Well, you are in for a treat, then."

As they crested the last step in the stairwell, John allowed his eyes to take in the scenery outside the windows—windows he feared only a couple of nights ago. His brain tried to make sense of the city's skyline. He subconsciously moved closer. Not only had he never seen such wonders, but he could never have imagined such architecture, the structures, the lighting, the way vehicles all defied gravity. It was all beyond his understanding.

Jean took time to point out some sights. She first highlighted the downtown walking area they would tour, then the science academy and the Empyrean John had already visited. Jean then allowed John some time to process everything he was seeing. Not wanting to waste too much time on the sky bridge, John turned toward the crew support building to let Nurse Jean know he was ready. As he turned, John caught an unusual shape from the corner of his left eye. Unable to fight the urge, John crossed the sky bridge to the other set of windows, as if drawn by a magnet. John looked down from his perch, and he could not believe his eyes. It was a ship... it was the ship.

This must be the ship I arrived on, he thought. The ship looked moored to the building like those at the Empyrean. It was smooth and curved, like the ceiling in the room where he woke after being taken from the pharmacy.

John knew he had to make the most of the opportunity and try to memorize every detail. Sitting atop the structure was another spherical compartment with a walkway leading to the crew support building. The ship floated between the two sides of the building. Its exterior had an almost iridescent quality. Then it hit John like a hammer. The ship was not in water; it hovered in the air. His eyes bulged in disbelief, almost popping out of his skull.

"You okay, John?"

"Oh, uh, yeah. That ship, it's… it's floating. It's remarkable."

"That's the SG331. We call it the Transporter."

"That's what they brought me here on?"

"Yes, that's how they brought everyone in the camp here. Come on, John. Let's get you into the city. There's plenty to see."

Jean led John out of the crew support building and into the city. Unlike when John snuck out on previous evenings, the walking area was teeming with life—both humans and Big Brains. Commercial vehicles cruised past them as they walked along a pedestrian pathway. John expected to feel the eyes of bystanders gawking at him as they walked, but everyone went about their business. Only a handful noticed him.

"This is one of the planet's newest cities," Jean said. "I don't know all the details, but as I understand it, the city grew out of what was originally a test site for some new technology the Big Brains were developing. If the stories are true, there was some concern that the technology was so risky that the Big Brains feared testing it near populated areas. We all assume it was the development of the transporter ship or whatever powers it. The Big Brains don't say much about it, though. Obviously, whatever it was, it was successful, so they built the Empyrean, the Science Center I showed you on the sky bridge, and… I guess the rest of the city just grew to support them and their missions to Earth."

John hung on to Jean's every word, hoping for any clue to help him get back to Mary.

"We've coexisted in harmony for quite some time now," Jean said. "We believe the first humans were brought here about thirty years ago. I guess back then, the Big Brains brought many more humans than they do today. About twenty years ago, they started moving newly arrived humans to their own place, the camp where you were."

As they walked, John fixated on the sights. While taller, the massive skyscrapers in New York and Chicago paled in comparison to the magnificence of the Big Brains architecture. From the dome-like structure of the Empyrean to the Science Center's near-perfect integration into the lush green hills that formed its backdrop, or the downtown area that would feel at home to humans from any walk of life, John marveled at what the Big Brains had built. Jean limited the tour to the walking area downtown. There were cinemas, restaurants, grocery stores, fun places for the kids, and much more.

"Looks familiar, doesn't it, John?"

"It really does. I… why… I… I don't understand. Why would—"

"Because we're here, John. As the city expanded, the Big Brains sought our input on how best to build a city that would be as enjoyable for us as it is for the Big Brain residents. They even started bringing things like movies back from Earth so we can watch them here in the theater." Jean pointed across the street to a theater, which caused John to stop walking. "Is everything okay, John?"

"Oh, uh, yeah, I'm fine," John said as he wiped the hint of a tear from his eyes.

"It's okay, John. What is it? That's why we do these tours. You can tell me."

"Oh, it's nothing. The movie that's playing—"

"Wizard of Oz? That's a favorite around here. We often joke that the Big Brains used it for inspiration on some of the architecture. Does it bother you?"

"No, no, that's when I met… I mean, uh, that's the movie I saw on a town pass from MCB San Diego. A theater there had a special showing."

"MCB?" Jean asked.

"Oh, sorry. MCB means Marine Corps Base. That's where I went to boot camp."

"Oh, you were a Marine?"

"Well, yes. I finished boot camp but never actually shipped out. My father passed before my unit left, and by the time I got back from leave, our orders were canceled, and I was discharged."

"I'm very sorry for your loss, John."

"Oh, uh, thank you. I appreciate that."

After a long walk through the city and a light lunch, Jean brought John to one of her favorite parks.

"I used to come here as a child all the time. It's just so peaceful," Jean shared.

"As a child?" John asked. "The Big Brains abducted children? That's horrible."

"Oh… No! Not at all. I was born here. My parents met here after the Big Brains brought them each here… before they started sending people to the camp."

"Why did the Big Brains start sending us there?"

"We're really not sure. Many of us think it's a population control measure, but no one really knows. Well, John, I think it's time we started heading back, okay?"

"Oh, uh, yeah, sure… thank you for this. I really appreciate the tour."

John felt at ease with Jean. He could drop his guard and speak with her like a friend for most of the day. As they returned to the crew support facility, they passed the manhole John used to find the Empyrean.

Like an excited friend, John blurted out, "That's how I got there." He said, pointing to the start of his escape route.

"Got where?"

"That shipyard place? What did you call it?"

"Oh, the Empyrean? You crawled through that? It's a wonder you made it at all."

John laughed and said, "No kidding. There were a few minutes where I didn't think I was going to make it out alive, for sure."

"Well, I guess you're not gonna do that again, right?"

"No, absolutely not."

"Promise?"

"That's a promise, Jean."

John's trust in Jean continued to grow, but her affinity for the Big Brains made complete trust impossible. As they entered the crew support facility, regret crept into John's mind as he fought against his instincts to believe Jean had his best interests at heart. He was glad to have spent time with her, but he wondered if she had ulterior motives. John resolved to accept the day for what it was and hoped Jean was who she appeared to be. He may have lost the maintenance tunnel as an escape route, but he learned where the Big Brains docked the ship. His mistake should not impact his ability to get back to Earth. John remained undeterred.

The security beep sounded as Jean led John back into his room. Jean remained in the doorway, keeping the door open as he settled in for the evening.

"I hope you enjoyed the tour today, John."

"I did, Jean, I really did. Thanks for taking me downtown."

"No, John, thank you. I very much appreciate you being so well-behaved. I stuck my neck out there believing in you, so I'm glad I wasn't wrong."

John nodded in appreciation and sat down to remove his shoes.

"We'll need you to get enough rest tonight so we can start the first procedure tomorrow."

"Procedure? What procedure?" John asked. His brows furrowed in confusion.

"It's the first step in your rehab, but it's a fairly significant step. We get through that smoothly, and it's easy going from there. Try not to worry, John. Everything will be fine. Just relax and get some sleep."

Jean turned and left, but no beep followed. John wondered if Jean set the security or if the beep never sounded because she never fully entered the room. *Should I try another excursion? I just promised Jean I wouldn't. Will the*

DETACHMENTS

procedure planned for the next day wipe my brain? What are the chances I'd successfully find the launch information if I tried again? John's mind toiled with the unknowns.

CHAPTER 20

The only thing he found more frustrating than the gaps in his information was whether to try the door to see if security was fully engaged. He stepped toward the door, then returned to his seat, a pattern he had already repeated a handful of times.

The door whooshed open, and in walked an orderly with his dinner. It was clear to John that the beep never sounded. Jean left the security disengaged. He was so distracted by the enticement that he never acknowledged the orderly asking how he felt that night.

As the orderly departed, John sat in deep contemplation for several more minutes. He looked over at his meal but had no appetite. His mind twisted in contemplation. He weighed the pros and cons of sneaking out of his room again. It would certainly offer a chance to learn when the ship was next scheduled to launch, but he had no solid lead for where to get that information. More questions filled his mind: *if I got caught, would I be back in restraints? Maybe permanently? Jean took a real risk trusting me, didn't she? Would she get into trouble with the Big Brains? Or perhaps the restraints and the tour were all tests? Is the door a test? Is this all a setup to get me to accept the treatment?*

It suddenly dawned on John. Every scenario he could contemplate ultimately hinged on whether he believed Jean was acting in his best interests. If she did, he should stay in his room. If she did not, then the door being left unlocked must be a test, and the Big Brains would capture him the moment he stepped out of his room. In that context, John's decision became easy. He would have to trust Jean. He would have to hope she was the good person she appeared to be.

Resigned to his circumstances, John set his bed to its sleeping position to get the sleep Jean recommended. Staring at the roof overhead, trying to calm his mind, John's thoughts drifted to Mary. How much he had missed her. He reminisced about the day he met her in San Diego. He had gone to watch a movie with a few other Marines when he saw Mary in line, waiting to buy popcorn. He had no interest in a snack, but he could not stop himself from getting in line to meet her. She had a natural elegance. She was undoubtedly a beautiful woman, but there was something more—something John could not quite place. She only glanced at him as he stepped in line behind her. It wasn't much, and perhaps it was more his uniform than John himself, but it was all the encouragement he needed. He started a conversation in line and ended up buying her popcorn. His friends were no longer a thought in his mind as he left them to follow her to a special showing of "The Wizard of Oz."

John continued to play back the memories of that fantastic day: every moment, every laugh, every stolen glance—a far more important story than the one on the screen. He lay there, thinking, smiling, crying, and, perhaps more than anything, longing to be back with Mary. He lost all sense of time and dozed off well past whatever Jean would have considered a good night's sleep.

John woke to the sound of the door closing against the frame; his medical team had already shuffled in. A second doctor had joined Dr. Harry and John's usual nurses, Jean and Clara. John stretched his arms above his chest as he rolled toward his visitors and cracked his eyes open to allow the light to creep in. Fully open, his bloodshot eyes revealed his condition.

Dr. Harry and his two nurses came into focus, along with a second doctor he had not met before. He wondered what the procedure could be and why they needed another doctor.

"Nurse Jean, did you not advise John of the importance of getting enough rest for the procedure today?"

"Yes, I did, Dr. Harry."

"We needed you to get plenty of rest last night," Dr. Harry said. "You don't appear to be well-rested. I'm very concerned this could jeopardize your procedure."

"I'm sorry. There was a lot on my mind last night. I'm not sure how much sleep I got, but I feel pretty good," John said.

Dr. Harry released a pronounced sigh as he shut his eyes and tried to smooth the wrinkles on his distressed forehead with his hand. "John, this stage of your rehabilitation process is delicate. It requires focus and attention. It can become quite frustrating when lost focus causes us to repeat exercises. Lack of sleep often exacerbates things. Do you feel you'll be able to proceed today? You won't become agitated if we need to restart… perhaps several times?"

Dr. Harry spoke in subdued tones, being careful not to sound harsh. John could sense the disappointment in his voice. He could tell Dr. Harry had dealt with challenging experiences during earlier attempts to conduct the procedures. Jean and Clara's eyes revealed their own story. They, too, must have experienced difficult times with previous patients. The other doctor, who had yet to be introduced, stood by the door. He looked on with no specific emotion John could discern. John deduced he must be a specialist whose time his regular medical team had requested.

"I'm sorry," John said. "I tried, but I simply couldn't calm my mind."

"Were you worried about the procedure?" Dr. Harry asked.

"No, no, not at all. I was… uh… well, I just had some things on my mind. Just, uh, memories, I guess… memories from home. That's all. Nothing about the procedure."

"Were you ever diagnosed with any mental—?"

Nurse Jean said, "Dr. Harry, after spending the day with John yesterday, I think he's being sincere, and the procedure wasn't what was causing his sleep challenges."

"Hmm." Dr. Harry contemplated. "Dr. Smith, I hate to ask this. I know your time is precious, but might it be better to treat John for—?"

"No!" John interjected, surprising the medical team. "It's nothing like that! I was just thinking about my family, remembering the good times. We can proceed. I'm sure I got enough sleep, and I'll be able to concentrate, even if it means we have to repeat some of it. I can do it."

Whatever the rehab treatment was, Jean's defensiveness and Dr. Harry's query to Dr. Smith all felt somewhat ominous. John concluded that whatever treatment Dr. Harry referenced was far worse than the current plan.

"Okay, John… okay. This is Dr. Smith," Dr. Harry gestured. "He leads the team waiting in the stasis room to see you through the next stage of your rehabilitation. We know some aspects of the procedure won't make sense to you and can often be uncomfortable, but if you do as you say you will, everything will work out."

"Wait," John held up his hand in a stop motion, "you're not coming with me?" He motioned to his original medical team, primarily to Nurse Jean.

"I'm sorry, John," Nurse Jean said. "We're not trained on those procedures, but we'll see you again when you come back from the procedure, and maybe we'll be able to go on another tour once you've fully recovered."

"Is it that much strain? How long will I need to recover? What exactly is this procedure?"

"Relax, John," Dr. Smith spoke his first words. "All we're doing in this step is installing some implants that will later allow us to work with you and help you live more comfortably here."

"Wait, wait, is this going to wipe my brain like they say in the camp?"

"What… wipe your brain? Where the…" Dr. Smith shook his head. "No, John, we don't—"

"Don't lie to me! I met Tom! I know you and the Big Brains wiped his mind!"

"Whoa, John, hang on there... Tom was a very extreme case. He had a terrible childhood trauma that led him down a path of violence. He needed extensive work—"

"So, you just wiped his mind, right?" John said.

"No, John, that's not what I'd call it, but we had to do a significant amount of work with him to make sure he wouldn't end back on a path of violence. Rather than think of it as a wipe, in Tom's case, try to think of it more as a series of alterations that allowed Tom to become the person he should have been."

"You're telling me, right now, when this procedure is done, I'll still know everything I already know? I'll remember being on the tour with Jean and all my memories from back home?"

"John, nothing we're doing today will affect your memories at all. All it does is energize parts of your brain in ways that allow us to help you later. Tom's rehabilitation took over a year, and we had to spend a lot of time together to address everything he needed. Tom helped us every step of the way. He wanted us to take the extensive actions we did. We would never change a person's memories without their consent."

John considered Dr. Smith's assurances and studied him for any signs of deception. Unable to convince himself whether to trust Dr. Smith, John's eyes shifted to Jean. She was the closest thing John felt he had to a friend. With a gentle nod and the look in her eyes, John knew she agreed with everything Dr. Smith had conveyed.

"What about you, Nurse Jean? Are you willing to promise this procedure will not take my memories? I won't lose who I am? This won't wipe my mind?"

"Yes, John, I'm absolutely willing to promise you that. We don't do that here."

With a deep breath, John placed his hands on the side of his bed, lifted himself to his feet, and said, "Okay, can you give me a few minutes to get cleaned up and dressed?"

"Sure thing," Dr. Harry said as the medical team departed to give John time.

About twenty minutes later, the door opened, and the team entered.

"John!" Jean called out anxiously.

"Almost done," John called from the restroom. "I'll be right out."

John stepped out a few moments later and saw the relief on Jean's face. He put on his footies and reached for his shoes from the previous day.

"Oh, you won't need those, John. We're just headed a little way down the hall," Dr. Harry said.

"Oh, uh… okay."

John stood up and followed the team out of his room. They turned left, walked down the hall, and passed five or six doors on the left before reaching the only door on the right—the door John left on his first night after he arrived from the camp. When Nurse Clara approached the door, the security beeped, and the door split from the middle. The group entered the corridor and reached the next door to enter the ship. The team led John in.

"This is the ship, isn't it?" John asked as he positioned himself on the map he had drawn in his mind of the medical building.

"Yes, John," Dr. Smith said. "The ship has certain capabilities that aren't easily replicated, so rather than build a dedicated room for these procedures, we simply use the ship. Clara, are all the ship's protocols in place for the procedure?"

"Yes, Doctor," Clara said.

"John, over here is the stasis room where the process will take place on the physical level of your brain," Dr. Smith advised as he pointed to the open door next to the ship's entrance. Bright blue lights illuminated the small room. There was a powered chair that looked something like a futuristic dental chair with head and wrist supports. The chair was adjustable for different-sized patients. Various monitoring equipment and medical devices adorned the chair, along with several adjustable lights around the room. The room was about half the size of John's room down the hall. There were several types of medical equipment John could not identify. All the machines were on wheels, so the staff could roll them to the chair as needed.

"Is everything ready to go?" Dr. Smith asked his team.

"Yes, sir. We have everything prepped and ready to go."

"Hop up into the chair, John," Dr. Smith instructed. "We've got to shave a couple of small areas of your head. It's unfortunately necessary."

John agreed with a nod as Dr. Smith summoned the nurse, who cleared John's scalp in the key areas. She then attached conductors to the clean skin to monitor John's brain activity.

The nurse then applied restraints to John's wrists, which caused him to jerk his arm away from the bedrail.

"Sorry, I should have warned you. When we wake people between the different stages, they often thrash about. We use the restraints so you won't hurt yourself or any of us." Dr. Smith cracked the slightest of smiles. John relaxed his arm and allowed the nurse to apply the restraints.

"Okay, John, we're ready to get going on the first step. For this part, we need you to be asleep, so we're going to engage a system that's a lot like anesthesia but has none of the nasty side effects. Nurse, go ahead and engage the stasis protocol, and let's put John under."

As the familiar feeling took hold, John realized what Dr. Smith meant by the stasis protocol and called out, "But wait—" John's words scarcely escaped his lips as the ship's stasis protocol took effect. Unprepared to fend off the induced sleep, John succumbed to its power.

CHAPTER 21

John woke to bright, white light that gave way first to shapes in the shadows and then to a human arm adjusting a medical instrument attached to his head. Another arm crossed over his chest with a shiny silver object. Muffled words exchanged between the people landed on John's ears. They, too, grew in clarity.

"Doctor! His eyes!" the nurse warned.

John instantly knew something was amiss.

As with his first experience on the ship, John had no voluntary movement, but he could feel his fight-or-flight response kick in, and his senses returned. A searing pain, like a drill, burrowed into his skull. It jolted through his body like lightning seeking ground.

"Get that anesthesia cart over here, now!" Dr. Smith ordered.

A scream burst from John's vocal cords as the anesthesia cart rolled to his side. It was such a horrific sound that only Mary's cries from that fateful night rivaled it. Dr. Smith covered John's mouth and nose with a mask. John faded back to sleep as he felt the cart bang into the chair's armrest.

"Wake up, John. We need you to wake up."

He remained groggy as the anesthesia's effects faded. He raised his hand to rub his eyes.

"That's it, John. Can you hear me, okay?"

"Muh… muh… Mary? Is that you?"

"It's Jean, John. You're back in your room. We've gotta get you up. We need to get you drinking and using the bathroom."

"Jean? Jean who? What are… where am I?" His vision once again cleared, and the cloud over his brain lifted.

"Who the fuck are you? Where the fuck am I?"

John jumped to his feet. Rage spread across his reddened face.

"I've never hit a woman, but I swear to Christ, if you don't start answering my questions, I won't be able to make that same claim tomorrow."

Jean and Clara bolted for the door as John rushed after them. Both women narrowly escaped as the door closed behind them, followed by a beep.

John slammed against the door, banged his fists, and screamed, "What the hell is going on? Get me the fuck out of here!"

After an hour, John had grown quiet—a voice called through the door.

"John, it's Jean. Are you okay? We think you had an adverse reaction to the anesthesia, but it should have worn off by now. John? Can you hear me?"

Following three firm knocks, Jean called once again, "John, we just want to make sure you're okay. I'm coming in to check on you. I won't hurt you."

With a short beep, the door slid open. John erupted from his room; Jean, unable to move in time, crashed into the opposite hallway wall. He turned to run down the hall and discovered two Big Brains hovering twenty feet in front of him. The blood drained from John's face. Fear drove him backward as he fell. He scrambled on all fours until a stumble sent him sprawling to the ground.

"John! John! It's okay! It's okay!"

"Get the fuck away from me," John snapped.

DETACHMENTS

By the time John could turn to stand and run, the Big Brain guards had already closed the distance and knocked John fast asleep on the cold hallway floor.

With the Serpentis leadership gone, the Drongs established their dominance in the camp. They became the most prominent gang almost overnight. Doc realized the Drongs were excited to gain more territory—the Hub, the market, and the entire camp. Spearheaded by their leader, Mick, the Drongs made their strength known, especially to the remaining members of the Serpentis.

The Serpentis did not stand a chance of survival in the camp without their two most important members. Even if Sal and Antonio did return, they would be useless. Their only hope depended on the Rev Rehab and the remaining Serpentis figuring out how to steal it. John had failed to get it for them, so they would have to do it themselves.

Nicola, who went by "Nick," had exalted himself as the new Capo of the gang, driven by the goal of getting the Rev Rehab out of the infirmary's pharmacy—a goal that would require not only contending with the Big Brains but also with the Drongs seeking the same prize.

The serum wasn't Nick's only priority, though. His spy inside the Drongs had disappeared, and Nick realized his rise to Capo had resulted from being fooled by the Drongs. To maintain power, Nick needed a scapegoat. That's at least what Doc suspected when Nick and his goons snatched him up and dragged him back to their hidden club. The Serpentis had Doc trapped there for two nights, and his friends knew something was wrong.

"Do you think he may have done something and was taken by the Big Brains?" Chris asked.

"I don't think so. We would have heard about it," Rex said.

The market bubbled with excitement that afternoon as if everyone in the camp decided to shop simultaneously. Chris and Rex walked along, talking as items changed hands.

"Something must have happened to him," Chris said. "I am sure of it. I have checked his room several times, but nothing. Something is terribly wrong."

"I'm betting the Serpentis are behind it," Rex said. "For Nick to be accepted as Capo by the Serpentis, he's gonna have to hold someone accountable for getting their leadership wiped. I'm betting he's gonna put the blame on Doc."

"I hope that is not the case. We better start looking for him," Chris said.

"That's not gonna be easy. They know every nook and cranny of this camp, so they probably have him stashed someplace. We're gonna need some help… from an unusual place," Rex said, slowly nodding his head in thought.

"Unusual? What do you mean?"

"Well, who else in the camp is gonna know the kinds of places to do the things the Serpentis would want to do with Doc right now?"

"Who would know? I don't know what you mean. Who are you talking about?"

"The Drongs, Chris. Who else would have that kind of insight except another gang?"

"You're kidding, right? Do we not have enough trouble with the Serpentis? And now you want to get mixed up with the Drongs, too?"

"I'm not saying it's my best idea, but do you got a better one?"

Chris looked up at the sky to his left as he rubbed the side of his head.

"I see those gears turning, Chris. You got nothing, right?"

Chris shook his head while he contemplated the challenge.

"Yeah, I didn't think so," Rex taunted.

"Do you think they will help us? They knew that Doc once tried to help the Serpentis get the serum. Even if they agree, you know they will want something in return. Maybe the serum… What if getting the Rev Rehab is their price for helping us? What are we going to do then?"

"You've got a point, no doubt," Rex said. "But do we have any other options?"

Chris shook his head again, recognizing their dilemma. They could either hope for the best that Doc was somewhere safe or they could enlist the help of the Drongs.

John slowly opened his eyes and rolled them about in their sockets, still unsure of his surroundings. He shut them back again and moved to wipe his eyes. John looked to see what had ensnared him and saw the restraints on his wrists and ankles. Rage once again flooded his face.

"Let me out of here," John screamed in his now hoarse voice. He was thrashing about like a cat that had fallen into water.

A moment later, a beep sounded at the door, followed by John's medical team. Dr. Harry and nurses Jean and Clara rushed in as though they had been waiting for the first sounds of John waking.

"John. It's Dr. Harry."

"Who? Who the hell is Dr. Harry? What happened to Mary? Why am I here? And what the fuck were those things that floated after me in the hallway?"

"John, you're in your room. Remember? We spoke this morning about the rehabilitation procedure?"

"Procedure? What fucking procedure? Tell me where the fuck I am."

"You're right where you were this morning, John. You're in Earth City, in the medical building here on planet Twin Moons."

"Planet what? Earth City? Is this some kind of joke? You better—"

"Hold on, hold on, John… Hold on now. Can you just answer something for me? Can you tell me the last thing you remember?"

"Yeah, I was watching a movie with this gal, Mary, and then I woke up here."

"You don't remember anything after watching the movie?"

"No, the next thing I remember is that nurse over there waking me up."

John noticed a tear forming in Nurse Jean's eye.

"Oh my God, Dr. Harry, have you ever seen anything like this from anesthesia?"

"This isn't a reaction to the anesthesia, Jean. Something isn't right. Clara, get someone from Dr. Smith's team in here, now!" Dr. Harry commanded.

"What's not right? Someone tell me what the fuck is going on!"

"John, calm down. You're just going to hurt yourself. We're going to figure this out. Don't worry."

"I'm so sorry, John. I can't believe this is happening. I promised you'd be fine, and—"

"Jean, get yourself together or leave."

"Yes, sir, yes, I... I'll be fine; I just feel awful."

"I know. We're gonna get this fixed, John... we're gonna get this fixed. We won't rest till we do. Now, what were you doing before you went to the movie with Mary?"

"I was, I... uh... oh my God. What the fuck is wrong with me? I can't remember anything! What did you people do to me?"

John thrashed harder, nearly toppling his bed. His breathing became erratic, and he almost reached the point of rage-induced distress.

"Jean, go get me a sedative. We've gotta calm him down before he goes into cardiac arrest."

Jean rushed out the door and was back in seconds. Dr. Harry held John's left arm down and administered the sedative. The sedative was strong enough to pull him out of his episode but allowed him to stay at least functionally aware of what was happening around him.

A few moments later, Nurse Clara returned with Dr. Smith.

DETACHMENTS

"Oh, Dr. Smith, I wasn't expecting you'd still be here."

"I was actually on my way out, but when I heard your nurse describe what was happening down here, I figured I'd better come to check on things myself."

"I appreciate that. John here is experiencing severe memory loss, and it's unlike anything I've ever seen. He seems to have no recollection of anything before or after running into a woman named Mary at a movie theater. Also, he's been impossible to console or calm without sedatives."

"Damn it, I was worried something might happen, but this sounds worse than anything I would have guessed."

"What do you mean? Did something go wrong?"

"Oh yeah! You bet it did! Son of a bitch woke up while I was installing the first implant in the cerebral cortex, and this guy opened his eyes. Then he let out this blood-curdling scream. I'd never heard anything like it before. We had to revert to traditional anesthesia to finish the procedure."

"Were you able to get the implant seated correctly?"

"Sure, I got all five of 'em seated exactly where they're supposed to be… all confirmed with imaging, ping rates, and standard diagnostic tests."

"Do you think, uh… could waking up disrupt the modification process?"

"I suppose it's possible since we don't fully understand how the technology works. The Big Brains just trained us on how to install the implants. We know the electrical signals in the brain power them, and we know that with the right training, they can dramatically affect behavior. They're quite remarkable, but the Big Brains don't share many details."

John was still high on sedatives. "Big what? Did you say… Big Brains?"

"Oh yes, John. The guards. We call their kind Big Brains."

"Okay, Big Brains… that's nice."

The door beeped and opened. A lone Big Brain floated into the room.

CHAPTER 22

All the humans stood up straight with their arms at their sides, like John did when standing at attention during basic training.

"Captain Meadowbrook!" Dr. Harry announced.

"Relax, everyone, relax. I just wanted to come and check on this one. I've heard some interesting stories."

Dr. Harry looked at Dr. Smith, surprised by the captain's awareness of the situation.

"You… hah… Big Brain, hehe he," John giggled.

"He's on a sedative, sir," Dr. Harry said.

Like the other Big Brains, Captain Meadowbrook had characteristic crinkles all over his body and large, black eyes emitting a dull blue glow around the edges. He moved with an aura of great authority.

"Sedative, huh? You've been dealing with some challenges, then. What seems to be the problem, gentlemen?" Meadowbrook asked.

"Sir, we're not sure just yet," Dr. Smith revealed. "Throughout his pre-stasis stage, he responded well to the procedure. His patterns were normal, and he showed no sign of anything that would suggest he would have any post-stasis challenges. He didn't seem to get enough sleep, but we opted to proceed."

"Would that have caused the problems we're seeing now?"

"Oh, no, sir," Dr. Smith said. "We never got to the part where his sleep would have been a factor."

"You never got to that part?"

"Sir, we believe the stasis protocol failed. He woke up while we were installing the first implant."

"He woke up?" Captain Meadowbrook asked, with a subtle lifting of hands and spreading his long, skinny fingers—a rare display of emotion.

"Yes, sir. I haven't checked with the maintenance crew, but I can only assume the ship's systems failed. So, we ended up having to use traditional anesthesia."

"Failed? That seems unlikely. How did he respond to the phase exercises after installing the first implant?"

"Because we used traditional anesthesia, we couldn't do the exercises, sir. That's why his rest didn't matter. We installed all five implants while he was under and brought him here for post-op."

"I don't feel like exercising," John joked, still feeling the sedatives.

"Hmm, I think that might be part of the problem. You did nothing wrong, but when we developed the implants, we never considered the possibility that the ship's stasis wouldn't be able to keep a patient under. This is quite interesting. Using traditional anesthesia was a wise decision. You made the right call installing the implants when you did. I think the delays the anesthesia would have caused between implants would have been well beyond limits. He almost certainly wouldn't have been sufficiently coherent for the exercises for the neuronet to initiate correctly. Did it pass all the diagnostic tests?"

"Yes, sir. Flying colors," Dr. Smith said.

"Well, I'll have to get my developers to work on this problem and see if they can figure out a solution. A more immediate question I have, considering the SG331 is scheduled to launch in six days, is how he could wake up, and if there is any risk of this happening with others?"

"Sir, you don't think it could be a malfunction with the ship?"

"No, I don't believe the ship is the issue here. In fact, this may all be my fault."

"Your fault, sir? How could that be?"

"He woke up on the ship before... three times while returning from our last trip to Earth. That's why I brought him back with us."

"I like Earth," John said.

"Has anyone else ever woken up on the ship?" Nurse Jean asked from the background.

Captain Meadowbrook turned to face her. "No, never. We've had a few other people who could resist our guards' sleep commands, but never the artificial system on the ship."

"How were those people able to resist the guards?"

"We're not sure, Jean, but powerful emotions could cause it. Maybe anger, hate, sorrow, or love, for all we know. There just haven't been enough examples to form a hypothesis yet."

"Love?" Jean asked. "Do you think this Mary person he mentioned could be a factor?"

"Mary?" Meadowbrook asked. "Who's Mary?"

"Mary! Mary!" John yelled and thrashed at his restraints as the sedative weakened.

"It's okay, John. It's okay." Dr. Harry held John's arm still and administered more sedatives. "Clara, let's get John on a sedative drip to keep him calm but awake. Hopefully, we can talk to him when needed."

Clara headed out to get the IV kit.

"And what about this Mary person?" Meadowbrook said.

"We don't know, sir. It could be nothing, but the only memory he claims to have is meeting a woman named Mary and watching a movie with her," Dr. Harry said.

"That's his only memory?"

"Yes, sir."

"Hmm, I'll freely admit that the emotions of Homo sapiens are still somewhat of a mystery to us. So, it's not out of the realm of possibility that it might explain some things, but how could a movie with this Mary person create an emotion strong enough to overcome the ship's safety protocol?"

"It's love, sir," Jean said. "It has to be love."

"Love?" Meadowbrook asked. "Why love?"

"I think all the pieces of information add up to that, sir," Jean concluded.

"How so, Nurse? All we have is his one memory of a woman at a theater," Dr. Smith said.

"Think about it, gentlemen. He was apprehensive about losing his memories. He's only been here a matter of weeks, but he was already trying to steal Rev Rehab on behalf of a camp gang. The first person he called for after the procedure was Mary, and she's the only person he remembers. Whoever she is, John is in love with her, and he's trying to get back to her," Jean said with near certainty.

"That seems like you're making a lot of assumptions there, but admittedly, it's not implausible," Dr. Smith acknowledged. "I suppose if John's thoughts had been so focused on this Mary person, it might explain why the neuronet is stuck and only allowing access to that one memory."

"He did say he had a lot going on in his mind, and that's why he didn't get much sleep. He could have been thinking about her," Dr. Harry said.

"Captain Meadowbrook, in the other cases where people could resist stasis by the guards, was there an emotional attachment to someone?"

"There have been a handful of cases, but the one I have personal knowledge of happened when the woman's mother had just jumped off an apartment building in the camp. Her daughter rushed to be with her, and the responding guards couldn't induce her to sleep."

"That could certainly be considered love," Jean said, and the doctors agreed.

"Okay, let me take this as another thing to get my team working on. We'll review the other cases of humans resisting the guards and make sure we can mitigate any concerns. This is disconcerting. I had hoped we brought our last human here five years ago. I don't want to take any chances until I know we can prevent this from happening again. We'll scrub any further SG331 launches until we figure this out."

"No more launchy, launchy. Ha ha," John teased.

"Sorry about that, sir. We, uh... we humans tend to react in odd ways to certain narcotics, but it's a lot better than how he was acting," Dr. Harry said.

"Not to worry, I understand," Captain Meadowbrook said. "I'm going to visit the infirmary to get a better understanding of what happened there. As for the two patients who arrived from the camp a few nights ago, let the other teams work with them. I want John to be each of your teams' top priority. We'll discuss it some more when I have answers."

"Yes, sir," both doctors responded.

As Captain Meadowbrook left the room, Nurse Clara returned and set up John's sedative.

"There's no sense worrying about the worst-case scenario. We can hope they won't demand such a high price, but I don't see where we have an option," Rex highlighted.

"Really? Are you sure?" Chris asked. "Do you not think they can come up with something worse?"

"I dunno. I just don't know."

"If we are going to do this, we should get moving. There is no sense delaying the inevitable. Where do we go from here?"

"They're usually over at the ball field. Let's give that a shot."

After checking the ball field and not finding the Drongs, Chris and Rex looked for Mick in his room. On their way, they saw Gus coming toward them with a look of concern on his face.

"What is going on, Gus?" Chris asked as he approached him.

"Ah, nothin', mate. Just been over to Doc's room lookin' for him for the bloody millionth time today," he said.

"Yeah, we're pretty worried about him. We think the Serpentis might have nabbed him," Rex said.

"Exactly what I was thinking," Gus said.

"We're looking for the Drongs to talk to them to see if they'll help us find Doc. The Serpentis may be a shell of themselves, but we're still no match for them. We need some strength on our side," Rex said.

"Reckon they'll agree, do ya?" Gus asked.

"There is only one way to find out," Chris said.

"Yeah... you might be right there, mate. Pretty sure I clocked 'em over by the infirmary," Gus said. "Looked like they were havin' a proper serious chat. Might still be there, yeah?"

The three friends made their way toward the infirmary. Chris was swelling with doubt about their plan. He was certain the Drongs would want the serum, or perhaps more. He pondered the myriad impossible conditions the Drongs might apply.

The Drongs gathered under a willow tree close to the infirmary, where there were three park benches for camp residents to get some fresh air away from the sun. Just another place that made life in the camp more tolerable.

Just like Gus told his friends, the Drongs were having a serious discussion. They all sat on the benches except Mick, who was talking to his boys. That all came to a halt when the three friends approached.

"What do you want here?" Mick asked with a steely expression.

"We are not here to cause any trouble," Chris said. He was neither intimidated by Mick nor by his men on the benches. The Drongs outnumbered Chris and his friends, but if necessary, they were ready for a fight. Being in the Drongs' presence hardened Chris's nerves. He had decided. He was full speed ahead. "We wanted to see if you might help us with something. It is very important."

Silence hovered over the interaction like a sword of Damocles. The Drongs were trying to process the nerve of the interruption. Chris, Gus, and Rex waited anxiously for any sign of Mick's next move. An angry Drong spoke up.

"I ain't helpin' no daoine gorm! Now get your ass outta here before ya find out exactly what I do to the likes of 'em," Paddy warned in his thick Irish accent.

"Settle down, Paddy. This might get interesting," Mick said.

Paddy respected Mick's wishes, but his glare at Chris intensified.

"What is it then? What do you want?" Mick asked.

Recognizing Paddy's racism might derail discussions, Rex took a few steps closer. Gus and Chris stood beside him like bodyguards.

"We think the Serpentis are holding our friend hostage. We don't know where, but we're hoping you can help us find him," he said.

"You mean Doc? Is that who we're talking about? The same Doc that spread a rumor my girl was getting it on with Sal? That Doc? Is that the friend you're looking for?" Mick asked, already fully aware of the answer.

"Yes, it is, and to be entirely honest, we were all involved," Rex said.

"Is that so, and you want me to help you? To help you find the man who created a mess for my boys and me? Do you realize what could have happened if things had gotten out of control from all the bullshit you peddled?"

"Jesus, you've got some neck showin' your face 'round here, so ya do!" Paddy said.

"I know you are not going to believe this, but we had to do that to help our friend... He learned so much about the Big Brains through those fights. For all we know, he is beyond the barrier right now, giving those Big Brains a taste of their own medicine," Chris said.

"You're right, I don't believe it. But what I believe doesn't really matter 'cause it all worked out for us. Sal and Antonio are gone, and now, I have Sal's girl, the camp... Hell, I've got it all now. So maybe, lucky for you, it all ended well enough for the Drongs," Mick said with a bit of an evil laugh.

168

DETACHMENTS

"That's all in the past now, ain't it? We don't gotta be enemies, do we, mate?" Gus asked.

If Paddy were the leader of the Drongs, Gus and his friends would wake up in the infirmary, wishing they were in Doc's shoes with the Serpentis. Gus could see the hatred written all over Paddy's face. But not Mick. Somehow, the leaders of both gangs had the wisdom to take advantage of situations their more aggressive deputies failed to see.

"Yeah," Mick said, "no need to be enemies. Okay, we'll help you," he said, nodding, implying there were strings attached.

"What? Ah, come on now, you can't mean that, brother!" Paddy said.

There was also a grumbling among the other members, expressing their disapproval of their leader's decision. The look of tension on Rex's face relaxed. The slightest smile cracked Gus's lips, while Chris maintained a plain expression.

"But there's a condition," Mick said.

Like setting a hook, Mick had three fish on his line.

"We want the Rev Rehab, and you're gonna get it."

Rex's face turned as gray as a cloud of smoke. Despite Chris's prediction, something about it being said aloud hit him with unexpected force. The other members of the Drongs lauded Mick's announcement.

"You look nervous," Mick said as he and his henchmen laughed.

"Now, don't you go worrying yourself. We've been putting together our plan here for the last hour. But instead of us taking the risk, you will. There's only one way to get that serum without getting snatched by the Big Brains—"

"A staff member?" Gus asked.

"Exactly," Mick said. "A staff member. So, all you boys gotta do is find you a staff member and convince them to help you get it. They all know we're Drongs, so we'd never be able to make that happen without getting our minds wiped. So, you're gonna do it for us. You bring us the Rev Rehab, and we will help you get your friend back. That's the deal, got it?"

169

Gus gave Rex a light tap on the shoulder and whispered something in his ear. The three moved away from the scene but returned a moment later.

"Give us till tonight so we can talk this over, okay?" Rex said to Mick, who had been waiting patiently for their response.

"Sure, take your time. I've got all day… you think Doc does, though? You think those Serpentis are being nice to him right now?"

As they turned and walked out of Mick's earshot, the three friends weighed their options.

"What do you think, guys? Should we do it?" Rex asked.

CHAPTER 23

R ex knew his decision but waited to see how Gus and Chris felt before revealing his thoughts.

"I dunno, mate. Sounds easy enough, yeah," Gus said. "Since we ain't the ones nickin' the serum. But how're we supposed to find a staff member up for helpin' us? And even then, how're we gonna suss out the right one to have a word with about somethin' like this?"

"That is what I was thinking, too," Chris said. "If we talk to the wrong person, it will ruin everything. They could inform the Big Brains, and who knows what they would do to us?"

"Listen, our problem right now is finding the right staff member. So, it sounds like we're all saying we're gonna take the Drongs' deal, right?" Rex asked.

"So, you are good with this, Rex?" Chris asked.

"Good with it? I wouldn't say good, but I don't see how we have any choice here, guys. Do you?"

Chris and Gus looked at each other, then back at Rex. With a subtle shake of their heads, they acknowledged that if they wanted to save Doc, they would need the Rev Rehab.

"The Big Brains trust the infirmary staff for a reason, ya know? I don't think they'll be too willing to betray that trust," Rex said.

"Oi, everyone's got their price, right? We could just offer 'em somethin', couldn't we?" Gus said.

"They get pretty much anything they want working for the Big Brains. What could we possibly offer?" Rex asked.

"My worry now is that if we go back to the Drongs and tell them we have agreed to their deal, but we fail... what will they do to us?" Chris asked.

"Ah, bloody hell! Wish you hadn't brought that up. I think we all know, don't we?" Gus said.

"Look, the Serpentis are much weaker than the Drongs right now. Maybe we can recruit a few guys to help us and take them on instead of taking a risk with the Drongs? Who knows? Maybe we can pull it off," Rex said with his trademark cynicism.

Chris glared at Rex in disapproval. It was as if he had the thought to slap this crazy idea out of his head but only uttered, "Have you lost your—"

"Alright, guys," Gus said. "It's clear as day, isn't it? The Drongs are our only option. We'll have to get closer to the infirmary, suss out the staff, and pick our mark. We all on the same page, yeah?"

"Yeah, agreed," Rex said as he nodded.

"Alright, we'll give the Drongs the heads-up at dinner," Gus conceded.

"Okay, yes," Chris said as they arrived in the courtyard.

Each flopped down on an available bench, catching a breather of relief from the stress they had just been through.

"What about John, then? Any clue when he's gonna be back at camp?" Gus asked.

"Today is day six, right? If they only gave him the normal first offense, he should be back soon, right?" Chris said.

"Maybe we ought to wait for him to get back before we give this a go? He's been to the vault before, ain't he? Might have a few good ideas. Could be we could nick the serum ourselves without ropin' in a staff member, you reckon?" Gus asked.

"Yeah, good idea," Rex said with a laugh. "I'm sure John will come back from his first rehab eager to give the vault a second go. Why didn't I think of that?" Chris chuckled. Even Gus got a laugh out of that one.

Nick and the man he made his deputy, Leo, walked along a path between rows of boulders. There were trees and flowers on both sides. The boulders formed a border along the length of the path. Dry leaves carpeted the ground. As they approached, Doc could hear the men's feet shuffling against the ground. This place looked like an abandoned cave sculpted by the landscape and the trees, but light still reached it. It was the Serpentis' private club.

Tied to a small oak in the center of the clearing, Doc looked up as the men entered. There were no bruises on his body, but he looked emaciated. His sunken eyes and torn shirt revealed his state. Doc's beard had grown beyond stubble in the few days the Serpentis held him. Bits of dirt from the ground filled his hair.

Two members of the gang were watching over him. The air around the place should have been refreshing, something Doc could have relied upon to rejuvenate himself, but the men kept poisoning it with the awful smell of a native plant they smoked. Despite the leaves being a valuable commodity for the Serpentis, smoking it was a favorite pastime. Doc had been breathing their thick smoke since his capture.

As Nick and Leo arrived at the scene, the men hailed them. One passed Nick a smoke; another shared with Leo. They both sucked on the weed as Doc's drained eyes looked on in despair.

Nick took one more puff of the weed before moving in closer to Doc, where he puffed the thick gray smoke across his face. Doc shut his eyes and held his breath to avoid inhaling the smoke.

"I think he likes it," Leo said, a half-smile forming across his lips.

His accent was thicker than that of the other Serpentis. Like Sal, the Big Brains abducted Leo from the old country.

"Yeah, he does," Nick said.

Doc opened his eyes to a painful, stinging sensation, forcing him to close them again. When he opened them the second time, they glistened with tears. Nick smiled as he turned his attention to business. "Your friend once told us he could withstand the Big Brains' powers. I want to know how he did that, and I want to know now."

Doc did not say a word. He shut his eyes to keep out the smoke billowing from Nick's mouth with each word.

"You don't seem to get it, Doc. I need that serum. You and your fucking friends practically gave this whole fucking camp to the Drongs. I don't enjoy being a violent man, Doc. Why do you think my men haven't laid a finger on you yet? So don't fucking push me. Look at 'em… I said fuckin' look at 'em!" Nick grabbed a handful of hair on the back of Doc's head and yanked it, forcing Doc's eyes open to see the Serpentis' ire.

"I hate repeating myself, Doc, so I'm only going to ask you one more time before I let my boys loose on you… the Big Brains ain't gonna find us out here, Doc… they're not gonna save you from this, and don't think for a minute I won't end your miserable life. Now answer my fuckin' question: How does your friend resist the Big Brains' powers? You've been with him this whole time. How's he do it?"

Doc could sense the seriousness of his situation. He could tell Nick was not a bluffing man. Doc looked up to make eye contact and forced a whiff of air from his lungs across his vocal cords, tattered by dehydration. "Just like he told you. He's got a girl and a baby back on Earth." The occasional thimble of water Doc received over the last three days had taken its toll on him.

"Something about his connection to Mary, channeling that love, helps him block out the Big Brains. That's the only reason it works. It took him some time to develop it, but he's got it pretty well mastered now."

"Wait, you want me to believe this crap about some love bullshit?" Nick mocked. "You must be out of your fuckin' mind. This ain't some fuckin' fairy tale. Now start talkin'!"

Leo cocked a brow and inhaled a deep draw on the narcotic plant. The other two men had made more wraps of the weed for themselves as they sat on some rocks.

Doc exhaled with a cough that ripped through his throat, decorating the weed cloud with a fine crimson mist that stained his dried lips. "Look, I told you how it works. You don't believe it because you don't have it in you. Think about it: Do you know anyone else in the camp who left someone behind on Earth? There's a connection there that John has that can't be faked," Doc said, knowing anyone as stone-hearted as Nick could never understand.

"This fuckin' guy," Nick released his head and turned away. "Leo, fuck this piece of shit up."

"It's true! Beat me all you want," Doc said as his voice faded. "It's true," Doc said again as he directed his head toward the ground and spat out the blood that had collected in his mouth.

The spectacle demanded that the Serpentis reflect on the moment. Leo turned to look for Nick's guidance, who motioned to pause the punishment. Nick drew in some smoke and blew it into the air away from Doc.

"Let's assume, for a minute, what you're saying is true. How did he figure any of this out?"

Doc's head hung motionless, the pain in his throat too much to bear.

"Doc... you better not fuckin' pass out on me. You little bitch, wake the fuck up! Goddammit, splash some water on his face. For fuck's sake, get him up!"

The cool water landed on Doc's face like rain, resuscitating a dry riverbed. Even though it tasted like dirt, sweat, and blood, Doc seized the chance to drink a few drops of the water as it drained from his face.

"Ah, Christ. Nick. Shit! Give him some water. That's fuckin' nasty," one of the stoned Serpentis said.

"Fine, give him a drink."

Leo snatched Doc's hair, raising his head to drink water. Leo poured the water onto Doc in a fashion closer to water torture than a drink, but Doc consumed all he could, gurgling the last gulps to soothe his smoke-scorched vocal cords.

"He figured it out himself," Doc said. "Apparently, he woke up three times before he even arrived at the camp."

"Bullshit. Do you think I'm stupid? No one wakes up before the camp."

"He needs a smack. Nick, lemme fuck 'em up a bit," Leo begged.

"You hear that, Doc? My men think I'm being too lenient. Maybe I am… what do ya think, Doc? Am I taking it too easy on you? I think you better stop with the bullshit, or I'm gonna get in better touch with my violent side."

"But it's true. He figured it out himself. I only helped him through the train—"

Before Doc could finish the sentence, Nick tore his vision to shreds with a thunderous slap. It was loud and shocked the other men into putting away their weed to watch. Nick grabbed Doc's shirt, wadding each side of the collar into a tight grip with each hand.

"You think I'm jokin' here? You think I'm fuckin' jokin'?"

Nick forced the remaining weed in his hand into Doc's mouth and then landed another slap. Doc spat the weed out. Blood oozed from his mouth down onto his chin.

Nick tore Doc's shirt, exposing his chest. "Give me that!" Nick demanded as he reached Leo. He grabbed Leo's burning weed and drove the searing ember into Doc's chest. Doc growled in agony.

"Get me another one," Nick said.

"Here, Capo," one of the other men offered his own.

He snatched another smoke from his men and jammed it into the same spot on Doc's chest. Thick mucus and blood in his mouth muted his howls to little more than a burbling sound. A long stream of scarlet syrup drained from his face.

"You don't wanna fuckin' tell me the truth? I'll make you suffer some real pain. You hear me?" Nick said.

Nick grabbed Doc's shirt collar again as Leo lit up another wrap of weed and handed it to Nick. He pressed it into the same spot as the first two, only deeper, exposing a hint of Nick's sadistic gratification. Doc forced another yell. The veins bulging on Doc's forehead threatened to burst.

"Okay, okay," Doc said. "I'll tell you... I'll tell you everything."

Nick could not resist one more shot and punched Doc in the face. "That was for making me fuckin' wait!"

Doc spat the fresh blood out of his mouth as Nick stepped away to admire his work.

"It was... it was Shirley," Doc revealed.

"Shirley? Who the fuck is Shirley?"

"She's Margaret's daughter... the woman who jumped off Apartment 19."

"What? She had a daughter?" Leo asked rhetorically.

"Are you kidding me? That freak? How the fuck could she know how to block out the Big Brains?" Nick asked.

"I don't know. All I know is she helped John figure out how to focus. You wanna know more? You're gonna have to ask her," Doc said, exasperated, unable to hold his head up any longer.

"Where can I find her?"

"I dunno, maybe Apartment 19." Doc faded into a blackout.

After two days of sedatives and anti-seizure medications, John's condition stabilized. He was no longer lashing out with uncontrollable violence and showed a more thoughtful approach to situations of increasing complexity. He also had better answers to the medical team's questions, though his memories remained a void outside of the single memory of Mary. The doctors and nurses had shown great devotion to his recovery, but John still struggled.

When left alone, he sat deep in sorrow. When engaged, his mood ranged from significant frustration over simple tests or misunderstandings to fits of rage that kept the medical team on edge. The team followed his progress closely, and he received the most care and attention in the medical building.

Besides John's aggressive behavior, he also suffered from migraines that accompanied his temper. The medication he was taking provided only temporary relief before the pain returned. Dr. Harry tried to encourage John to remain hopeful by suggesting that the migraines were John's memories fighting with the neuronet.

John also received carefully structured psychotherapy sessions as part of his treatment. The treatment scheme aimed to help him relearn basic coping mechanisms. It included problem-solving, better recognition of right and wrong, and understanding the consequences of his actions. Individual counseling to identify the causes of behavior was always part of the rehabilitation process with problematic patients, but the team had never had a patient who needed so much focus. Even Tom's rehab left him starting at a place far more advanced than John's.

John was sitting in the chair in his room. He sat with his arms wrapped around his legs as he held his knees toward his chest. He stared down between his legs when he heard the door beep and slide open.

CHAPTER 24

His medical team entered the room with Captain Meadowbrook. The looks on their faces made it clear they were not bringing him good news. Jean's eyes were glassy; she was on the verge of tears. Whatever they had come to discuss with him, he knew it would not be a pleasant conversation.

"John, do you remember Captain Meadowbrook? You were pretty out of it the last time he was here with you."

"Dr. Harry. Uh, yes, I, uh, I do." John rose to his feet in a show of respect. He offered Captain Meadowbrook a chair, but it remained empty throughout their discussion.

"John, we wanted to give you an update on your treatment. We're happy with how much progress you've made in such a short time—" Dr. Harry started.

"But?" John said.

"But we're very concerned that we've reached the limits of what we can do without help from Captain Meadowbrook's technical experts."

John listened intently. "Technical experts? What do you mean?"

"John, I don't expect you to fully understand what's happening here, but the procedure you underwent was supposed to be completed in very specific stages, with important exercises between each stage. You may have heard us discussing this, but because you regained consciousness during the first stage, Dr. Smith had to skip the exercises and finish all five stages of the procedure at once."

"I don't understand. What do you mean I woke up? What were these exercises supposed to do?"

"The exercises were to help us ensure the neuronet implant initiated and didn't impact regular brain function. Those implants help us work with you to make your time here more enjoyable, but we're afraid the unforeseen circumstances in your procedure may have caused irreparable damage to your brain."

John looked over at Jean as tears filled her eyes.

"Is that why I can't remember anything? Anything except the day I met Mary?"

"We aren't a hundred percent sure, but we think so. Captain Meadowbrook's experts suspect you were thinking about that memory when you woke during the procedure. Since Dr. Smith had to complete the installation of the neuronet without the exercises, we think the neuronet initiated in the wrong sequence, which caused the malfunction. They believe that's why you've been experiencing these symptoms and why you've lost your memory."

"Can it be fixed?" John's eyes lit up with hope. "Can I get my memories back?"

His excitement lasted only a moment as the dam holding back Jean's tears gave way. They streamed down her face as she apologized. "I'm so sorry. I never imagined anything like this could have happened. I never—"

John cut her off, "So... I can't? My memories are gone. Is it your fault? Is that why you're so upset? Did you do this to me?" John's voice rose in anger.

"Yes, it's all my fault. I'm so sorry." Jean broke down and rushed out of the room.

"John, calm down," Captain Meadowbrook said, asserting his presence. "This was not Nurse Jean's fault."

DETACHMENTS

"No, it was not," Dr. Harry insisted. "Nurse Jean blames herself because she promised you something like this could never happen, and she was the only one of us you trusted, even if only in a small way."

The explanation calmed John, and he dropped his head into his hands as the news settled in his mind. "Am I understanding you right, then? I'm stuck this way? I'll be this empty brain mess for the rest of my life?"

"John, that's why we're here. We wanted to discuss some options with you. We can continue with the traditional approach we have been using and keep you here with us. After several years, our treatment may help you build the coping mechanisms and skills you need to live on your own."

"Years? Several years? There's gotta be a better way. There has to be."

"Well, there may be," Dr. Harry suggested as he looked to Captain Meadowbrook to further the conversation.

"John, my experts have come up with an idea they think might work to at least give you a fulfilling life here. To do it, though, we will need to bring you back to where we did the first procedure. Do you have any memories of where that was?"

John stared at Captain Meadowbrook in amazement. The captain's mouth never moved while he was talking. It was as if his weighty voice somehow existed in John's imagination.

Sensing his wonder, Captain Meadowbrook said, "Our voice doesn't work like yours, John. Our lungs don't push air over vocal cords, as with your species. Instead, our thoughts directly interact with your brain. Your brain then interprets those signals and creates the effect of something like a voice inside your head. People from all over your Earth, regardless of what language they speak, can still understand us. This is why you call us Big Brains. When we mention our species to your kind, your mind interprets our signals as the words 'Big Brains,' but what we're actually saying is something closer to how quickly we can calculate equations."

"But how can that be? You mean, like, you can read minds? You can control what we think?"

"No, not at all. It's more like our brains emit electrical signals that any mammalian brain can interpret. We can speak to any mammal on the planet within the limits of that mammal's intellectual capability. Likewise, our brains interpret the electrical signals in human brains that control speech. Think of it like this: when you see a school of fish on your planet and how they all move in unison, it is almost like they share one brain. That's a decent analogy for how our brains work with our species and how we can communicate with you and other mammals. For us, speech is closer to another sense than to a language."

John nodded in appreciation of Captain Meadowbrook's explanation. "I guess that makes sense. I just, well, now I have a million questions, like why are we here, humans, I mean, and—"

"In good time. Right now, I want to talk more about your treatment."

"Oh, yeah... of course."

"Do you remember anything about where we performed your neuronet procedure?"

"No, not at all. Why?"

"We use a special system there that allows us to put you under without drugs. That system didn't keep you under last time, so we're concerned about using it again with you. That's why I'm here, John."

"Okay," John said, with confusion.

"The system I'm talking about is an artificial version of a defense mechanism my species uses. It's how we protect ourselves from threats, since our vestigial arms and legs don't give us the ability to fight off threats like your species can. Instead, we effectively move things telekinetically. Now what—"

"Teleka? Teleka what?"

"My apologies. The human brain often interprets how we describe our ability as telekinesis or moving things telekinetically. That's not a terribly accurate description, but you must have heard that word at some point for your brain to interpret my signals that way. Does that make sense?"

"Yes, I think so. You can move things with your mind, and my mind interprets that as telekinesis. Right?"

"Yes, that's right. Our telekinetic abilities allow us to put living organisms into a stasis-like state for as long as needed to ensure our safety. This technique has no lasting effects, and most species awaken feeling well-rested."

John's mouth was wide open in complete disbelief at what he was hearing, thinking, or sensing; whatever the means, Captain Meadowbrook was communicating with him.

"Why are you telling me all of this? What does any of this have to do with fixing my brain?"

"Well, we're very concerned about the lengthy nature of the work we need to do on the neuronet in your brain. We're concerned you may wake up again, and we think this time it could kill you. No one wants that, John. No one."

"Is there anything we can do to make sure that doesn't happen?"

"Unfortunately, the only way to be a hundred percent certain is to rely on traditional treatment. But if you permit me, I'm willing to stay here to test whether the stasis will work in your current condition."

"What do you mean, test it?"

"Since the stasis room works on the same principles as our defense mechanism, I want to put you in stasis with my mind and see if I can hold you there long enough for the procedure. Are you okay with me trying that?"

"Right here? You want to do that now?"

"Well, yes, but I want you to try to stop me from doing it. We think whatever you were thinking about may have caused you to wake from the stasis. Are you up to trying this?"

John thought about it momentarily. "If this works, you're going to do the procedure on me? The next time I wake up?"

"No, no. We're just going to test it here today. Once we're satisfied it's working, we'll ask if you want to proceed. Is that okay?"

"Okay, yeah, I'm okay with that. I'm ready when you are. What do you want me—"

Before John could finish his sentence, Captain Meadowbrook placed him into stasis.

After about fifteen minutes, Captain Meadowbrook released the stasis, and John woke up.

"Oh, sorry, I must have dozed off. Did you want to test that stasis thing?"

After a muted laugh, Dr. Harry said, "He already did. Did you have a nice nap? He had you out for about fifteen minutes."

"Actually, yes, it was a pretty nice nap indeed. So does that mean it's safe to do the procedure?"

"No, not yet, John. That was just a first test," Captain Meadowbrook revealed. "Did you have any dreams or memories while you were out?"

"No, I don't... no, I don't think so, no."

"Okay, I want to try this again, but this time, concentrate on the memory you told us about—the one about the day you met Mary. Could you do that for me?"

"Oh sure, that's a wonderful memory. I'm happy to."

"Okay, now, while you're concentrating on that, I want you to stay awake. Do you understand what I mean?"

"I understand, yes, but is that even possible?"

"There have only been a few people in unique situations where they have been able to do that. We're thinking you might be like those people, which could explain what happened with your procedure."

"Okay, I can try. Are you ready for me to give it a shot?"

"Yes. Now, focus on that memory."

John shut his eyes and concentrated his mind on that one memory— the only memory that remained of Mary. In a moment, he was out.

After another fifteen minutes, Captain Meadowbrook released John from stasis.

"Lemme guess," John said as he woke. "It worked again, didn't it?"

DETACHMENTS

"Yes, John, perfectly. I'd like to try one more test before we consider moving forward. I'm going to put you into stasis and keep you there until morning. Once again, concentrate on that memory of Mary, okay? If all goes well tomorrow morning, we'll decide whether to move forward with the procedure, okay?"

"Yes, that's okay. That works for me."

"Okay, have a great night's sleep, John. We'll return in the morning. If you have any problems tonight, just hit the call button. Nurse Clara will be here all night. Sleep well."

Unbeknownst to most of the camp residents, the stage was set. A battle for the Rev Rehab was inevitable. Doc's friends had teamed up with the Drongs to save him from the Serpentis. The Serpentis leaders were looking for Shirley. She was already their partner, whether she wanted to be or not. The staff at the infirmary were unaware of the brewing war. The camp's rival gangs were on course for a head-on collision, and John's friends were committed inextricably to it.

Doc remained in the custody of the Serpentis, but they had grown bored with actively torturing him. He continued a miserable existence in their captivity, provided only with the basic needs to keep him alive, existing in a kind of limbo between life and death. Since Doc's last encounter with Nick and Leo, his only reference point for the time of day was the occasional visits from the Serpentis with food and water and the twice-passing of the two moons overhead.

With Doc receiving more regular food and water, he regained some of his strength, and his throat started to heal. He was alone in his thoughts, its own kind of torture. He was thankful for the solitude from the beatings and constant smoke. His mind often drifted to whatever might happen with John. *Did my help once again lead to a friend's death? Is John undergoing rehabilitation? Is he dealing with some fresh horror?*

185

Unbeknownst to Doc, that was precisely what John was experiencing on the eve of the most significant decision of his torn-asunder life. He wanted to believe John had already found his way back to Earth, that at least one of them might escape the Big Brains' oppression or the Serpentis' wrath—a wrath that Shirley, too, was soon to endure. Doc lamented how he had been so weak to have served her up to the Serpentis on a platter. The depths to which they might stoop to force her to help them filled him with guilt beyond any he had ever experienced. At least with his two attempts to help friends escape, they were both willing participants. Shirley had no warning for the hell that was coming her way, and he could do nothing to protect her. Perhaps it was already too late. Perhaps the Serpentis had already done their worst to her.

In the distance, Doc heard the crushing of leaves, steadily growing louder—the telltale sound of the Serpentis returning.

CHAPTER 25

Lunch had only been a couple of hours ago. This was not a welfare call. Something was happening. Doc heard a voice as the Serpentis approached. "Did he say why?"

"No, he just said to get back here."

Two Serpentis breached the entrance. Doc did not recognize them as anyone in particular. Perhaps they had been two of the men who tortured him, but he could not be sure. As the men settled onto a rock, Doc could hear more people coming up the path toward him.

"Can you fuckin' believe that bitch?" It sounded like Nick approaching.

"I dunno. She might be telling the truth." The accent was unmistakably Leo.

"Don't give me that shit. She's lying because she doesn't want to help us," Nick responded as he and Leo entered Doc's vision.

Nick paused and looked around, then focused on the two Serpentis that had arrived before them.

"Where the fuck is everyone? It's just you two?"

"Uh, I dunno, Capo. We just got here a few minutes ago."

Another couple of men shuffled into the area, followed by a few more. Eventually, all ten men Nick expected had arrived. "It's about damn time. You know we're trying to win a fuckin' war here. Sit your asses down. Here's the deal. We finally found that bitch, Shirley. She admitted to having been able to shut out the Big Brains once but refuses to help us. This bitch expects me to believe she can't do it again. So, we're gonna have—"

"She can't!" Doc exclaimed.

"What the fuck did you just say? Have you not been getting enough attention from us lately? You need some more beatings, Doc?"

"No, no, I just—"

"Nick, like I said, I didn't sense she was lying, and I'm usually pretty good at these things," Leo said.

"Shut the fuck up. You're just thinking with your dick. You see a pretty face, and suddenly she can't be fuckin' us over?"

"It was just the one time. That's what she told John and me... that's what she told you, right? It was just once, wasn't it?" Doc asked.

Nick turned around and slapped Doc hard across the face. "Are you out of your fuckin' mind? You just like the beatings or something?"

Doc shook off the sting of the slap. "I'm just trying to tell you she helped John focus on the loss of his girl and his baby, but her mom has been dead for years. The pain and anguish of the love lost has faded, so she can't do it anymore."

Nick turned, looked at his men, and realized Leo was buying into Doc's assertion.

"You... gag this fuckin' piece of shit before he says something that earns him a one-way trip to the infirmary."

Nick's goon jumped up and taped Doc's mouth.

"Here's what we're gonna do," Nick said. "We're gonna drag that bitch over here, and we're gonna show her what happens to a woman when they don't cooperate with the Serpentis."

The men hooted and hollered at Nick's implication since it had been some time since either of the gangs had jumped a woman in. It was the morale boost the Serpentis needed before going to war with the Drongs for the Rev Rehab. Leo sat quietly, slowly shaking his head.

"What, Leo? I thought you liked this woman. Why so quiet? Shut up, shut up, everyone... quiet down. Let me make this clear: No one... you hear me? No one gets so much as a look at Shirley till Leo has had all he wants. Have I made myself clear?"

The gang all nodded in agreement and returned to their grotesque celebration. Leo sat, distressed by his capo's announcement. He felt there was no amount of horror they could unleash on Shirley that could increase her ability to help them steal the serum. She did not deserve the hell the Serpentis planned to inflict upon her.

Doc looked upon the atrocity he had unleashed on Shirley but was helpless to intervene.

"All right. All right. Settle down. Settle down! I need two volunteers."

It was clear Nick had already formed a plan. Every hand but Leo's shot up to the sky.

"Now, before any of you get too excited, let me explain. I don't think any of you are gonna like what I want you to do."

The group grew more silent, confused about what their capo might have in mind.

"Okay, we're gonna attempt to steer her near here to keep the Big Brains out of our way. Once we've got her close enough and she realizes she's run out of places to go, she's gonna try to run. That's where the two volunteers come in. They'll be the initial strike. She can't weigh more than a buck-o-five. Should be easy for any of you pussies to manage," Nick goaded his men.

"I'll do it, boss. I got this."

"Hang on. You haven't heard the hard part yet. Now, here's the critical part: as soon as Shirley hits the ground, I need these two volunteers to have a knockdown, drag-out brawl with each other to distract the Big Brains while the rest of us scoop her up and run her back here before the Big Brains are onto us. So, who's my volunteers?"

Suddenly, the group was silent, with no hands in the air and no celebrating—only the sound of muffled laughter from the background that earned Doc another smack from Nick.

"Now look. I know I'm asking a lot from you, but think about it. If we get Shirley, we get the serum. If we get the serum, we can fix you as soon as they bring you back to camp."

Doc could see the heads of several Serpentis nodding in agreement. Nick was gaining support for his plan.

"Ah, fuck it! I'll do it."

"No, I don't think so, Leo. Not you. We're not waiting a week for you to get back before we have our party with Shirley. You missed out on the other women we've jumped in, but you're leading the way this time. My deputy gets all the perks." Nick grinned with enthusiasm for the reward he was giving Leo.

"Yeah… thanks, Capo. I, uh… I'm grateful."

Doc could tell Leo could never force himself on Shirley. He was a brutal man. Doc was sure about that, but apparently, he had limits.

"Who's it gonna be, then?" Nick asked as he surveyed his gang.

"Dang, okay, we'll do it. This serum bullshit better work."

The two men who first arrived for the planning meeting volunteered for the brawl.

"Great," Nick said. "You guys are usually hanging out together. Are you gonna be able to make this believable?"

"Oh yeah, I'm gonna kick this fucker's ass. Don't you worry."

"Bullshit, you're mine, motherfucker."

The men all laughed and continued their banter as their capo tried to bring the group back to the task at hand and finish their evil scheming for Shirley's planned capture and rape. Nick walked them through his idea. Since she had met Nick and Leo, they would have to lead the effort. Since Shirley rarely ever left Apartment 19, their plan would have to start there. Nick and Leo would be the first to show their faces. They would move in on her, pushing her toward the other Serpentis in pre-positioned areas. If Shirley tried to evade Nick and Leo, the other Serpentis would be there to corral her into their trap. They all agreed, and then, like breaking a football huddle, the men left the area to go recon where they would need to hide for the plan to work.

The beep at the door ended John's slumber.

"Good morning, John," Nurse Clara greeted him as she entered. "How was your sleep?"

"Well, considering my memory situation, I can honestly say that was the best night's sleep I can remember ever having," John said with a chuckle that caught Nurse Clara a bit by surprise.

"Oh, well, I'm glad you're feeling pretty good then. I've brought you a change of clothes. The medical team will arrive soon, so if you get cleaned up, we'll be back in a bit."

"Okay, uh… thank you."

The door beeped, but John called out before the nurse could leave, "Oh, Nurse Clara, will Nurse Jean be with the team today? I was hoping to apologize for yesterday."

"Oh, sorry, John, I don't think Nurse Jean is ready to get back on this case. She's still pretty upset."

"Oh no. I'm sorry to hear that. Could you tell her I'm very sorry for how I acted? And tell her that if I once trusted her, she must have done something pretty special. There's no way she could have been at fault for this situation. Would you do that for me?"

"Sure, John, I'll let her know," Clara said as she departed.

John cleaned up for his visit with the medical team. About thirty minutes later, the door beep sounded once again. The medical team and Captain Meadowbrook entered, but Jean was not with them.

"John, how are you feeling?" Captain Meadowbrook asked.

"I feel fine. I slept through the night with no problems."

"That's very good to hear. Since that went so well, I'm willing to authorize the procedure my technicians would like to try. That's, of course, only if you're interested in continuing."

"I'm honestly not sure yet. Can you give me a sense of what the risks will be?"

"If I'm being entirely honest, we aren't certain. The human brain is extremely complex. On this planet, it's second in complexity only to ours. We've figured a lot out, and the neuronet is a direct result of that work, but there's still so much we don't understand, especially as it relates to human emotions. All that to say, I think there's a real possibility things could get worse, but it's only a remote possibility, according to my specialists. They believe the most likely outcome is that they will be able to give you a functioning baseline so you can live a normal life, make friends, and enjoy hobbies here—"

"Here in the medical building?" John impatiently asked.

"No, with other humans here on Twin Moons as well. We have a camp with a few thousand humans living there. We think you'll find it like the life you knew on Earth."

"A camp, like a prison camp? Is that what you mean?"

"It's not a prison. Think of it more like a reservation. It's a home for your people. You'll have everything there you would ever need, but it is an isolated camp in that you cannot visit other areas of the planet. Like many places on your Earth, there is some crime and violence, but most people have a very enjoyable life there. We understand it's not a perfect solution, but it's the best we can do for the humans we end up bringing back here."

"What do you mean, it's the best you can do? Why do you bring us here at all? What are you doing to us? Even with the little sense I've got left, I know you can't be doing this for our benefit."

CHAPTER 26

John could sense the unease in the room and on the faces of his medical team. He knew Captain Meadowbrook was holding back.

"John, I will share this with you to keep you calm so you can decide whether to proceed with this plan. We Big Brains live very long lives, some of us over three hundred of your Earth years. I, myself, am a hundred and seventy-five. Unfortunately, about seventy-five years ago, we suffered an outbreak that initially killed many of our species. We developed some remedies to keep the symptoms at bay, but it still decimated our overall life expectancy. After a technological breakthrough that made it possible for us to travel in ways we never thought possible, we researched other species that we believed had developed immunity or resistance to the pathogen. That research led us to your Earth and your species. Your species had the right attributes, allowing us to combine your resistance with our immune system."

"So, you just take us away from our families? You kidnap us so you can survive? What about our lives?"

"I understand why it looks that way, John. In the early years, we had no choice but to bring people here. The ship we use today, though, the SG331, has everything we need to extract the samples, so we rarely have to bring humans here anymore. You're the first one I had to bring back with us in over five years. The SG331 is where we'll bring you today if you want to proceed."

"So you abducted me, took samples from me so some Big Brain could live longer, and now I never get to see my family again?"

"Actually, John," Nurse Clara said, "the Big Brains only choose people who don't have a family. It's one of their rules in case they have to bring someone back here."

"That's right, John. We have safety protocols to prevent that," Captain Meadowbrook said. "So, you see, you couldn't have a—"

"But wasn't it a safety protocol that failed when I lost my memories? If that protocol failed, how do you know I don't have a family?"

"It's true, John… we can't know for certain. We're terribly sorry for what has happened—"

The door beeped, interrupting Captain Meadowbrook. Nurse Jean walked in. "Captain Meadowbrook, I just wanted to let you know your technicians have arrived, and they're in the stasis room awaiting guidance."

"Thank you, Nurse."

As Nurse Jean turned to leave, John called out, "Nurse Jean, please, could you wait a moment?"

John stepped down from his bed and walked toward Jean. "I wanted to apologize for my outburst, and I'd like you to continue to be part of my medical team. I've got to choose whether to continue with this procedure, and after learning everything, I'm not sure I want to. Would you please stay? I'd especially like to hear your opinion on the matter."

Jean turned back toward John. "John, you have nothing to apologize for. I was never upset with you for how you reacted. I was upset about how awful your procedure went and what it's done to you. If it helps you for me to be here, I will stay. I just wasn't sure if my presence was more harm than good."

"Please stay, Nurse. I'd very much appreciate it." John returned to his bed, and Jean remained near Nurse Clara as the conversation continued.

"You were saying, Captain?"

"I was saying… we're very sorry for what happened to you, and while there is a remote chance that people we bring here have some family, we do everything we can to prevent that. I'm afraid, though, we've found ourselves in a situation where, if that occurred, we don't have a way of undoing it, especially given your current state. I'm afraid the best we can hope for is to give you as good a life as we can from this point forward."

Captain Meadowbrook's comments landed heavily on John, and as much as he wanted to debate or yell, he believed he had limited options.

"Is there anything else I need to know before I decide?"

"I think we covered everything. Do you have any questions left?"

"How will I know if it was successful?"

"Ideally, you won't. You'll wake up in the camp as if none of this ever happened, with no memory of me or this conversation. You'll just be ready to enjoy your new life with the other humans in the camp."

"And what do you think, Jean?"

"I… I don't, uh… oh God… I don't think you want to know what I think."

"No, I do. I want your opinion more than anyone else in this room. Please."

"John, I think… I think this has been an absolute tragedy. The one memory you have is of someone you love. I don't know if she loves you. I don't know if she's even alive, but I believe in my bones that she's someone you care deeply about. As a human—" Jean glanced with a hint of prejudice toward Captain Meadowbrook. "As a human, knowing that if you go through with this procedure, that one memory you have of Mary will be gone forever makes my heart ache. But as a nurse and a care provider, I know with near certainty that if you don't go through with the procedure, you have a much higher chance of going mad with that one memory in your brain than you have of gaining any of your memories back. I think you will live a much happier life here if the procedure works as expected. I just don't see how any other option can give you that potential for happiness. We're so sorry this happened. I only hope that somehow, in some way we can't yet understand, you'll one day be able to forgive us."

John stared off somewhere between Jean and Captain Meadowbrook, lost in contemplation of Jean's waterfall of wisdom.

"Can I have a few minutes to myself?"

"Certainly," Captain Meadowbrook said. The team left, with Nurse Jean taking one last look back at John as though she had just tucked her child in for bed.

As the door closed, John collapsed to his knees. He did not fully understand why. Something moved him… no, compelled him to pray. His eyelids shut as tight as drums, squeezing a lonely tear from each. His mind turned to his only memory of Mary. He did not know what she meant to him. He did not know if their lives together ever included a second date, but he prayed that if she were the love of his life, they would one day find each other again. John stood, wiped the tears from his eyes, and lay down on his bed as the door signaled his medical team's return.

"Let's do it," John said in a soft but resolute tone.

"Are you sure?" Captain Meadowbrook asked. "I will put you under as soon as you confirm."

"I'm sure."

"It's been very nice talking with you, John."

Those were the last words John heard as the world dimmed.

Still in captivity, Doc felt the hunger growing in his stomach as the scraps he received for what could be called breakfast had faded hours ago. What the Serpentis offered as lunch was already later than usual. His mind refused to focus on anything but whatever evil the Serpentis had planned for Shirley.

Doc heard a commotion off in the distance—yelling and screaming. Moments later, he heard the crunching sound of leaves revealing quick, heavy steps.

"Come on!" he heard one voice yell.

Two Serpentis burst into the hide with Shirley over one of their shoulders. Doc could tell she was unconscious as blood seeped out of a cut just below her swollen left eye. The Serpentis' plan had succeeded, and they had their prize.

The men dropped her to the ground. Her head bounced off the dirt. Doc rolled his head back in anguish and screamed through his gag, "Careful!"

"Stop your bitchin'. She'll be fine."

Nick, Leo, and the other Serpentis trickled in shortly thereafter. Eventually, all but the two volunteers returned.

"Yeah!" Nick yelled. "Uh... how 'bout that? The plan worked like a charm. Now we just gotta get this bitch to cooperate. Wake her the fuck up."

One of the Serpentis grabbed her by her shirt and lifted her chest off the ground. Her head slumped back like that of an unsupported infant. The ghouls then slapped her across the face to bring her around.

"Stop, you fucking idiot!" Doc tried to yell through his gag. No one understood a word he was saying.

"Gimme some water," Shirley's current abuser demanded. He threw water in her face. She did not react at all.

Doc continued to scream through his gag until Nick relented and removed the tape from his mouth.

"What the fuck are you bitchin' about, old man?"

"You dipshits are gonna fucking kill her. I wouldn't be surprised if she's already in a coma. That idiot over there dropped her. She's probably got a concussion. She needs a doctor. If you don't get her to the infirmary, she might die."

"She's not going to the infirmary, Doc. So you better start telling us what to do to make sure she survives."

Doc said, "I need to examine her."

"Yeah, that ain't gonna happen now, is it? So how 'bout you walk me through whatever we need to do?"

197

Doc sighed in disbelief at what was happening before his eyes. "Fine, just lay her down and prop her head up so it's above her heart. Then I need you to open her eyes and tell me what her pupils look like."

The Serpentis did as Doc instructed.

"The pupils—that's the black part of her eyes, right? They're fuckin' huge."

"Did they change at all when you opened her eyelids?"

"Didn't look like it. I don't think so."

"You don't think so? I can't do this! You've gotta let me down."

"Forget it, Doc, not gonna happen."

"There's no way I can make sure... fuck... fine... whatever, we're wasting time. Does anyone have a flashlight?"

"Yeah, here ya go." One of the Serpentis handed it over to the man who helped Doc examine Shirley.

"Okay. Now here's what I need you to do. With one hand, hold one of her eyes open. With the other, I want you to sweep the flashlight across the open eye, shining the light directly into her eye. Tell me what her pupil does."

"Whoa... it got really small."

"Okay, okay... that's good. Now check the other one."

"It's not—oh no, wait, yeah, it's getting smaller, just not as fast as the other one."

"Are they both perfectly round?"

"They are. Yes."

"Okay. Look, Nick, whatever you wanted from this poor woman isn't happening. She's at least got a concussion, and she may have a serious brain injury. The fact that the right eye isn't constricting like the left tells me there's pressure on her brain."

"Fuck!" Nick yelled. "You better not be jerkin' my chain, Doc."

"I swear, I'm telling you the truth. Your thugs hit her too hard, and bouncing her head off the ground almost certainly made it worse. Check the back of her head. I'll bet she's got a good lump back there."

Nick motioned to the Serpentis member, who acted as Doc's hands. Nick's pawn ran his hand around the back of Shirley's head, stopping to look back at Nick to confirm Doc was right.

"How bad is it?" Doc asked. "How far does it stick out? How wide is it?"

"It's sticking out more than half an inch. It's a good two to three inches around."

"That's a pretty good-sized lump. You won't listen to me, but she needs the infirmary. If you're not gonna do that, we need to get ice on both the lump on the back of her head and the swelling on her cheek. We do that, and we get a cool compress on her head, and if we're lucky, she might wake up when the swelling comes down. Otherwise, you probably just murdered her."

Nick was unfazed by the idea of Shirley dying. Unfazed, besides no longer having an advantage in gaining the serum. Regardless, the infirmary was off the table. He sent his men to get the ice packs and cold compresses to treat her. Nick then leaned into Doc.

"You better fuckin' hope she lives. If she can't help us, you can bet I'm gonna make you find a way." Nick reapplied the tape to Doc's mouth.

"Leo, watch over these two. When the boys get back with the supplies, send them all to the Hub. I don't want anyone else out here but you and me in case things take a turn."

"Understood, Capo. Will do!"

Nick departed the area, leaving Leo, Doc, and Shirley to spend the night in the Serpentis' club.

John rustled about on the bed. He yawned and stretched until his skin nearly snapped. He opened his eyes and let the world around him unfold.

As he surveyed the area, his surroundings came into focus. It was his room in the camp; of that, he was sure. It had all the familiarity, but John had no specific recollection of ever being there.

He sat up in his bed. He felt weak for reasons he did not understand. His room was littered with books, clothes, and personal necessities. He got off the bed and went to his window to verify that what he saw matched his expectations. It was nighttime, but the lights revealed he was right where he expected to be—in the camp.

He stood at the window for some time, looking beyond the lights and through the darkness. He saw some residents moving from one place to another. The entire experience felt almost dreamlike, but he knew it was no dream.

Unconvinced, he moved over to the mirror on the wall. Standing before it, he stared at the face looking back at him. He searched for signs of change. His hair was shorter than usual, and he had a few freshly shaved patches. He did not know why, but somehow he expected them to be there and was not concerned. Still, something did not feel right. He took a deep breath to settle his mind and went outside. He looked around his untidy room to get used to what appeared to be his home.

John left his building. He did not have a particular destination but knew where to find everything he might need. He roamed about, trying to make his existence feel more natural. As he turned the corner, he saw three figures in the shadows approaching him.

"John!" Gus yelled.

CHAPTER 27

Rex and Chris realized who they saw and rushed to greet him. Each of them shook hands and hugged. John reciprocated despite not recognizing the men. Regardless, he felt warmed by what he assumed was a customary embrace. Like everyone who returned from the city, he was calmer, smiled more, and genuinely connected better with people. John was no longer preoccupied with returning to Earth, no longer singularly focused on pursuing his goals. Ultimately, he was no longer John.

"How you feelin', mate?" Gus asked.

Chris added, "You have been gone awhile, my friend."

"Do you remember what happened? What'd they do?" Rex asked.

"I don't know. I… honestly, I just, I… uh… I really don't know. It all seems like a dream right now. I'm sorry to say I can't even remember how we know each other, but I know I like all of you. I can feel that. And I'm just so glad to see you all right now."

John's comment garnered sympathy from his friends as their faces drooped in sorrow. None of them had ever had a friend brought beyond the barrier. The stories they heard about Tom and others never directly affected them. This hit close to home, giving them a sense of loss.

"Do not worry about that, brother. We are here for you. We know people come back different. But we will help you in any way we can," Chris said, speaking for the group.

"Thank you, uh—"

"Chris. I am Chris, this is Rex, and the big guy over here, that is Gus."

"It's great to meet or see all of you again. It's nice to know I've got some friends. Where were you guys headed?" he asked.

"I'll tell you what. Your room's the closest. Why don't we head back there? We can catch you up on what's been happening around here. Sound like a plan?" Rex asked.

John nodded in agreement and led them toward his room.

"At least you seem to remember where you're going, anyway?" Rex teased, testing John's boundaries.

"It's the weirdest thing. I feel like I know this place. It's like I belong here, but I can't say I recall ever being here. Does that make any sense?" John said in an unconcerned tone.

"Yeah, I suppose I can get where you're comin' from," Gus said as they reached John's door.

The men entered the room, and each found a comfortable chair. Two sat at the table in the small breakfast nook, and one on the couch. John turned his desk chair to face his friends and sat down.

Rex kicked off the inquisition. He was always the most direct of the group. "John, what do you remember about Mary?"

"Mary? Who's Mary?" John asked. "Is she someone here in the camp?"

John's friends froze. Rex's question surprised them, but John's response left them in shock. Their faces blanched, and their eyes widened in horror.

"John, my friend, you don't remember Mary?" Chris asked.

"No, I don't, but I didn't remember any of you either, so that doesn't seem too odd, does it?"

DETACHMENTS

"Look, I don't wanna make this awkward, but what d'you remember, mate?" Gus asked.

John looked up in search of his memories. "Honestly, I can't say I remember, well... anything," John said with no sense of alarm or worry, as though he had no expectations of having memories.

"John, this might be a bit hard to take, but," Gus said, "we ain't on Earth. These Big Brains nicked us, all of us, and now they're makin' us live in this camp."

Unfazed, John said, "Oh, yeah, that. I feel like I knew that already, so what does that have to do with this Mary person?"

"Mary was... uh... is... she was your girl back on Earth, John. She was pregnant with your kid. You were takin' her to the hospital to have the baby when those Big Brains snatched you, mate."

The weight of Gus's words landed like sand pouring into a basket on John's chest. At first, he almost disregarded it, but as the basket filled, the weight of the knowledge became unbearable until John could no longer hold his cheerful demeanor.

"But how can this be? How can I not have memories of this person? What happened to me?" John asked in near desperation.

"It's the Big Brains, mate. When someone gets caught fightin' or doin' somethin' they shouldn't, the Big Brains drag 'em off to their city and, sometimes, wipe their memory. This was your first screw-up, though. We didn't think you'd cop a full wipe, not like they did with Tom," Gus said.

"What did I do? Why did the Big Brains do this to me?" John asked. While unsure, he suspected the Big Brains had a good reason.

With that, the men explained to John what had happened since he first arrived at the camp. They described his and Doc's plan to return to Earth and how they spread rumors so John could practice fighting off the Big Brains. They described the serum the Serpentis tried to make John steal, the huge fight they caused between Antonio and Sal, Doc's captivity, and their agreement to get the serum for the Drongs in exchange for their help to rescue Doc.

"You are back, though. That changes things. Even without being able to fight off the Big Brains, you are a powerful guy. Maybe with your help, we don't need the Drongs after all," Chris wondered aloud.

"I... uh, fight? I—"

Before John could finish, Gus said, "Oi, let's give John a bit of time, yeah? He's only just got back and needs to rest up. No need to go through all this tonight, is there?"

With that, the men all agreed, and John's friends left his room for the evening.

Shirley remained peacefully on the ground, her head still propped up. Leo applied ice packs to her injuries at intervals, as Doc recommended. He believed Leo genuinely hoped she would make it through the night. He was unsure if that was more out of concern for her or more for the good of the Serpentis, but Leo was worried. There had never been a murder in the camp, so no one knew how the Big Brains might react to such a crime. Leo would catch some sleep on and off throughout the night. He slept beside Shirley on the ground, waking at the faintest noises that might suggest distress.

This night was no different for Doc. He would catch some rest here or there, still tied to the tree, but at least he was no longer gagged. Leo had grown tired of taking the gag off whenever he needed advice to care for Shirley. Doc was more skeptical that she would survive. He had seen people survive worse injuries without medical treatment but believed such hope was ill-placed, given her injuries. He started to nod off again when a faint choking sound drew his attention. It was subdued, but loud enough to pull Leo from his slumber.

"Shirley, you there? You awake?" Leo startled Doc to full alertness.

The choking sounds grew louder and more pronounced.

"Roll her on her side!" Doc shouted.

Leo complied as he rolled Shirley to her side. She began coughing up phlegm, mucus, or perhaps vomit. Her body then went stiff, and moments later, she was convulsing.

"Doc, what do I do?"

"You gotta cut me down. I can't do anything from here."

"There's not a fucking chance. Tell me what to do!"

"Fuck! Protect her head… especially where that lump is. Use your wallet or something soft to keep her from biting down and hurting her tongue."

"Wallet? You think I'm carrying a fucking wallet around?"

"Okay, try to keep her on her side so she doesn't choke to death, and try to keep her mouth clear."

Leo followed Doc's instructions, fluid still dripping from Shirley's mouth. The seizure continued into the second minute. Her eyes rolled back deep into her head. Sweat poured off her brow. Doc could see her dark skin had become ashen.

"She's having a seizure! Check her heart rate!"

"It's racing, Doc. No… no. Wait. It seems to be slowing now. Hang on. I can't… lemme check here. I can't—"

"Is she still breathing? Can you feel her breath?"

"I don't think she's breathing. I can't find her heartbeat! What do I do? What do—"

"You gotta cut me the fuck down! There's nothing you can do. Either cut me down or sit there and watch her fucking die!"

Leo could take no more. He stood up and cut Doc free. Doc rushed to Shirley's side and checked for a pulse. Nothing. He laid her onto her back and began rhythmic chest compressions.

"Come on, Shirley… don't you let go. Not you too, come on! Leo, get over here and take over."

Doc guided Leo to the exact spot where he wanted him to perform chest compressions. Once Leo got the rhythm right, Doc tilted Shirley's head back, opened her mouth, and reached in with his fingers.

"What are you doing?"

"Just keep at those compressions! I'm making sure there's nothing still left in her mouth. She might be choking on vomit. I'm gonna try something."

Doc performed mouth-to-mouth resuscitation while Leo continued chest compressions. She had been without a heartbeat for close to a minute as Doc gave her several breaths. After some initial resistance, the air flowed easier, and Doc could fill her lungs. Leo and Doc kept at it for another thirty seconds when Shirley coughed violently.

"She's alive!" Doc screamed. "Quick, let's roll her back on her side."

Doc kept giving her stiff pats on her back while she coughed up whatever debris she had previously inhaled or Doc inadvertently forced into her lungs. The dark honey-brown color of her skin returned as she opened her eyes. Her coughing continued, bringing up more of the substance that nearly killed her. She spit it out on the ground as she worked to catch her breath.

"What the fuck? Why the fuck is Doc down from the tree? Are you fucking kidding me?" In the commotion, neither Doc nor Leo heard Nick approaching from the path.

CHAPTER 28

Leo scrambled to his feet. "Nick! She's alive. She's gonna be all right. She's gonna be all right, isn't she, Doc?"

"I don't think—"

"I'll tell you what I don't think. I don't think Doc should be off that fuckin' tree. Are you outta your fuckin' mind?"

"Are you not hearing me, Nick? Shirley died! She was dead. Doc just brought her back to life. If I didn't cut him down, she'd be dead, and any hope of getting your precious fuckin' serum would be gone."

Still catching her breath, Shirley tried to speak, managing only a few grunts and groans.

"It's okay. Everything is gonna be okay," Leo said as he consoled her.

Shirley struggled to open her eyes and understand what was happening around her. After several minutes of trying to regain some composure, Shirley scooted closer to Doc in a more upright position, almost instinctively trying to hide behind him.

Doc put his arm around Shirley. "It's okay, Shirley, you're okay. Now, take it easy. You've still got two pretty nasty head injuries."

"What happened? Oh my God! It's you two? What do you want from me? How did I get here?"

"Okay, someone better start explaining," Nick said.

"She started choking, I—"

Doc took over the explanation. "I'm pretty sure the concussion caused some nausea, and she vomited a little while she was unconscious. That caused her to choke, and she started convulsing. I walked Leo through treating her, but eventually, her breathing and her heart stopped."

"So, I cut him down!" Leo asserted in defiance.

"It's a good thing, too," Doc added. "Without Leo helping with the chest compressions while I cleared her mouth and lungs to give her mouth-to-mouth, there's no way she'd have made it. Leo saved her life as much as I did."

"Saved my life? What happened? What did you two do to me? I remember seeing you both and trying to get away from you and your goons, but nothing since. What have you done?" Shirley asked, still exhausted from her trauma. Her words trailed off.

"It's my fault," Doc said. "It's my fault. I caused all of this. Nick and the Serpentis believe you can help them steal a serum that will undo the effects of the Big Brain mind-wipes. I told them you helped John learn to prevent the Big Brains from incapacitating him. I'm so sorry I wasn't strong enough to protect you from them."

Nick lost his patience. "All right, enough of this bullshit! She's gonna live, and she's gonna do the job we need her to do. Now help me tie this piece of shit back up."

Nick and Leo tied Doc to the tree as the sun crept over the horizon. Nick then turned his attention to Shirley, for what would be an excruciating interrogation. Doc briefly considered trying to fight back against the men, but he did not want to risk reinvigorating Leo's ire. They had saved a life together, and perhaps that might pay dividends later.

The next day, Rex and the others were in the lunchroom having breakfast while trying to make plans to rescue Doc. Upon entering the lunchroom, John noticed the men, grabbed his food, and headed toward them. He sat down, gulped some water, and looked at Rex while he was talking. John was eager to engage. Rex took one look at him and stopped talking, allowing John to interrupt.

"I guess you were talking about Doc and the gangs, weren't ya?"

"Yes," Chris acknowledged. "We are in a real bind and do not know what we will do about it."

"Man, I'm sorry. From what it sounds like, this was all my fault. I got Doc and all of you into this mess trying to help me."

The men sat, surprised by John's conclusion. He had always been so obsessed with his pursuit that he never showed this type of concern for his friends.

"Oi, listen. We'd have done this for anyone, knowin' what you'd been through," Gus said.

"Yes, I know Doc would say the same," Chris said.

"I dunno about all that. I had nothing better to do, so…" Rex joked.

John grinned. He found Rex's humor refreshing. "I appreciate that. It also explains why I'm gonna help you get Doc back."

"What? He's in, yeah… we can—"

"Hold on, hold on," John said. "Listen, I said I'll help, but don't go getting excited about me fighting anyone. I'm just not the violent type. Honestly, I'm having a hard time believing I ever was… it just seems so, I don't know, foolish? I guess?"

Chris shook his head as he processed John's words. Gus took a deep breath to speak when Rex beat him to the punch and summarized the situation perfectly.

"And… we're fucked."

"Now hang on. I'm sure we can think of a good plan that doesn't require violence, even if these aren't rational people. I'll bet if we put our heads together, we'll figure this out."

"We've been racking our brains for four days now, and we haven't come up with shit. Now you think we can come up with a non-violent way? Man, they did a number on you," Rex said.

"Look, we ain't been gettin' anywhere on our own, have we? So who knows? Let's see what John's got to say, yeah?"

"Thanks, Gus. Listen, I'm not sure yet, but I wanna help. So, can you run me back through everything that's happened since I've been gone? Maybe then I'll have some ideas."

The men finished their breakfast and wandered about the camp. They described in more detail everything they knew about Doc's apparent capture, his unknown whereabouts, the deal they made with the Drongs, the Rev Rehab serum, and, of course, the fight between Antonio and Sal that allowed the Drongs to take over pretty much all the illicit activity within the camp.

"Let me ask you this: have you told anyone else my mind has been wiped?"

The men all looked at each other while shaking their heads as if they had not.

"Okay, no one knows I can't fight the Big Brains then, right?"

With a glint of recognition for John's plan, Gus said, "Nah, no one… not even the—"

"Drongs!" Chris chimed in.

"Exactly," John said. "If they think I can shut down the Big Brains, maybe we can get them to tell us where the Serpentis are hiding, Doc, and we can rescue him ourselves."

"I dunno, I don't see them helping us until we get them the serum," Rex shared his doubts. "We agreed to get them the serum first. Face it, we're fucked."

"Guys, you agreed; I didn't. If they want the serum bad enough and believe I can still take out the Big Brains, they'll want my help. Doc's whereabouts are my price. We might just be able to pull it off."

"Okay, hang on. Let's assume the Drongs buy it and they tell us where Doc is. Then what?" Rex asked. "It's still just the three of us against the Serpentis, and since you're not gonna fight, we're gonna get killed."

"That's true. I'm not gonna go looking for a fight. I'm sorry. But didn't you say the Big Brains will come and stop people from fighting?"

"But the way the Serpentis block the doors at the Hub? They know how to keep the Big Brains from intervening. They must be holding Doc where they feel safe from that," Chris said.

"If we can get the Drongs to spill where he's at, we might be able to get the Big Brains to step in before we catch it too bad. Worst case? We end up back here a bit like John is now," Gus said.

"Are you serious? Like John? You're nuts. I don't want them messing with my head, man. We gotta find a better way," Rex said.

"Rex, mate, we've been at this way too long already. I've got no clue what they're doin' to him, but I reckon Doc ain't holdin' up too well. Look, we could get done in by the Drongs for not nickin' the serum, taken out by the Serpentis tryin' to save Doc, or maybe the Big Brains step in, and we come back… well, not quite ourselves. But for Doc? That's gotta be worth the risk, ain't it?"

The men pondered what Gus had to say without finalizing their plan. Regardless of how to get Doc freed, they knew their next step was to get Doc's whereabouts from the Drongs. If the plan failed there, all remaining options were irrelevant.

Nick had limited patience and was ready to start in on the barely conscious Shirley, but Leo set clear boundaries for what he would tolerate.

"Nick, fuckin' relax! There's no rush here. She just came to. Even if she can help us with the Big Brains, she's not gonna have the strength to do a damn thing unless we give her a chance to recover."

Nick could see the wisdom in Leo's point. "Even if she can? Oh, she can, and she will! Isn't that right, Shirley? You're gonna help, right, Shirley?" Nick's voice rose, trying to break through Shirley's exhaustion and semi-conscious state.

"Look, Nick, she's in no condition to help. Hell, she can barely talk. Why don't you let me deal with her till she's strong enough? She's had nothing to drink in nearly a day. Let me get some water in her. Have one of the guys bring back some food from the lunchroom, and we'll see how she is later tonight."

Nick glared at Leo's insubordination but lacked any valid argument against Leo's suggestion.

"I'm gonna give you till nightfall. After that, we're doing things my way. You got me?"

"Sure, Boss, I got ya. Just send someone back with some food, and I'm sure she'll be in a much better place by nightfall."

Nick barely acknowledged Leo's response as he walked off from the Serpentis' lair. He was barely out of earshot when Leo turned to Doc.

"I bought her some time. How far did I stick my neck out there? Is there a chance she'll be able to talk to Nick tonight? Can she do the job?"

"I dunno, get some water in her, and maybe she can answer some questions, but she needs the infirmary. As far as the Big Brains—"

"I can't..." Shirley pushed the words past her lips as Leo grabbed some water and helped her sit up in a better position to drink.

Doc could barely believe his eyes as Leo showed genuine concern for Shirley's well-being. The sight of this hardened brute softening was almost impossible to believe.

As Shirley gulped down the water, Leo cleaned the dried and gritty blood from her face, her striking features coming into focus once again.

"I can't," Shirley repeated, this time with more clarity. Her breathing was heavy from having held her breath too long while trying to take in so much water. "It was only that one time I ever could. I just did it... There wasn't time to think."

"Relax, don't worry about that now," Leo instructed, bringing the water back to her.

Trying to take advantage of Leo's increasing bond with Shirley, Doc said, "Leo, she needs a doctor. She needs to go to the infirmary."

"It's not an option, Doc," Leo said, shaking his head in shame. "We'll do the best we can, but I'll be in that infirmary right next to her if I try anything like that."

"Leo, it's right there—"

"Doc. I said it's not happening. Now, unless you want the gag back on, I suggest you let it go."

A few moments later, a Serpenti returned with food for Shirley and her caregivers. Doc got his normal ration, while Leo ensured Shirley received all she wanted before taking his first bite of the day.

"How you feelin' now? Now that you got a little food and water in you?"

"I'm just, I'm just tired. I wanna rest."

"Doc. Hey, Doc. She says she's tired and wants to rest. Is that okay?"

"Check her eyes again like we did last night. How's her pupils reacting?"

Leo grabbed the flashlight and had Shirley look straight ahead while sweeping the light back and forth across her eyes. First, her left, then her right.

"They're both acting the same now. Both seem to get small pretty quick."

"Shirley, we're gonna let you nap, but Leo's gonna have to wake you up in a bit to make sure you're okay."

Leo nodded his understanding of Doc's instructions and helped Shirley into a more comfortable position.

"She might still experience some nausea, so keep her on her side to stop her from choking again."

Leo and Doc watched over her throughout the morning, waking her every hour to make sure she wasn't slipping into a coma. Leo ensured she received plenty of water between her naps. As the day progressed, she grew noticeably stronger when sitting up to eat her meals. When her dinner meal arrived, the rest, the water, and the food significantly aided her improvement. She could sit up independently and no longer required Leo's help to eat or drink. Her recovery was going about as well as anyone could hope.

Lunch had come and gone. The men were too caught up in developing their plan to be bothered. They rehearsed their approach to help John pretend he could still thwart the Big Brains' defense mechanism. He was going to have to lead the way with the Drongs. Chris, Rex, and Gus had already sealed their fate. John presented their only way out.

"Do you feel like you are ready?" Chris asked.

"Yeah, I guess so. I'm probably about as ready as I'm gonna be. Where do we find the Drongs?"

"From what I've seen," Rex said, "once the Drongs took everything over, Mick has mostly been hanging out at the Hub. Let's start there."

"Okay, let's do this," John said.

"Whoa! Easy there, mate. Uh, is it just me, or is anyone else feelin' a bit peckish?" Gus asked.

The group chuckled but quickly agreed that Gus was making a good point.

"Yes. We should eat some dinner before we do this. If things do not go well, we may not get another chance for some time," Chris said.

The group headed toward the lunchroom to grab their meals. None of the men finished their plates, all too distracted by their task.

Rex was the first to break the silence as the men sat around the table contemplating the coming events.

"I guess there's no sense delaying the inevitable." The men nodded in agreement and headed out of the lunchroom for the Hub.

CHAPTER 29

Gus entered the Hub first and looked around the casino area as Rex, Chris, and John filed in behind him.

"There he is," Chris motioned toward Mick, sitting at one of the Hold 'em tables that remained intact after the brawl between Antonio and Sal.

The men walked across the room, unaware they had already captured Paddy's attention. Rex was a heartbeat from calling out Mick's name when Paddy and four other Drongs grabbed the men and spun them around.

"The fuck are ya doin' here?" Paddy barked in his thick Irish accent. "You've no business with the Drongs unless you've got the bloody serum in your hands."

"We need to talk to Mick," Rex said.

"The fuck ya do. What ya need to do is get outta here, right now."

"We got a plan—"

"You ain't got nothin', but about another day before we finish this— and you along with it."

"Look, do you want the serum or—"

"Shut the fuck up, you idiots," Mick spun around from his table in frustration. "Can't ya see I'm trying to play a fuckin' hand here?"

"Mick, we need—"

"I said, shut up. What about 'shut up' do you not understand? Take these fuckin' idiots up to the tennis courts and wait for me there."

"You heard the man. Get fuckin' movin'," Paddy snapped as he shoved Rex backward toward the elevators. Paddy and his cohorts shoved the men into the elevator and proceeded to the tennis courts. Despite his earlier experience with the Serpentis, John had no recollection of the grimy haven for gang activity, but he could sense the anxiety it was causing his friends. Sweat formed on Gus's brow, and Chris could not stop fidgeting.

"Would ya stand the fuck still, for fuck's sake?" Paddy said as the elevator doors opened and the Drong pushed the man out of the elevator toward the courts. They opened the gate and led John and his friends to their reckoning.

"Get on your fuckin' knees, now!" Paddy ordered.

Before they could react, the Drongs pushed them all down to the ground, kicking the back of their legs to guarantee they would bend. Their knees all hit hard on the ground. Gus had to catch himself with his hands to keep from falling flat to the floor.

"Get up! Straight on those fuckin' knees. I swear to Christ, if your ass so much as touches your legs, I'll break your fuckin' jaw!"

The men tightened their posture, putting virtually all their weight directly on their kneecaps, grinding them hard into the court surface. Paddy had clearly used this tactic to wear down other victims. Seconds ticked by in excruciating stillness. The men each tried to shift their weight from one knee to the other to relieve the pressure—an exercise in futility.

Gus was the first to break form as his buttocks fell to the back of his legs for an instant. Paddy's hand rapped across Gus's face. The slap instantly stunned Gus back to the expected position.

John wasn't far behind because of the weight of his upper body, formed from years of back-breaking ranch work. It was too much for him. He did not know how long he had endured the stressed position. It may have been a couple of minutes or fifteen. He only knew the pain he felt. He rocked back toward his feet, shifting his knees to avoid sitting down. That did not stop Paddy, who delivered a proper backhanded slap across John's face that knocked him to the floor.

"Get your ass back on your knees, now!"

John worked his way back to the requisite position. Rex and Chris were both slender men, but Gus neared his breaking point again as Mick arrived.

"All right. All right. You can relax," he said, looking over at Paddy with a chuckle. "You had 'em like that the whole time?" Paddy grinned with pride. Mick shook his head with a smile in appreciation for the joy Paddy derived from punishing their victims.

John and his friends sighed with relief as they took the weight off their knees, giving them a much-needed break. Rex stood to stretch his legs and quickly learned with a slap from Paddy that "relax" did not mean they could stand up.

"Okay then, where's my fuckin' serum?"

"We don't have it yet, but that's why we're here," Rex said.

"Without the serum, you're just wasting my time. You're getting nothing further from me till I have the serum."

"But we've got somethin' for you," Gus said.

"Oh? What is that? Excuses? Whining? More begging for help? What do you have?"

"Me, they brought me. They want me to help get you this serum."

"What's so special about—"

"He can stop the Big Brains," Chris said.

"He can! I've seen him do it," Rex confirmed.

"John? Is this the John I've heard about?"

"Yeah, I'm John."

"And that's all true?"

"It's more like I can prevent them from stopping me, but yeah, I can. I've gotten pretty good at it, too."

"So, why the fuck are you here? Go help your friends get the serum and bring it back."

217

"Friends? They're not my friends. They've been trying to talk me into helping get this serum since I got back from the Big Brains' rehab. The only friend I remember having from this place is Doc. He was the only one willing to fight to help me get back to my family on Earth."

"So, you don't remember these guys, but you remember Doc and your girl on Earth? If that's true, why would the Big Brains let you keep those memories?"

"What do you mean, keep my memories? I've got all my memories, at least as far as I know; they just made it so I won't be violent anymore."

"Ha, we'll see about that," Paddy snickered as he landed a straight right jab to John's nose. John rocked back from the shot as blood trickled from his nose and his eyes watered.

"Why would you do that?" John responded without a hint of anger. "Listen, do you want my help or not? I know where the serum is and can get through the Big Brains. I'm the only chance you have. These guys obviously can't get it, or I wouldn't be here."

"I reckon you're gonna help 'em, or by tomorrow, they won't be seen 'round here ever again."

"What good will that do you?" John asked. "You still won't have the serum."

"Ah, fuck this! Listen here, ya piece of shit! You're gonna get that fuckin' serum, or you'll be joinin' these three by tomorrow. No one'll hear from any of you lot ever again!" Paddy emphasized his point with a slap across John's cheek, catching enough of his nose to increase the trickle of blood to a light stream.

"So be it," John said, unfazed by Paddy's strikes. "I've got nothing to live for, anyway. I'm stuck here, and I'm never gonna see Mary again. What's the point of even living?"

"Why the fuck did ya even bother showin' up?" Paddy asked in anger.

"Are you not listening? Doc! I just told you, he's the only friend I've got here. The only one that was willing to help me. I owe him! If I can help get him away from the Serpentis, I will."

"Look, we told your mates to bring us the serum, and we'll help ya get Doc back, so we will."

"Yeah, and none of us believe you're gonna live up to that, so here's the only deal on the table. I'll help these guys get your serum if you point us in the right direction to find Doc. You don't have to help. All we need is for you to show us the way, and we'll take all the risks. If we're successful, Doc can help us get the serum. He's a doctor, so he can help us trick the staff. Between my ability to counter the Big Brains and Doc's medical knowledge, we can get it. That's it, that's the deal. It's your only chance of getting that serum."

"Nah, that's not happenin'. You're bringin' us the serum first, so you—"

"It's not gonna happen. I need Doc to help get the serum, and we already know we're dead if we don't. What I'm saying is, if you don't give us the info we need to find Doc, you might as well kill us now."

"Wait, what? Kill us now?" Chris said.

"You heard 'em, we're dead anyway, so there's no sense waiting around for it," John rationalized. Turning back toward Mick, he said, "So get it over with, come on! Do it! End it already! Or maybe you want that serum more than you want us dead? What's it gonna be, Mick?"

Mick pondered John's words as he sought Paddy's counsel, and with a slight twist of his head, Paddy understood Mick's assessment of the situation. "It's down a path behind the infirmary, then off to the right. They call it their club, but it's more like a campsite. They've got drinks and a bit of weed, so they're always hangin' out there. We reckon the Big Brains can't keep tabs on the place. They've had some proper scraps out there, and the guards never showed up, so they didn't."

"Now, let me make this clear," Mick said. "Whether or not you get Doc back from them, no one will enjoy a moment of peace until I have my serum. If you know what's good for you, you'll make it quick."

The men worked their way up from their stiff knees and walked off the tennis courts and out of the Hub to find their friend, Doc. All their planning paid off, so the first step was complete. Mick realized their proposal was his only legitimate chance of obtaining the Rev Rehab and believed John's abilities could be the key. In the end, the Drongs risked nothing to provide the information. Their worst-case scenario was that they still would not have the serum.

The sun fell beyond the horizon. Leo knew Nick's return was looming. He knew he would come for Shirley. Leo believed she could not prevent the Big Brains from knocking her out, and she would never help the Serpentis secure the serum. He knew she would face Nick's rage.

Shirley was alert. She had rested much of the day and regained some of her strength. She could once again carry on an entire conversation, and she and Leo had been talking for at least an hour. Their conversation mostly revolved around Leo's upbringing in Italy. Shirley tried to compare it to her experience of having grown up in the camp. They had been talking since she finished her dinner.

"It sounds so beautiful there. I wish I had had a chance to see Earth, or, for that matter, anything other than this camp."

"I guess I always took it for granted. I was too focused on myself and surviving to pay much attention. I pretty much grew up on the streets, constantly getting in trouble... hold on."

Leo could hear men coming up the path to the lounge. It was Nick, for sure. From the sound on the path, several Serpentis accompanied him. He knew Shirley's brutal interrogation was imminent if he could not convince Nick that she was useless to their plan.

"Nick! Hey, brother. Shirley's doing a lot better. I've been asking her questions all day."

"What'd she tell ya? Anything useful? She gonna be able to help us?"

"Brother, she can't do it."

"What? Are you fucking kidding me?"

"Hang on, hang on," Leo said, trying to calm Nick. "She said she could do it that one time when she saw her mom die."

"Is that right?" Nick turned his glare to Shirley.

"It is. I only knew what happened enough to tell Doc and his friend what to focus on, but I've never had to try... uh... I, uh, never could do it again. I just didn't have the emotion to make it work."

Nick sensed Shirley was holding back. "When was the last time you tried?"

Shirley, realizing what her stumble had revealed, said, "I, uh, well, I haven't—not since my mother died. I've never been around Big Brains since."

"Well, good news... we're gonna give you a chance."

"No, I'm sure I can't. Maybe if it had been right after I lost my mother, but there's no way I could do it today. I know how much emotion I had that day. I can't fake that!"

"Looks like you're gonna have to, 'cause you're all we've got. Besides, you may not have enough emotion over your mom still, but I'd be willing to bet my boys here will make you pretty emotional when I let them loose on you. You want—"

"Nick! You said she's mine first," Leo said, settling the other Serpentis' excitement down. Shirley could tell Leo's interruption was for her benefit and not Leo's actual desire to harm her. She realized Leo would do what he could to protect her from being violated by the gang members.

"Relax, Leo, you're still first, but if this bitch don't stop playing games with us, that pretty face of hers won't be so pretty."

"Now listen to me, bitch... you're gonna tell us the truth! Can you stay awake near the Big Brains or not?"

"No! I—"

"Don't you fucking lie to me!" Nick said. "You did this once, so you better fuckin' figure out how you're gonna do it again!"

Tears formed in Shirley's eyes. "I don't know—"

"Yes, you do... I know you do!"

"Nick, man, I don't think she's lyin' to us, brother." Leo tried to appeal to Nick's better senses.

"What the fuck is the matter with you, Leo? Are you forgetting your place here?"

"No, I just... I've been questioning her all day. If she could still do this, she'd tell us."

"Really? Did she tell you she's never even tried since her mom died? Did you find that out during your questioning? No? So, I dunno... maybe I'll run the fuckin' Serpentis and decide when someone is telling the truth? You okay with that?"

Leo realized he had pushed too hard and only enraged Nick further. That fact became all too clear when he returned his attention to Shirley.

"You can still do it, can't you, Shirley?" As she shook her head, Nick sprang across the gap between them and brought his hand down to slap her face. He stopped himself only inches from contact. The other Serpentis leaped to their feet to cheer their Capo on. Leo winced for Shirley, expecting the blow to land solidly on her face.

"I'm not gonna stop myself next time," Nick assured Shirley.

Nick's badgering continued, obsessed with getting Shirley to admit she could defend herself against the Big Brains. He all but lost sight of the serum as a goal. Shirley grew numb to anything the Serpentis might do to convince her.

Nick had been tormenting Shirley for about an hour when John and his friends made their way to the Serpentis' club. The men traced their way through the hidden path Mick put them on. John led the way as they all moved in.

CHAPTER 30

The stench of the Serpentis' club tainted the air. The men had to cover their noses to make it through.

"This is an awful place to keep someone," Gus said.

"Keep quiet. If they know we're coming, we're fucked," Rex reprimanded.

They walked carefully to avoid stepping too harshly on the dried leaves. They veered through the paths until Chris spotted Doc through the brush, still tied to the oak. The Serpentis had tied Shirley to a tree on Doc's left. Her hair was messy and matted, her lips pale, and her face swollen. Besides Nick and Leo, six Serpentis were in the club—a formidable force.

The four friends ducked behind a boulder. They would have to strategize better to save the two victims. They could see Nick had utterly lost his patience, and only a thin thread held him back. His men flanked beside him.

The leaves on the trees rustled in the wind, concealing the crunchy sounds made by the rescuers as they fanned out.

"You gonna keep fuckin' lying to me?" Nick asked Shirley.

"I am not lying to—"

Nick snapped. He raised his hand with clear intent to land a slap, but Leo jumped in and held it in the air. Nick was stunned. The other Serpentis were as well.

"That's not gonna happen," Leo said, throwing Nick's hand aside.

He stood beside Shirley, watching the pairs of eyes around him for the slightest movement.

"What the fuck, Leo? Get out of the fuckin' way," one of the onlooking Serpentis pleaded.

But Leo stood his ground.

"No, fuck off, no one is going to lay a finger on her. You almost killed this woman for no fucking reason. We're not gonna sit here and beat on her for some belief she can do something she—"

Nick threw a punch at Leo's chin before he could finish talking, but again, Leo caught it in the air. The only thing the Serpentis found more shocking than Nick's punch was Leo's reflexes. Leo threw off Nick's fist and stood his ground.

"Nick, I don't wanna fight. We're brothers. We don't need to do this. Shirley can't help us, brother."

Nick wasn't taking this insolence. He was walking in circles, pacing, thinking of what to do next.

"I see what's going on here," Nick said. "You caught feelings for this bitch, didn't you? Somewhere between saving her life and spending time with her all day today. Unbelievable… fucking Leo. You're the last person I thought—"

"I don't care what you think the reason is. I'm not letting you hurt this woman. She's been through enough. The only thing that's gonna happen to her is the proper treatment at the infirmary," Leo said.

Nick and the other Serpentis pounced on him. Like a bullfighter, Leo parried Nick's charge as he countered with a hard left to the back of Nick's head. As the punch landed, another Serpentis member dove on Leo to bring the behemoth to the ground. Leo rolled his shoulder, throwing the man to the ground, and followed it with a straight shot to the side of his head.

In his crouched position, three more Serpentis reached the scrum, knocking Leo to the ground as Nick regained his composure. Nick took his frustrations out on Leo's rib cage with repetitive hard kicks until Leo's thrashing tossed some men off him.

John and his friends quickly seized the opportunity and stormed in. Gus untied Doc and Shirley while the rest fought with the gang members, trying to stop them. Realizing he had help, Leo got back to his feet. Doc's excitement over seeing John motivated him to summon his remaining strength and join the fight, taking control like a battlefield commander.

"You three, take Shirley to the infirmary now! Tell them about the fight happening here. Go!"

"John, help Leo fight off the Serpentis."

"I, uh, I can't—"

"What the... dammit! The Big Brains seriously fucked you up, didn't they? You can't... okay... uh, hang on, I got an idea." Doc shoved John into the fray, knocking down a gang member. The Serpenti got up and pummeled John, who would not fight back, but he instinctively employed an effective defense, bringing his hands up to his face and blocking the strikes with his forearms. The blows rained down on him, but they only connected with his arms before he got to his back and shifted his hips to center the gangster between his legs. He used his feet to block his attacker's hips as a guard.

Leo ensured no hands reached Shirley as Gus, Chris, and Rex cut her loose and led her away.

"Make sure you tell the staff where we are. Run! We're not gonna survive long."

"Protect yourself, John. It won't be much longer."

Just as Doc had hoped, the Big Brains arrived within a few minutes, confirming for Doc that Shirley was safe in the infirmary and that their friends had informed the staff about the brawl. Salvation was at hand. The Big Brains closed in, and the men succumbed to their imposed stasis.

John awoke from the influence of the Big Brains' induced sleep to the sound of Dr. Harry and Nurse Jean's voices. John could barely make out the words at first, as his mind was still foggy from sleep.

"—again, so soon?" John did not recognize the male voice.

"Neither did I, Doctor. It seemed like he was going to be okay."

"He passed all the tests before we sent him back to the camp. I don't—"

"Back to the camp?" John asked.

"What do you mean? I've been here before? Is this where you wiped my brain? What are you going to do to me?"

"Oh, he's awake. John, it's okay. Everything is going to be okay," Nurse Jean said. While not familiar to John, he believed her.

"Yes, John. You've been here before. We tried to help you, but the implant process was disrupted when—"

"Nurse, perhaps we should, uh… check his vitals before we get into any details that might cause him some distress."

"Oh, sure. Certainly, Doctor."

Jean reviewed the vitals John's bed revealed while Dr. Harry continued the conversation. "As Nurse Jean mentioned, your procedure was interrupted when we had an… uh… an anomaly with our equipment. This caused the complication that unfortunately resulted in your near-total amnesia. We can't express our sympathy enough for that," Dr. Harry said as he made brief eye contact with Jean.

"That's why I can't remember Mary and the baby? That's why I couldn't remember any of my friends in the camp?"

"I'm afraid so. That was never our… did you say… baby? Oh, uh… right. John, that was never our intent. We only wanted to make life in the camp and separation from your loved ones more bearable. We just wanted your life here to be enjoyable."

Feeling more alert, John sat up in bed to continue the conversation. "So, what happens now? Is Doc okay?"

"Doc's going to be fine. He was severely dehydrated and weak from a lack of nourishment, but he's been getting intravenous fluids and supplements. He should be back to normal in no time."

"Are you going to wipe our brains? Are you going to erase my memories again?"

"No, John, we don't wipe brains at all. Our method helps people adjust to life here and avoid violence. It sometimes requires blocking out certain memories, but we discuss that with our patients to ensure they understand. We never intended to do that with you. While some people who came in yesterday will need significant behavior modification before rejoining the others in the camp, Doc probably won't need much."

"But Doc could end up like me?"

"No, no, of course—"

"But what if you experience an anomaly during the procedure, like with me?"

"Oh, that? That won't happen again, John. We figured out the precise cause of the anomaly in your case. That won't ever happen again."

Jean looked over to Dr. Harry as he continued to avoid alerting John to his past ability to disrupt the Big Brains' artificial stasis technology.

"Was it related to how I can resist the Big Brains?"

With a heavy sigh, Dr. Harry's head dropped. "I take it your friends told you that, no?"

"They did, yes. So, was it an anomaly with the equipment or something to do with me?"

Sensing Dr. Harry was about to lose any chance of gaining John's trust, Jean stood and walked over to John's bed, looking at Dr. Harry to confirm he would not stop her from asserting control over the situation. Jean said, "There was an anomaly with the equipment, John, but you're right. Something about your unique abilities caused that anomaly. Apparently, you woke during the implantation process, and it caused nearly catastrophic damage to your brain. We're so very sorry," Jean said as she wiped the tear forming in the corner of her eye.

"We had never seen anything like this happen before. You were in significant pain and required a lot of drugs to keep you from going insane. Our specialists developed a secondary technique that successfully ended the pain and normalized your mental well-being without drugs, but we were unable to restore your memory."

Dr. Harry nodded along as Jean regained John's confidence.

"You needn't worry about Doc, John."

John gained some comfort from Jean's explanation. "What about me, though? Will I have to go through another procedure?"

Jean looked to Dr. Harry to provide the answer. With a slight tilt of her chin, she made it clear she expected him to respond in a manner she would find acceptable.

"Well, uh, John, seeing how well you've handled this conversation, and since you don't appear to have engaged in any offensive violence at the camp, I suspect that won't be necessary. We have some diagnostic tests we'll need to perform, but I don't think you'll have any problems."

John exhaled in relief, and even Jean found comfort in how Dr. Harry revealed his opinion.

"Okay, John. We've brought you some fresh clothes, and you'll be able to clean up in there." Jean pointed to the bathroom area. "Your lunch will be here in about an hour, and we'll be back sometime after that to run through some tests with you, okay?"

John nodded in agreement as Dr. Harry and Nurse Jean turned to the door. John heard a beep and watched as Jean pressed an area on the wall, causing the door to slide open.

The day had been dragging along, and Nurse Clara had come and gone with John's lunch. He sat alone, pondering the few memories he had formed recently, ruminating on the information he had learned from his friends and his medical team. *How could I have been so attached to Mary to withstand the Big*

Brains' powers but have no recollection, no sentiment toward her at all? He could rationally understand how important she must have been to him, especially having been pregnant with his child, but could not form any emotional connection to the concept.

A beep at the door startled John from his thoughts. Jean walked in, pushing a cart with medical equipment John had not seen before.

"Hi, John. How are you feeling? Was the food okay?"

"I feel pretty good... lots of questions... but I feel fine."

"I'm sure you do, and that's good news because the diagnostics we're going to do just require us to have a conversation. The bad news is I've got to shave those three spots on your head again. I'm afraid your hair growth is just a bit too much to use these," she said as she held up the stick-on pads that would communicate with the machine.

"What are they for?"

"They let me attach this machine to you so we can interpret how your brain functions as we talk. The doctors will review the results and determine the way ahead for you."

"And... if I fail, I might have to get another treatment?"

"It's not a pass or fail thing, John. Not at all. It's much more of a verification that everything is working the way it should. We would not be doing this test if we thought we would need to conduct a more invasive remedy, like the one we did before. This is just to confirm that our diagnosis is correct."

"Oh, okay, I guess I'm ready."

"Great. Well, hop back into your bed so it can monitor your vitals, and we'll get started."

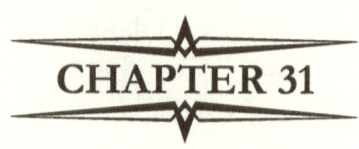

CHAPTER 31

John stood up from his chair, sat on his bed, and adjusted it to a more upright position to sit comfortably. Jean applied some cream to the areas she needed to shave and, in no time, completed the job and attached the stick-on patches to the three freshly shaved spots on John's head. She connected the machine to the electrodes on the patches and turned the machine on. It generated a low hum that filled the room.

"Okay, before we start with a more free-flowing conversation, I have some standard questions I need to ask. Is that okay?"

John nodded his head in agreement.

"Great. How have you been sleeping?"

"Other than the first night back in camp, I think the only sleep I've had was induced by the Big Brains. But that was fine," John said with a chuckle.

Jean grinned as she looked at the reading on the machine. "And what about the night in the camp? How did you sleep that night?"

"Seemed pretty good, I guess. I don't remember waking up or being overly tired the next day."

"And how would you describe your eating habits so far?"

"They've been pretty sporadic: breakfast and dinner yesterday in the camp... that was yesterday, right?"

"Yes," Jean laughed, "it was yesterday."

"And then lunch earlier today. Everything seemed fine, though."

"How has your mood been?"

"Fine, I guess. I feel like I should be more upset about things that have happened, but somehow, it all just seems okay. Does that make sense?"

"It does, John, sure. Have you been worried at all or been unable to stop being worried about something?"

"No, honestly. When we were planning to face down that gang to get Doc back, I probably should have been worried. But I don't know, I just felt like we were right to do it."

"Hmm, that's interesting. Okay. How confident would you say you are in your abilities? For example, when you were going to face down the gang, did you feel confident you'd be able to protect yourself?"

"Not really... well... confident. I guess I was confident I wouldn't be violent. Does that make sense? I helped come up with the plan, but I told my friends I knew I wouldn't be able to fight. But when one of the Serpentis threw me to the ground, I was confident I could protect myself from him hurting me without needing to punch back. So, I guess you could say I was confident in my abilities, even if they were just defensive."

"Okay, good. One more standard question, and then you can ask me any you might have, okay?"

"Sure. Go ahead."

"Can you tell me about your hopes or dreams for the future?"

"I guess I just hope my friends will all be fine, and Doc and I can go back to the camp as we are, but for a dream of the future... hmm." John cocked his head to the side and looked up to the left as he contemplated. "I guess it would be nice if there weren't any gangs in the camp at all. If we could all just be nice to each other and try to live happy lives, I'd like that very much. I know that sounds almost utopian, but it would be nice."

"Okay, well... that's, uh... good, that's good. Now, what—"

"Was that not okay? Did I say something wrong?"

"No, not at all, John. I think the doctors will be quite happy to hear your responses, especially regarding your hopes for the future."

"Are you sure? You seem—"

"I'm sure, John. You've got nothing to worry about."

"Okay, I, uh… well, can you tell me more about the last time I was here?"

"Wow, that's quite the question. You were quite a handful there for a while. How 'bout we start with something more specific? The reading will be better if we do shorter questions and answers rather than me just talking for a while, okay?"

"Yeah, that's fine. What was it that made me such a handful?"

"That's an easy one. You kept trying to leave. The first night you were here, the Big Brain guards caught you trying to open a restricted access door, and then you got caught two nights later all the way out at the Empyrean."

"The Empyrean?"

"Oh, that's the… well, it's like a combined air and sea craft port, but it's almost a mile away. We're not even sure how you made it there without being seen by anyone." Jean shook her head in good-humored amazement.

"Was that before the first procedure?"

That question quickly removed Jean's smile, as she knew there would be no further opportunity for laughter.

"It was. Yes, John."

"Was that why that process was necessary?"

Jean's expression was all the confirmation John needed, but she said, "It was definitely a factor. When you came in from the camp, the Big Brain guards had caught you trying to steal a controlled serum—"

"The Rev Rehab?"

"Yes, you had even forced a nurse at the infirmary to help you, and then you knocked out a Big Brain guard. You nearly killed him."

"Oh, so I was going to need the procedure anyway?"

"Yes, in fact, we had you scheduled for a routine implant followed by a next-day return to the camp until you tried to leave the first night. That forced us to reevaluate our initial plan."

"That seems silly. Why did I try to leave? Where was I trying to go?"

"At the time, we didn't know, but now things make more sense."

"Mary?"

"Yes, and apparently your baby?"

"Yes. My friends said I was taking Mary to the hospital when she was in labor. I guess that's when the Big Brains took me."

Jean's voice cracked, and her eyes glistened with moisture. "I never imagined the Big Brains could do anything like that. I don't want to believe that's true."

"The way my friends described it to me, it sounded like all I cared about was trying to get out of the camp and back to my family."

"I just... I can't believe the Big Brains, especially Captain Meadowbrook, could do such a thing," Jean reiterated.

"I never told you any of this?"

"No, not at all. We didn't know anything about Mary till after your first procedure."

"I still remembered her after the first one?"

"No, well, not really. This is so awful," Jean said, brushing away tears. "I'm so sorry to tell you this, but you only had one memory. It was of the day you met Mary at a movie theater." A tear formed in Jean's eye. "We worked with you for days trying to help restore your memory with treatment, but nothing worked, and you would become dangerous and violent if we didn't keep you on the right sedatives and medications."

"Let me get this straight. I only had one memory left of Mary, and you even took that away?"

Tears were streaming down Jean's cheek as she nodded. "Yes. That's exactly what we did, John, but we had no choice. We talked about it with you when you were stable enough to understand everything. We told you that might be a risk, but it was either the second procedure or continue with the drugs and likely a miserable life."

"You're telling me I agreed?"

Jean again nodded. John remained unfazed by the information, taking it all in.

"Did I make the right choice?"

"Oh, God... I wish I knew for certain. But of the options we had, I think you chose the one that gave you the best chance of living a normal life here." Jean wiped the tears from her face and lifted her head to see how well John was dealing with the new information. "I, uh, I think we've got enough data for the doctor to review. Let me get these off you."

Jean stood up, shut off the machine, and removed the stick-on pads from John's head.

"There we go. Tomorrow, you'll meet with Captain Meadowbrook. He'll make the final decision on whether any further procedures are necessary before we send you back to camp. Do you have any other questions for me before I go?"

"No, I, uh, I'm good. I'm sorry if I upset you."

"You didn't, John. Your case has taken an emotional toll on all of us. I'm just glad you seem to be adjusting to life here fairly well... now." Jean's words hinted she felt a modicum of disappointment—a hint John noticed.

"You don't think I should have agreed, do you?"

"No, no, it was the smart choice."

"The smart choice? Wait... just because it was the smart one doesn't mean it was the best. Was there a better choice? Was there a right choice?"

Jean looked at John, frozen. John could tell she was struggling to find the words.

"Let me ask you this: would the person I was before I lost my memory have made the choice I made?"

"Not a chance. Knowing what I know now, there's no way you would have agreed to the secondary treatment."

CHAPTER 32

John barely reacted to Jean's revelations—accepting the information and only nodding in understanding.

"What do you know now that you didn't know then?"

Tears again formed in the corners of Jean's eyes.

"I just, well… after we talked this morning, I spoke with the nurse from the infirmary. She cleared some things up for me. And, well, now I know there was an option Captain Meadowbrook hadn't shared with us. One that you didn't have a chance to consider."

"And you think I would have chosen that option?"

"I don't know, maybe. It would have been extremely dangerous, but I don't know. You may have. The Big Brains never would have allowed that option, though. I realize that now."

"Why? What option? Why wouldn't they allow it?"

As Jean was about to answer, the door beeped and slid open. Nurse Clara walked in with John's dinner.

"Oh. Hey, Clara," Jean said as she wiped her eyes. "I was just wrapping up with John."

"As I was saying, John, you'll be meeting with Captain Meadowbrook in the morning after you've had breakfast. Do you need anything else before we leave?"

"Uh, no, I'm good. Thank you both."

Clara set down the food for John, and the two nurses left the room.

John woke from his slumber and ran through his morning routine. Breakfast had come and gone. He sat waiting for Captain Meadowbrook's arrival to learn whether his behavior would require more modifications or if he was ready to be sent back to camp. The door beeped, and Dr. Harry walked in with Nurse Jean.

"Oh, good. I see you're ready," Dr. Harry remarked.

"Good morning, John. How are you feeling this morning?"

"Good, Nurse. I feel just fine."

"John, Captain Meadowbrook should join us here shortly. I assume you don't remember having met Captain Meadowbrook before. Is that right?"

"No, that's right, Doctor, I don't. I met him here the last time?"

"You did, a couple of times. We had to perform a series of somewhat experimental techniques with you, so he wants to have a chance to… uh… make sure everything is okay before deciding whether—"

"I get to head back to the camp?"

"That's right, John. Now, there's nothing to worry about here. Just answer his questions about how you feel. There's no wrong answer, John. This isn't a test or anything."

"Okay. And this Captain Meadowbrook… he's a Big Brain? Like the ones that brought me here?"

"That's right. Yes."

"I never got to see them up close. One minute, I was blocking punches, and the next, I saw several floating above the scrum."

"John, you're about to get your—"

The door slid open. The sight of Captain Meadowbrook coming through the doorway caused John to shuffle back into his chair in surprise.

"Good morning, Captain Meadowbrook. How are you today, sir?"

"I'm doing well, Doctor. How's our most intriguing patient doing?"

"He seems to be doing well. The secondary procedure your specialists performed seems to have done the trick."

"Good morning, John."

John, still trying to take everything in, recognized the high degree of respect both Dr. Harry and Nurse Jean showed. He nervously extended a greeting. "Uh, good morning, uh, sir?"

"No need for formalities, John. You can call me Meadowbrook if you like."

Noticing the same curiosities John expressed the last time they met, Meadowbrook said, "We Big Brains don't speak with vocal cords like you do, John. To communicate with you, our brain signals directly interact with yours, so you can understand our meaning without language."

"We've had this conversation before, haven't we?"

"Indeed, John. We have."

"You're telepathic?"

"No, no. Not at all. Our brains can directly interact with you to communicate, but we cannot know your thoughts. Our ears still process sounds, and we need those sounds to receive your brain's signals that handle speech. So, until we hear your voice, we can't interpret your thoughts or feelings behind it. Does that make sense?"

As if to test Meadowbrook's assertion, John only thought about his response.

"John, does that make sense? Are you okay? John, are you try—"

"You really couldn't hear me answer?"

"No, John. Only when you speak. Now, do you have any further questions before we get started? It's fine if you do. I don't want you too distracted, okay?"

"You can't speak at all? Is that right?"

"That's correct. It's how we've evolved over the last million years."

"Evolved to not speak? Why would a species evolve to not speak? That doesn't make sense to me."

"Well, one of our earliest ancestors, a species we call Improved Brains, was hunted by the then-dominant lifeform. We call that lifeform the False Brains. The False Brains weren't a biological species like us; they were a technological one. They had vastly superior capabilities over the Improved Brains. They could even detect and track vocal patterns anywhere on this planet. They hunted and killed many Improved Brains, believing them to be a threat. Over a couple of hundred thousand years, the Improved Brains adapted to communicate without speaking and evolved into a species we call New Brains. The New Brains eradicated the False Brains and became the most intelligent species on the planet. Several hundred thousand years of evolution later, we no longer have vocal cords."

"And your species killed off all the New Brains then, right?"

"Oh no. Not at all. The New Brains went extinct long before my species ever existed. In a desperate attempt to kill the much more powerful New Brains, the False Brains created a highly adaptable virus. It eventually wiped out the New Brains and the species from which we directly evolved, which we call Fine Brains. We were on the road to extinction ourselves until we discovered your species."

"How were the New Brains so much more powerful than the Improved Brains?"

"Well, like the Improved Brains, the New Brains could communicate without speech, but over much greater distances and with many more New Brains at once. More importantly, they could do all of that without the need for technology that the False Brains could attack."

"And that was enough to destroy the False Brains?"

"Not exactly, John. No. They also developed another adaptation— a defense mechanism that the Improved Brains lacked. It allowed the New Brains to quickly and literally crush the False Brains."

"They crushed them?"

"Not entirely, just their brains. Whenever a New Brain felt threatened, their defense mechanism would instantly crush the brain or brains of the attacker."

"Brains? The False Brains could have more than one brain?"

"Well, in a way, yes. Because they were a technological species, their form was virtually unlimited. They were much closer to living machines than biological organisms like you and me."

"And the New Brains could just crush their brains? How?"

"It's like how we can make humans and other species sleep. It's also how we float and move things with our minds. That's actually what I wanted to talk to you about today," Captain Meadowbrook explained as he tried to focus John back on his treatment.

"Oh, yes. Sorry. This is all just fascinating."

"I understand, John. It's fine. I guess you're aware, though, that we've struggled to keep you under. Is that right?"

"Yes. Yes, sir. That's what my medical team told me yesterday."

"Well, let me explain how it all works so we can discuss our plans from here. We call it telekinesis. Now, the word you heard in your head is inaccurate for what I'm saying. Your brain can't process the mechanism I just described, but it's good enough as a starting place. Like muscles, the stronger the mind, the larger the object that mind can move. But we can also affect things that are extremely small, even microscopic."

"So, when you glide through the air, you're moving yourself with your mind?"

"Yes, well, not exactly, but effectively, yes. We're technically not moving anything, at least not like you might with your hands. What we're truly doing is manipulating gravity around a given object. When you see us floating, we're actually reducing the gravity beneath us and creating a gravitational force above us and in the direction we wish to travel."

"So how does manipulating gravity put us to sleep?"

"We just change the gravity around a small area within your brain. It's just an evolution of the New Brains' defense mechanism. We have quite a bit more control over the forces, so instead of crushing the brain of a threat, we can induce a kind of stasis that isn't harmful. See, as our species grew more dependent on our brain's abilities, our appendages became of little value for manipulating tools, weapons, or even our body weight. That left us with limbs that are useless for anything more than expression and presenting a larger physical appearance to some of the more predatory animals here on Twin Moons."

"Wait, wouldn't the gravity necessary to lift yourself, an object, or even to knock me out also affect everything else around the object?"

"Yes…" Captain Meadowbrook said with a subtle nod, impressed by John's question. "That's quite perceptive, John. The details are quite complicated, but essentially we can isolate gravity to only those things we want to affect. The New Brains couldn't control gravity like we do, though. We think their ability locked onto brain signals and created a small but powerful gravitational effect that would implode everything within a few inches of space."

John looked on with amazement. Captain Meadowbrook could tell he had not satiated John's thirst for clarity and waited for the next question.

"So, unlike New Brains, Big Brains can control the size and power of the gravitational field you create, and you can shield everything you don't want to affect?"

"Yes. Exactly. Like your muscles, our minds are only so strong. Individually, we can't lift much more than a human or two. Studying this is the basis of my life's work. You're here, Dr. Harry, Nurse Jean, all of you— even this city we're in right now—all came from this line of curiosity. This is truly fascinating. They mentioned this was possible, but I never imagined your cognition would improve this drastically."

"Wait, you made me smarter? What exactly did you do to me?"

"We installed a system in your brain. It's a series of five implants that allow us to change a person's reaction to stimuli. It's a kind of technology your brain won't be able to translate into something you would understand, but think of the implants as a system that can replicate the signals in your brain. I believe Dr. Harry and the other Homo sapiens call it a neuronet. Is that right?" Captain Meadowbrook turned to Dr. Harry, who confirmed the use of the term.

"When you awoke during the implant process, it forced us to use traditional anesthesia, preventing the proper initiation of the system. When our specialists developed their solution, we had to force the system to use different parts of your brain than we originally intended. That required the creation of a new baseline of knowledge and the ability to learn new information. So, in a sense, yes. The system has made you smarter. And clearly, noticeably so."

John quietly contemplated the new information, leaving an opening for Captain Meadowbrook to focus on his reason for visiting.

"John, as I mentioned, this is why I wanted to visit with you today before approving your return to the camp. We'd hoped not to see you back here at all, let alone after only a couple of days. I take it your friends from the camp have shared some details about your time there with you. Is that right?"

"That's correct, yes."

"And what else have they told you?"

"They told me about Mary, of course, and that she was pregnant with my child when you abducted me and brought me here."

"Yes, that was never our intention. We're truly sorry. How does knowing that information make you feel about being here?"

"I wouldn't say I have any feelings about it. From a moral perspective, I know you and your kind wronged me, but I'm not angered, if that's what you mean."

"It is, yes, that's exactly what I meant. And what about Mary? How do you feel about her now?"

"About the same. I know she exists or existed, but I can't say I have any attachment to her right now."

John noticed Jean's eyes beginning to shine as she blinked to dam the tears fighting to break through. Noticing his glance, Captain Meadowbrook turned to Jean.

"And Nurse Jean, how were his vitals and the diagnostics on the neuronet?"

"Oh, uh, they all looked good, Captain. No signs of degradation in the neuronet, and all the synapses observed fired within range... elevated... but all within range."

"Very good. Glad to hear that. So, here's what I'd like to do, John. With your permission, I'd like to use my ability to put you into stasis for just fifteen minutes. Are you comfortable with that?"

"Sure, that's fine, but, uh, why?"

"Well, we didn't expect to see you back here, and with the experimental remedy we had to use, we're not exactly sure how using our stasis abilities on you might affect the stability of the neuronet. Does that make sense?"

"It does, yeah. So, what do I have to do?"

"Let's get you back up in the bed so you're more comfortable, okay?"

John agreed and adjusted the bed to a slightly upright, yet comfortable, reclined position.

"Okay, I'm ready."

A moment later, John was out until the promised fifteen minutes had elapsed. His eyes opened with rapid blinks as he rubbed them for more clarity.

"How are you feeling, John?"

"Fine, sir. Any concerns?"

"No, John. That seemed to go very well. This time, focus on what you learned in the camp from your friends over the last couple of days, especially about Mary. I want you to take everything they told you about her and try to feel how you think you should feel about Mary, okay?"

"Okay, I can do that, sure."

"Great. I'll give you a few minutes. When you think you're focused and ready, let me know, and we'll proceed."

John searched his mind. His thoughts wandered over all he had learned from his friends. He considered how much he must have loved Mary, how hard he fought to return to her, and his conversation with Nurse Jean the day before—so moved by his attachment to Mary that she wept over his lost memories. The love he must have had for Mary was powerful. John focused his thoughts and signaled to Meadowbrook that he was ready.

As with the earlier test, John was out the next instant.

After the expected fifteen minutes, John awoke and asked, "How'd it go?"

"Perfect, John. Thanks for your cooperation on that. I think I've got everything I need."

"Am I able to return to the camp, then?"

"I don't see why not. We'll keep you here another day or so for observation, but everything looks great."

With that, Captain Meadowbrook left the room.

"John, do you need anything before we go? I'm betting you're getting hungry. Lunch should be in any minute now."

"No, no, Nurse, I'm fine. Lunch would be good, but I'm fine. Thanks."

"Okay, then we'll check in on you again tomorrow. Feel free to buzz if you need anything."

Captain Meadowbrook and the team departed, followed by the beeping noise that had become normal. Lunch and dinner passed with little fanfare. John's thoughts drifted toward returning to the camp with Doc. He had heard so much about him from his friends that he felt he knew him and hoped to renew their friendship.

A few hours later, a beep at the door surprised John.

CHAPTER 33

Nurse Jean entered in a frenzy. She was not wearing her traditional nurse uniform. Instead, she appeared to be dressed for a night out.

"John, I have something important to tell you. I know you don't really know me and you don't remember our walk in the town or that you trusted me, but I'm hoping you can trust me now."

Jean's sense of urgency took John aback.

"Trust you? Why? What's going on? Is Doc okay?"

"Doc? Doc? Oh, your friend. No, no, he's fine. At least I don't have any reason to think he's not fine. I'm not here about Doc. I'm here for you. John, I think you're in danger."

"Danger? Why would I be in danger? The visit with Captain Meadowbrook went well, didn't it? What happened?"

"I thought it did, too, but I don't think so anymore. They took me off your medical team, and they told Nurse Clara to prepare you for a visit from the Big Brain guards tomorrow. They're going to put you in stasis and transport you to the Science Center."

"The what?"

"The Science Center. It's where all the Big Brain scientists develop the technology that supports their missions to Earth. That's also where they developed the neuronet." John could not believe the words he was hearing.

They landed on him like Jean was speaking a foreign language. "Let me make sure I understand. Are you saying they're not sending me back to the camp?"

"No! I think you're about to become a science experiment."

"A what? An experiment?"

"I think they're afraid of you, John. It sounds like when you thought about Mary, Captain Meadowbrook had a difficult time keeping you in stasis. I think he's worried you'll regain your ability to prevent them from using the stasis power on you."

"Why? How do I scare them? They know I'm not violent. I'd never hurt anyone, even if I could prevent them from knocking me out. They'll never need to."

"I just think they're scared that the more you learn about Mary, the more you'll realize what you've lost and could rebel against them."

"I don't understand. What does Mary have to do with any of this?"

Jean sighed heavily, realizing how she had overwhelmed John with her concerns.

"Okay, this will take a minute, so let's sit down so I can explain."

Having calmed down, Jean recounted John's Twin Moons experiences, the procedures, and their theory that his love for Mary enabled him to resist the Big Brains' stasis powers.

"It's something about how complex human emotions are. They think your love for Mary is what made your ability possible."

"What do you think is going to happen to me?"

"I don't know. I just know Captain Meadowbrook is worried, and they plan to lock you up."

"Why wouldn't they just keep me here? Why at the Science Center?"

"I don't know, I don't know. None of this makes sense, John."

"No, it doesn't at all. I mean, with all the humans here, how can I be the first person who loved someone?"

Jean's eyes widened, nearly leaping from their sockets. "Oh my God, that's it!"

"What, oh—" John seemed to clue in on Jean's realization.

"That's what they're afraid of. That's why they want you in the Science Center. You showed them something they didn't know was possible. They must be worried that all the humans here can form the same love you had for Mary. Especially here in the city."

"Yes, I can see how they'd find that a grave threat. Do many humans have families here?"

"Just in the city, yes. About twenty years ago, the Big Brains started sterilizing abductees and putting them in the camp to ensure the human population and birth rate wouldn't exceed their own."

"But if enough humans could resist their power, they'd effectively be defenseless against us since we're so much stronger," John opined. "That must be it. They must intend to use me to figure out how to make sure they can defend themselves."

Jean nodded in agreement. "What else could it be?"

"Now what, then?"

"I don't know, John. But we gotta get you out of here, and I don't think we have much time."

"I don't, I just don't—"

"Look, John. I'm sticking my neck out for you here. I shouldn't be here at all. But I've done all I can do without asking some friends for help. If we do this, I need to know you'll make sure the risks we're taking are worth it and we're not throwing our lives away here for nothing."

"I understand, Jean. I won't let you down."

"Okay, I've got to leave you for now. If I'm not back for any reason, you need to be gone before breakfast tomorrow. You understand?"

"But where do I go?"

"Remember what I told you about how you escaped last time? Just down the hall, up the stairs, across the skywalk, and back down the stairs to the exit. Once you're outside, you'll see a manhole across the street. You can hide in there. If I don't come for you by nightfall tomorrow, something went wrong, and you're on your own."

"By nightfall? I guess it's good that I had a big dinner tonight."

"Okay, John, I plan to be back before breakfast, so be ready."

"But what about Doc? What's going to happen to him?"

"I'm sure they'll just send him back to the camp."

"But he knows how I did it. Won't they worry he'll be able to get other people to realize they can, too?"

"Hmm… that's a good point. Especially if you never show back up in the camp. Okay, I'll try to figure out what they've got planned for Doc, and we'll cross that bridge when we come to it, okay?"

"Yeah, that's fine, okay."

"All right, I'm gonna leave the security off. To exit, you'll need to push right here," Jean pointed to the virtually invisible button on the wall. "I'll try to come back again tonight so we can figure things out. I know your mind is racing right now, but try to get some sleep."

"Yeah… I'll do that," John remarked with a hint of sarcasm. Jean left the room, and the door closed silently behind her.

John set the controls on his bed to ensure he would awake well before breakfast. Despite Jean's news, John drifted off to sleep with relative ease.

Four hours before breakfast, Jean returned, dressed in her nurse's uniform.

"John," Jean called out in a hushed tone to avoid startling him from his sleep.

"John." Her voice grew louder. "John, I need you to wake up."

With no response, Jean moved closer. "John, you need to wake up." Jean shook John by the shoulder.

"What, uh, Mary, is that… oh, uh, sorry, I meant Jean. You're back! I'm so glad I didn't have to find my way out of here alone."

"John, focus. We have very little time. Breakfast will be here in four hours."

John raised his bed to a more upright position. "Okay, okay, what do we have to do?"

"We have to decide, John. Well, really, you do. I found out Captain Meadowbrook ordered a supply of Rev Rehab for the Science Center."

"You think that's for me, don't you?"

"I do, yes."

"Isn't that the serum that's supposed to undo the procedure they did to me?"

"Yes, it is, but according to Nurse Helen, it might also kill you. It depends on how reliant your nervous system has become on the neuronet. She said it doesn't technically reverse the rehab process. That's just what our brains hear when the Big Brains ask for it."

"But what does it do?"

"It kills the neuronet. None of us fully understand the technology, but apparently, the devices are like living organisms, and the Rev Rehab is toxic to them. Helen says they only ever use the Rev Rehab if the neuronet has become unstable and is causing the patient extreme pain that medication can't control. They've only ever used it on one patient, and she only lived long enough to throw herself off a roof in the camp."

"Shirley's mom!"

"Who?"

"Oh, uh, sorry, the woman who killed herself. Her daughter was a friend. Well, I guess she was. That's one of the things I learned while I was back in camp. The Serpentis captured her with Doc. They wanted her to help them steal the Rev Rehab."

"John, the infirmary nurse who helped you, gave me a treatment that was supposed to go to the Science Center. I have it here with me now."

Jean's remark floored John. "You have the serum? With you?"

"I do. That's part of the decision you have to make."

"I, wow! I, uh… that sounds very risky—"

"Before you answer, I've got more information you need to know."

"It's not good news, is it?"

"No, John, it's not… it's Doc. They're going to administer the first rehab steps on him in the morning. Then, they plan to use the procedure they did with you, the new baseline. They're actually going to wipe his mind, John."

"Why? What did he do? He just helped me. The Serpentis were the violent ones."

"I guess before he helped you, there was another person he tried to help escape. That person ended up killing himself. To make matters worse, the Serpentis we just brought here, along with the last two that we treated… they all made it look like Doc was responsible for almost all the recent gang violence in the camp. Something about spreading rumors to stoke the violence."

"This is awful, Jean. We have to get him out of here. I can't leave him behind. Where do we go? Can we hide in the city?"

"John, it's going to be hard enough for you to get free, so trying to get both of you out simply isn't realistic."

"Jean, there's no way I'm leaving Doc to be wiped. We have to find a way."

"There's no time to debate—"

"You're right. You're just gonna have to accept he's coming with me."

Jean recognized if John was this determined before receiving the Rev Rehab, she had no chance of convincing him to leave Doc if the serum proved successful. Jean groaned, "Ugh… I guess it's possible we could get you two into the city. The Big Brains rarely go downtown, but we've never had anything like this happen. There's no way to know how hard they might look for you two. I think I have a better idea."

John looked on, eager to hear Jean's recommendation.

"They're preparing the ship to go back to Earth, John. It will launch in twelve hours, shortly after they've installed Doc's neuronet. I… I think you and Doc need to be on that trip."

"And go back to Earth?"

"I think it's your only chance. The crew is typically only two Big Brains; Captain Meadowbrook will be commanding, and they board from the other building. You and Doc can hide in the holding bay till they get to Earth and start collecting specimens from the humans."

"And then what do we do? The Big Brains will just knock us out."

"They will... true. Unless—"

"The serum works?"

"Exactly. That's what you have to decide. Take the serum, maybe get your memory and abilities back, and try to return to Earth. Or don't, and you and Doc can try to hide from the Big Brains the rest of your lives in Earth City."

"This is insane. I can't believe this," John said.

John toiled over the information, trying to consider every workable option. He struggled to develop something Jean had not thought of, some other way out with a higher chance of success. Jean tried to remain patient while John deliberated, but they had already been talking for thirty minutes, and their window for action was quickly closing.

"John, the serum can take up to an hour before it works, so if we're going to do this, we need to do it now."

CHAPTER 34

Jean's words hovered over John like a dark cloud. He knew what he had been told about Mary, the baby, Doc, and the heartbreak he had experienced—details detached from emotion. John had to risk everything and endure Rev Rehab for a chance at the life he once had but never knew. He drew a long breath and exhaled almost instantly. "Okay, let's do it. Give me the treatment, and let's get Doc and me on that ship."

Jean nodded with approval. A faint smile nearly fractured the purposeful look on her face, but only for a moment.

"Okay, Helen said the serum causes excruciating pain. We need to get you up on your bed and strap you down. Let's also get those footies off so the bed gets better readings in case you go into cardiac arrest—the bed will hopefully save you."

"Hopefully?"

"John, you're young and strong, but if you were Doc, I don't think we'd be trying this. It's not too late if you want to change your mind," Jean advised as she tightened the final restraint, strapping John securely to the diagnostics bed.

"No, I know the risks. Let's do it."

Jean prepared the syringe, drawing in the thick blue fluid and pushing a drop of the substance from the tip of the needle to clear any air.

"Okay, here we go."

Jean readied John's vein for the injection. "It's thick, so we have to go slow, and it's going to burn as it goes in, John. After a few minutes, you'll feel pain all over. Try to hold still while I administer the full dose, okay?"

Jean inserted the needle and slowly depressed the plunger, forcing the blue substance into John's vein.

"That's one cc, John."

"Wow, you weren't kidding about the burning sensation."

John grimaced as the searing pain radiated up his arm like venom.

"That's two, eight more to go. Hang in there."

John's muscles contracted with escalating intensity.

"That's three."

Sweat began forming on John's brow. His feet stiffened and locked, then stretched far back toward his shins. His fingers spread wide on his hands as they tensed.

"That's four."

The searing pain continued, but the pain he felt throughout his body almost overshadowed it. Every muscle ached, as if each were being stretched and torn simultaneously.

"We're halfway there, John."

John did all he could to hold his voice back, but random, hushed grunts escaped. His body started shaking. Jean did all she could to hold John's arm still to continue delivering the treatment.

"Six!"

Jean broke into a sweat herself. John convulsed against the tie-downs on his hips. They strained to keep his body tight to the bed.

"Seven."

John was no longer coherent, writhing in pain. His eyes rolled back in his head as the alarm on the bed sounded for a high heart rate. Jean leaned her elbow hard on John's arm and secured the needle. With the same hand, she shut off the alarm, using her access card to prevent another nurse from responding, then resumed the injection.

"Eight."

John passed out as his heart rate dropped.

"Nine... and ten." Jean removed the needle and bandaged the injection site. John lay motionless on the bed, his muscles still contracting.

Ten minutes, fifteen, twenty—John remained unconscious. His vitals were weak.

After twenty minutes, John's vital signs stabilized. Thirty minutes passed, and his tense muscles relaxed. He lay motionless, drenched in sweat. Jean applied cool compresses to his forehead to keep his temperature down. Another ten minutes passed. John rolled his head slightly to the right, then back to the left. His eyes briefly opened.

"You with me, John? Can you hear me? John, do you know where you are? Wake up, John?"

"Yeah, I, uh, I do, Jean. Is that you?" John opened his eyes as the first smile he'd experienced in days, if not weeks, adorned his face. Tears streamed from John's eyes. "Jean, I remember Mary, I remember my baby, and oh my God, I... I remember everything. Jean, you did it. You gave me my life back!"

Jean could no longer control her emotions. She leaned down to John, still secured to his bed, and embraced him, sobbing on his shoulder. After a few moments, Jean realized the awkwardness of the embrace.

"Oh, hell, let me get you out of these straps."

Jean freed John from his tie-downs. He sat up and embraced his nurse. The two of them held one another like long-lost family members.

Jean released her embrace and composed herself. "Okay, John, now the hard part begins."

They both laughed at the absurdity of what Jean had just said. As brutal as the treatment had been, they both believed everything next would almost certainly be more challenging. They had two more hours before breakfast would be served, which left precious little time to devise a plan to rescue Doc and get them both on the ship.

Doc had received treatment for his injuries, dehydration, and malnourishment. At that point, his medical team shifted their focus to Doc's preparation for rehabilitation. His mind was at ease with his decision to allow the complete wipe. He blamed himself for so much that had gone wrong. For Doc, the decision offered a logical way to restart his life and not suffer the anguish of his failures. A beep at Doc's door cracked the early morning silence, but it did not wake him.

"Mr. Blake, are you awake?" Jean whispered into the unlit room as the door slid closed behind her.

"Mr. Blake, wake up."

"Desmond." Jean's voice increased to a near-conversational tone, to no avail.

"Doc," Jean said, raising her voice further while shaking Doc's shoulder.

"What? Huh? Oh, damn, you scared me. What, what is it, Nurse?"

"Doc, listen—"

"Who are you? Where's my nurse?"

"Doc, calm down. I need you to listen to me."

"Listen to you? I don't even know who you are. How do you know my friends call me Doc?"

"Calm down, and I'll explain everything."

"Fine then, start explaining!"

"I'm Nurse Jean. I'm on John Calloway's medical—"

"John? You know John? What have you done with him? Is he okay?"

"Doc, you've gotta let me talk. There's no time. John is in grave danger, and we have just over an hour to figure things out. He's doing fine. He's very sore and weak from the Rev Rehab right now, but he's fine."

"The Rev Rehab? Why did he need the Rev Rehab?"

"Didn't you... oh, I guess you didn't know. John's rehab went terribly wrong. He woke up in the middle of the process. It really messed his mind up, and Big Brain specialists had to come in and try an experimental procedure to stabilize him. The procedure worked, but he lost all his memories of you, his friends, and even Mary and the baby. Without his memories of Mary—"

"He couldn't resist the Big Brains," Doc said, finishing Jean's sentence.

"Exactly. And now we think the Big Brains are worried that other humans here who have formed families will—"

"There are humans here with families?"

"Yes, Doc... we don't have time for this. The Big Brains seem worried. They're gonna use John as a guinea pig to figure out how he does it so they can stop it."

"Okay. What do we need to do?"

"Doc, the only way for him to get out of here is for him to return to Earth. The Big Brains have a mission planned for tonight after—" Jean looked on with a hint of concern, almost searching for the right words.

"After what?"

"After... after your first treatment in the rehab process."

"Oh, yeah, that's scheduled for this morning."

"You didn't object to it?"

"No, well, I wasn't, but now that I know John is okay, I'm gonna help him."

"He knows, Doc. There's only one problem. The ship is the only place they can implant the neuronet. If you escape with us now, the ship won't launch until the Big Brains find you."

"Can you help him escape without me?"

"I think so, yes. He's weak from the serum, but I think he'll manage as long as we get moving."

"Sounds to me like you don't need me for anything, then. Why are you wasting time here with me at all?"

"John wanted to make sure you were okay with going through the first step in the rehab. It just installs what we call the neuronet. That has to be done on the ship to keep you knocked out and properly activate the devices. Once they're installed, the rehab process—the part where your mind is first altered… that's done here in your room."

"I was going to let them do it anyway, so that's fine. But if I'm not needed for John's escape, then I'll just be a liability."

"John said he needs you to come. He couldn't explain why. He said he was certain you had to be there with him."

"That's nonsense. If he's got his memories back, he doesn't need to worry about the Big Brains. I'm useless."

"Doc, I already tried to convince him it would be too hard to get you on the ship, that there just isn't enough time, but he refuses to leave without you."

"Damn kid, he's so damn stubborn."

"I know, Doc, but he insists it's the only way."

"Fine, fine, whatever. I'll go. What's the plan?"

"I'm going to get John out of here before they come to take him to the Science Center. The Big Brains already think he's regained his ability to fight them off, so it should look like he escaped alone. He's going to hide in the city till nightfall, and then I'll help him get you both on the ship."

Doc agreed. Jean left the room.

John gained enough strength to lift himself from his bed and stretch his muscles from the havoc the Rev Rehab had wreaked upon them. It sapped his strength, but his mind was buzzing with energy and excitement. Memories dashed through his mind; those from Earth and the camp before his rehabilitation merged with those from after.

After about twenty minutes, John's door opened, and Jean rushed in.

"Doc's in. He doesn't think you need—"

"No, I absolutely need him. I know it. I don't know why, but I know this all fails without him."

"Okay, well, we're running out of time. Are you ready?"

"I'm about as ready as I'll ever be."

"And you remember where we had lunch, right?"

"Yeah, yeah, I can get there."

"Okay, go there and eat. Make sure you grab something you can bring with you and some water bottles. The ship's never gone for very long, but you'll need something, I'm sure. Don't worry about Doc; he'll have a chance to eat again. I need to get to the nurse's station before Clara arrives. Give me ten minutes before you head out. Here, change into these."

Jean handed John a pair of shoes suitable for walking around outside and a fresh set of clothes.

"You can use that carry bag to bring some supplies."

"Doc's room is just three doors down from yours. Listen, you need to be on that ship no later than two hours before launch when they detach the loading connector. Once that's detached from the medical bay, there's no way to board other than through the crew module. Understand?"

"Yeah, I got it. I... I can't tell you how much I appreciate your help."

"No thanks needed. I'm just so happy for you. I'm so glad you've got your memories back. I pray you and Mary will reunite."

John hugged Jean lovingly, the only way he could convey his appreciation that his words failed to communicate. Jean patted John on the back to acknowledge her understanding. The two ended their embrace, said their goodbyes, and Jean left.

John changed his clothes as the prescribed ten minutes elapsed. He opened his door and checked that the hallway remained clear. He left his room and headed down the hall. As he reached Doc's door, he paused, contemplating that this might be his last chance to see Doc if things should go wrong.

When John heard the clatter of breakfast carts being readied for rounds, his sense of urgency returned, and he made haste for the exit. John accepted that the only way he would see Doc again was to ensure he succeeded with their escape plans.

Doc finished breakfast. He tried to settle his mind as he awaited his medical team's arrival. He wondered if his friend had made it to safety and if he would have any complications like John. Mostly, he wondered if they could pull off their escape.

Doc's medical team arrived later than expected, but he was glad he had the extra time to prepare himself physically and emotionally for the procedure.

"Well, Dr. Blake, are you about ready?"

"Please, I told you, call me Doc."

"I keep forgetting, Doc. My apologies. Let me introduce you to Dr. Smith. He's the specialist who will carry out the treatment today."

"Good morning, Dr. Smith."

"Good morning, Dr. Blake. I'm sure you're very curious about how this works, but we're a bit pressed for time. I'll happily address details with you afterward, but is there anything that concerns you that we need to discuss now?"

"No, no, the medical team here has been very helpful in explaining what I should expect. Why are we pressed for time? Would it be better to wait for another day?"

"We should have plenty of time to complete the procedure, but we had a situation this morning that delayed our arrival. That's nothing for you to worry about, though. Let's get you over to the stasis room and get you prepped."

The medical team escorted Doc down the hallway, led him through the double doors, and eventually onto the ship. Dr. Smith's medical team was already waiting in the stasis room, ready to begin.

"Dr. Smith, everything is ready to go. All the ship's stasis systems are working normally."

"Great. Okay, Doc, if I can call you that as well?"

"Sure, Doc's perfect."

"Okay, Doc. Well, hop up into the chair here so we can get you situated. We'll need to shave a few small—" noticing Doc's primarily bald head, "well, maybe just a couple of small spots on the back of your head to apply these pads."

"We're also going to apply these restraints to make sure there are no unplanned movements once we get the procedure going. For this first step, we're going to put you out. It will feel very similar to the Big Brains' stasis power."

Doc nodded in understanding.

"I think we're ready if you are, Doc. This will all seem pretty quick to you. Are you ready?"

"Sure, I'm ready. Go ahead."

CHAPTER 35

D r. Smith nodded to his nurse. She reached under his chair, then a blue light flashed above his head, and Doc's world went dark.

"Okay, can you open your eyes?" Dr. Smith asked. "Open your eyes for us, please."

Doc's eyelids opened.

"Don't try to do anything else. We need you to keep still. Just open your eyes."

With a few rapid blinks, Doc's eyes widened as he took in the light above him.

"Okay, great. There is no need to talk yet. If you hear me, I want you to look as far to your right as possible without turning your head."

Doc shifted his eyes hard to the right.

"Now, do the same thing and look back to the left."

"Excellent. Now, up and then down for me, please?"

"Perfect. Okay, now tell me your full name."

"It's, uh, it's Dr. Desmond Richard Blake. Just call me Doc," he said with a gentle smile.

"Understood, Doc. We sure will. Okay, just a couple more tests, and we'll put you back under, okay?"

DETACHMENTS

Dr. Smith tested Doc's reflexes and sensitivity at each of his extremities.

"Okay, things look perfect here. We're ready to put you under again if you are."

"Sure thing, I'm ready."

Doc drifted into stasis. A moment later, he awoke to Dr. Smith's voice.

"Great, Doc, things are going very well. Now, I want you to tell me your earliest memory from as far back as you can remember."

Doc thought for a few moments. "I only have fragments in my mind, but I remember digging in the dirt with a friend of mine. He was using a claw-type hammer, and I guess I leaned in too close, and he brought it down on my head. I remember going to my mother for a towel to stop the bleeding, but I ended up getting stitches. I think that's when I first became interested in pursuing medicine."

"And how old were you then?"

"I would have been about three, I guess."

"Okay, that's perfect, Doc. Now tell me, what's your nurse's name?"

"Anna, it's Nurse Anna."

"Great. Let's get you back under and finish the next three implants. When we wake you up from each of those, we'll have you do some exercises with your arms and legs to make sure the implants are working correctly. You all set?"

Dr. Smith installed the subsequent two implants without issue, waking Doc after each for the exercises. Dr. Smith put Doc under for the last time, installed the final implant, and woke him to complete the procedure.

"Doc, how are you feeling?"

"I feel good, relaxed... good."

"Great. It's not unusual, but also not typical, that you might develop a headache in the first twenty-four hours. If that should happen, alert your medical team, okay?"

"Sure, easy enough."

"Let's see… okay, vitals all look good. Let's get you up and back to your room for dinner."

"Dinner! It's dinnertime already?"

"Not quite, but we're well past lunch. We've been at this for about five hours. Let's get you down from there and see how you do walking. Give me about five steps, turn around, and walk back. Everything feel normal?"

"Yeah, you couldn't have gotten rid of the pain in my knee with all of this?"

Dr. Smith snickered, "Yeah, nothing I did will change that. Sorry, Doc."

Dr. Smith's team led Doc back to his room, where he waited for his meal and hoped John would soon visit. He still did not feel the need to go with John, but he wished for one last chance to see him. Doc felt like he had nothing to return to on Earth, and the peace the rehabilitation promised was an attractive way to enjoy the rest of his life without guilt. He still hoped he had not failed John and that somehow he would make it back to Earth and, perhaps through some miracle, find Mary and their child alive and well.

The sun slipped below the horizon, and the planet's two moons were visible in the sky. John had to make his way from downtown Earth City, where he was safe from Big Brains that might search for him, and return to the ship. Big Brain security would be tight as he neared his goal. John used the tunnel entrance near the Empyrean. He knew that would at least get him close to the entrance of the crew support building. He took a long, deep breath and lowered himself down into the passage.

His muscles were still sore from the Rev Rehab, but he regained much of his strength throughout the day. The shoes Jean gave him allowed him to make quick work of the wall-walking necessary to straddle the muck below. John reached the exit across from the crew support building and popped open the cover to breathe in fresh air. As John caught his breath, he surveyed the increased security he would have to navigate. To his surprise, he saw no guards patrolling, no lights sweeping across the property, no fencing, or anything to suggest security was as tight as he had imagined.

John slinked out of the passageway and tucked himself behind a bush, expecting a trap. He lacked the time to contemplate the myriad possibilities and stood to make his first move across the road. The lights of a nearby vehicle caught John's eye. He dove to the ground; his heart jumped, and he gasped for air to recover from the fright as the vehicle continued out of sight.

John crept around the greenery, made one last scan of the area, and darted across the street to the entrance. He hugged tight to the wall next to the door and checked for any sign that his dash had alerted the Big Brain guards... nothing.

He pressed his hand to the door and concentrated, trying to sense whether a Big Brain could be on the other side. John climbed the stoop and opened the door. It made just a whisper, but enough to cause John alarm. He peeked around the corner of the door and noted no resistance. He closed the door gently to ensure he remained undetected.

The stairs to the riskiest part of his mission lay only a few feet in front of him. He climbed each step, allowing each foot to land purposefully and silently. His eyes crested the floor of the sky bridge. Ever so slowly, he ascended. Once he exited the stairwell, he knew he would have to traverse the entire chokepoint. If the Big Brains had planned to ensnare him in some form of trap, the next fifty feet of his journey would be ideal for an ambush.

John stepped from the stairwell onto the connector between the crew support and medical facilities as he snuck across the sky bridge and looked at his goal. The ship remained connected. *Thank God, it's still there*, he thought. He could see the coupling between the medical facility and the ship's loading bay was still in place. John had not missed his chance. His pace quickened. He expected he had about half an hour to get Doc and get on the ship before the crew pulled the coupling away.

John's breathing quickened as he closed in on the staircase that descended to the medical facility. The anticipation of a surprise attack from the Big Brains became all-consuming. His foot reached the stairwell, and still, there was nothing. While he by no means felt safe from the Big Brains, the tight confines of the stairs would make a swarm difficult. That comforted him. He could resist the Big Brains' stasis powers and focus his energy on the closest Big Brain. He surmised he could land several punches, enough to get free of many Big Brains.

As he continued to think through potential scenarios for how to deal with an attack, he realized he had not used his abilities since he received the Rev Rehab. His memories were all restored, and he was confident he could focus the way he had practiced, but he could not prevent doubt from seeping into his thoughts. Worse, John worried that the doubt alone could be enough to degrade his one advantage over the Big Brains. He tried to distract himself from his concerns. *Indeed,* he thought, *the Big Brains were too wise to fight in such a confined stairwell.*

John descended as fast as possible and slowed as he arrived in the area where he remembered the Big Brain guards were staged. This time, he could hear no voices in his mind and could feel no sign of their presence. If they weren't in their hold, perhaps they were waiting for him in another location he had not yet contemplated. Regardless, he felt he had passed the point of no return, and any interaction moving forward would be a fight—something only hours ago he would never have dreamed of contemplating. He paused momentarily. Perhaps there was some wisdom in choosing a nonviolent path he had not considered. If there was, though, that path eluded his thinking as he clenched his fists and readied himself. He stepped out of the stairwell and into the main hallway. Doc's room was his next stop.

To John's relief, the hallway was clear, and he quickly made his way to Doc's room. John pressed the button, and the door slid open.

"It's about damn time. What the hell took you so long?" Doc joked as he rushed over to greet John with a firm handshake and hug.

"Damn, it's good to finally see you again, Doc."

"Same here, kid, same here. I started to wonder if you made it out of here this morning at all. My medical team was late getting me into the procedure. I'm betting it was because of you, but they never said for sure."

"The rehab. How are you feeling? Did everything go well?"

"It did, yes. No issues at all. I just finished dinner about thirty minutes ago. Speaking of which, you have little time, so you better get on that ship."

"You mean, we."

"Nah, kid, I've been sitting here thinking. I don't think it makes any sense for me to go with you. I helped as much as I could. Well, hopefully, I helped. I dunno."

"Doc, there's no way I could have done any of this without you, and there's no way I'm getting on that ship alone."

"Kid, what good can it be for me to come with you? I'll be a liability if we have any run-ins with the Big Brains."

"Listen, I'm not leaving you here to go through God knows what with that shit they put in your brain. I'm not going without you. So, what's it gonna be?"

"Jesus, you are one stubborn son of a bitch. Fine. I'll go, but if something goes wrong, don't go blaming me. I warned you this was a bad idea."

John laughed and nodded his head in agreement.

"All right, let's get going. That link to the ship is gonna detach soon."

John approached the door.

"Now, it's possible that when we open this door, everything could go to hell in a handbasket. You ready?"

"As long as you are, kid. You're the one who can stop the Big Brains. I'm just along for the ride here."

"Honestly, it's been shockingly easy getting here. Leaving this room and entering the ship seems to be the last two places they could try to stop us."

"All we can do is try. Worst-case scenario, we're still stuck on this planet," Doc said. "Let's do this!"

John nodded and pressed the button on the wall. The door opened, and again, no resistance impeded their progress. The men left the room and went to the double doors that led to the ship.

John focused, trying to ensure their success thus far had not lulled him into a false sense of security. He pressed the button to open the doors and saw the clear path ahead to the ship's main holding area. The men entered the ship as the loading door closed behind them.

"Holy shit, I can't believe we're really—"

"What's that? Quick, get in the stasis room."

John pushed the button on the ship's wall, opening the stasis room where both men experienced their rehabilitations. They could hear the double doors connecting the medical bay and the ship open as they entered the chamber. John leaned his ear against the stasis room's door to listen for any sign of what was happening.

"It sounds—yeah, it sounds like footsteps. I think they're humans."

"They could still have Big Brains with them. Sit tight. Maybe, hopefully... they're not looking for us."

John held up his hand to silence Doc, as he believed a Big Brain was right outside the door. Both men sat quietly, expecting the door to open but praying it would not. They continued to balance on that razor's edge for what seemed like an eternity.

A voice from beyond the door shattered the silence. "READY!"

"CLEAR!" a second voice shouted from slightly farther away.

"RELEASE!" the first voice shouted, followed by a loud metallic bang. The ship rocked slightly as John heard footsteps walk away from the door. Then he heard the voice call out again.

"TWO READY!"

Followed by a faint "CLEAR!" from even further away than the earlier response.

"RETRACT!"

Following the "retract" command, John heard a rhythmic rotating sound, like gears turning. The sound lasted for close to a minute. A whoosh followed shortly after that sounded like the double doors closing, but louder, faster, and closer.

"I think they're gone, Doc. I think they released the coupling to the med bay."

"Sit tight, John. Let's give it a minute before we check."

John pressed his ear against the door to listen for any movement. "I'm gonna check it out," he said.

Doc nodded, accepting that John had already decided.

John stood and pressed the button, opening the door to the main area. As the door opened, John saw the gurneys that filled the holding bay, no doubt awaiting humans the Big Brains would abduct. John looked back at Doc from the doorway.

"Yep, the ship is closed up. They must have retracted the link to the med bay. That means we've got about an hour and forty-five minutes before we launch."

"Well, I suggest we stay in here, John. There's much more to hold on to in case things get rough."

"Agreed."

John turned back into the stasis room and sat on the floor with his bag of supplies.

"Why don't you hop up in the chair? It's gotta be more comfortable."

"Nah, you go ahead, Doc. I'm fine here. You need a bottle of water or anything?"

"I'm good. It's better to save all we can, just in case. I don't know how their technology works, but imagine this will be a long trip."

"Fair enough, Doc."

The men settled in and prepared for launch and the long journey to Earth. They both sat quietly, with only occasional time hacks from John.

They feared alerting anyone to their presence but remained shocked they had made it so far.

"Should be about an hour from launch now. The crew should be boarding," John said.

About fifteen minutes later, the lights on the ship blinked, and the low hum they barely realized existed in the background went silent. A moment later, a loud sound of pressure being released, like popping the cap off a soda bottle, echoed through the chamber. A pumping sound immediately followed, something the men could feel through the floor. The pumping gave way to a light groaning noise, like an engine turning over; then the low hum returned. A moment later, the lights turned back on, followed by a few beeps in the stasis room and somewhere in the main bay of the ship. The entire sequence took less than thirty seconds.

"Well, uh, that was interesting."

"I was thinking the same thing, John. Too late to change our minds?"

Both men laughed. They started to believe they would succeed.

"Thirty minutes to launch."

"Ten minutes to go."

"Should be any minute now, Doc."

Another fifteen minutes ticked by, then thirty more.

"We've gotta be well past launch time, Doc. What do ya figure is going on?"

"I dunno, kid. You think they're onto us?"

"I… I think if they were, they would have found us by now. It's not like there's any place to hide."

"Let me get a swig of that water, John."

John handed Doc a bottle. He cracked open the top and took a quick drink. "You want any?"

"No, I'm good. I think I'm gonna go out there. It's an hour and a half past launch. Something's wrong."

DETACHMENTS

Doc agreed with John's assessment and nodded, even if somewhat begrudgingly. With his tacit concurrence, John stood up, walked toward the stasis room door, and pressed the button.

CHAPTER 36

As soon as the doors slid open, John could feel the familiar sensation of stasis powers being used against him. He focused his mind, closed his eyes, and, with a moment of concentration on his love for Mary, fought off the sensation with ease. Relieved he still could fight off the Big Brains, John reopened his eyes to an astonishing sight. What John saw was so jarring that he stumbled back into the stasis room, dumbfounded. The door shut again, closing off the chamber from the main holding area.

"John, are you okay? What's going on? Are the Big Brains here? Are we toast? Talk to me, John."

"You're not gonna believe this, Doc."

"What? John! What?"

"We're here; we must be. What else could explain it?" John asked.

"Yes, we're here on the ship. Did they find us?"

"I guess that makes sense. No, it... it has to be; what else—"

Doc grabbed John's shoulder and shook him to get his attention. "John, John, what the hell did you see? What's going on?"

"Oh! Uh... shit. Sorry, Doc. Sorry. You're not gonna believe this, but I think we're here. I think we're back on Earth."

"How the hell can that be? What did you see? What's going on out there?"

"The gurneys, Doc, they're half full of people. They're already abducting people. We have to be on Earth already."

"How is that possible? We didn't even feel the ship launch, so how could we have gotten to Earth so fast?"

"I don't know, but I think I know how we didn't feel any movement."

"You do?"

"Maybe. Captain Meadowbrook, the Big Brain I met, said the way they float is by manipulating gravity and shielding it so it doesn't affect anything other than the object they're moving. He said he had been researching that his whole life. I think this ship uses some kind of gravity drive, and since we're inside it, we can't feel any of the movements."

"Well, look at the big brain on John," Doc teased. "I'll buy that for why we didn't feel anything, but I don't see how that explains getting here so fast. Regardless, we may not have much time. For all we know, we're already on our way back to their planet."

"Let me check again. The main bay has the stasis on, so don't get too close to this door."

John opened the door again. "Looks like there's more people, so I think they're still collecting samples."

"How many—"

"Oh wait, hang on. The floor is opening up. It's… it's… oh my God."

"What is it, John?"

"It looks like they're returning the people now, so they must have already collected their samples. They're just floating off the gurneys and right out of the bottom of the ship."

Doc moved a little closer to witness the sight.

"Don't get any closer to me, Doc. I can feel the stasis here."

John squatted down to give Doc a better view of the bay. They were both transfixed as they watched the people being lowered through the floor of the holding bay one by one. The longest part of the process between transfers was the time it took to lower the people back down to Earth.

"They can't all be going to the same place. Can the ship be moving that fast, and we don't even feel it?"

"It must. I guess the ship doesn't need to stop for long if they can shield the people like the ship. They can lower the people down while the ship is still moving. They only need to stop for a moment to put them back. It's pretty incredible when you think about what they can do."

"There's only three more, John. We're gonna have to make our move soon."

"Let's wait till the last one is off. I want to make sure we don't inadvertently hurt any of these people or, worse, get them taken back to Twin Moons," John said.

"Twin Moons?"

"Yeah, that's what my medical team called the Big Brain planet."

"One more to go, John."

"Yeah, there he goes."

"Okay, let me see if I can get to the crew module. Wait here, Doc."

As John walked between the gurneys, he approached the center of the room and could see through the bottom of the ship to the Earth below. They were far too high to consider escape, but John at least pondered the choice, knowing how daunting it would be to force Captain Meadowbrook to take him home.

"Doc, I think it's safe. I don't feel the stasis anymore. Doc? Can you hear me?"

The door to the stasis opened with Doc standing in the doorway.

"Yeah, I hear ya, kid. I think you're right. Otherwise, I'd probably be out by now."

Doc worked his way through the gurneys and over to John.

"All right, let's find the door to the crew compartment."

John and Doc made their way over to the side of the holding bay. The smooth walls made the loading doors and, apparently, the crew module virtually invisible. John felt around the walls, looking for the button to open the door. Before he found it, he sensed the faint feeling of a Big Brain's stasis power.

"Doc! Get back, get on the ground!"

Doc knew precisely what that meant. As he reached the floor, the door to the crew module opened, and a Big Brain emerged, causing Doc to succumb to its power. Seeing John unaffected, the Big Brain held his skinny arms out in front of him, signaling for John to stop.

"You're John, aren't you?"

"Yes. Now wake my friend up, or I'm knocking you out." John closed his fists and brought them up into a fighting stance, ready to engage if the need should arise.

"Okay, okay, I don't want to hurt anyone. Captain Meadowbrook said you might be here. I'm only—"

"What do you mean? He said I might be here?"

"When he learned you escaped from the medical bay, he thought you might try to get on the ship. He told the guards not to search for you until we returned from this trip and not to stop you if you found your way here."

"What? Why? Never mind... none of that matters right now. Wake my friend up!"

"I just... I just need to close the bay," the Big Brain explained as he motioned toward the opening they used to return the abducted humans to Earth.

"You're not doing a fucking thing till you wake my friend up. Do you understand me?"

"John, I told you I won't hurt you or anyone, but how do I know you or your friend won't hurt me?"

"You're going to have to worry about me hurting you if you don't wake my friend. You know you can't stop me with your stasis power. I'm stronger than you. Don't make me do this."

"You seem to forget something, though, John."

"Oh, what's that?"

"You may be able to resist our stasis, but—"

John felt a sensation he had never experienced as his feet lost contact with the floor. He floated off the ground along with the two gurneys he stood between. Panic coursed through John's body as he flailed about in a weightless prison of gravity.

"We're not violent, John. If I wanted to hurt you, you would already be in pain. We don't believe in violence. That's why we use our stasis ability. Now, I'm going to put you down, and if you're willing to talk rationally, I'm willing to discuss waking your friend."

John nodded, accepting that he could not fight against the Big Brain's ability to manipulate gravity. Whoever this Big Brain was, he was strong.

"Now, I'm going to close this loading bay and bring you to the crew module to talk with Captain Meadowbrook. Like I said, he thought you might be with us and is eager to speak with you."

"Will you please wake my friend up?"

As the Big Brain finished closing the bay by turning a lever in the room with his mind, he turned back to John and responded, "Yes, but only after we leave the holding bay. Is that okay with you?"

John looked over at Doc, resting comfortably on the floor. He looked back at the Big Brain and nodded in agreement.

"I'm Ensign Stonemiller. It's nice to meet you. I've heard a lot about you, John."

John remained skeptical of this Big Brain's motives, but he had known Captain Meadowbrook to be reasonable in earlier discussions.

"Yeah, uh, nice to meet you too," John forced the salutation.

"Come this way, John." The Big Brain opened the hatch to the crew module and motioned for John to enter the narrow stairway first.

John went up the stairs as Ensign Stonemiller entered the stairwell behind him. He heard the door slide shut behind them with a beep that

274

caused John to pause. He looked back at his escort and said, "Is there a need for security to be engaged?"

"There's a lot of sensitive equipment on the ship, John. It's not designed for humans. One of you in the command module is risky enough, so two of you in there is far too much risk to accept."

John returned to climbing the stairs to the command module. As he approached the door, it beeped and slid open at Ensign Stonemiller's control.

Doc felt the cold floor against his face as he opened his eyes. He was alone in the holding bay. The center of the floor was closed. He worried about how long he had been out and whether the ship had returned to Twin Moons. He was most concerned about what had happened to John. Doc went over to where he had seen the door open before passing out from the power of the Big Brain. He felt around the wall until he found and pressed the button for the door, but it had no effect.

Doc searched around the holding bay for anything that might force the Big Brains to return to the holding bay, reunite him with John, and, most importantly, allow them to stay on Earth.

As John stepped through the threshold, Captain Meadowbrook spun around and made eye contact with him. Unsurprised, he slowly rotated back toward the control area as he spoke. "You can sit over there, and I'll be with you in a moment."

John watched Meadowbrook struggle to control the ship. Though he made no physical movements, his intensity was clear. He controlled the ship with his mind. John's patience was running short.

"I'm not sure what you're doing or where you're trying to go, but you need to take us back to Earth."

Captain Meadowbrook extended his left arm toward John with one finger held up, as if to tell him to be patient for another minute.

After a few moments, Captain Meadowbrook finished whatever feverish activity he was doing and turned back toward John.

"I'm sorry, John. I had to plot our course before I could speak with you. There are some storms in our path, and when I'm piloting the ship directly, they're not a problem. But to carry on this important conversation, I can't focus enough to keep the ship safe. Now, what were you saying?"

"I need you to return us to Earth. We're not going back to Twin Moons."

Before Captain Meadowbrook could respond, the ship shuddered unexpectedly. The captain returned to his control panel with some urgency.

"Your friend seems to be trying to cause some problems, John. Ensign, John's friend has opened the bay again. Go shut it and activate the holding bay's stasis protocol to keep him under control."

"You better not hurt him!"

"Ensign, make sure he goes under gently."

"Yes, Captain."

"You and your friend can be quite the challenge, John."

"Maybe you shouldn't have abducted us then."

"No, you're right; we shouldn't have. Especially you, John. I'm very sorry. We did not know about Mary. By now, you've already figured out we only select people with no familial attachments. Our records, however, aren't perfect. They depend on how your people record information—like births, deaths, marriages, etc. We couldn't find any records suggesting you were married or had children. We knew your parents had already passed, and we found no birth records for children or siblings. That's why we chose you. We never intended to bring you back to Twin Moons, but when you woke up in our holding bay, we knew that would have a traumatic effect, and your... how should I say this... we thought you would have a better life on Twin Moons. Truly, John, that's the only reason we bring anyone back."

"You're telling me all of those people you abducted today—none of them had any familial connections, and you just put them back to live the rest of their lives like nothing ever happened? None of them woke up?"

"That's right, John—none of them. You're the first person who has woken up since we started doing the sampling on the ship. Before then, we brought everyone to the medical center where we docked the ship. For many years, we didn't put people back at all, but the population of humans was growing far too quickly, so we had to devise new methods."

"But surely some people in the camp would have gone on to meet someone and start a family if they had been returned, but now that family will never exist."

"No, John, that would not have happened."

"How can you know? Maybe a passerby could've helped Mary and me. How can—"

Before he could finish his question, the door to the command module opened, and Ensign Stonemiller entered.

"Is the friend in stasis?"

"Unfortunately, no, sir. He's hiding in the stasis room and somehow blocked the door to prevent me from subduing him. The holding bay is closed now, though."

"Let's hope he doesn't do anything crazy in there."

"Yes, sir. Agreed."

"Okay, start plotting phase two. We should be ready to proceed here shortly."

Doc pressed hard on the makeshift wedge he fashioned, using a medical tray and some surgical tubing wrapped over its edge to provide the friction needed to hold the door closed. A few minutes had passed since the last time he felt the door trying to open, and he wondered if the Big Brain had returned to the crew module.

Doc released his hold on the tray, which stayed wedged in the seam. He looked around the room for anything he could use as a weapon against the Big Brain. He lifted attachments from various medical equipment around the small room, rehearsing a strike with each to determine its suitability. As he lifted the next contender, the metal tray wedging the door slipped out and slammed to the floor, making a loud clanging sound that seemed to echo for days—a noise Doc was sure would invite any waiting Big Brain to enter.

Doc froze for a moment, then gathered his composure. A minute ticked by, then another. Doc concluded he was alone and returned to the door to confirm. While he had not found a weapon, he accepted that even if he had, he still would not stand a chance against the Big Brain.

Doc cautiously approached the doorway to the holding bay to confirm it was clear. He leaned against the wall as far away from the door's button as possible but still within reach. With a deep breath, he opened the door, and as it slid open, he took a quick look into the holding bay and slumped to the ground in sleep.

Doc woke up to find himself on the floor of the stasis room. The door had closed while he was out, and the instrument tray remained in the same spot on the floor by the door. He realized the Big Brains had enabled the holding bay stasis. Had the Big Brain subdued him, Doc would have woken back up in the medical center on Twin Moons.

Doc racked his brain to figure out what he could do to escape the stasis room, rescue John, and get the Big Brains to return them to Earth. He knew he did not have a chance if the stasis was on in the holding bay, so his first order of business was to find some way to deal with that. He looked around the room for anything that might impact the stasis power.

Then it hit him. If other humans could remain in the stasis room during his procedure, there must be a safety feature to keep the main bay from activating when the stasis room is in use. *It's a long shot*, he thought, *but perhaps activating the stasis room would deactivate the holding bay.*

Doc searched around the procedure chair in the area where the nurse had been standing when she activated the stasis during his neuronet procedure. He pressed one button, and the chair raised; then another caused the back to recline, and still a third turned the light on above it. Doc pressed another button and noticed a blue light the size of a dime on the ceiling. The light shone down on the chair in a faint blue circle where a patient's head would rest. Doc surmised, perhaps optimistically, that the light indicated the stasis was active and marked the area where it was unsafe for the medical team.

Doc returned to the door and positioned himself to avoid injury if the stasis remained active. He pressed the button. The door opened. Doc inched closer. He reached the threshold and was no longer affected by the stasis. The system was deactivated. Now Doc needed to find the crew module.

"Calculations complete, sir. Ready for your confirmation."

Captain Meadowbrook turned back toward the control panel.

"Calculations confirmed. Load and prepare to initiate."

"Initiate? Initiate what? What are you doing? Where are you taking us?"

"John, I need you silent right now."

"Calculations loaded, sir."

"Initiate."

Doc proceeded to the door for the crew module. He knew if he made his way up to it, he would have no chance against the Big Brains. *If I could get one to come down to the holding bay and surprise it,* Doc thought, *I might have a chance.* With nothing to use as a weapon, he determined a gurney would suffice. He rolled one into position to push the gurney into a Big Brain as soon as the door opened. He concluded he could hit it before it could defend itself.

Doc locked the wheels into place and headed for the controls to open the holding bay. It had drawn the Big Brains' attention last time, and perhaps it would be enough again. Doc threw open the controls, and the bay opened. The ship rocked violently, and gurneys careened across the bay before the ship stabilized.

The turbulence tossed John to the floor of the command module and shook the craft. Ensign Stonemiller and Captain Meadowbrook avoided injury. Their ability to manipulate gravity allowed them to compensate for the ship's movement.

"What the hell happened?" John said.

"Sir, the gravity shield momentarily failed, but we emerged successfully. The controls are yours."

"It's not… I can't… it's not responding. Something's wrong. Go get John's friend and bring him up here."

Doc picked himself off the floor just as the Big Brain appeared from the doorway. He took one look at Ensign Stonemiller before collapsing back to sleep.

The door in the command module opened, and Doc floated in, followed by Ensign Stonemiller, who had immobilized him. The ensign laid Doc gently on the floor as John watched. Captain Meadowbrook focused intently on the control panel. John could tell he was struggling. Something was wrong, but he had no insight into the damage done.

DETACHMENTS

A few moments passed before the captain turned away from the panel and looked at Ensign Stonemiller. The Big Brains never expressed much emotion, but John sensed the nonverbal communication between the two and realized something catastrophic had happened.

"John, I'm afraid we've lost the ability to control the ship. We're going to crash. Please pay close attention to what I'm going to tell you. Ensign Stonemiller and I almost certainly won't survive the impact. We're going to wake Doc. I need you to make sure he stays calm and listens."

CHAPTER 37

John agreed, and Ensign Stonemiller pulled Doc out of stasis to tell him about his and John's fate.

"Doc, everything's okay. Wake up."

"John, what's… John, behind you!"

"I know. They need to talk to us, Doc. There's no need to fight; the ship is going to crash. They don't think they'll survive the impact, but believe we will."

"Where are we, John?"

"I think we're back on their planet, Doc. Here, sit up, and we can ask."

John looked at Captain Meadowbrook for the answer.

"Yes, gentlemen, we are on our planet. In a way, though, we never left it."

John and Doc looked at each other. Both perplexed, they looked back at Captain Meadowbrook for more clarity.

"But we saw humans. We had to be on Earth. Will you please just be honest and level with us?" John asked.

"John, do you remember our discussion about evolution and the False Brains?"

"Yes, of course."

DETACHMENTS

"Remember, I told you the False Brains modified a pathogen from a species that preceded the Improved Brains to use against the New Brains? Well, John, that earlier species is Homo sapiens. You never left Earth. Twin Moons is Earth. Your planet is our planet. We live more than a million years after your species went extinct. Your species created the False Brains. When your species lost control of them, Homo sapiens integrated themselves with technology to compete. The integrated humans evolved to become the Improved Brains. This ship, and only this ship, is how we travel back in time to collect our samples from your species to fight the False Brains' virus."

"What the hell are you talking about?" Doc asked.

"John will explain all that later, but we're very short on time. Now, I've been able to slow the ship's descent and speed enough to where it should be within survivable limits for both of you, but it will not be for us. The straps on the bulkhead here should fit around you, so get strapped in."

John and Doc quickly stood and made their way to the emergency restraints. Designed for the smaller frames of the Big Brains, John had a somewhat tricky time locking the restraints. When he settled, the reality of what Captain Meadowbrook said hit him as well.

"My God, we're stuck here? We're going to crash and be stuck on Twin Moons forever."

"No, John, we're stuck in the time of your species, and I need you to convey this to your people. This ship is the only means we have to collect samples. Without those samples, our species would go extinct. Your people's DNA, stem cells, and antibodies are critical to maintaining our birth rate at levels that sustain our population. You must ensure your people secure the remains of this ship, work to rebuild it, and return it to my time."

"How are we going—"

"I've already loaded the proper calculations into the ship's systems. Here's the most important part: your people must continue to repair this ship until it's operational, even if it takes thousands of years. My species will survive if the ship is returned using the calculations I preprogrammed."

"I don't understand. Thousands of years? How—"

"John, you won't understand how time travel works, but your people can eventually operate this ship. Once it is operational, they'll need to start the ship's return sequence. Unfortunately, according to Nurse Jean, you've already had the Rev Rehab; is that right?"

John was stunned that Captain Meadowbrook knew that not only had John taken the Rev Rehab, but that Nurse Jean was responsible.

"John, relax. I spoke with her before we launched. Why do you think no guards were trying to catch you? Who do you think ordered the Rev Rehab for you, anyway?"

"You?" John asked, surprised by the insinuation.

"Yes. I didn't plan for you to receive it in the Medical Center, but I had hoped it would restore your full memories and do so safely."

"And... you weren't worried that other humans in Earth City might have developed the ability to resist your stasis?"

"Worried? No, not at all. The humans who live in Earth City are very peaceful and live among us as friends. We've never had violence between Big Brains and humans in Earth City. Was I curious how your brain could resist us? Absolutely. Would I want to understand that more? Certainly. But just like the rehabilitation, we'd only ever use treatments that have your consent."

"Unfortunately, though," Captain Meadowbrook said as he looked toward Doc, "the ship will require a functioning neuronet to operate."

"Doc, you will not live long enough to start the sequence, but your neuronet will survive for about fifty years after your brain functions have ceased. As long as your people develop the technology necessary to sustain the neuronet indefinitely, they'll eventually learn how to interface it with the ship's systems."

Doc nodded, acknowledging the challenge but accepting the responsibility he had.

"Gentlemen, I know you have many questions, and we have very little time. But that is the most critical technical information I need you to convey to your people's scientists. The most important thing you must impart to your political leadership is that they must not attempt to use the technology on this ship for any other purpose. This ship must not fall into the hands of people who might misuse the technology; it must be kept secret until it is naturally developed. I'm sorry to say, though, that won't happen until well after your species has gone extinct. The technology within this ship can destroy the planet itself. In fact, we think this technology is what caused the moon to split, which resulted in the largest mass extinction since the asteroid that killed off the dinosaurs."

"Let me make sure I fully understand this," Doc said. "You're from a million years into Earth's future. You sample our species to sustain yours, and you only take people who have no families?"

"That's right, Doc, exactly. We've been able to obtain records for your people to make sure we only abduct those whose future wouldn't be altered by knowing we exist, like you, Doc, and all the other humans on Twin Moons. But as I mentioned, our records are limited by how well your people keep them."

"But how did you know I'd never have—"

John stopped himself before finishing the question, as the answer he most feared slid into his mind. Captain Meadowbrook could tell John was connecting the dots of the totality of the process.

"Yes, John, we start with death records. Then, we look at whether someone had a family. Since you and Mary were never married, we had no reason to believe you had any family."

"Then I must have—"

"Yes, John, our records showed your wounds were self-inflicted," Captain Meadowbrook said with the closest thing he could muster to a sympathetic tone. "Right there, where we sampled you. That's where your life was meant to end. Many of the people we have sampled took their own lives. That's true for you as well, Doc. The samples we need require humans to be between twenty and forty years old. Deaths by suicide are often unattended, so we can collect our samples without being detected by people we can't take with us."

John fought hard to choke back the tears as he struggled with whether he wanted to know more. "So Mary and the baby? They died that night too?"

"We don't know, John. All we know about Mary is what we've learned from you. After an incident we had, I believe you know her, Shirley? Well, after her mother's tragic death, we no longer considered pregnant women suitable samples. So, we would not have researched Mary's death once we realized she died with child."

"She could be alive, then... the baby could be alive too, right?"

"At this moment, she must be. John, phase two was our plan to get Mary and bring her back to Twin Moons to be with you. We were on our way to where we first found you, the one place we knew she'd be."

"Oh my God, Doc, she's alive! Mary's alive!" Tears formed in John's eyes as Captain Meadowbrook suddenly turned away in concern.

"What... what's the matter?" Doc asked.

"We have one minute to impact, John. I've tried to steer the ship to a field near a domicile where, hopefully, someone can help you get to Mary. Ensign Stonemiller and I will use all our strength to help stabilize and protect the ship during impact. You will not have much time, but hopefully, you can save her and your child. I'm so very sorry for the challenges we've caused you and hope you both have long and wonderful lives. I hope you will forgive me and help save my species."

The ship slammed into the earth. Captain Meadowbrook and Ensign Stonemiller bounced about the crew module, doing their best to use their gravity defenses to shield themselves from hitting the walls of the crew module. It was clear Ensign Stonemiller succumbed to his injuries before the ship came to a stop. Captain Meadowbrook maintained his defenses throughout the ordeal but remained motionless on the floor as John and Doc hung nearly upside down from their emergency straps.

The control panel lights had faded away, and the cabin lights dimmed and flickered. John and Doc released their harnesses and rushed to check on Captain Meadowbrook.

"Doc, is there anything you can do?"

"I don't know anything about their physiology. He still seems to be with us, but barely."

"Go save Mary before it's too late and you can no longer help—" Captain Meadowbrook said as he faded away.

"He's right, John. There's nothing I can do. Let's get to Mary."

John accepted the reality of the situation. He and Doc then climbed to the only light remaining in the crew module, an emergency light near the stairwell to the holding bay. The door was wide open already, an apparent emergency feature. They entered the inverted winding stairwell and scaled the narrow passageway to the holding chamber, hoping they might find an exit. As they reached the bay, emergency lights from the doors to the crew chamber, the stasis room, and the loading bay cast sufficient light to reveal a jagged mountain of gurneys and twisted metal. Aside from the narrow opening in the center of the floor from when Doc attempted to open it, the ship was largely undamaged.

Time was of the essence as John charted his path up the wreckage to the opening through the floor above. As he reached the top, he called to Doc, "I can see the sky, and if we can get through, I think we can get out. Find something we can use as a pry bar to wedge this thing open some more."

Doc found a gurney leg that had already been bent over ninety degrees. He stood on the toppled gurney and repeatedly bent the leg back against itself until the metal weakened and gave way. Doc tossed the leg up to John, and he got to work trying to create enough space to wiggle through the gap. After a few moments, John squeezed through to the other side. He climbed through the floor's opening into another compartment, the bottom half of the ship. The compartment was virtually identical in size and shape to the holding bay but was filled with various equipment, wiring, and unidentifiable components that must have been the technology that powered the ship. John looked up and saw a three-foot-diameter hole several feet above that led to the ship's exterior.

"Doc, there's not a lot of room to move around in here, but climb up, and I'll pull you through."

Doc made his way up the shaky, makeshift scaffolding. Gurneys creaked and slipped on one another along the way. He reached through the narrow opening. John grabbed and pulled him through as the top gurney slipped from its perch and slammed into the ceiling below.

The hole directly above their narrow confines was out of reach for John's best jump. Without contemplation, Doc recognized their dilemma and knelt on the floor. John stood on Doc's back and grabbed hold of the rim of the exit. He pulled himself up and through, then reached back down for Doc.

"Give me your hand."

Doc stretched up as John leaned as far into the hole as he could for Doc's hand, but they were still more than a foot apart. Doc jumped to reach John, but he could barely touch his fingertips. Gaining a firm enough grasp to escape was out of reach.

"I'm gonna climb back down through the floor and see if I can find something to get out with," Doc said.

"We don't have the time. What if you fall trying to get back up? It's too dangerous."

"We're never going—"

"Hold on, quiet. I hear something," John said. "It's headlights! Someone's coming! Over here! Hey! Over here!" John yelled at the top of his lungs as a farm truck approached.

The truck arrived at the site and skidded to a stop. The driver jumped from his vehicle, shotgun in hand.

"Who the hell are you? You get your hands up!" the man yelled as he leveled the shotgun to his shoulder, both barrels zeroed in on John.

John held his hands up as he stood atop the wreckage. "Sir, we just need some help. Please help us! My friend is trapped, and my, uh, my wife, she's in labor down the road." John lied about Mary being his wife, but he knew how conservative people in the area were and thought it best to call her his wife.

"What's your name, boy?"

"Sir, it's John. John Calloway."

"John Calloway? John Calloway. That name's familiar. You from 'round here?"

"I believe so, but I'm not exactly sure where we are. I live in Torrance County at my father's old place."

"I got good news then. You're very close. You're in Lincoln County and on my ranch. Why don't you come down from there, nice and slow?"

"Sir, you gotta listen to me. I know none of this makes sense, but you have to help me get my friend out of this ship. He's a doctor, and my wife needs his help right now."

"I don't think I'm gonna do anything of the sort. Now, how 'bout you come on down here?"

"Sir, can I ask your name, please?"

"My name? What do you need my name for?"

"I've worked on a lot of the ranches around here, so I wouldn't be surprised if this was one of them."

"Is that so? You don't look familiar to me, boy. But, uh, you can call me Mac."

"Mac? Mac Brazel? From the Foster Ranch?"

"How the hell do you know my name?"

"It is you! Oh, thank God! I know exactly where I am. Sir, I worked your ranch a few months back. I was part of the crew Bob Sullivan brought to help herd your sheep to new feeding grounds. Please, sir, can you hand me some rope so I can get my friend out of here so we can go save my wife?"

Mac, convinced John was on the level, put the shotgun back in his truck, grabbed a rope from the bed, and threw it to John.

"Here you go, son."

John lowered the rope down to Doc and pulled him from the ship. They climbed down, brushing aside several large pieces of the ship's iridescent skin. The unusual material amazed John. It was light and flimsy, but somehow it returned to its original form when they crumpled it up and threw it to the ground.

"Sir, I'm truly indebted to you," John said as Mac helped him and Doc down from the ship. "Can I ask one more favor? Could you take us to my wife?"

"Hell, yes, I can. Here, you drive since you know where you're going."

"I don't know how I'll ever be able to repay you, sir."

"Son, you can start by not calling me sir. It's Mac."

"Well, okay, Mac. I can't thank you enough. This here is Doc."

The men jumped into the truck and sped off.

"Look, you boys, just drop me off at the house. You'll need the room for your wife, anyway. You get her safe and get the truck back to me as soon as you can."

As John was racing Mac's truck back to his house, Doc broke the silence. "I hate to ask, but do you have any medical supplies?"

"I've got a bag with some stuff for emergencies, sure. You can take that. Anything else?"

"I think a bucket or some water jugs would also be good."

"That shouldn't be a problem. Just pull in here, and you can help me get it together so you two can hit the road."

John kept the truck running as Mac helped Doc load the supplies. A few minutes later, John and Doc were back on the road to find Mary. John could barely hold back his emotions, but he knew what that cost him last time—a mistake he would not repeat.

"You still remember the spot where you were taken, right?" Doc asked.

"Yes, I know exactly where I'm going from here," John assured. "Hold on, Mary, we're coming for ya!"

CHAPTER 38

The truck's headlights tore through the blackness created by the dense clouds hiding the moon above. After a few turns and about fifteen minutes of driving, John crested the last hill before reaching the straightaway where his truck should be. The lights settled onto the dirt road below. John's body tensed with anticipation, expecting his truck to come into view, but there was nothing. He quickened the pace to reassure himself he miscalculated. Mac's truck reached the end of the downslope, and doubt crept into John's thinking.

Could Captain Meadowbrook be lying? Have I forgotten the way from Mac's ranch? Could my memory of where I left Mary be faulty? For several moments, John pondered silently before speaking to Doc.

"I don't understand. It should be here."

"Give it a bit, kid. Maybe it's just a bit further up."

"I dunno, I dunno. I thought that last hill was where I first saw the light from the ship."

"You had a lot going on that night, John. It may be a good bit further than you remember."

As John reached the verge of hopelessness, a faint silhouette formed on the horizon.

"Wait a second. Maybe. Yes! There it is!" John said as he pointed.

Any remaining doubt that it was his truck subsided as the dents and scratches on the body and the faded Ford logo came into sight. John strained his eyes, looking for any sign of Mary in the lights illuminating his truck's windshield. To his chagrin, there was nothing. Fatalistic thoughts entered his mind as he noticed the driver's door was wide open.

He vividly recalled having shut that door when he went to examine the cause of the vehicle's failure. Could Mary have tried to go for help? Did someone come and take her away? John continued to conjure the worst-case scenarios as he reached the truck and brought Mac's vehicle to a stop in front of it. John opened the door and heard the worst possible sound: silence.

"Hang on, Mary, I'm coming. I—I found a doctor to help you," he cried out before he confirmed she was there.

He ran as fast as he could to his truck, nearly tripping on the overnight bag he had packed before they left their home, a byproduct of Mary trying to find some modicum of comfort in her distress. As he rounded the corner of the open door, he caught the first glimpse of his long-lost love. He found her lying unconscious across the bench seat of the two-door pickup. Her head was propped up on the passenger door, with her feet barely dangling over the edge of the driver's side of the seat.

"Doc!" John screamed.

John reached across the seat and gently tapped her warm, pale cheek.

"Mary, wake up! Mary! Can you hear me? Please, Mary, please, God! Please wake up!"

Doc arrived at John's side with his makeshift medical kit.

"John, I need you out of my way."

"Mary! Come on, Mary. Wake up!"

John was near panic as tears formed in his eyes.

"John!" Doc shouted with unusual authority.

"I need you to move. Get out of the way, John!"

John's wits returned as he pulled himself out of the truck. He moved aside to give Doc the space he needed. Doc leaned in and checked Mary's pulse. He then reached across the seat and lifted each of Mary's eyelids.

"How is she, Doc? Is she gonna make it?" John asked, his voice still stricken with panic.

"Yes, she is. I think she just passed out. Probably been pushing too hard for too long. This baby wants out, John, and we're gonna need her to push. We're gonna be in serious trouble if we can't get her to wake up. Go around to the passenger side and open the door."

As John ran to the passenger door, Doc supported Mary's head and pulled her closer to the driver's side of the truck, far enough to prop one leg on the steering wheel and the other on the back of the seat behind the driver's position.

"Good, now keep her torso up, but keep her head below her knees."

Doc reached into his bag of supplies, opened a bottle, and pressed a clean cloth against the opening. He tipped the bottle onto the cloth to soak the rag.

"What's that?"

"It's ammonia." Doc placed the moistened fabric under Mary's nose, and within a few seconds, she gasped for air and coughed as her eyelids spasmed to clear the sting of the ammonia vapors.

"Mary! Mary!"

"John, is that you? Where are we? What happened?"

"Oh God, Mary, thank God you're alive! The truck broke down, and I, well, I, uh, I found this doctor here. Dr. Blake. He's going to help us."

"Oh, thank God," Mary sighed with relief right before another contraction sent her writhing and screaming in pain. She bore down and pushed.

"No!" Doc yelled. "Not yet! I need you to relax and breathe through the pain. Do not push. Do you understand, Mary?"

Mary panted through the contraction as she nodded. "Yes… I… I understand."

Mary collected her thoughts as the contraction subsided.

"Where have you been? I woke up all alone, and you were gone."

"You passed out, Mary. I didn't know what to do, so I… I had to run for help."

"Where could you have gone? Where did you find a doctor all the way out here?"

"Mary," Doc said, distracting her. "I need to examine you."

Mary nodded in agreement, and Doc checked her cervix. Just as he completed his examination, another contraction rocked Mary.

"Okay, Mary. This baby is ready to come out. I'm gonna need you to push, but only when I tell you. Do you understand?"

Mary nodded as she grimaced in pain and squeezed John's hand with all her might.

"Okay, here we go. Now push, Mary, and give me everything you've got. Two, three, four… you can do it. Just a few more seconds… seven, eight, nine, and relax."

Mary let out her breath in one giant exhale as she sucked in air. She needed to prepare for the next push.

"Good, Mary. That was great! You were pushing non-stop before when you passed out, I'll bet, weren't you?"

Mary nodded in agreement.

"Okay, take a deep breath, and let's do this again. Are you ready?"

Mary took a deep breath.

"And… push. Harder, Mary, harder. Keep going, seven, eight, nine, and relax."

Mary recovered from the strain before Doc had her repeat the process until the baby crowned.

"We're almost there, Mary. Give me one more big push. Here we go, and… push! Give me everything you've got, just a couple more seconds, and… relax. Don't push."

With a rush of exhilaration, the intense pressure Mary felt gave way to the sound of her baby's cries echoing throughout the cab of John's old pickup.

"It's a girl. It's a beautiful baby girl!" Doc announced with glee as Mary and John overflowed with excitement. John embraced Mary, and the two wept as Doc tied off the baby's umbilical cord and introduced her to her parents. Doc let out a sigh of relief for a few minutes, then went right back to work to deal with the afterbirth before concluding his treatment.

John and Mary remained in wild adoration of their new baby girl while Doc gave them some time alone. Doc inspected under the hood of John's truck. He discovered the culprit for the truck's failure: the radiator hose split just shy of its connection to the radiator. The engine must have overheated, causing the fluid to push through a weak spot in the old hose.

Doc fetched a knife from the supplies he grabbed from Mac's place and cut the hose where it split, trimming approximately an inch. A bit of the still-warm coolant in the hose drained to the ground as Doc removed the clamp and tubing remnant that was still attached to the radiator. Doc reconnected the slightly shortened hose, which had enough slack for the improvised repair. He retrieved a jug of water from Mac's truck and filled the radiator back up, hoping the overheating had not caused irreparable damage to the engine. He sealed the radiator and returned to the cab to check on John, Mary, and their baby girl.

"John, Mary, how's everything going?"

"Other than the fact that this girl sure can cry, we're doing great, Doc."

"That's okay. We want her to cry. That'll clear those lungs out and get them nice and strong. Listen, I think she's doing great, and you're going to be fine as well, Mary, but we've still got to get you both to a hospital, okay?"

Mary nodded, and John said, "Okay, Doc."

"I think I found the problem with your truck. Looks like you blew a radiator hose and overheated it. I fixed the hose, so if the engine wasn't damaged, we might be able to get this thing going. Mary, are you able to sit up so we can give this thing a shot?"

"Yeah, I think I can… maybe with some help?"

Doc helped lower Mary's feet from the seat, below the steering wheel, and onto the floorboard as John helped get her to the passenger seat. Mary cringed in pain, but it paled in comparison to what she had been through.

John rolled down the window and held Mary in place with his left arm while he reached around the door frame, through the open window, and braced her. Once clear, John rested her gently against the door as he closed it. He then walked to the driver's side, turned the key still in the ignition, and cranked the engine. After a few moments of cranking, Doc told John to stop.

"Whoa, hold on a second." Doc inspected his repair and found no evidence of leaking. He leaned down, shined his flashlight under the car, and checked for anything else that might suggest a problem.

"I don't see any obvious signs of an oil leak. There's no metal on the ground or anything, and it turned over, so I think the engine is good. Try giving it some gas."

John cranked the engine again, and this time pumped the throttle. The engine sputtered a few times, then roared to life. "All right! I think we're in business here. You're a miracle worker if I ever saw one."

John cranked up Mary's window so the cool night air would not be too much for her. He leaned her back against him and placed their overnight bag on the passenger floorboard. "Doc, follow me, and we'll take Mac's truck back to his place. We've gotta go that way to get to the hospital."

"Okay, kid. Sounds like a plan. Listen, everything is gonna be fine. There's no rush, okay? Let's not push that truck and find out I'm not nearly as good a mechanic as I am a doctor."

"Okay, Doc, I'll take her easy."

Less than half an hour later, they safely returned to Mac's ranch. When they pulled up, Mac came out of his house to meet the men and rushed to John's truck, unconcerned with his vehicle.

"Oh, I'm sure glad to see you back so soon. How's your wife doing?" Mac asked as he approached John's window and saw the baby asleep in Mary's arms.

"She delivered? Already? Right there in the truck? Well, ain't that the darndest thing? How's she doing?"

"They both fell asleep about ten minutes back, but she's doing really well. Mac, I can't thank you enough."

"Oh, there's no need to thank me. I just done what anyone else in my shoes woulda done."

After parking Mac's truck, Doc handed him the keys before returning to the passenger side of John's pickup. He opened the door and squeezed inside, doing his best not to disturb Mary, who was still sleeping on John's shoulder. Doc pulled the door shut as quietly as he could while John finished his conversation with Mac.

"We're gonna get these two to the hospital and get them examined, but I need one more favor. Would you mind?" John asked.

"What is it?"

"The ship. We'll contact the sheriff after we get Mary and the baby checked out. If anyone shows up, though, don't let them near the ship unless they tell you they talked to me. I have vital information I need to pass on, and I need to make sure it gets into the right hands. Can you do that for me?"

"What the hell is that thing, anyway?"

"Mac, you wouldn't believe me if I told you, but I can't. It's just too risky. Please make sure if anyone comes asking that hasn't talked to me, tell them I said it was too dangerous to be near—"

"Whoa, is it dangerous? Do I need to get my wife out of here?"

"Oh, no, it's not dangerous at all. Just tell them that, so they come and talk to me before they try to mess with it. Will you do that for me?"

"I dunno, John. Will I get in trouble for that?"

"When I tell them what that thing is, they're not gonna have time to worry about whether you were completely honest with them. I wouldn't worry about that."

"How 'bout I just tell them I haven't messed with it, and you told me to tell them it was too dangerous to get near, but you could help them? That be okay?"

"That'll do just fine, Mac. Okay, we gotta get going. Thank you again, sincerely."

John backed the truck off Mac's property and began the remaining drive to the hospital.

Doc and John's family arrived at the nearest hospital. The journey from Mac's house took longer than expected as John drove carefully to avoid waking Mary or the baby. Of course, that journey represented barely a fraction of John's journey from his home, which he still could not believe technically only began five or six hours earlier. The weeks he had spent on Twin Moons or future Earth felt like an eternity. He still had a tough time wrapping his mind around it all.

With Mary and the baby in his arms, John followed Doc into the hospital's emergency center. Doc advised that he had delivered the child with no complications or hemorrhaging, but that Mary had passed out at least twice during labor. The hospital staff quickly got Mary to an exam table, assessed her as dehydrated, and set her up with intravenous fluids to help her rehydrate and regain her strength. After about an hour, the staff settled her into a room where John awaited additional information on Mary and the baby's well-being.

The sun shone through the window as its first rays peeked over the horizon. The staff had been in a few times to check on Mary and the baby, and each time, all went well. Doc, John, and Mary all took turns sleeping. The baby had her first feeding from Mom, and for John, everything seemed right in the world.

Another hour passed before the OB/GYN arrived to check on Mary. "Good morning, everyone. I hear we had an exciting night last night. Tell me, how's Momma and... it's Carolyn, right?"

"Yes, Carolyn, Carolyn Jean."

John and Mary had thought about the name early in the pregnancy but had planned for her middle name to be Gloria; however, John needed to honor the woman who made his return, Mary's survival, and Carolyn's birth all possible. So, he changed her middle name from Gloria to Jean, knowing Mary would agree once he told her the whole story.

The doctor checked Mary's vitals while she slept to ensure she was recovering well. Moments later, a nurse entered the room. "Mr. Calloway, we contacted the sheriff as you asked. He'll be along soon. We've also got this ready for you. Can you review it and make sure we've got all the information correct?" The nurse presented John with Carolyn's birth certificate application that they had prepared.

John smiled the widest of smiles as he looked at Doc, who nodded in understanding. John's exuberance caused his voice to tremble as he read aloud from the application. "Carolyn Jean Calloway, born to Mary Rose Lewis and John Gordon Calloway on this day, the twenty-fifth of June, in the year of our Lord, nineteen hundred and forty-seven, in this place, the town of Roswell, New Mexico."

About an hour later, Sheriff Wilcox arrived at the hospital to learn of John's concerns regarding the handling of the ship. At John's request, the sheriff contacted Roswell Army Airfield, bringing Major Marcell to the hospital later that day. John provided all the necessary information to Major Marcell, who put together the initial cover story that the sheriff and Mac would have to use if it ever came to the attention of the press. Major Marcell advised that, depending on the specifics of any news release, they would adjust as necessary.

"And that's when all hell broke loose," John said. "Somehow, word got out after we arrived here at Fort Worth with the ship. The next thing we knew, the Roswell public affairs office put out an article about the ship. I guess it took some convincing to get Mac to lie about discovering the wreckage and reporting it to Sheriff Wilcox, but apparently, the searches after July 4th found more debris. Major Marcell had all that stuff shipped up to Wright Field as part of the weather balloon cover story he created. I guess they were having a hard time getting that story to stick, so they even brought out a general to say it and to take the heat off us and the ship being kept here. Anyway, here we are three months later, telling you the whole story, Agent Carroll."

"Gentlemen, thank you for running through all that with me. I know you've had to tell that story several times already. Right now, though, this is the nation's most closely guarded secret. That's why they brought me in from the FBI to ensure security transitions smoothly to the new Air Force. We can't take the risk of anything going wrong with something this unprecedented."

"We understand, of course. But, uh, Agent Carroll, what will become of us? Of my family and Doc here?"

"Please, gentlemen, call me Joe. I certainly understand your concerns, and I'm happy to discuss that with you. I don't think there's any need for us to continue recording, though, so unless there's anything else you'd like to discuss about the Big Brains, the ship, or your experiences, I'm going to turn this off so we can talk about what happens next, okay?"

"No, that's fine. You can turn it off."

EPILOGUE

The last sound captured by the microphone was the click of the stop button on the original reel-to-reel system used to record Agent Carroll's interview with Doc and John. The digital recording I had been listening to ended with the slapping sound of the tape wrapping around the receiving reel. I could not believe everything I had just heard. My mind was still trying to process it all. The confirmation of the Roswell incident being a ship at all would have been beyond shocking, but I never could have imagined that visitors from Earth's future were responsible.

I spent nearly thirty years working on some of the most sensitive investigations and operations in the Air Force Office of Special Investigations, or OSI—the very agency General Joseph Carroll created in 1948. I could not believe the origin story I had accepted for almost my entire adult life hid the most incredible truth. My mind was completely blown.

I replayed all the Area 51 and alien conspiracy theories I had heard over the years: the revelations about Project Blue Book, Project Mogul, and even the ongoing investigations into Unidentified Aerial Phenomena, or UAPs, today. How could it be that none of those hinted at the truth I learned on my first day—my first morning—here at OSI's most secretive unit, OSI Detachment X? I could not believe my agency had managed to not only keep this secret but to do so from almost all of its employees. Truly remarkable. I glanced at the non-disclosure agreement I had signed a few hours earlier. I had been 'read in' to so many programs over the years that I had practically forgotten many of the details, limitations, and punishments for revealing anything associated with the various projects to which I had been privy. With each of those, I could see the staggering cost to national security if any of the details were discovered by our adversaries. None of those programs were in the ballpark of the risk posed by the technology I was now charged with protecting.

I had been sitting with my mouth open in silent contemplation for a heartbeat too long when Agent Johnson's voice cut through the air. His voice startled me, causing the same adrenaline rush I would get from indirect fire when I was deployed to Iraq in 2008. Agent Johnston, or Al, as I'd called him for years, was about to retire, and the command needed a senior agent to take things over for him. Al and I went way back, so even though I was never particularly interested in Detachment X, his assurances that he had a fantastic crew of agents swayed me to take the gig as my own swan song assignment.

"Pretty fucked up, ain't it?"

"Dude! What the actual fuck did you sign me up for?" My sarcasm was clear. Al knew I was overjoyed by my new adventure.

"I told you, brother. This place is crazy."

"I just... well, damn... I just can't imagine. So, fill me in on what's happened since the interview. What's happened in the last, what, seventy years?"

"Well, apparently, the counterintelligence and security program General Carroll developed for this project was a major factor in why the SECAF was so keen on bringing him in as the command's first director. His insistence on moving the project from Fort Worth to a more secure location was a driving force behind building this site."

"You're telling me OSI made Area 51 happen?"

"I wouldn't go that far," Al snickered. "I think that whole experimenting with technology that can warp spacetime was a bigger factor. But securing it more easily helped get the money to make it all happen.

Apparently, there was a lot of gnashing of teeth over even trying to repair the ship at all. A lot of folks opposed building this site for fear it would encourage experimentation. But recognizing the safety and security benefits of keeping the project out here helped win a lot of decision-makers over."

"Spacetime? I thought the Big Brains were manipulating gravity?"

"Yeah… that's what I thought when I got here, too. But the physicists around here will be quick to remind you that everything John told us about the Big Brains was filtered through his understanding of the universe. Apparently, he wasn't tracking on Einstein's theory of relativity. So, everything Meadowbrook described, John could only understand through Newtonian theories of gravity. Our best understanding now is that the Big Brains could warp spacetime, but apparently even Einstein wouldn't be able to fully understand how the Big Brains do it because most theories today preclude the possibility of traveling back in time."

"Einstein's theory of relativity? Newtonian gravitational forces? Spacetime? Dude, what the—"

"Don't worry, you'll be fine. I'll leave you my copy of 'Astrophysics for Dummies' here in the desk."

Al laughed while showing me the book from his desk.

"So, wait a minute. Since everything is filtered through John's understanding of things, are they really called 'Big Brains?'"

"Hey, I think you're starting to get the hang of this," Al said, summoning his best impression of Rex. "We still use 'Big Brains' here, but our biological anthropologists are sure that 'brains' almost certainly refers to something related to processing power or calculating operations, like a computer processor. They assume the False Brains were some form of sentient artificial intelligence we'll eventually create, with significantly more powerful processors than anything we can currently imagine. We think the Improved Brains were basically just Homo sapiens with neuro implants—"

"Like what Doc had?"

"Oh, nothing that advanced, but some kind of implant to increase their brain's ability to process information to compete with the False Brains.

We think the enhancements must have been enough to worry the False Brains and prompted their eradication of humans from the planet."

"Man, it's a lot to wrap your head around. What about Doc, John, and his family?"

"They lived on the base at Fort Worth till we moved them out here in '55. Doc passed in the early seventies of natural causes, I'm happy to say. He was an active participant in the program for pretty much the rest of his life. In fact, he played a crucial role in helping us make some initial progress in understanding how the Big Brains controlled the ship. He seemed to enjoy the work."

"Yeah... he had a purpose, right? What about John and Mary?"

"John and Mary lived out here well into the 1990s. John had the most insight into how the ship's stasis powers worked. We're nowhere near being able to replicate the way the Big Brains could harness spacetime, but the concepts John explained led to remarkable developments for some of the other weapon systems we keep here at the base. Crazy! Those weapon systems are some of the most sophisticated and sensitive capabilities in our arsenal, and yet, being here, they help keep our biggest secret."

I continued to take it all in, shaking my head in disbelief the whole time. But I had to know more. "And Mary? What about Mary?"

"Ya know, from what it sounds like, Mary was the most incredible person. Not only was she John's rock that got him through his time at Twin Moons, but I guess he never really experienced depression again with her by his side. Apparently, it took a little coaxing to get her to commit to living here. She was completely in once she decided, though. Legend has it that everyone here used to call her mom. She was like royalty. It wasn't just her personality, either. In fact, she was even the one who came up with the idea to release the true Project Mogul information when it became clear the weather balloon story for the Roswell incident was no longer cutting it."

"And their baby? Carolyn, right?"

"Yeah, she goes by her middle name, though, Jean. She's still here with us. A remarkable woman. She was a little rebellious in the sixties, and keeping her here voluntarily proved to be difficult. Once we read her into the program, she played an active role in the engineering work to get the ship functioning. She's retired now, though, and mostly relaxes at her home on the other side of the range."

"It doesn't work yet, then, huh? The ship, I mean."

"I wouldn't say it doesn't work. Since I've been here, they've managed to get the gravity drive—that's what they're calling it anyway—functioning in a limited way. The craft can hover, but they haven't yet been able to communicate with the ship's systems enough to do anything else. One of the first things we figured out was the ship's artificial stasis. It was still functioning in the stasis room after the crash."

"I guess we've never flown it, then?"

"Nope, not yet. Folks around here seem to be getting pretty excited, though. I think they feel like we're nearing the first test flight. I wanted to be here to see that, but it is what it is."

"Why retire then? You still got a couple of years before mandatory, don't you?"

"Yeah, I don't turn fifty-seven for a little over two years, but this COVID thing's got my wife pretty freaked out. They keep saying the vaccine is coming, but who knows? Her brother was only three years older than me when he died from COVID pneumonia in the hospital back in May."

"Damn, I hadn't heard. I'm really sorry to hear that."

"Yeah, she took it real hard and doesn't like me out and about much… she knows I take this thing off every chance I can get," Al said as he lifted his mask from the desk.

"Well, brother, I'll tell you what. If it happens during my time, I'll try to get a special accommodation to bring you out to witness it."

"Dude, that would be great. I know it's a long shot, but I'd really like that."

"Still, something I don't quite understand yet, Al."

"What's that?"

"If this is the only ship the Big Brains could use, and we've never flown it, what are all the UAP sightings people have described? Isn't there a whole task force that just stood up? What about all of that?"

"Oh man! Are you sure you're ready for this?" Al laughed.

"Dude, just give it to me, I'll manage," the sarcasm was getting thick.

"The truth is, we don't know. I mean, the government technically isn't lying about unidentified aerial phenomena," Al used air quotes, almost mocking the terminology. "I mean, technically, they are unidentified. We can't explain it, but—"

"But we're lying our asses off," I said with a laugh.

"No, technically, we're not. Think about it. The sightings could be all kinds of phenomena we can't explain, but once you throw time travel into the mix, things get very murky. Could they be sightings of Big Brain missions from before the Roswell incident? You know, the thousands of people on Twin Moons? Maybe they're sightings of our test flights using the ship at some point in the future? Maybe they're Big Brain flights after we eventually return the ship to them? The truth is, we just don't know. Hell, it could be all of the above for all we know."

Al was right. I wasn't ready for this. My mind twisted, trying to think through all the possibilities besides everything I had just learned about Doc, John, and the Big Brains.

"Dude. Yeah. I, uh, I think that's gonna take some time to think through, I guess. Jesus, talk about Pandora's box."

"No kidding, right?" Al asked.

"Yeah, alright, brother, I guess I'm about sapped and ready to get some lunch. One more quick question I gotta know, though: with all the conspiracy theories about alien bodies and whatnot, what did we do with Captain Meadowbrook's and Ensign Stonemiller's bodies?"

"Oh, Jesus Christ, you would ask. That, my friend, is not a quick question. That's a whole 'nother non-disclosure agreement.'"

The end?

ACKNOWLEDGEMENTS

Despite all the words I've used in writing, editing, and completing this manuscript, I find myself at a loss for words to express my gratitude for the tremendous encouragement, support, mentorship, and love I've received from family, friends, colleagues, and the real "Big Brains" who have shown me what is possible. While I know I won't remember every person who has helped me over the years, I would be remiss not to acknowledge those listed below, many of whom continue to work tirelessly in extremely sensitive programs to keep America safe. I have omitted surnames to protect their identities: Al F., Amanda L., Andria A., Anna A., Anthony A., Chris C., Chris H., Chuck B., Chuck M., Darren G., DeWayne D., Eddie G., Fred D., Heidi B., Irene R., Jason T., Joe G., Joe O., Joel W., John H., Kaitlyn A., Karla A., Kat P., Khalid B., Kim R., Kristoffer C., Larry W., Lance W., Linda C., Monica S., Pete A., Randy A., Richard A., Rick M., Sierra A., Spencer K., Vern D., and Wendy A.

"Fiction reveals truth that reality obscures."
Jessamyn West

DETACHMENTS